SHATTERED LIVES

BOOK ONE IN THE SHATTERED TRILOGY

PHOENIX WOLFE

PHOENIX WOLFE PUBLISHING

Contents

DEDICATION

To Chad and Sherry

for helping me heal,

and to Cody and Madison

for giving me a reason to.

LETTER FROM THE AUTHOR

Dearest Reader,

As an author and survivor of sexual assault, I felt it was important to show a realistic portrayal of the lingering aftereffects of such a traumatic event. The road to recovery is long. It is not linear, and no two people's journeys look exactly the same. It took me many years – decades – to reach what I would consider "recovered", yet even now, specific triggers can catch me off guard and cause me to struggle temporarily.

I understand that not everyone can read about such events without reliving his or her own trauma. As such, I strongly recommend reading the trigger warnings page to see if Charlie's story is a fit for where you are in your situation. You may also view a sample chapter at the following link: **https://phoenix-wolfe.com/sample-of-chapter-one**

For those who have survived sexual assault, I stand with you and support you. What happened to you was not your fault, and despite the lies your inner critic may whisper, you are never too damaged to be worthy of love. For those whose lives have not been shattered by rape, perhaps this book will provide insight into the long-term struggles survivors face.

I urge anyone who has survived any type of traumatic event to seek help, even if your trauma is not recent. Many people cope by trying to forget what happened, rather than dealing with it. I'm one of them. I tried to forget, and in the end, I still had to unearth the past and address it. Repressing and burying pain is merely a stop-gap measure. Eventually, you have to deal with the pain of your past. Talk to someone – a counselor, your health care provider, a psychiatrist, support group, or spiritual leader. You can also contact the **National Sexual Assault Hotline** 24 hours a day by calling **1-800-656-4673.** If you prefer, you can go to **online.rainn.org** and chat with someone online.

Additionally, if you or someone you know is considering suicide, I urge you to reach out for help. **You can call, text, or chat with someone from the Suicide and Crisis Hotline by dialing 988.** You can also **text the word HOME to 741741 for free, confidential support** from a Crisis Counselor 24/7. You can also reach out to the **American Suicide Prevention Foundation at 1-888-333-2377.** Please, seek help. Your life is valuable, and **you matter**.

Recovery is a journey, not a destination. You are not alone.

Standing alongside you,
Phoenix Wolfe

TRIGGER WARNINGS

This book contains references to physical injuries, physical assault, sexual assault, kidnapping, PTSD, depression, anxiety, suicidal thoughts, and graphic violence.

Please read the note from the author and a sample of the first chapter for free on my website at **www.phoenix-wolfe.com/sample-of-chapter-one** to see if this book is a fit for you.

CHAPTER ONE

CHARLIE

SOULLESS BLACK EYES GLITTER as the man eyes my naked body, lingering on my curves, and he leers, exposing crooked yellow teeth. He spits words at his devoted minions, his tone guttural as he gestures toward me and smirks at the others eagerly awaiting their turn. His intent is clear, and he's performed these theatrics more times than I can count. His sadistic glee hardens my resolve. I force down my fear and focus on my anger.

Bastard.

He surveys me, licking thin lips at my gritted teeth and taut jaw. The bastard delights in sexual violence. My stomach churns. Fighting back only inflames his lust, but I'll die before I surrender. He smiles in anticipation, his fervor palpable. The Chihuahua enjoys inflicting pain.

He lifts a stubby hand toward my face, curling it as if to stroke my cheek with his knuckles. Instead, he backhands me with enough force that the cell around me goes black, and I taste blood. As soon as my vision clears, I snarl and buck as hard as I can against my restraints. The barbed wire suspending me from a pipe in the ceiling bites deeper into my wrists with my movement, and warm blood drips up my arms. His dark eyes gleam with satisfaction, and he licks his lips as he unbuckles his belt.

No!

I jolt into alertness at the sound of three rapid blasts of gunfire. I hurriedly scan my surroundings without lowering my weapon. I'm panting, soaked with cold sweat, my heart skittering like a jackrabbit as my eyes dart wildly, searching for my attacker.

But there's no one.

My gaze falls on the plump beige sofas and reclaimed wood tables in the next room. I stare down at the gun gripped in my right hand, recognizing the smell of hot sulfur as comprehension creeps over me.

I'm home.

Not there.

I'm safe.

Dammit! Not again!

A split second later, my cell phone alerts, playing the custom ringtone Lila and Tucker recorded for their frequent nocturnal interventions. Lila's voice is calm yet firm. "Charlie, you're safe now. No one can hurt you. Listen to my voice, Charlie. You're safe now. No one can hurt you. Pick up your phone." The words repeat in a loop until I answer it with trembling hands.

"Charlie?"

My lips won't form words. I nod instead.

"Charlie, wave your hand if you're with me." Her gentle tone steadies me, and my eyes flash to the camera Tucker mounted in my foyer ceiling as I lift a shaky hand.

"Good job. We've got you on speaker. Can you put down your gun?"

I stare at the gun still clenched in my hand, then place it on the table to my right.

"Good. Do you think you can talk to me?"

I shake my head.

"That's alright. You're doing fine. Put us on speakerphone. We're going to take some slow, deep breaths now. Do it with me. Breathe in. Nice and deep." I hear her inhaling deeply, coaxing me along. "Breathe out. That's it. In. Nice and easy. Out."

I close my eyes and match my respirations to hers, feeling my erratic heart gradually calm. It's several minutes before I'm settled enough to open my eyes.

"I'm okay." My voice comes out raspy, and I clear my throat.

"Name four things you see."

Lila's making sure I'm grounded in the present and oriented to my surroundings.

Making sure I'm safe to be alone.

My eyes scour my foyer. "There are wrought iron drawer handles on the table to my right. The red and cream rug at my front door needs to be straightened. The picture of me and Mark in Afghanistan is on the table beside my gun." I sigh as my eyes land on the far living room wall leading into the kitchen. "And I've got three new bullet holes."

Lila sticks to the protocol. "Describe three things you can touch."

I reach down, seeking different textures with my fingertips. "The bench cushion feels warm and nubby. My yoga pants are soft like a T-shirt. The bench is cold and smooth."

"Two things you hear."

I concentrate. "The hum of the heater." I listen harder. "And the wind is rattling the windows. And I can smell gunpowder," I add, already knowing her next question.

I hear Tucker chuckle, and I wave halfheartedly at the camera. "Sorry, Tucker."

"Don't apologize. Do you need us to come over?" His deep voice echoes off my foyer walls.

"No," I blurt quickly. I swallow, then aim for a more measured response. "No, I'm okay."

"Are you sure?" I can almost hear Lila biting her lip through the phone.

"I promise, Lila. I'm fine. What time is it?"

"A little after four," Tucker answers through a stifled yawn, and I cringe. This is the third night in a row I've woken them up.

"I'm going to make coffee and take a shower. I'm good now. Thanks, Lila. You too, Tucker. I'm really sorry."

"Stop apologizing. And call if you need me," Lila insists.

When they hang up, I get to my feet, still tremulous and sweaty. I pick up my red throw blanket off the floor and drape it over the bench before sliding my handgun into my spandex belly-band holster. I wave up at the camera again before heading to the kitchen to start coffee brewing. I need high-octane caffeine.

Actually, I need a lot more than caffeine, but it's a starting point.

Upstairs, I blast old-school Eminem, finding an odd solace in his angry lyrics and pulsing rhythms while hot water pounds my body. I scrub ferociously, trying to scrape away the sensation of filthy hands, leaving my skin a furious pink when I emerge. Afterwards, I cocoon myself in a thick towel, leaving the mirror fogged until I'm fully dressed. I don't look at my reflection until I've put on my layered bracelets. I've been wearing these particular bracelets for several months, alternating strands of green malachite beads that match my eyes with ones of bronzite, a warm brown stone flecked with gold, like my hair. My bracelets are part of my armor, like my clothes, concealing my scars from view.

They let me pretend to the rest of the world that I'm just like everybody else.

But it doesn't matter.

Hidden or not, my scars are an inescapable, suffocating weight, as much of a prison as my night terrors. My gut-wrenching dreams aren't dreams at all. They're abbreviated memories that attack when I'm defenseless. For a while,

I'd improved, only experiencing them once or twice a week. Not anymore. Now they're happening almost nightly. These past few weeks have been the most intense since I was in Walter Reed. Even asleep, my night terrors fill me with rage, and I reflexively erupt. I wake up yelling. Sometimes I find myself crouching on the floor. Sometimes I fight.

And sometimes – most of the time, now – I fire my gun.

The interior walls in my living room and hallway have been completely rebuilt from chunky 6x6's, and the layer of drywall on top of them gets replaced so frequently that the local hardware store thinks Tucker's taking on contractor jobs as a side hustle.

I may be home, but I'm just as shackled now as I was over there.

Maybe even more so.

All I want is peace. It's why I moved to the middle of nowhere, to a tiny town with fewer than three thousand people. I live in a big, quiet house surrounded by lush forests and mountain streams, with only animals for neighbors. Yet despite the serenity of my setting, inner peace is unattainable.

Peace is a unicorn, a beautiful fairy tale that never materializes. It's not an option. I'm a train wreck masquerading as a functional adult.

I bring my coffee upstairs to sip while I get ready, twisting my shoulder-length hair up and securing it with a clip. I'm forced to spend extra time applying makeup. The lack of sleep and ever-darkening circles beneath my eyes makes me look paler than usual, demanding more attention to camouflage my wan complexion. I add a dusting of bronze eyeshadow and swipe mascara across my lashes to disguise my fatigue. I finish with lip gloss and gold hoop earrings before assessing my reflection. If I plaster on an artificial smile, I don't look half-bad.

It's still dark after my second mug of coffee, but I'm too edgy to sit still. I head through the breezeway to our clinic next door, disabling the security alarm long enough to enter. I perform the same routine I do when I return home alone, silently sweeping the building, gun raised, turning on every light and checking each room to ensure I'm safe. When I'm satisfied, I retreat to my office and tuck my gun in my desk drawer.

I designed my private office to be a sanctuary. The room exudes a spa-like feel with soft sage walls and fluttery white sheers that ripple along the floor with the breeze. Plants thrive on the cherry wood surfaces, sprawling across shelves and tables. A fountain on top of my credenza infuses the space with the soothing sounds of trickling water.

Like my home, my office is a serene setting, but here, I can lose myself in work and forget the rest, at least temporarily. Being at home has become increasingly difficult. I'm naturally introverted, and being around people drains my energy. I've always been like that, preferring quiet to chaos, and I need solitude to refill my tank. But for the past few months, there's been an undercurrent of tension, and I find myself unable to relax and recharge. I've been running on empty for too long, with no end in sight.

I stifle a groan at the sight of my desk. I need an uncluttered work surface for mental clarity, but every evening, Tom, Lila, and I deposit our daily paperwork here for me to manage. Running a healthcare-based business means mountains of papers, from maintaining client records and billing insurance companies to sending updates to physicians. I have two enormous piles on my desk from this week alone, and it's only Thursday. I ought to use this time to catch up before it becomes unmanageable, but I'm too keyed-up to focus on paperwork. I've slept fewer than three hours a night for more than a month, and my constant influx of adrenaline and caffeine leaves me feeling like a zombie on speed. At this point, my spirit animal is a squirrel.

Not just any squirrel, mind you. I'm not happily flitting from branch to branch, squawking at bluejays and chasing chipmunks. No, I'm the squirrel trapped in the middle of an eight-lane freeway, trying desperately not to get squashed by huge vehicles bearing down on all sides, driving me further and further from the safety of the shoulder.

But it's not trucks spewing diesel exhaust that threaten me. It's my crippling past. Like the safety of the roadside, my deepest desire is beyond my reach.

All I want is a peaceful, normal life, instead of this irreparably broken mess.

MARK

Nothing has gone as planned this week.

I've doubled our patrols and increased the number of soldiers on each team to a minimum of four men. There's fresh activity in an area east of us, a region we've cleared top to bottom three times over the past year. Each time we stabilize it, a new group of bullies barges in to tyrannize the locals who live near our base camp. Their mere proximity to us creates suspicion that they're American sympathizers. As a result, we've rushed to their aid multiple times to protect them from overzealous nationals.

Unfortunately, our assistance only increases the distrust they face. It's a no-win situation for people who only want to live their lives in peace.

I'd planned to video chat with Charlie both yesterday and the day before, but with things going off the rails here, I haven't been able to. Both times I dashed off an apologetic email and let her know I was safe, that work got in the way. She understands. She's lived it. She was an Army medic for eleven years, with her last six years in my unit with Lila, another medic, and Tucker, my right-hand man.

Charlie and I were best friends long before we enlisted. Lila and Tucker are an unexpected gift, a perfect complement both to each other and to me and Charlie. My parents are long dead, and I was an only child. Charlie's parents were killed right before we enlisted, and she was an only child, too. Lila grew up bouncing around the foster system. Tucker's the only one of us with a real family outside the military. We formed our own family unit on a battlefield, and the three of them mean everything to me.

I've just finished conferring with Colonel Sherman, a good man I've worked closely with for over a decade. He's also concerned about the uptick in activity to our east. Our meeting ran long, and it's two-thirty in the afternoon. I calculate the time difference halfway around the world, realizing it's roughly four am in Colorado. I really wanted to chat with Charlie, to read her facial expressions and listen to the inflections in her words, but military life demands flexibility. I'll record a quick video and follow it with a longer email. I set up my webcam, and when I'm ready, I smile broadly and press record.

"Hey, Baby Girl. It's two-thirty in the afternoon here, so it's about four in the morning your time. This was the only time I could grab. I'll email when I have a few minutes. Things in the Sandbox are about the same. Winter in these mountains is a pain in the ass. At least it's not snowing. Maybe this weekend, though. It's so cold, even the mountain goats are bitching." I grin at my pathetic attempt at humor. "But the hot chocolate you sent is a big help, and so are the extra thick socks." I lift my cup for the camera even though it currently holds coffee. "I'm hoping to take leave next month if things are stable. I'll fly to the states, maybe crash on your couch for a couple of weeks if you don't mind. Oh, and the old bird made me promise I'd tell you he misses you." I grin again, wishing the Colonel were here to scowl at my nickname for him. It's a term of affection for a man who's the closest thing I have to a father.

My smile fades at a sudden flash of Charlie as she once was, with laughing green eyes and an unguarded smile. "I miss you, too. I hope –" I swallow hard at the sudden emotion rising in my throat. "I hope you're doing okay. You sound different in your emails." There's a vagueness to her letters, something she isn't saying, and I'm positive something's troubling her. I stare into the camera and chew my lip. "You know you can talk to me, Charlie. Always. About anything." I rub the back of my neck, wishing I were there instead of here.

I draw a deep breath and paste my fake smile back in place. "Anyway, I need to run. Tell Tucker and Lila I miss them. I miss you most of all, Baby Girl. Take care of yourself, okay? Love you." I thump my right fist twice over my heart, a gesture she and I have used for years to say "I love you", then reach forward and stop the camera.

When the red light is off and I'm certain it's no longer recording, my smile evaporates and my shoulders sag.

Something's definitely off with Charlie. I've noticed it over the past several months. She still sends emails a few times a week, but they've become centered around Tucker and Lila and work. She doesn't discuss herself or how she's doing.

How she's really doing.

Charlie keeps her cards close to her chest, but she and I have always been open with each other. If we hadn't, we'd never have survived the crap we've been dealt, like losing my mom when I was a kid, or my dad committing suicide not long after, or her parents taking me in, then dying when she was eighteen. Charlie and I have been inseparable since we were kids.

It's not that I don't believe what she's telling me. I'm certain everything she's saying is true. I'm more concerned about what she's holding back. She no longer talks about her day-to-day life, when she always used to include stories or anecdotes to remind me of the world outside this place. She never discusses what's on her mind or what's happening in her life. She doesn't talk about her physical or emotional health or share anything deep or personal any more. Everything she writes is surface-level information. That worries me, because Charlie's been through hell, and I need to know she's okay.

Really okay.

And if she won't tell me, all I can do from halfway around the world is entrust her to Tucker and Lila. At least I know they're watching out for her. I trust the two of them with my life. If I can't be there myself, they're the next best thing.

I take a deep breath and tap out a quick email, apologizing for the short blurb and promising a more detailed one soon. I attach the video file and hit send.

Even if my mountain goat joke was pathetic, I hope it makes Charlie smile.

CHARLIE

I'm drumming my fingers on my desk, struggling to find something else productive that doesn't require mental focus. I've vacuumed the rehab gym, washed a load of massage towels, scrubbed the community fridge, and recycled the outdated magazines. When I hear keys jingling, my hand automatically slides toward my gun, but I stop myself. *Intruders don't have keys.*

"It's me, Charlie," Lila calls as she resets the alarm.

I groan. "It's barely seven. You didn't go back to sleep?"

"Better. I went for a run." I hear the smile in her voice, and I know she's trying to keep me from feeling guilty about waking her. It doesn't work. "Besides, Tom's bringing doughnuts. He wants to hear the latest Winner versus Whiner results."

Winner versus Whiner is what Tom has dubbed my revolving door of Wednesday night blind dates. They started several months ago when I finally surrendered to Lila's "assertive encouragement". She knows I long for normalcy, and as she's pointed out repeatedly, that requires achieving a basic level of comfort around males. After numerous disastrous interactions since returning to civilian life, I caved to her incessant demands.

Lila began her quest by setting me up with single guys she or Tucker knew. When that didn't work, I reluctantly joined a dating website — a true picture of futility in action. Though I'd mostly done it to shut her up, a small part of me acknowledges a need to be able to socially interact with men. Besides, drinks or dinner in public should be relatively painless.

"Relatively", however, is, well, relative.

Somehow, my utter lack of enthusiasm evolved into Lila selecting my dates, something Tom strongly objects to. Tom is the nicest guy I've ever met. When Lila and I graduated from massage school and opened our wellness clinic, we posted an ad for a physical therapist. Our clientele is primarily wounded veterans, a group she and I are comfortable with because of our own years of service. I'd intended to hire a female therapist because ever since Afghanistan, I'm uncomfortable around men, but the second Tom walked in, we both knew he was the one. Tom exudes a calm energy that defused my anxieties immediately. He's one of those rare individuals who easily connects with people, and he's relaxed in every situation because he's comfortable in his own skin. Our male clients like him because he's a boxer, built like a bulldog with a broad chest, muscled arms, and a nose that's been broken at least twice. Even though he's never served in the military, his masculinity gives him man-card credibility. Our female clients adore Tom because he's easy on the eyes. His boyish grin and twinkling brown eyes could melt the hardest of hearts, and he has a great sense of humor. Women swoon in his wake, but he and I have a sibling-type relationship. It's almost a shame we see each other that way. He's practically perfect, especially when you throw in his daughter, Maya, whom I adore.

Tom's a good friend, and for me, those are the exception, not the rule. My list of friends comprises four souls: Mark, Lila, Tucker, and Tom. It's a short list, but I'll take my handful of ride-or-die friends over a gaggle of fair-weather acquaintances any day.

Lila pops into my office with three huge paper cups in a cardboard tray. "Vanilla blueberry swirl," she announces. She doesn't look like someone running on five hours of sleep. She looks perfectly styled despite our bland work attire of khakis and loose white shirts. Blond curls tumble down her back and her violet eyes sparkle, perfectly matching her jewelry and manicure.

I eye her as she holds out a cup that smells strongly of blueberries. "This is coffee, right?"

She laughs. "Yes, silly. Tom's bringing blueberry doughnut holes. I thought we should stick with a theme."

Of course. Because nothing improves a discussion about my pathetic dating life more than a fruit-based theme.

Right on cue, I hear his key in the front door as he whistles a cheery tune. "It's me, Charlie." Tom always ensures I know he's approaching, and he instinctively avoids walking behind me or inadvertently trapping me in a corner.

Like I said, good friend.

"Back here," I call. He saunters in, dressed in his usual black scrubs. His brown hair is still damp, and I smell his clean, soapy scent mingling with the aroma of fresh pastry and blueberries.

"Still warm." He lifts the white bakery bag and produces a wad of napkins. "Desk or couch?"

"Couch," Lila answers. She selects a spot on the white sofa and hands him a coffee while he fills a plate with doughnuts. I sit beside Lila, and Tom flops into a chair across from us.

I bite into warm deliciousness and sigh as sugary icing melts over my tongue. "I really needed this."

He chuckles. "That answers my question."

"What question?"

"Winner or whiner."

I narrow my gaze. "Really? No polite chit chat? No 'How are you, Charlie?' or 'Did you sleep well, Charlie?' Just straight to 'How badly did your date suck this time?'"

He grins. "I didn't ask if he sucked. I inferred it from your comment."

"So how badly did he suck?" Lila asks.

I roll my eyes. "He would have had to improve to suck."

Tom tilts his head toward Lila. "Why do you let her rope you into this?"

I sigh again, and not from carb-induced bliss. "Because Lila wants me to be happy. Normal. Which means I need to work on finding the perfect man."

Tom raises an eyebrow. "There's no such thing."

I smile and gesture in his direction. "Present company excluded, of course."

"Naturally."

Lila frowns. "Time out. I never said you couldn't be happy without a man. You need to be happy with yourself, with or without a man. No man should be the sole thing that makes you happy, regardless of how wonderful he may be. I simply said you need to learn to trust again and be open to the possibility that all men don't suck."

"I never said all men suck. Mark doesn't suck. Tucker doesn't. Tom doesn't."

"I definitely don't," Tom grins. "I'm an exceptional human being."

"An exceptional human being with terrible taste in women," Lila interjects. Tom snorts, and they're off.

I watch in amusement as they squabble good-naturedly over Tom's girlfriend-of-the-month, Whitney. Whitney is the anchor of a local morning news show, a willowy platinum blonde with a spectacular figure and luminous blue eyes. Lila insists she's had significant cosmetic assistance. ("No boobs that big don't have some natural sag unless they're fake, and those nipples could poke someone's eye out. Plus, when she smiles, nothing above her cheekbones moves.") I can only speculate about her gravity-defying breasts and weaponized nipples, but Lila's dead-on with her assessment of Whitney's facial features. When she smiles, the corners of her eyes don't crease, and when she attempts to affect a look of faux-sincere concern for her viewers, her perfectly arched brows remain motionless.

Their bickering about Tom's busty blond companion continues as Tom insists she's perfectly nice. There's something in his eyes, though, something he's not saying. Lila argues Whitney is phony and superficial and that Tom could do better. While I silently agree, I remain outwardly neutral. When it comes to Tom's taste in women, I'm Switzerland.

Eventually, the conversation winds back to me when Tom points at me with a pastry. "None of that explains why you let Lila pick your dates."

I reach for another doughnut hole. "Theoretically, you can tell from their profile if you're compatible before you ever have to meet them."

"You're assuming they're being honest. And you realize you just said '*have* to meet them', right?"

"Mmmm," I agree, chewing. I sidestep his comment about having to meet men. "Last night's Whiner was definitely less than honest."

Lila glances over. "How dishonest?"

"Six inches shorter and at least fifteen years older than his profile said."

Her mouth drops open as Tom leans back, rubbing his hands together. "Do tell."

I grin at his enthusiastic interest in my riveting dating life. "It started with the usual questions. I asked him to tell me about himself. His name is Chase, and he owns a used car dealership."

Tom groans as Lila shakes her head. "Seriously?"

"I know. His bio only said he owned his own business. An intentional oversight, no doubt," I add. "I told him I co-owned a wellness clinic. I asked him to tell me one thing he wanted me to know about himself. His answer was that I was much more attractive in person and that he couldn't wait to get me naked."

Tom's eyebrows lift as his mouth tightens.

"When I said I had PTSD and intimacy issues, his response was – and I quote – 'So there's no chance we're having sex tonight?'"

Tom's frown deepens.

Lila shakes her head. "What an ass."

"It gets better. When I informed him I didn't make a habit of sliding between the sheets with total strangers, he threw down sixty bucks and hooked up with a blonde at the bar."

I glance at Tom. His jaw muscles flex, but he's silent. I shrug. "Trust me, he was no great loss. They hadn't taken our order yet, so the server got a huge tip."

"This happened before dinner?" Lila's outrage is palpable.

I shrug. "My suffering was short-lived, and I had a lovely glass of red wine. Besides, my cute waiter gave me his number. Not that I'll call him," I add. "He just turned twenty-one."

Neither of them point out that I wouldn't have called him anyway.

Tom casts an accusing look at Lila. "I can't believe you picked this guy."

I shake my head. "It's not her fault." I pull out my phone and open his dating profile. "Chase Roberson. Thirty-five. Black hair, brown eyes. Six one, one hundred eighty pounds. Business owner. Enjoys quiet evenings by a fire and moonlit walks." I pass him my phone. He gives it a cursory glance and his jaw tightens again. "Now compare that photo to this one." I retrieve my phone and swipe to a photo I snapped of Mr. Wonderful. He's leaning on the bar in profile, one hand on the blonde's ass, his salt-and-pepper hair and pot belly in full view.

"Six one and thirty-five, my ass," Tom grumbles.

I chuckle and pass the phone to Lila, who makes a face. "What a douche."

"Like I said, no great loss."

"At least let me vet these guys," Tom says. "I grew up with sisters. My jackass radar is strong."

"It's fine, Tom. This is a necessary evil. I'm not expecting to find Mr. Right. I'm simply retraining my lizard brain to understand that most guys aren't a threat, even the jackasses."

Tom frowns again when I say "necessary evil", but that's what this is. I'm not opposed to meeting the right guy eventually, but for now, I'm essentially in desensitization mode. These Winner versus Whiner dinners are the dating equivalent of allergy shots – brief exposures to small doses of an irritant to help the body stop overreacting to their presence. Likewise, I tolerate casual dates in reasonably safe environments to become more comfortable in one-on-one situations with men.

Lila shakes her head. "Chase. What a perfect name for a man whore," she mutters.

I grin. "My waiter's comments were far more derogatory and entertaining."

CHAPTER TWO

MARK

Colonel Sherman and I have decided to recon the areas to our east. Satellite images aren't revealing much, and sometimes, there's no substitute for boots on the ground. At dawn, I take a dozen men to scout the area where we've seen more activity. The plan is to divide into two teams and check out a couple of the I.S.'s former not-so-secret safehouses. They appear deserted, but this enemy excels at hiding in plain sight. We arrive at first light, and I huddle up with Sergeant Rivers to go over the plans for his team one more time.

One minute I'm talking to Rivers on my left, standing near the back of a tan MRAP tactical vehicle as we examine the map.

The next, I'm flat on my back as my brain struggles to make sense of the scene around me.

What happened?

Thin patches of pale blue sky peek through thick black smoke that billows and undulates above me like a writhing snake. The acrid stench of chemicals, burnt flesh, and blood is overpowering. I can't hear anything except the ringing in my ears.

We've been hit.

Where's Rivers? Where's my team?

Get up.

I shift my eyes left toward the eight o'clock position. The vehicle is flipped over, orange flames surging from a yawning hole in its side. Soldiers lie scattered on the ground.

My men.

I see figures, but I can't make out who they are as a red haze obscures my vision.

As the ringing in my ears fades, I hear their screams.

My men need help. I have to help.

I blink to clear my eyes and roll my head left. I move too quickly, and dizziness and nausea wash over me. I squeeze my eyes shut until it passes, then open them. A man lies a few feet from me, but I can't tell who it is. His head faces skyward, and he's covered in blood. Crimson liquid saturates the sand around him. His right arm is just beyond my reach. I scoot toward him, fighting another wave of nausea.

I have to help.

It's hard to move. Why is it so hard to move?

One inch. Two.

I stretch out, barely able to grasp his fingertips. I tug once. Nothing happens. I slide over another inch, get a firmer grip, and pull harder. His head lolls toward me. A chunk of blackened metal protrudes from the left side of his throat. His lower jaw is missing. Sightless brown eyes stare at me from charred flesh.

Rivers.

He's gone. Let him go.

Help someone else.

More yelling. Pleas for help. I angle my head, looking past my left leg. More dizziness, even though I'd moved slowly. I shut my eyes again, waiting for it to pass.

A soldier howls and flails his right arm. No. Part of his arm. His forearm and hand are gone. Blood spurts skyward, splattering as it lands, staining the pale sand. Beyond him are two others.

They don't move.

They don't scream.

They need help. Get up.

I try to move, but my body won't respond.

Something's wrong. It's getting hard to breathe. I gulp, sucking in air, but it doesn't help. I try to roll to my side to catch my breath, but I'm not able to.

Why won't my body cooperate?

Intense, searing pain in my right leg seizes my attention. My head pounds ferociously. I take a deep breath to get a handle on the pain, but it's getting harder and harder to inhale. It's like I've got sandbags crushing my chest, keeping me from taking a full breath.

Get up. They need help.

Get up!

My eyes swim. The pale blue bits of sky melt away. The red haze dissolves as inky blackness encircles the edges of my vision, moving toward the center. My ears stop ringing as sounds fade.

Everything disappears.

Everything except the darkness.

CHARLIE

When Tom and Lila leave, I return to my desk chair with two hours until my first client appointment. Fully fueled with sugar and caffeine, I check my email to see what needs to be dealt with first.

My heart leaps as my eyes zero in on an unexpected gift – not just an email, but a video from Mark. A video means he's alive and well, and I can't tear my eyes away from the screen.

Pale blue eyes contrast with his tanned face, and the camera field captures his broad shoulders and desert camos. His dark blond hair could use a trim. Despite the fatigue etched in his features, he smiles, and it reaches across the miles like a reassuring hug. When he says, "Hey, Baby Girl," his familiar voice soothes my ragged soul. The time stamp shows he recorded this right after my nightmare, as though he felt my distress halfway around the world.

I scribble a note to mail him more cocoa, socks, and his favorite cookies. I grip my desk and suppress a squeal upon hearing he might visit soon. When he calls Colonel Sherman "the old bird", I laugh, missing the colonel's faux-offended reaction when we'd call him that in private.

Then Mark hesitates, furrowing his brows and pressing his lips together.

He's worried about me.

He knows something's wrong, even though I've been exceptionally careful with my emails. I refuse to burden him with my struggles. He's in a dangerous situation that demands his full attention. Being distracted by something he can't fix jeopardizes his safety and the safety of those under his command. But Mark and I have had a special bond since we were kids.

I stare, transfixed, as he continues. "You can talk to me, Charlie. Always. About anything." He glances away, rubbing his neck, his mind elsewhere. Then he looks back and smiles again.

"Anyway, I need to run. Tell Tucker and Lila I miss them. I miss you most of all, Baby Girl. Take care of yourself, okay? Love you." He thumps above his heart twice before the frame freezes and goes dark. My fist lightly taps my own chest two times in response.

When his face fades from view, my soul aches, and I watch the video over and over, long after I've memorized every detail, every word, every expression on his tired face.

I wish Mark were here.

Military life isn't for the faint of heart, both for the deployed or for those waiting at home. It's hard when your best friend is on the other side of the world. It's even harder when he's in a war zone that's no longer officially designated a war zone because of political machinations. It's harder still when weeks go by without knowing if he's dead or alive.

I never thought twice about it when I served because my parents were already gone, as were Mark's. Neither of us had anyone stateside to worry. He and I only had each other. We enlisted together after my freshman year of college. I became a medic; he chose infantry. We both shipped off to the Middle East, but it wasn't until several years later that I transferred into his unit. By that time, he was a platoon leader in one of the most dangerous regions of Afghanistan. That's where I met Lila, a fellow medic, and her now-husband Tucker, one of Mark's sergeants.

They say foxhole friendships are the deepest, and while we were never in foxholes, we were definitely battle-tested. The four of us are more like family than friends, and each of us would unhesitatingly take a bullet for the others.

Lila and I were medically discharged four years ago. Tucker followed the next year to join Lila here in Cedar Ridge, Colorado. They married several months later. Mark stayed in. Military life suits him – the discipline, the strategy, the control. He excels at seeing the big picture, at manipulating the pieces on the chessboard into proper positions. Just five more years and he'll hit his twenty-year mark, though I can't see him retiring. The Army is as much a part of him as breathing.

I think back to his pale blue eyes and easy smile, missing the man I know almost as well as I know myself.

I can't wait to see him next month.

MARK

I slowly become aware something's happening around me. There's a familiar thrumming sound, but I can't place it. I try to open my eyes, but my eyelids are too heavy.

Are those helicopter rotors? I need to check. My men need Air Evac.

My head pounds like a bass drum, throbbing in conjunction with every beat of my heart. I must be alive. Death would be far less painful.

Where am I?

I feel like I'm at the bottom of the ocean. Voices murmur in the distance, too far away for me to understand what they're saying. Someone moves me, slowly rocking me to one side and then the other. I'm jostled sharply, and intense pain rushes over me. I think I groan, but I'm not sure. A deep voice speaks near my ear. His tone is reassuring, but I can't make out his words.

Everything vanishes into darkness.

I surface partially at a blast of frigid air. Jumbled voices surround me, talking too fast for me to grasp their words. Strange, unidentifiable odors drift by, smells I associate with hospitals. There's pain, terrible pain. My head feels like it's going to burst and my right leg throbs mercilessly. I groan again, or at least, I think I do. I struggle to open my eyes, but I can't. The blackness overtakes me.

This pattern continues.

Over.

And over.

And over.

In time, the voices change from mostly male to both male and female. I don't recognize them, but their tones are soothing.

Someone lays a soft hand on my cheek and speaks close to my ear. A sweet, gentle voice, like an angel.

Am I dead?

Someone should tell me if I'm dead.

I still can't open my eyes. They're too heavy. And I hurt all over.

I fade in and out as the voices come and go, interspersed with only darkness and pain.

CHARLIE

Hot blood snakes up both arms, carving fresh ruby paths through older dried brown streaks before dripping into the clotted puddle on the stone floor. My shoulders scream for relief as the barbed wire suspending me gouges deeper into my wrists. The throbbing low in my belly and between my thighs has intensified. My breasts sting, and my back blazes with fiery heat.

My mouth is parched, my lips cracked. I'm so dehydrated that the sandy dust in the air can't stick to my tongue. The particles settle on my bare skin, mingling with my blood.

My entire body tenses as raucous laughter approaches from behind. I wrestle against my restraints, trying to wrench free. Heavy boots pound closer, venom in their harsh strides. I struggle harder, but the wire only chews deeper into my raw flesh.

Metal clangs as the door bangs open behind me. I cease bucking, but my body still sways, hanging several inches above the floor. The foul stench of soured bodies assaults my nostrils.

The Chihuahua steps in front of me, and an involuntary shiver races down my spine. I don't take my eyes off the rusty blade in his hand. He smiles as he pierces my chest with it, not deeply. He carves a shallow slice through the flesh of my left breast – painful, but not fatal. I grit my teeth as blood trickles down my body. He moves lower, dragging the jagged tip lightly across my abdomen, but not cutting flesh. He watches my face as he toys with me, a cat tormenting a trapped mouse.

Fucking bastard.

I know what's coming, and my body tenses. He repositions his knife at the apex of my thighs, grinning evilly as my eyes lock with his.

Deep-set, heavy-lidded, soulless black eyes. Small and hard, glittering with deep loathing and cruel satisfaction.

He sneers, thrusting his blade upward. Sharp pain follows the invasion of his filthy knife, but instead of crying out, I growl like a wild animal and bare my teeth.

I awaken to the blast of gunfire, down on one knee in my foyer, gripping my gun in both hands. Sweat runs in rivulets down my back. My breath comes in pants as I scan for the threat.

I'm in my foyer. Safe.

Fuck.

Four days in a row.

I hear my cell phone somewhere behind me. "Charlie, you're safe now. No one can hurt you. Listen to my voice, Charlie. You're safe now. No one can hurt you. Pick up your phone." Breathing hard, I lower my gun and place it on the table. It takes a minute to locate my phone beneath the bench. I flop back on the floor, my back resting against the bench as I answer, automatically putting it on speakerphone.

"Sorry, Lila."

"It's me, Charlie," Tucker answers. "Lila's in the shower. You with me?"

I nod, waving a hand at the camera in the ceiling.

"Tell me what you see," he prompts.

"I need to sweep under the bench. There are two dust bunnies that I'm counting separately. And my phone is in my lap and I'm wearing red socks. I'm okay, Tucker. I'm sorry. I'm sorry to keep doing this shit to you guys every fucking night."

Without warning, tears flood my eyes, and I swipe them away and swallow against the growing lump in my throat.

"It's fine, Charlie. I was already up. Wait, are you crying?"

I shake my head and lean forward so he can't see my face.

"I can hear you sniffling. We're coming over."

"No," I insist. "I'm fine."

"Is she crying? What did you do?" Lila's accusatory tone echoes in my foyer.

"Nothing. She just started crying."

"I'm not crying," I insist. "It's allergies."

"Bullshit," they reply in stereo.

"Not bullshit," I say, getting to my feet, my legs quaking. "I'm fine. What time is it?"

"You're late today. It's almost five-thirty," Tucker says.

At least I let them sleep a little longer this morning. "I'm sorry," I apologize again. "I'm fine. I'm going to shower. I'll see you at work, Lila. Thanks, Tucker."

"Quit thanking me. You'd do this for me."

I allow myself a good long cry in the shower, an ugly cry, the kind where you're glad there's no one to witness your blotchy face and runny nose.

I'm so tired of being broken.

I saw a psychiatrist twice a week for over a year. I thought I was better, but I'm still a fucking train wreck.

Maybe this is as fixed as I get to be.

That thought depresses me more than I thought possible.

When I get to work, Tom's already there, setting up for his clients in the rehab gym. "You're early."

"Hey," he says, his boyish smile lighting up his face. "I didn't sleep much. Figured I'd come in and get a head start. You're here early again, too. Not sleeping well?"

I shrug. "I heard a noise, and once I'm awake, I'm awake. I envy people who can go right back to sleep."

My attempt at distraction doesn't work. Tom knows I have PTSD and difficulties with men, but not why. Lila's told him what happened to her, so he has a general idea, and that's enough. It's not that I don't trust him – I do. I just want one friend who doesn't know how fucked-up I really am.

Since the best defense is a good offense, I tip my chin at him. "So what's the real story with you and Whitney?"

He freezes. "What do you mean?"

"I'm not buying that 'everything's fine' speech."

He frowns. "Why not?"

"Your eyes didn't match your words. And this?" I gesture to him. "Avoiding my question? That says I'm right."

He scowls. "You see too much." I wait with crossed arms until he sighs in surrender. "Maya hates her."

Maya is Tom's enthusiastic, precocious ten-year-old. If she likes you, you're friends for life; if not, there's little chance she'll reconsider. For one so young, she's surprisingly perceptive.

"Did she say that?"

He exhales in a burst. "The words 'shallow' and 'diva' were tossed around."

I silently agree with Maya. A few weeks ago, Whitney offered Lila and me autographed headshots while she was waiting for Tom.

Autographed. Headshots.

From the co-anchor of a six am local news show.

In a town with two stoplights and three times as many farm animals as people.

Lila had glanced at me with a look of "Is she for real?" on her face, something that did not go unnoticed by Whitney, who'd snatched her photos up and stalked off at Lila's polite declination.

Maya's assessment is spot-on.

"How are you and Whitney handling it?"

"Whitney pretends not to notice while Maya finds creative ways to not-so-subtly insult her. The other night at dinner, she detailed each point of a five-paragraph essay she wrote, contrasting the uselessness of fleeting beauty against the enduring resilience of character and intelligence."

I fight a smile, thoroughly impressed with Maya's ingenuity. "Maybe the three of you can work through this." Tom could do a lot better than Boobzilla, but I want him to be happy, and his daughter hating his girlfriend is a no-win situation for him.

"I don't think either of them wants to."

"I'm sorry. Can I help?"

He shakes his head. “I don’t think so. Thanks, though.” He returns to sorting colorful therapy bands before glancing up. “By the way, I was informed I needed to invite you to dinner tonight.”

I grin. “You were informed?”

He nods. “By two very insistent females. Maya and Skyler are making spaghetti.”

“I’ll be there.”

He chuckles. “Maya said you’d agree as soon as you heard the word spaghetti.”

“I'd have agreed anyway, even without my weakness for pasta. What time?”

Tom shrugs. “Seven-ish? My chefs are a bit unreliable. There’s a distinct possibility we could end up ordering pizza.”

“I’ll take my chances.”

My day passes quickly. I provide therapeutic massage to five regular clients, all disabled vets between twenty-five and forty years of age. I schedule six new VA referrals and send updates to physicians, working through the papers stacked precariously on my desk. I’m hanging up the phone at the front desk just before closing when the door opens and a familiar figure saunters in. Shaggy blond hair brushes the collar of the white linen shirt clinging to his muscled chest. Steely blue eyes twinkle above his crooked nose, and he flashes me his trademark lazy grin.

“Charlie,” he purrs, “you look beautiful today.” He leans on the counter, his eyes fixed on mine.

I smile. “You say that every day, Blake.”

He winks. “Because it’s true.”

“You’re a shameless flirt. You know that, right?”

Blake Wilson is the most flirtatious man I’ve ever met. He’s good-looking, and he knows it. He’s also extremely appreciative of the feminine form. I’ve never seen him meet a female without complimenting her. It doesn’t matter if she’s eight or eighty, hot or homely. He finds something attractive in each one, whether it’s how her scarf brings out the color of her eyes, the way her smile lights up a room, or how her clothes hug her curves. It’s surprisingly charming, even if it does scream man-whore.

“It isn't flirting if it’s true.”

I roll my eyes. “Tom should be done in a couple of minutes. You’re welcome to wait in the reception area in the rehab gym.”

He ignores my blatant dismissal. “I prefer the view here.”

Blake is Tom’s assistant boxing coach at the center for disadvantaged youth. He’s also a life coach – one of those annoyingly positive people who yammer on about visualizing what you want and seizing the day and making your dreams come true. Maybe that’s why he’s so persistent in his flirtation.

And in all honesty, despite his constant stream of compliments, part of me enjoys it when he drops by, because I'm guaranteed a self-esteem boost.

I return my attention to the files from today's visits. Blake taps the counter with one long finger. "So, when are you having dinner with me?"

"I wasn't aware that I was," I reply without looking up.

"How about tonight?"

"Sorry, I have plans." Thanks to Maya and Tom, it's true.

"Tomorrow then. Have lunch with me."

"Plans," I repeat. I'll do something with Lila so it won't be a lie.

"Sunday afternoon," he insists.

I shake my head. "Sorry, Blake. I have something going on already." Sundays are when I clean the house and go grocery shopping.

Without warning, he reaches across the counter and strokes my cheek. I freeze as my blood turns to ice and iron bands grip my chest.

"One of these days, I'll wear you down," he murmurs, oblivious to my panic. He straightens up just as Tom comes around the corner.

"Hey, man, I thought I heard you out here," Tom says. "Come on back, I'm almost done."

Blake walks away, unaware of my distress. My breathing grows rapid and shallow, and I squeeze my eyes shut, dipping my head and pressing the heels of my hands to my forehead.

Breathe in.

Breathe out.

Slow and deep.

"Gimme a minute. I'll catch up to you," I hear Tom say, and I sense his approach.

"Charlie?"

I don't open my eyes. My fingers fist against my forehead.

Tom squats down but doesn't touch me. "Hey, Charlie. It's okay. You're safe. I won't let anything happen to you. Take some nice deep breaths."

I nod, my eyes still closed.

Breathe in.

Breathe out.

"Do you need Lila?"

I shake my head no and focus on slowing my breathing.

Breathe in.

Breathe out.

It only takes a minute or two before I'm able to unclench my hands, and another one until I'm calm enough to open my eyes. Tom's worried brown eyes are the first thing I see.

"Thanks," I mumble, my face growing hot.

"Anytime." He gets to his feet, his eyes lingering for a moment before glancing questioningly across the room.

That's when I catch sight of Blake's curious stare. Embarrassment turns to complete humiliation as I realize he's just gotten a front-row seat to my shitshow of a life, all because he innocently brushed his thumb over my cheek.

Just fucking awesome.

Because I needed two more people to see exactly how fucked up I am.

CHAPTER THREE

CHARLIE

I'M NOT EVEN HALFWAY to Tom's front door that night when Maya bursts out and bounds toward me. I hoist my bakery box over my head and laugh as she flings her arms around my waist. "Easy, kiddo. These cupcakes won't taste nearly as good without the frosting."

"I've missed you!" She peeks up at me with huge brown eyes identical to Tom's, though her bone structure matches her supermodel mother's, with high cheekbones and a perfectly sculpted nose. Her skin is a perfect blend of Chele's warm chestnut tones and Tom's ruddy complexion. Copper-colored highlights artfully streak her springy dark curls.

I kiss her forehead. "I've missed you, too. Now what's this I hear about spaghetti?"

She pulls me through the comfortable craftsman-style house to the kitchen. The aroma of tomatoes, peppers, onions, and garlic hangs in the air, and my mouth waters.

"Dad told us how to make the sauce and supervised. It's been simmering for two hours because that's how Italian old ladies do it." I grin at her description. "There's water heating for the noodles, and Dad watched us make garlic butter and spread it on the bread. When the spaghetti goes in the water, the bread goes in the oven. And Skyler and I have almost finished making salad." Her voice is full of pride as she gestures around the kitchen.

"Hi, Skyler." I wave to Maya's best friend, a petite girl with gorgeous red hair and brilliant blue eyes, perched on a barstool, chopping a cucumber. "Everything smells delicious."

"Hi, Charlie. What's in the box?"

"Triple chocolate cupcakes."

Both girls squeal as the back door opens and sharp toenails scrabble across the floor. A split second later, a massive red dog barrels toward me. I put down the cupcakes and drop to my knees just in time to be pushed onto my backside by an overly-enthusiastic pit bull. Her entire back half wags as she covers me in sloppy kisses.

"Bella, down," Tom commands as he enters the kitchen. Bella's butt hits the floor immediately, but she continues to snuffle and lick. Skyler giggles. I push Bella's big muzzle away from my face before rubbing her loose jowls with both hands. Tom frowns. "I wish I could break her from that. She's going to hurt someone."

I shrug. "She's still a puppy. She'll learn. Besides, I'm used to it."

"Whitney hates it," Maya chimes. Tom's expression tightens.

"Stay, Bella." I tell her. Tom reaches a hand down to help me up. I hesitate briefly before taking it. As soon as I'm upright, I automatically tug my hand free, my body tensing. Hurt flashes in his eyes.

Dammit. He's safe.

I shut my eyes briefly. "Sorry. Reflex."

I need to learn to relax around the male population in general, but my top priority is to break my ingrained panic reflex with Tucker and Tom. Neither of them would ever hurt me; in fact, I'm certain both of them would do anything to protect me. Despite that, the simplest touch from either of them elicits my fight-or-flight response, and I hate it.

Tom's face relaxes. "You did great. You took my hand."

I reach forward and let my fingers graze his wrist, loathing the way my stomach instantly clenches at the contact. "Hey, thank you for earlier today. For being there. It helped."

He shrugs lightly, smiling down at his wrist where my fingertips sit. "No thanks needed. And look at you. You're improving by the minute. Good job."

Maya rolls her eyes. "Dad, you're using the tone you use when Bella learns a new trick."

At the sound of her name, Bella jumps to her feet and rockets down the hall toward the living room. A loud hiss follows an angry yowl. "Eddie, settle down," Tom calls. A black and white blur streaks past us with Bella in hot pursuit before doubling back. Tom sighs at a loud crash.

"I think you lost another lamp, Dad."

"I think so, too."

Dinner is delicious. The girls light candles and serve sparkling grape juice in wine glasses. Maya finds a playlist titled "Italian dinner music", and it's a perfect backdrop to the evening. Skyler and Maya fill me in on the latest details. School is in that dreadful time after Christmas break but before spring break, and the girls are ripe with complaints. Apparently, snow only falls on weekends (thereby costing them potential snow days), there are too many word problems in their math homework, and the PE teacher is far too excited about wind sprints.

It's nice to know some things haven't changed.

After dinner, I insist on doing the dishes. Tom and Skyler take Bella for a walk, but Maya opts to stay and help me. Her reason becomes obvious when I'm elbow-deep in soapsuds.

"I wish you could be Dad's girlfriend," Maya blurts without warning. My head jerks toward her, and I'm startled to see she's on the verge of tears.

Shit.

I reach for a dish towel and dry my hands, scrambling to find the right words. "Your dad already has a girlfriend."

"But if he didn't, you could be his girlfriend, right?" Her chocolate eyes shimmer.

I kneel in front of her, taking her hands. "Maya, I adore you, and your dad and I are really good friends, but that's all."

"Don't you think he's good-looking?"

I smile up at her indignant expression. "He's very good-looking," I assure her. "But I don't have many friends, and sometimes when people break up, there are too many hurt feelings for them to stay friends. I would never risk losing you and your dad. You both mean too much to me."

"Maybe you wouldn't break up," she says hopefully.

I pause. *How much do I tell an innocent child?*

"I'm not good at relationships, Maya," I confess. "I have a hard time letting people get close to me, and that creates problems."

That's as honest as I can be with a ten-year-old.

She studies me, her eyes serious. "Can we be close? You and me?"

I reach up and tug one of her curls. "Always," I promise.

"No matter what?"

I nod soberly. "No matter what."

She pulls her hands free and wraps her arms around my neck, and I hold her as tightly as she's holding me.

It slices through me without warning, like a knife ripping through my heart, and suddenly I can't breathe.

This is what I want, more than anything.

I want a house full of love and kids, of dogs the size of miniature ponies and three-legged cats who take offense at said dogs. Pasta dinners with messy faces and chocolate cupcakes and fallen noodles that rapidly disappear into a giant slobbery muzzle. Papers about fleeting beauty and science projects and last-minute bake sales. And a man who loves me, who doesn't see me as broken, who doesn't treat me like I'm broken.

Not this house or this man or this family, though I do love them.

No. I want one of my own.

And I don't merely want a man who doesn't see or treat me like I'm damaged. I don't want to be damaged at all.

But I am.

Wishing I wasn't a train wreck doesn't change a damn thing. Those bastards destroyed any hope of a happily-ever-after for me.

The painful revelation of wanting something I can never have shatters my evening, and when Tom returns, I go home, feigning a headache, though my head is fine.

It's my soul that's in anguish.

MARK

Pain. Searing, godawful pain. My right leg. Both thighs. My chest. Everywhere, just differing levels of pain.

The pressure inside my head hurts the most. It feels like my brain's going to explode.

Explode.

Something tugs at the edges of my memory. *There was an explosion...*

I try to recall more, but it's like sifting through dry sand in search of a single grain of salt.

Darkness overtakes me again, maybe for minutes, maybe hours. Maybe days. I drag myself up from deep underwater again, catching snatches of conversations around me.

"We need to increase his dose. He's biting the tube."

A murmur of voices. One male. Two females. I try to open my eyes, but I can't.

"Has his commanding officer notified the family?"

"There's only one person to notify, and his colonel apparently knows her. He's going to call."

They're going to notify my family.

I'm dying.

But it doesn't frighten me. It's okay. Just more blackness. No more pain. Just peace.

Wait. Family...

Family means Charlie.

The pain is so intense, death would be a welcome relief, but I'm all Charlie has left. I can't die. She needs me, and I need her.

The voice comes from my left. "This should put him back under."

Darkness.

CHARLIE

My dejection leaves me unable to relax when I get home. I've never experienced a strong desire for my own family before tonight. Realizing it's something I'll never be able to have is soul-crushing, though I don't understand why losing something I'd never craved before has filled me with such deep despondency. I try to push it from my mind. I take a hot shower, check the door locks four times, drink two cups of chamomile tea, and fail epically at my attempt at meditation. It's half-past one the last time I glance at the clock from my perch on the foyer bench, gun in hand. I close my eyes, envisioning a cool mountain stream, imagining the sound of water tumbling over moss-slicked rocks and rushing around fallen logs. I can smell the crisp damp air and hear chirping birds and chattering squirrels, but every time I almost drift off, the images fade, just beyond my reach like everything else.

It's shortly after two when sharp rings pierce the foggy haze somewhere between sleep and wakefulness. I'm instantly alert, raising my gun as I scan the area until I realize the noise is my cell phone, not an intruder.

Colonel Sherman's name is on my screen.

Oh God.

My mouth goes dry. Colonels don't make calls at this hour.

My hands are shaking even before I answer. His baritone voice is gentle, urging me to fly to Brooke Army Medical Center in San Antonio immediately.

There's been an attack. An explosion, an IED. Multiple fatalities. Mark is in critical condition with a severe head injury. They've placed drains in his skull to relieve the pressure, trying to prevent permanent brain damage if he survives.

Dear God.

If.

There's more, much more, and he keeps talking as my stunned mind staggers to keep up. Mark's on a ventilator. The force of the blast ruptured his spleen and tore his liver. He has multiple broken bones, dozens of shrapnel wounds, and burns. The last thing he says is that the explosion shredded his right lower leg.

He uses that word, *shredded,* and I nearly vomit.

Shock rapidly turns to adrenaline, and moments later, I'm sprinting upstairs, dialing Lila. I put it on speakerphone, willing her to pick up as I hurl my suitcase onto the bed.

"Charlie?"

"I need a ride to the airport. Colonel Sherman called. Mark's been hurt." My brisk tone belies my panic as I fling clothes and necessities haphazardly into the case.

Lila gasps. "What do you mean, Mark's hurt? What happened?" There's brief static as she switches to speakerphone for Tucker's benefit.

"I don't know all the details. An IED exploded and Mark was thrown against an armored vehicle. They stabilized him and flew him to San Antonio."

"From Afghanistan?"

"The field hospital, then Landstuhl, then to Brooke." I stuff toiletries in around the edges of my suitcase.

"So he was burned." Her voice quavers. As former medics, we both know BAMC specializes in burn victims.

I grab my carry-on and start filling it as well. "Second and third degree, but he didn't say where or how much. He's unconscious with a bad head injury, on a vent. He had surgery to stop internal hemorrhaging. And –" I sink onto the bed. "And he said the blast shredded his right leg."

"Jesus Christ." Tucker's voice is barely a whisper. "But he's alive?"

"For now." I swallow hard. "But it's bad, Tucker. Really bad."

In the background, I hear the rapid clicking of computer keys. "I'm booking your flight," Lila says. "Pack fast."

"We're leaving now," Tucker says. "Unlock the chain on your door and leave your gun."

Tucker hurtles at top speed to get me to the airport, shadows flying past me in the dark before I can identify them. I make my flight with no time to spare.

The red-eye flight is agonizing. The interior of the plane is dimly lit as other passengers doze, but I couldn't sleep if my life depended on it. I can't stop trembling, my stomach in knots as one terrible question swirls through my mind. *What if?*

What if Mark doesn't make it? What if he lives, but has severe brain damage? What if he loses everything that makes him Mark – his memories, his brilliant mind, his sense of humor, his charisma?

What if I'm forced to keep a promise I never should have made?

An unwanted memory shoves to the forefront, playing like a movie in my mind. It was back in Afghanistan, late one night, with the four of us huddled around a fire. A few days before, we'd shipped out four of our guys with critical injuries sustained in an IED blast, and we'd received word that Taylor hadn't survived. The others were alive, but they'd never be the same. Jameson and Hardaway were missing limbs, and Brock's head injury was bad enough that they suspected he'd spend the rest of his life in a vegetative state.

Ryan Brock was twenty-two, just a kid, with a cheery smile, dancing eyes, and a mouth that would have shocked a sailor.

It wasn't fair.

We spent every day surrounded by the brutalities of war, driven by duty and denial. Horrible things happened all around us, but each of us believed we were immune, that it wouldn't happen to us. We had to. Hearing about Brock had ripped away our sheer veil of invincibility.

Tucker's light brown hair looked golden in the firelight, and though I couldn't see them in the semi-darkness, I knew his dark blue eyes were somber. His hands flexed repeatedly as he looked toward me and Lila, tipping his head toward us. "Would you want to live if you'd been badly injured? If you weren't the same?"

Lila made a face. "If I'm beating and breathing, yeah. I'll fight my way back."

I stared at orange sparks flying skyward as the tower of burning wood in the firepit shifted, taking my time before answering. "It would depend on what I'd lost."

Lila's head whipped around. "What does that mean?"

I shrugged. "There are things I wouldn't want to live through. I think I could deal with physical injuries. But TBI's? Traumatic brain injury," I clarified for Tucker. "Ending up like Brock, with my body intact and my mind gone?" I paused. "I don't want to be trapped in a healthy body with no idea who I am or who anyone else is. We've seen it too many times. The brain is fragile. I don't want to be completely oblivious for years until I finally die from pneumonia or an infected bedsore. I want to go out fighting."

Mark had silently walked me to my barracks later that night. I'd turned to go in when he caught my hand. "I won't let you go out like that, Baby Girl."

I turned back to look at him, his face half hidden by the darkness of the starless night. "How? Fighting? It's a little late to avoid that."

"No. Dying oblivious, trapped in a healthy body. I won't let that happen to you."

"I'm not sure you can prevent it."

He studied me, deliberately choosing each word. "If you truly wouldn't want to live that way, and I knew you really weren't in there anymore –" He'd hesitated. "I wouldn't make you live like that. It would be wrong to make you suffer."

The shadows playing across his face emphasized the weight of his words, and I shook my head. "I would never ask you to do that, Mark. That's too much. It's not right."

"You aren't asking, Charlie. I'm offering. I'll make sure you don't have to worry about living that way if we both know you wouldn't want to." He hesitated again. "For what it's worth, if it's me? If I'm not in there anymore, if my body hangs on, but I'm gone?" He'd tapped his chest. "I don't want that either. There's a difference between existing and living. If I'm merely existing, I'd rather die."

I remember wondering if we were actually having this surreal discussion, two best friends discussing mercy-killing each other if the unthinkable occurred. It was a possibility, albeit a remote one. Just having the conversation unnerved me.

His pale blue eyes were sober when I hugged him. "I hope it never comes to that."

He kissed my head and held me tight. "Me too, Baby Girl. Me too."

That conversation haunts me the entire flight.

I owe Mark my life, but if it comes down to it, am I strong enough to honor his wishes? Not just let them turn off the machines if he's unable to survive without them – as painful as that would be, I know I could make that call. But what if his flesh survives and his essence is gone? What if his body is merely a vessel for a vacant mind, the thing we'd both feared most? Am I strong enough to do as he asked? Am I strong enough to help him die?

By the time the flight lands, I'm a wreck. His words play on an endless loop in my mind.

If my body hangs on, but I'm gone? I don't want that.

There's a difference between existing and living. If I'm merely existing, I'd rather die.

Head injuries are tricky beasts. I've seen soldiers' heads wounded so badly, they're missing a chunk of skull, yet many heal without long-term deficits. That open area of skull gave the swelling somewhere to go, avoiding further injury to delicate brain tissue. I've seen other soldiers' heads bloodied and bruised, swollen like water balloons. They look so horrific immediately after the trauma that survival seems impossible. But despite their appearance, they may fully recover, because bleeding and swelling do far less damage outside a rigid skull.

Then there's the third type of head injury, where soldiers look like they're just sleeping. They don't have external bruises or bleeding. They've suffered a whiplash-type injury, where the head slung forward, stopped sharply, and snapped back, though their head never struck anything.

But their brain did.

The brain doesn't fully fill the skull; it's surrounded by fluid. Much like a crash dummy striking an airbag, when the head whips forward, the front of the brain smashes into hard skull. When the head snaps back, the back of the brain slams into the back of the skull, creating two separate brain injuries. The same thing happens in shaken-baby syndrome. Innocent-looking head injuries are often the most deadly.

And I have no idea what type of head injury Mark has sustained.

There's a difference between existing and living. If I'm merely existing, I'd rather die.

I swallow hard. I'm not strong enough for this.

I find an extended-stay hotel half a mile from the hospital, tossing my bags on the generic beige carpet of my room before racing to the sprawling brick complex. I pause at a desk and ask for Mark's location, dodging people milling through identical vanilla corridors like rats in a maze. When I find the correct ICU, a blond nurse asks my name and ushers me into an empty waiting room. "Dr. Paxton will be in to speak with you shortly. Make yourself comfortable."

She offers me coffee, but I'm too nauseous to drink anything. When she leaves, I perch on the edge of a chair, surveying my surroundings. The lights are low, with tissue boxes all around the room. Twelve tissue boxes, scattered around a room with only fifteen chairs.

I chew the inside of my lip. This isn't a room for delivering good news. My stomach clenches, and the familiar bands tighten around my chest.

Not again.

I draw a deep breath and close my eyes, then take another, and another, and another, until finally a feeling of calm strength starts to spread through me.

I can do this.

I have to. I'm the only one he has.

There's a quiet knock before a tall man in a white coat and a petite dark-haired nurse enter, closing the door behind them. My throat tightens.

Please let Mark be okay. Please.

The man has a runner's build, long and lean, and close-cropped brown hair. He holds out his hand. He has elegant fingers, like a pianist. "I'm Dr. Paxton, one of the trauma surgeons, and this is Monica, one of our nurses. Are you Captain Chandler's wife?" He takes a seat facing me. She chooses a chair to my right, angling her body toward me.

I shake my head. "He's not married. I'm Charlie Emerson. Mark is my best friend. He'll be coming home with me."

His tone is gentle as he glosses over the situation, likely trying to avoid inciting panic by speaking in smooth generalities. "Mark has multiple severe injuries. It's too soon to predict his prognosis with certainty, but his condition is critical."

I raise a hand to stop him. "I spent eleven years as a battlefield medic. I've seen horrors most people can't imagine. I need specifics. I can handle it."

Dr. Paxton's dark eyes study me carefully. Then he unearths a tablet from his voluminous lab coat and treats me as a colleague. He opens full-color photos of Mark's injuries, zooming in to show the full extent of them in horribly graphic detail. He shares Mark's labs, CT scans, X-rays, medication lists, and vital signs. The sheer volume of data leaves my mind whirling like a tornado. Of everything he says, his most terrifying words are "possible permanent brain damage". I know how to fix Mark's other injuries. There are protocols to follow, specific steps to take. But with brain injuries, all you can do is wait.

Patience is a virtue, but it isn't one of mine.

Dr. Paxton's staggeringly detailed information allows me to slide into my clinical mindset. The ability to separate ourselves from the pain and gore was drilled into us in medic training. Emotions are an unaffordable luxury on the battlefield. Empathy makes you emotional, but the wounded need you to be levelheaded. Emotions disrupt efficiency when seconds literally make the difference between life and death. Wounded soldiers need to be assessed quickly and objectively. If their injuries are unsurvivable, particularly in a mass casualty situation, ease their pain and move on to someone you may be able to save. It sounds cold, even brutal, and in a lot of ways, it is. Battlefield medicine requires you to shut down your compassionate side. It's an acquired skill, one I'm positive will get me through this.

I discover how wrong I am when Monica leads me to Mark's room. She halts outside his door, stopping me with a gentle hand. Her brown eyes are serious, her voice soft.

"Charlie, you and I have learned to detach our emotions from our patients. It's how we cope with the all-too-frequent tragedies we see. But you won't be able to do that here. It isn't some stranger in that bed. It's someone you care for, and it's going to hit you hard. Take as much time as you need to prepare. When you're ready, we'll go in together."

I dismiss her well-meaning words and reach for the door handle. I've spent the majority of my adult life taking care of trauma patients in the field. By the time they get to Monica, they're all tidied up. They don't have intestines spilling out of gaping belly wounds, raw burnt flesh, raggedly-torn limbs, or spurting arteries. No matter what's on the other side of that door, I've got this.

I should have listened to Monica.

I stand in the darkened room, staring, searching for some semblance of the man I know almost as well as I know myself, but the man in the bed in front of me is completely unfamiliar.

Maybe there's been a mistake. Maybe Mark is fine, and this is someone else.

Anyone else.

Anyone but Mark.

The man's dark blond hair has been shaved in spots, and two tubes crusted with dried blood drain excess fluid through small holes in his skull. A band of gauze encircles his head, leaving small tufts of hair poking out like sprigs of dry grass. His face is horribly swollen, blurring his features into one shapeless, unidentifiable mass covered in violent purple bruises and peppered with black sutures. Both eyes are swollen closed.

The hair color looks right, but the face is so deformed by swelling, this could be anyone.

Jesus. What if this *is* Mark? My heart skips a beat, then takes off at a gallop.

A breathing tube protrudes from his mouth, and the attached ventilator with its ribbed blue tubing hisses, pushing warmed air into his lungs. Monitors blink and beep quietly in the background. I turn away, studying the numbers and waves on the screens, fighting to regain control of my emotions by concentrating on clinical data, but it's not working.

Monica watches unobtrusively from the foot of the bed. I take another deep breath, steeling myself before scrutinizing the man again.

The longer I look, the more certain I am this isn't Mark. I start to say so but stop, knowing how ridiculous my words would sound. Instead, I examine the muscular chest and shoulders, bare above the blankets. My eyes travel down the bed, halting abruptly at the flattened area where his right lower leg should be.

Of course, it isn't there.

The jarring realization makes my stomach roll, and I sway unsteadily.

Monica appears at my side, steering me with firm hands into a chair near the head of the bed. "Take his hand. Talk to him. He'll know your voice. It will soothe him."

I collapse into the chair, trembling. I study the stranger again, searching for even one recognizable detail while simultaneously praying this critically wounded man isn't Mark.

When I see the pale Y-shaped sliver on his right shoulder, my racing heart slams to a stop.

I know that scar.

Mark got that scar when we were kids pretending to be cowboys. We snuck off to ride a neighbor's cranky horse, and he bucked us off. Mark's shirt and arm caught on the barbed wire fence, and he ended up with stitches while both of us got a very stern safety lecture.

That thin white sliver obliterates my wispy hopes, and my shallow breaths turn to rapid pants.

This isn't a dream. This is real.

That's Mark.

My soul shatters into a million pieces.

I squeeze my eyes tightly closed, drowning in panic. That's when I start hearing voices.

Well, just one voice. Mark's. It's part memory, part meltdown.

It pops into my head as clear as day. We were alone in my hospital room at Walter Reed after a particularly traumatic therapy session. A panic attack hit me hard and fast. Iron bands clamped around my chest. I struggled to breathe, but the faster I gasped, the less air I seemed to get, and the tighter the bands grew. Mark had stepped directly in front of me, cupping his hands loosely around my face, tilting it up so all I could see were his pale blue eyes.

“Breathe,” he’d said gently. “Slow and easy. I’m right here with you, Baby Girl. I’ve got you. Just breathe.”

The clarity of his voice inside my head stuns me, enough that I’d swear he’s speaking audibly. He can’t, though. He’s unconscious, with a machine helping him breathe. Still, I let the memory of his warm voice wrap around me, cocooning me like a blanket.

Breathe, Baby Girl.

Slow and easy.

I’m right here with you.

Just breathe.

I’ve probably lost my mind, but I don’t care. I clutch whatever part of Mark I have left.

I obey his soothing tones inside my head, slowing my breathing despite my tears. I become aware of Monica squeezing my shoulders, murmuring words of consolation. She places a box of tissues beside me. “I’ll give you some privacy. Call me if you need me.” Then she slips out, leaving me alone to wrestle with my emotions.

Breathe, his voice insists inside my head.

I’m right here, Baby Girl. Breathe.

When I can finally speak, I move my chair closer.

“Mark?” I whisper, seeking his right hand beneath the smooth sheets. I uncover it, clinging to it, inspecting his battered fingers. “Mark, I’m here. You’re going to be fine.” My laugh is shaky. “You didn’t have to do this to get me to visit. I’d drop anything for you.” My voice trails off as I study his bruised, swollen face. I recognize the thin scar embedded in one puffy eyebrow. Its familiarity gives me hope that he’s still in there. That he’s listening.

That he won’t leave me.

I stand and lean close to his ear, dodging his numerous tubes and lines. “I’m here, Mark. You’re going to be okay. I won’t give up on you. Just please don’t quit on me, please. I need you too much, Big Guy.” I press a soft kiss to his purpled cheek, then sit in the chair again, leaning against his bed. I grip his large hand and whisper the same words over and over, hoping he’ll hear me and listen. “Please don’t leave me, Mark. Please. I need you.”

I wake much later, still grasping his hand, my head on the bed beside him. Someone’s tucked a blanket around my shoulders. A folded piece of paper sits beside the tissue box. I open it to find a short note written in neat script.

IT’S ALWAYS DARKEST JUST BEFORE THE DAWN. BE STRONG.

MONICA

CHAPTER FOUR

CHARLIE

I'M EXHAUSTED BY THE time I return to my hotel room. It's just after midnight, but it feels like I've been awake for days. I drop my keys on the desk beside the paper sack containing a sandwich and toe off my sneakers. Then I flop on the bed with my phone, calling Tucker and Lila for a video chat. I'm under orders to call them as soon as I return to the hotel.

"Hey, Lila," I say when her worried eyes come into view. "Sorry it's so late."

"Hang on, Tucker's coming," she says, glancing over her shoulder.

Sure enough, within a few seconds, Tucker's dark blue eyes are peering at me from beside her. "You okay, Charlie?" he asks.

I swallow hard, my throat tight. "He's bad, Tuck. Really bad."

"Tell me everything the doctor said," Lila says. Her voice is firm, but she's twirling her curls around her fingers, the way she does when she's nervous.

"He has a Coup-contrecoup head injury," I say quietly. "Bleeding and swelling in the frontal and occipital lobes. He's got Burr holes and drains. Even with them, his intracranial pressure is high, and he may need surgery. They can't tell yet how much damage he's sustained."

"Time out," Tucker says. "Contray-what?"

"It's like shaken-baby syndrome," I tell him. "It's the same type of head injury." It's the one I was most worried about, because it's insidiously dangerous, invisible to the naked eye.

I wait while Lila explains about a fragile brain smashing into a rigid skull, trying desperately not to picture it as she speaks. I know Tucker understands when his expression freezes.

"So – so Mark has brain damage?"

"Head injuries take time," Lila says, trying to reassure him. She's shifted into clinical mode, the way I'd tried to earlier, but unlike me, she's successful, probably because she's seven hundred miles away and not staring at her best friend lying broken in a hospital bed. "We won't know anything until the swelling's gone down and he wakes up."

"But he will wake up?" Tucker asks.

The bands around my chest grow tight again. "Everything's very touch-and-go right now."

"What else?" Lila asks. "Don't leave anything out."

I give her a full head-to-toe clinical report, using medical jargon Tucker won't understand, knowing she'll break it down for him when I'm done. I close my eyes against the image of Mark lying helpless, surrounded by tubes and wires. It doesn't help. "His vitals are borderline. His temp's around one hundred and his white count's twenty-seven. He's tachycardic in the one-twenties with a BP in the nineties, even with norepinephrine. He had multiple rib fractures with floating ribs on the right, fixed with titanium plates and screws." I tick items off on my fingers as I mentally work my way down his body. "He's got a right-sided pneumo with a pigtail catheter and blast lung with bilateral chest tubes. He's intubated and on propofol. He had a large liver laceration and a ruptured spleen, so they operated at the field hospital and stopped the hemorrhaging. His hemoglobin stabilized at ten after eight units of blood here plus however many they gave him before he arrived. He's got second and third degree flash burns to both thighs with skin grafts on the right. His right femur was fractured. They tried to repair it at the field hospital, but they weren't successful, so he had surgery for that again when he got here. It's pinned, plated, and screwed. His right lower leg was partially amputated by the blast. They worked on it at the field hospital, but when he got here, it was infected, so they had to revise it and remove more tissue. He's got roughly two dozen shrapnel punctures and lacerations, including a large lac that severed the big artery in his right upper arm. He's septic. His lactic acid was six, but it's coming down. His creatinine is three, so there's kidney damage, but that should come down as his sepsis resolves."

Lila turns to Tucker, who's waiting impatiently for her interpretation. "Okay. Mark has a systemic infection from all the crap that penetrated his body and got into his wounds. That makes his heart rate and temperature go up and his blood pressure go down. The infection on top of the massive blood loss has injured his kidneys. With antibiotics, IV fluids, and blood transfusions, that should improve. He's on one infusion to keep his blood pressure up and one to sedate him while he's intubated. A pneumothorax is when air leaks into the chest cavity. Mark's was probably caused by a broken rib puncturing his lung. They use a tiny tube to let the air escape from the chest cavity so his lung can re-inflate properly."

"What's blast lung?" he asks, his gaze intently shifting from Lila to me and back.

I let Lila field his questions. "Lung tissue is very delicate, like single ply toilet paper. The shock wave from an explosion damages it. White blood cells rush to heal the area, causing a buildup of fluid that makes it harder to breathe. They've placed tubes to drain the fluid away."

I watch as Tucker frowns, processing what we've told him. "So he's got bleeding and swelling in the front and back of his brain, drains to remove fluid and lower the pressure inside his skull, and he may have permanent brain damage," he says. I nod, my chest tightening at the thought. "He's got three tubes in his chest and a machine helping him breathe." I nod again. "He was bleeding into his belly, but they stopped it." I nod a third time. He takes a deep breath. "And he's got a broken right thigh and an amputation below his right knee."

"And burns to both thighs," Lila adds, "with a skin graft on the deeper one."

Tucker nods, then glances at me hesitantly. "How does he look?"

My eyes sting as I recall Mark's swollen face, his features blurred into a shapeless mass of purple bruises and black sutures. "Unrecognizable," I whisper, barely swallowing over the enormous lump in my throat.

"It's just the swelling," Lila reassures me. "It'll go down, Charlie. Soft tissue can swell without too much damage, and the bruises will start to fade in a few days."

She doesn't understand. She hasn't seen him.

She correctly reads my expression and says, "Send me pictures. I'll feel better if I can see him."

My spine stiffens. "I'm not taking pictures of him, Lila."

"I need to see Mark with my own eyes."

"Not like this," I say firmly. "Trust me. This is a memory you don't want to have."

"We should close the gym and clinic and fly down," she says suddenly, glancing at Tucker.

I shake my head. "No. Not now, anyway. There's nothing you can do. There's nothing any of us can do right now except wait."

"You shouldn't be alone," Tucker says, his eyebrows pulling together.

"I'm okay," I lie. "Besides, we don't know how long he'll be unconscious. There's no point in leaving our clients stranded while we sit and stare at him. This could go on for a while."

"I don't like you down there by yourself," Tucker insists, rubbing his hand through his hair.

I see the concern in his eyes. He's dancing around what he really means: he's not sure how I'm going to cope with Mark barely clinging to life when I was already struggling with daily life back home. Frankly, neither am I. But closing both our businesses won't help Mark.

Lila sighs heavily. "Unfortunately, she has a point. Mark could be unconscious for three days or three weeks." *Or three months... or forever.* My throat tightens. "The three of us watching him lie there won't make him heal any faster."

Tucker frowns. "Mark's got an entire team of people taking care of him. Charlie's got no one."

His protectiveness warms me like a cozy blanket. "I'm not helpless, Tucker," I say gently.

He blows out a frustrated breath. "I know you're not, but this isn't something you should be dealing with alone."

"I'm not alone. You guys are just a phone call away. If he gets worse or I need you here, I'll call. I promise. But for now, as lousy as it is, all we can do is wait and see."

Tucker doesn't look happy, but he finally sighs. "Fine. We'll stay here for now, but if anything changes or you need us, we're on the next plane."

"Thanks, Tucker."

"Have you eaten anything today?" Lila asks.

Of course not. I spent most of the day trying not to throw up from nerves, but I don't mention that. "I bought a sandwich on my way back to the hotel, but I wanted to call you guys first."

"Eat," she says firmly. "Then get some sleep. You need to keep your strength up."

After we hang up, I do as instructed, eating my now-soggy chicken sandwich before heading for the shower. The water streaming down my face blends with my tears as images of Mark's bruised and battered body fill my mind. I start shaking, unable to stop. It continues after I'm out of the shower, even after drying my hair, even after huddling beneath the blankets and clutching a pillow to my chest, facing the hotel room door.

I can't lose Mark.

I *can't.*

I'm not strong enough to do this without him.

MARK

The blackness fades in and out as voices come and go. They must be angels. I wonder what they look like and if they have wings and harps. I don't hear any harps, though. Just voices.

I feel myself being shifted sometimes. I'm like a ragdoll, unable to move on my own, positioned by whoever is in charge here. Sometimes I hear different voices from far away, and I sense painfully bright lights beyond my eyelids.

My eyes are still too heavy to open. Maybe the bright light is the one I'm supposed to go to. If it is, I hope one of the angels will tell me.

That's my last thought before the darkness returns. It always returns.

Then I hear her. She's here. *Charlie's here!*

She's crying.

Don't cry, Charlie.

I need to tell her not to cry, but I can't push through this fog. Darkness overtakes me again.

I partially resurface later, though I don't know how long it's been. I'm still engulfed in a thick haze, but I hear her voice again. Charlie's still here. She's talking.

What is she saying?

Her voice is gentle, but I can't make out her words. I try to turn toward her. She's on my right, but I can't move my head, and I can't convince my eyes to open.

Why won't my body cooperate?

I try to growl my frustration, but nothing happens.

Darkness.

Every time the darkness starts to lift, I hear her voice, husky and sweet. Sometimes I hear music, familiar but distant. It reminds me of her.

Charlie's still here. She hasn't left me.

I need to wake up. I have to talk to her. But the darkness is too strong. I fight it with all my might, but it keeps overpowering me.

At least I can hear her. I don't know what she's saying, but she's with me. Her presence comforts me. Soothes me.

Charlie's with me.

Darkness.

CHARLIE

Despite my physical and emotional exhaustion, I can't sleep. I'm too anxious. I toss and turn in the bed, relocate to the firm recliner, and even try lying sideways across the second queen-sized bed in the room, but it's no use. Every time I close my eyes, I see Mark's broken body. The images seize my heart, compounding my fear he won't wake up. Or worse, he will wake up, but he'll be gone – an empty vessel devoid of *him,* leaving me forced to keep a promise I never should have made.

Eventually, I rifle through the packets at the small coffeemaker in the tiny kitchenette and find tea bags. I brew myself some green tea, sipping quietly, trying to envision my happy place in the woods beyond my house. I close my eyes and picture the solitude of the mountain stream. I can almost hear the water splashing over the rocks and feel the damp moss beneath me and the rough bark of the tree at my back. I breathe deeply, drawing on the peaceful image in my mind. When my mind is calmer, I turn on the ceiling fan for some white noise and crawl into bed.

But it's not meant to be.

An hour later, I'm crouching on the floor beside the bed, drenched in sweat from another night terror. I scan the room, temporarily disoriented by my unfamiliar surroundings. Then it all comes crashing back, and for once, the memory of my present situation is worse than my past.

I drag myself through the shower again, hoping the steamy water will wash away my fatigue. It doesn't. I unpack my bags and settle into the hotel room, wishing I'd brought a backpack or messenger bag. I check my phone and find a twenty-four-hour superstore nearby. An hour later, I'm back at my hotel, armed with snacks, bottled water, and a faux-leather tote large enough for my laptop, tablet, and the contents of my purse.

I return to the hospital before daylight. In the dark, the enormous brick and glass complex shines with lights from at least half the windows despite the early hour. Hospitals aren't for sleeping, they're for healing, and anyone expecting a night of uninterrupted sleep is in for a rude awakening.

My Uber driver drops me off, and I hurry inside, bracing myself against the brisk January winds. I find my way through the maze of hallways to the ICU more easily today. When I slip into Mark's darkened room, I pause, scrutinizing him. He looks the same as yesterday, swollen and battered and bruised, not at all like my Mark. My chest constricts.

The room has a beige vinyl couch that folds out into a cot-sized bed, a recliner beside the window, and a straight-backed chair for me to choose from. I drop my bag on the couch and move toward the monitors attached to

Mark, gauging his condition based on objective data. His heart rate and blood pressure are mildly improved, and his ventilator settings are unchanged. These are good signs – he's stable, and slightly better than yesterday.

I glance briefly up at the stethoscope dangling above the ventilator and hesitate a split second before reaching for it. I listen to his heart and lungs with a practiced ear. His lungs still have fluid at the bases, but his heartbeat is reassuringly strong. I return the stethoscope to its hook and glance thoughtfully at him before deciding I might as well assess the rest of him. I'll feel better if I do. Besides, if he were conscious, he'd let me. I've patched him up plenty of times before.

I take a deep breath and gently pull down his covers. The absence of his right lower leg makes my stomach clench. Limb loss isn't easy for alpha male soldiers to cope with, and Mark is one of the most alpha males I know. His limb now ends five or six inches below his knee. It's hard to tell exactly because thick gauze wraps all the way to his hip, presumably also covering his burns and the incision from his femur surgery. Flat metal bars run down either side of his thigh to his knee. They're held by velcro straps to brace his repaired femur. His bandages are clean, except for some yellowish-brown drainage near the amputation site. His left leg is swollen and splotched with dark purple bruises, and assorted dressings cover several shrapnel wounds and his thigh burn.

I pull the blankets back up to Mark's waist, then loosen his gown and slide it up to examine his torso. It, too, is covered in angry bruises and assorted gauze dressings – one at each of his three chest tube sites, one spanning the width of his upper abdomen from the surgery to repair his liver and remove his spleen, and a vertical one along his right chest wall where they repaired his free-floating broken ribs. There are also several smaller dressings over shrapnel punctures.

I tug his gown back down and straighten his covers, smoothing them lightly over his chest. Then I reach for his right hand and squeeze it as I lean down to kiss his swollen cheek, avoiding his tubes and lines. "Morning, Big Guy. How about waking up and talking to me?"

He doesn't, not that I'd expected him to.

I just hope he wakes up soon, and that when he does, he's still Mark.

Because if he's not, I don't know what I'll do.

I watch him, pretending he's just sleeping as I drag the recliner over to his bed and sit down, sandwiching his right hand between both of mine. Mark and I have been best friends almost since we met. He and his parents moved next door when I was nine and he was eleven. Not even two weeks later, he rescued me. We'd met twice already, once when my mom and I took over a tray of cookies to welcome his family to the neighborhood, and again when my dad lent his dad a drill because his hadn't yet been unearthed from a moving box.

The day Mark became my hero, I was on the soccer field after school, practicing dribbling and cutting maneuvers. He was there practicing, too, but we weren't practicing together. I'd lost control of my ball, and it rolled off the edge of the field and down a slight incline behind the back corner of the gymnasium. I trotted after it, startled to find Corbin Holmes lurking back there. Corbin was a big, mean, nasty-tempered bully a couple of years older than me. He grabbed my soccer ball and refused to give it back. When I attempted to pull it out of his meaty hands, he let go of it, and I fell onto my backside. Before I could blink, he'd flipped me onto my stomach and was kneeling on my back, shoving my face into the gravel. I was furious, trying to buck him off, swearing I'd knock his teeth out when I got up – a rather ambitious threat, considering he was a full head taller and at least forty pounds heavier.

I'd heard quick footsteps crunching on the gravel right before Mark had appeared, tall and skinny, with long arms and legs and pale blue eyes that immediately assessed the situation. He didn't waste a second before snatching Corbin up by his collar and dragging him upright, then jerking his arms behind his back. He'd called Corbin a pussy for picking on a girl half his size. Corbin snarled, but there wasn't much else he could do. Then Mark had tipped his chin at me. "You wanna keep your promise?"

I'd gotten to my feet, brushing the dirt off my scraped knees and frowning at the tear in my favorite tee shirt. Stupid Corbin Holmes. "What promise?"

"To knock his teeth out."

I'd looked at Mark in surprise, and he'd grinned. Then I marched right up to Corbin, drew back my fist, and planted it solidly in his mouth. I'm not sure who was more surprised by the sudden flow of bright blood – me or Corbin. "You're dead," he threatened, spitting on the ground.

Mark had hitched Corbin's arms higher behind his back, enough to make him squeak in pain. "I don't think so," he'd said calmly, "because if you hurt her, it'll be the last thing you do, pussy. Mess with her, and you're messing with me. And you don't wanna do that." Then he'd hurled Corbin facefirst on the ground, taken me by the hand, and led me forward, both of us tromping right across Corbin's back.

I developed my first crush that day.

"Thanks," I'd told him when we got to the field.

He'd looked at me and frowned. "You're bleeding," he'd said. He'd glanced down at his dirty shirt, then pulled it up and used the inside of it to wipe the blood from my lip where Corbin had shoved my face in the gravel. "Nice punch," he said. "I don't think you knocked any teeth out, but you cut his lip up pretty good."

"You think he'll tell on me?" I asked, suddenly worried about getting called to the principal's office. I was pretty sure my parents wouldn't like that.

But Mark had laughed. "He's not going to tell anyone that a girl beat him up."

I'd eyed him. "You shouldn't say 'pussy'," I said. "It's crude."

He grinned. "Tell you what. I won't tell anyone you punched him in the mouth if you don't tell anyone I used crude language."

I'd agreed, and from that moment on, we'd been inseparable, always at each other's houses, hanging out together, and watching each other's backs. My childhood crush faded away, replaced by deep friendship. I helped Mark practice football passes from the time I was ten until he graduated from high school, and I can still throw a decent spiral. He tutored me in algebra and chemistry so I could pull off a C in both, something both I and my parents were immensely grateful for. When my jackass of a boyfriend Kirk dumped me for KiKi Carter two days before my prom, Mark asked if I'd go with him instead. I said yes, and Mark made sure we danced right next to the two of them. KiKi flirted her ass off with Mark the entire night, batting her big doe eyes and angling her body to give him an eyeful of her impressive boobs. He ignored her, and she and Kirk both ended up pissed off – KiKi because Mark gave her the brush-off, and Kirk because KiKi had lost all interest in him when compared to Mark, Lakeview High's former star football player. Mark and I stayed out all night, going out for huge, messy burgers (because what else would a hot guy in a black tux and a girl in a backless white prom dress eat?). Then we laid in the bed of his truck, listening to music and watching the stars until the sun came up. Mark had rescued me again, and my crush on him returned in full force. I kept it to myself until I left for college a few months later, unwilling to make a fool of myself by acting on it.

It wasn't all good times for us, though.

When Mark was thirteen, his mom was diagnosed with advanced breast cancer. By the time they'd found it, the cancer had already spread to her brain, lungs, and bones. She'd endured chemo for her family's sake, hoping for a miracle that wasn't meant to be. When she died, he and I leaned against each other in my basement for hours, him trying not to cry and failing, me rubbing his shoulders, unsure what to say or do. At eleven, I'd not dealt with the death of an adult before.

Two years later, his dad died. I didn't understand until later that his car accident hadn't been an accident at all. He'd intentionally driven into a concrete bridge abutment at seventy miles an hour, disguising his suicide. He couldn't handle losing his wife, and his unrelenting grief caused him to abandon his son. Mark didn't cry that day. He was too stunned. I'd wrapped my arms around him while he sat there, numb, both of us shaken by the irrefutable evidence that youth is no guarantee against pain and loss.

That's when Mark moved in with us. My parents converted our finished basement into a teenager cave, with a bedroom, bathroom, kitchenette, and living room. It was a mini-apartment in our basement, and he and I hung out there constantly – except when he'd sneak his girlfriends over. Then I ran interference for him, keeping my parents distracted. He'd do the same for me, letting me use his man-cave to sneak my boyfriends over.

Tragedy continued to find us, though. I'd finished my last final exam of my freshman year of college and was headed for a party when Mark showed up at my dorm, his eyes red and swollen. A drunk driver had hit my parents' car head-on. There were no survivors. Mark took the news as hard as I did. He'd lost his parents, found a second family in mine, and lost my parents, too. Everyone Mark cared about, he lost. I was the lone exception. I suspect that's subconsciously why he's always avoided any substantial long-term relationships.

A groan from the hospital bed yanks me back to full attention, and I sit up straight. "Mark?" I tighten my fingers around his bruised hand, then stop, afraid I'll hurt him. "Mark? Can you hear me?" He moans again, and I jump up, cupping his face gently between my hands, careful to avoid his breathing tube. "I'm here, Mark. You're okay. Everything's going to be okay." I press the button for the nurse, and he groans a third time. A moment later, a tiny blond woman with a hugely pregnant belly hurries in.

"Hi, dear. Did you need something?"

"I think he's hurting," I tell her, just as Mark groans again. She whips out a penlight and checks his pupils, asking him to squeeze her hands and open his eyes, but to no avail.

"Any change?" I ask.

"Responding to pain is good, but we don't want him hurting. I'm going to get him something for the pain."

The shot stops his pained moans, but even when he falls silent, I can't take my eyes off him. He's got to be okay. He's got to. Mark is my person. He's my best friend, my hero, my rescuer. He knows me better than anyone, and he's the most important person in my world.

He's got to be okay, because I can't do this without him.

CHAPTER FIVE

CHARLIE

DAYS AND NIGHTS BEGIN to bleed into each other. I stay past midnight and return before dawn every day, leaving just long enough to shower, catch an hour or two of fitful sleep, and shower again. It's nerve-wracking being unarmed in a strange location. I can't doze for more than a few minutes without waking in a panic to scan my surroundings. I finally resort to catnapping upright against my hotel room door so I know no one can sneak up on me. Lila comments on my exhaustion during one of our video chats, and when I confess my struggle in a moment of weakness, Tucker has two soft-grip telescoping tactical batons delivered to me by the end of the day. When extended, they can shatter bones; collapsed, they're innocuous looking, barely longer than a tube of lip gloss. That night, I sleep for a solid four hours.

Spending so much time in a military hospital again is also adding to my tension. While BAMC isn't Walter Reed, it's still populated by uniformed officers and soldiers alongside healthcare providers in white coats and scrubs. The cloying perfume of efficiency and disinfectant combines with the constant auditory and visual stimulation, leaving me feeling like every nerve in my body is raw. My days are a gumbo of fear and anxiety, heavily seasoned with intrusive memories of a time I've tried desperately to forget.

I cope by pouring all my energy into Mark. If he can hear me in his comatose state, then I intend to do everything possible to prevent memory loss. I talk to him incessantly. I discuss anything and everything – what the doctors said, what today's goal is, what they're serving in the cafeteria. It doesn't matter what I talk about, so long as I'm engaging his brain and maintaining our connection. I talk until my voice gives out, then switch to his favorite music or audiobooks.

Monica spends a lot of time in Mark's room. She lets me assist with whatever she's doing for him, not because she needs my help, but because she understands my need to stay busy.

"Tell me how you're related," she says one day while we're changing his dressings. "Brother and sister? Cousins?"

Monica was born and raised in Colombia and still has a slight accent. Her olive skin is dazzling, and her dark eyes and long dark hair emphasize her brilliant smile. She's intelligent and kind, and I'm glad Mark has her.

"We're not. We're best friends. His family moved next door when I was nine and he was eleven. His mom died of breast cancer when he was thirteen." A flash of sadness hits me at the memory of his mom transforming from a vibrant, lively woman to little more than a skeleton, gray and gaunt. Mark's dad underwent the same evolution, but from grief. "His dad couldn't handle losing her. He committed suicide when Mark was fifteen."

Monica rubs Mark's leg. "So tragic," she murmurs. "So much pain."

"His dad made arrangements before his death for my parents to become Mark's guardians. Our parents had been best friends. My folks were crushed when his parents died."

She gives me a quizzical look. "If you aren't related, why does the military consider you his next of kin?"

I smile. "Because any guardian's family member can be designated next of kin."

"So your parents, will they be coming?"

My smile fades. "No. They died when I was eighteen. It's just been Mark and me since then. We enlisted after they died. We were barely grown, not sure what to do with our lives. The Army offered purpose and structure, and we needed both."

"You left the Army and he stayed in?"

Time stops for a moment, and my breathing stalls briefly as icy memories tighten my stomach. "Yes. I've been out for four years. Mark had planned to stay until he hit twenty years."

She smiles. "I'm glad he has you here. He's going to need you."

The times I'm alone with Mark without distractions are hardest. That's when I'm forced to face horrifying possibilities I'm not strong enough to deal with.

What if he doesn't survive?

I can't do this without Mark. I just can't.

What if he lives, but he's not in there? Can I truly help him die?

I hear his voice in my head every time that question crosses my mind – which is often. *There's a difference between existing and living, Charlie. If I'm merely existing, I'd rather die.*

I'm a wreck, barely sleeping, barely eating, haunted by fears I'm too afraid to face. Every other day brings a new surgery. Explosions force debris deep into the body, creating wounds that have to be reopened and cleaned frequently. Every other day, it's more anesthesia, more risk, more chances of losing him. I'm hanging on by the thinnest of threads. I tell myself over and over he'll be okay, and I clutch at that hope with every ounce of my strength, but in those moments when my guard is down, fear consumes me, and I can barely breathe.

No one can tell if there's permanent brain damage yet. Mark might still be in there, or he might not. He's heavily sedated until his lungs improve, and until he's off sedation, they can't accurately assess his mental status. Not knowing is wringing me out, and if it weren't for my frequent talks with Lila and Tucker, I don't think I'd survive. I don't tell them that, though.

Days blur together. I measure time by milestones. I can't tell you what day of the week it is, but I know that the fifth day after my arrival, they're pleased enough with his CT scans to remove the drains from his skull. Three days later, his lungs have improved enough to lower his ventilator settings, encouraging him to breathe on his own with the tube still in place. The next day, Dr. Paxton approaches me in the hall.

"I'm removing his breathing tube. He's done well with minimal sedation, and I think he's ready." He pats my upper arm reassuringly.

If Mark can't manage without the tube, it will mean a tracheostomy – a permanent hole in his throat for breathing. It's yet another thing he wouldn't want, and I pace in the hall until Dr. Paxton comes out, reassuring me that everything went perfectly.

Good news is a welcome relief.

I spend all afternoon by his side, talking and holding his hand. Most of his facial swelling has resolved, and the purple bruises have faded to green and yellow. He's breathing easily, with simple nasal oxygen for support, but he's still asleep, so I keep talking, stubbornly prodding him, willing him back to me.

"I have a house in the mountains. You'll like it. It's in Tucker's hometown, a place called Cedar Ridge. He and Lila live just a few minutes from me, and they've got horses and goats. Can you believe it? Lila has goats, ten or twelve of them, all girls, all named after supermodels. I'm sure they'd be offended if they knew. The models, I mean, not the goats." I chuckle. "I think you'll be comfortable at my house. It's way too big for just me, but it spoke to my soul. Sounds weird, I know, but it's true. It's in the woods where it's green and quiet. You know me. I need the quiet. It has five bedrooms and tons of windows, and the views are incredible, with the most amazing sunsets I've ever seen. The sun paints the mountains this brilliant red. That's how they got their name. Sangre de Cristo? It means the blood of Christ. I think they were named by a priest. Or maybe it was an explorer? I can't remember –"

"You talk a lot, Baby Girl."

I nearly jump out of my skin at the hoarse whisper. Mark's pale blue eyes are open, and he has a tired smile on his haggard face. I shriek and launch myself at him, burying my face in his chest and bursting into tears. He leans forward and kisses the top of my head, slowly dragging his right arm up to stiffly rub my shoulders. "It's okay, Charlie. Don't cry." His voice is gruff, sandpapery.

His words finally register in my exhausted brain. He called me Baby Girl! He called me Charlie!

"You remember me!" I sob, and he stops moving. "They weren't sure you would," I ramble, wiping my eyes and sitting up, catching his befuddled expression. "I'm sorry. You're the one who's been through hell and I'm over here falling apart." I cradle his face in my hands. "I was so afraid I was going to lose you." Fresh tears stream down my cheeks. "I can't lose you, Mark. I can't."

He shakes his head, then winces. "I'll never leave you, Baby Girl. You're stuck with me."

"I'm holding you to that." I dry my eyes again and press the call button. "I've got to tell Monica you're awake." I kiss his stubbled cheek, resting my head on his chest again. We've finally turned a major corner.

Things progress erratically once he regains consciousness. Mark makes steady advances in some areas but lags behind in others. The morning after he wakes up, I'm delighted to find him up in the recliner, staring at the pink and orange clouds streaking the sky. He still has numerous tubes and lines, and he's pale, thin, and scruffy, but he's upright, and his mind seems fully intact.

"Tell me you brought real coffee." His voice is still raspy from the breathing tube. "This stuff is horrible."

I smile, holding up two cups. "I sensed your desperate need for caffeine." I pass him the taller cup and kiss the top of his head. He slides an arm around my waist and I lean gently against him, thrilled at how much he's improved in twenty-four hours. "How are you feeling?"

He purses his lips. "I made it to the chair. I never thought that would be an accomplishment."

I rub his upper back. "Baby steps, Big Guy. Yesterday you were still intubated. This is a massive improvement."

Dr. Paxton had been pleased to see Mark awake last night, but when Mark pressed him about his recovery, he'd been direct.

Very direct.

"Your body has taken some extremely hard hits, Captain," he'd said, dragging a chair to his bedside. "Your lungs are healing, but it will take months to regain stamina. Recovery from your brain injury could take a year or more. It's normal to experience memory gaps, mood swings, angry outbursts, inappropriate emotional responses, depression, and anxiety following a head injury, and it's possible to see those changes linger for years or even decades, though medication can reduce the symptoms. Your abdominal injuries are improving, but your core muscles have to knit together before you can begin strengthening them. You'll be more prone to infections without your spleen, so before procedures, you'll require antibiotics."

Then he'd pulled the covers back to expose Mark's right leg, or more accurately, what remained of it. Mark's jaw tightened. I slipped my hand in his and he gripped it tightly, tension radiating from him in waves.

Dr. Paxton raised the hospital gown to Mark's upper thigh and gestured to the swath of thick gauze encircling his leg from his hip to where it ended several inches below his knee. "You sustained a large burn along the outside of this thigh. The explosion produced a flash burn, hot and fast, so the damage was relatively confined. We removed the damaged tissue and placed a skin graft here." He traced the outline with his fingertip. "There's another burn along your left inner thigh, but it was shallow enough that it didn't require grafting. Your right leg took the majority of the damage."

I'd glanced at Mark's face, but it remained expressionless, his stare fixed on Dr. Paxton's face. He remained motionless but for the repeated flexing of his jaw.

He didn't look down at his leg even once.

"Your right femur was shattered," he continued. "They attempted unsuccessfully to repair it at the field hospital. When you arrived, we rebuilt your femur with plates, pins, and screws. That will take several months to fully heal." Dr. Paxton hesitated. "Your lower leg was ripped apart by the blast. The bones ended in splinters just below your calf, and what little tissue remained was torn to ribbons. The medics stopped the bleeding and flew you to the field hospital. The field hospital amputated lower than what you see now. When you arrived, it was infected, and we had to remove additional tissue to preserve the limb." He studied Mark, gauging his reaction. "Down the road, when your femur fully heals, you'd be ideal for a procedure called osseointegration. We would implant a porous rod in the center of your remaining bone, allowing you to use a mechanically-connected prosthesis rather than one that slips on over your stump."

"I hate that word," Mark growled.

Dr. Paxton nodded. "I don't blame you. It's a lousy word for a lousy situation." He'd waited, but Mark said nothing else. "If your femur heals properly, I believe you would benefit tremendously from osseointegration. You're young and strong, and it should allow you to achieve optimal function."

He looked at Mark's expression, then plunged ahead. "Your other injuries will take time. Broken ribs heal slowly, and the wound to your right bicep will limit your ability to use crutches for now. Your other wounds are healing well, and I don't foresee long-term issues from any of them. But I don't want to downplay your challenges. You've come a long way, but you still have an uphill battle."

I'd raised my chin and moved closer to Mark. "He won't be fighting alone," I said, putting my hand on his shoulder. Mark reached up to cover my hand with his own, and despite his stoic façade, I'd felt his hand tremble.

Dr. Paxton smiled. "A solid support system is crucial, and this young lady has barely left your side. You're in excellent hands, Captain." Then he'd gotten to his feet. "If either of you have questions, just ask. The nurses can reach me day or night." Then he'd gone, leaving us to collect the shattered pieces of Mark's world.

MARK

An amputee.

I'm a fucking amputee.

Some assholes in the sandbox set off an IED packed with ball bearings and rocks and shards of metal and shit, and now I'm missing half a leg. And that's not all. I've got tubes coming out of every orifice, and when there weren't enough holes, they made more. Holes in my chest. Holes in my skull. I've got broken bones, a body full of shrapnel, and burns.

And a goddamned stump where I used to have a leg.

The trauma surgeon comes to see me after I regain consciousness. Charlie's with me when he talks to me.

He's straightforward. Blunt. Surgical, eviscerating me, gutting my hopes. Not that I want him candy-coating anything, but still.

I'll heal eventually, but I'm damaged goods. Best case, I'm looking at a prosthetic leg after more surgeries. Worst case, my head injury permanently fucks me up, mentally and emotionally.

After fifteen years of protecting the weak from the bullies, I go out like this? A fucking cripple? What a load of horseshit.

But Charlie won't let me wallow. She pushes me forward, even when I feel mired in quicksand. She spends all day at my side, coming early and leaving late. She patiently waits while I'm in PT and helps with wound treatments and dressing changes. And she never flinches, not even when they clean my burns and the stench of dead flesh fills the air.

Not even when they unwrap and redress my stump.

God, I hate that word. *Stump.* It brings to mind a dead tree. Which is accurate, I suppose. A useless, dead chunk.

I hate the word 'stump' almost as much as I hate what my body has become. Repulsive. Weak. Vile.

But Charlie is relentlessly positive. Because it's her, I try to control my negativity, but sometimes it surges, and I behave like an ass.

And then, because things weren't shitty enough, the phantom pain starts. What was once a prickling sensation emanating from my non-existent foot morphs into crippling agony.

Holy fuck.

It's ferocious, debilitating, and infuriating. I don't have a fucking leg there anymore, so why do I have such excruciating pain? It doesn't make sense.

Maybe I am fucking crazy.

As my body slowly recovers, I start seeing a shrink. It's mandated, and because it's a military hospital and I'm not yet officially discharged from the military, I don't have a choice in the matter. Dr. Friedman is perfectly nice, but he pushes me to take pain meds for the phantom pain in my leg. I've refused, because there's no leg there. It's not logical for something that isn't there to hurt. I finally surrender after I miss a PT session because I'm in so much pain I can barely breathe. I take the damn pain meds. I have to go to PT. It's my only hope of achieving anything close to normalcy again.

Dr. Friedman also keeps pushing me to take an antidepressant. Fuck that. After all this shit, who wouldn't be depressed? We talk a lot about depression, anxiety, mood swings... well, he talks, and I sit in stony silence, running out the clock. I'm not taking any more pills. If I were stronger, I wouldn't even need pain pills, but that phantom pain is a motherfucker.

My body continues healing. I'm getting stronger. My physical and occupational therapists are teaching me how to manage my miserable new reality. As my body improves, my internal resentment heightens. I'm always at a low boil, and every little thing sets me off. I'm biting the heads off nurses and therapists, but they don't engage or bite back. They look at me with pity. They never say it, but I see it on their faces. Pity for the useless cripple.

I'm like a taut cable, ready to snap. I'm even bad-tempered with Charlie, but she lets it slide. Sometimes she'll raise an eyebrow or disappear and return with coffee or food. She doesn't pity me, thank God. If I saw pity in her eyes, I couldn't stand it. But Charlie looks at me the same way she's always looked at me. We've always had a connection far deeper than mere friendship. I don't know how to describe it, except to say she's everything to me, and she's all I have.

But even our bond isn't strong enough to hold my temper in check.

CHARLIE

Dr. Paxton hasn't exaggerated about the challenges ahead. Mark has his burns debrided again a few days later. Dead and infected tissue gets scraped away until only healthy pink tissue remains. It's brutal, but necessary. After that, he begins daily hyperbaric treatments that promote healing but leave him utterly exhausted.

I'm exhausted as well. Despite my tactical batons, I'm barely sleeping. Every door closing, every bus honking, every person talking in the hall, every parade of excited high school or college kids sprinting past – my anxious brain registers all these as lethal threats, keeping me in a perpetual state of hypervigilance. I'm averaging an hour and a half of sleep at night, broken up into two or three brief spurts between panic attacks and night terrors.

To hide my weariness, I act as Mark's personal morale booster, buying a cheap printer and covering his hospital room walls with photos and humorous sayings. I pick up outside food or treats most days to give him something to look forward to. I also schedule video chats every evening with Tucker and Lila, and he seems more relaxed after talking with them.

A few days later, Dr. Paxton sees us making our awkward laps in the halls. Because of Mark's bicep injury, I act as a human crutch on his right side. His injured arm rests along my shoulders while I grip his canvas gait belt. He uses his left crutch normally. Dr. Paxton stops to examine Mark's arm. "We can remove these sutures today. Maybe soon you'll be able to use crutches with both arms."

Mark is eager to try, but ambulating using two crutches causes pain in his broken ribs and healing abdominal wounds. He persists, ignoring his aching bones and burning muscles, convinced that stubborn determination is all he needs. More than once, he's forced to rest on a hall bench to avoid collapsing.

Dr. Paxton comes in the next morning as we're drinking coffee. I tense at his resigned expression, knowing immediately that it's bad news. "Put down your coffee, Captain. I just reviewed your femur x-rays. I'm taking you back to surgery this afternoon."

Mark's screwed-and-plated thigh bone isn't healing. The bone fragments stubbornly refuse to fuse together. The new plan involves a Humpty-Dumpty-esque plan involving external pins and a device resembling a roll cage. It's a last ditch effort. If the bones won't heal, he could end up losing his upper leg as well. But Mark doesn't know that, and I'm sure as hell not going to tell him.

Dr. Paxton removes all the old hardware before scuffing the bone surfaces and cementing pieces together, filling gaps and adding bone grafts. Then comes the new hardware: internal pins, plates, screws, external fixators, and the external cage. It's an extensive surgery, nearly five hours long, and all I can do is hope it's enough.

Because if it's not, I don't know what we'll do.

CHAPTER SIX

CHARLIE

Mark's additional femur surgery puts him back at square one. He's under strict orders regarding his activity, and rule number one is that he's not allowed to get up without help. This has been stated ad nauseam. Monica even wrote it in capital letters on his whiteboard. Despite the warnings, a few mornings after surgery, I enter his room to find him getting out of bed alone. He's upright, but his bedsheet is tangled around both the cage and his crutch. "Freeze, Big Guy."

Mark glances up with a guilty expression. It quickly turns to annoyance when he realizes I'm not the nurse. "I'm not a fucking invalid," he snaps. "I'm a goddamn soldier. I'm going to the bathroom and I don't need an escort."

"Well, Captain, perhaps you should unwrap the sheet from your leg and crutch." My voice is calm, my expression neutral as I kneel in front of him.

He dips his head, seeing the fabric caught around his leg and the crutch. "Lean on your left crutch," I instruct, and when he does, I lift the right one, freeing it and the cage from the offending sheet. "You're good now."

"Charlie," he begins, his face reddening, but I shake my head.

"Bathroom." I point, barely resisting the urge to add, "Soldier".

When he returns at a snail's pace, he still looks sheepish. "Sorry." He eases onto the bed, slowly positioning his caged thigh on a pillow and moving gingerly, wincing with every movement. Normally he'd be up in the recliner, watching the sunrise. Today he's pulling the covers up, his expression tight, the shades still down.

"Want me to call for something for pain?"

He glares. "No."

I'm not surprised. I can't recall Mark ever taking anything stronger than an aspirin before this. Whatever discomfort he had, he pushed through. Pain medications are one more thing forced upon him. His expression sours every time the nurses administer pain meds, but it's a necessary evil. If he can't participate in rehab, he can't achieve his recovery goals.

"I'm going back to sleep. It was a rough night."

"Want me to wake you for breakfast?"

"Powdered eggs and soggy bacon? I'll pass." He drags the covers over his head.

Hostility oozes from him, composed of layer upon layer of frustration. The abrupt end to his career. The loss of his identity, nearly inseparable from the military after all this time. Losing the only home he's known for fifteen years. His surviving brothers-in-arms he couldn't tell goodbye. The brothers who fell beside him and never got up. Survivor's guilt. Lackadaisical healing. Pain. Body image issues. Being trapped in a hospital. His loss of independence. And now phantom pain. It's agonizing, seeing him struggle under the weight of his growing despair.

Phantom pain is understood by few, even within the medical community. After an amputation, particularly traumatic ones, amputees sometimes experience severe, unrelenting pain that seems to originate in the missing limb. The only proven treatment? His nemesis, pain medication. As a result, discouragement and depression have crept in, black panthers slinking through the darkness after scenting their prey.

Mark views his phantom pain as a failure because it forces him to take pain medication. I'd hoped Dr. Friedman could get through to him. He's one of BAMC's top psychiatrists, and he specializes in head injuries and limb loss. They've been meeting twice a week, discussing depression, anxiety, mood swings, and pain – or rather, Dr. Friedman discusses them. Mark ignores him. Therapy is another thing Mark equates to personal failure.

Dr. Friedman has explained that shrugging off a headache is far easier than coping with the brutality of burned flesh and shattered bones. He encourages Mark to view his pain as a healthy response to overwhelming trauma. That might have been a concept Mark could accept, but as soon as he brought up psych meds, Mark tuned him out. To him, if pain signifies weakness, depression is even worse. He dismisses every suggestion of meds for his emotional turmoil.

"Try viewing medications as one more tool in your arsenal," I encourage him one day over pineapple and pulled pork sandwiches from the nearby deli. "They're a resource to boost your recovery. You're learning to cope with your injuries by using crutches to walk and climb stairs. Meds can help you push through the pain and bolster you emotionally."

My words fall on ears that choose to be deaf.

Not only does Mark adamantly shun antidepressants, he starts ditching his mandated appointments with Dr. Friedman. In a military hospital, that flies about as well as a lead balloon. Dr. Paxton pays him a stern visit with the psychiatrist in tow.

"Captain, we were discussing your progress in our interdisciplinary care meeting. You've failed to attend your last three sessions with Dr. Friedman. Those sessions are every bit as critical to your recovery as PT, and you will attend. If necessary, I will arrange for officers to accompany you. Am I making myself clear?"

Dr. Friedman balks at the idea of punitive participation. "I don't think that's necessary. Perhaps Captain Chandler was unaware of the importance of these visits. I'm sure he'll make every effort from now on." His eyes hold Mark's from across the room.

Mark grudgingly attends, but he still refuses meds and shuts down any conversations about his worsening emotional state. His discouragement and depression snowball into irrational outbursts and angry tantrums with physical therapists, nurses, and even me. His angry highs are higher, his depressed lows lower, and his outbursts increasingly volatile. Dr. Friedman pulls me aside a few days later to offer some insight.

"Picture Mark's emotional distress as an infection, brewing below the surface and thriving in darkness. Bacteria breed and form noxious matter that spreads unchecked until the body overcomes it, whether alone or with help. The mind responds that same way to depression and self-loathing. Poisonous self-talk forms deep roots. Mark's self-talk is toxic because his self-image is toxic. He needs a catalyst, a breakthrough, to help him see more clearly."

I envision Mark's depression and self-loathing as a huge purple amoebic blob, engulfing everything it touches and growing exponentially. "How can I help?"

Dr. Friedman smiles, his steel-blue eyes softening. "Keep doing what you're doing. It's not you he's angry with, it's his situation. Because he trusts you, he knows it's safe to 'lose it' with you, because you'll still be there for him. It's a terrible compliment."

Now nine weeks out from the explosion, Mark's thigh bone is finally fusing, his burns have mostly healed, and he's fully recovered from many of his other injuries. Measurable PT achievements boost his mood, but only temporarily. His primary focus of contempt is the appearance of his injured leg. Angry purple scars track from his upper thigh to just above the knee. The newest one, still pink, runs almost directly down the center of his thigh; two others run down the outside. A dozen or so punctures from the external femoral pins dot the surface, connecting to the cage. Pale rectangular patches highlight his skin grafts, and a thin lavender scar crosses the tip of what remains of his limb after they reshaped it following the amputation.

Mark's now in a (mandated) support group for new amputees. The meetings are led by experienced disabled vets who initially had difficulty coping with their new reality and have opted to help "newbies" learn things it took them years to discover on their own. One topic they've discussed at length is phantom pain, and while nothing besides medication seems effective, he's learned he isn't alone.

Mark's mentor from the group is a brawny, boisterous double-leg amputee named James Mackey, though he goes by the nickname "Stubbs". I meet him when he stops by the room one afternoon.

"What are you doing in that bed?" demands a deep voice, startling me. A huge man strides into the room, dressed in camo shorts that come to his knees and a khaki tee shirt that's tight across his broad shoulders. He's easily six-five, with rich mahogany skin, a massive chest, and muscled biceps bigger than my thighs. He reaches for Mark's covers and yanks them down. "Let's go, Pretty Boy. You can lay around when you're dead, and you don't look dead yet to me."

"I'm damn close," Mark mutters. "I just got back from three hours of PT."

The man snorts, then catches sight of me in the chair. He lays a huge hand on his chest. "Apologies, ma'am. I didn't see you there. Sorry for busting in. I'm Stubbs."

My eyes drop to his matching carbon-fiber prosthetic legs. *An amputee named Stubbs?* My exhausted brain doesn't catch up to my mouth in time. "Seriously? Your name is Stubbs?"

He smiles broadly, showing perfect white teeth. "Actually, it's James, but I go by Stubbs."

"On purpose?"

Damn exhaustion.

He laughs, unoffended. Maybe he's used to dealing with people whose brain-to-mouth filter doesn't work. "Do I look like somebody who'd put up with name-calling? Stubbs is my nickname, spelled with two B's, because I'm black and beautiful, baby."

"Clearly, there's no H for humble," I say with a wry smile.

He chuckles. "Humility isn't an affliction of mine." Then he turns to Mark. "Let's go. You're late for the meeting."

Mark pulls his blankets back up. "I'm not going today. I'm tired."

"I wasn't asking. You can go voluntarily, or I'll carry you like a little girl, but you're going."

Mark glowers at him. Stubbs crosses his arms and plants his solid body like a redwood. After a minute, Mark concedes defeat, throwing back the covers. "Fine. Get out of my way."

I hide my smile as Stubbs passes him his crutches. "You need to check your hair or fix your makeup?"

"Fuck you, asshole," Mark mutters, and Stubbs laughs out loud.

Stubbs is exactly the push Mark needs. He calls Mark on his bullshit in a way only military brothers can. He's a Marine ("no such thing as a *former* Marine") injured in an incident similar to Mark's. Stubbs swaggers through the hospital like he owns the joint, his cheerful bellows echoing down the halls. He stops by frequently to visit and "take the emotional temperature," judging the caliber of the day by Mark's mood. If he's bitchy, Stubbs bitches right back, somehow unruffling Mark's feathers, at least temporarily.

Two weeks before Mark's discharge, his tension erupts like Mount St. Helens.

My night terrors are the worst they've been since I was first hospitalized immediately following my rescue from Afghanistan. I spend every night backed against the hotel room door with my tactical batons, always awakening in a panicked crouch, panting and drenched in cold sweat.

Every. Damn. Night.

It happened again this morning.

The Chihuahua taunts me, holding his makeshift whip in my face. I clench my jaw, steeling myself, and he smiles evilly before stepping behind me and flaying my back again. The whip bites my flesh, and hot blood drips down my hips and legs. Then I see his leering face and cruel eyes, and once again, I wake up backed into the corner, crouching, my batons raised to strike even though I'm a trembling, sweaty disaster.

Fuck. No matter how hard I try, I can't escape those soulless black eyes.

What if they torment me for the rest of my life?

Despair settles over me like a wet blanket. I can't keep doing this night after night.

I'll give therapy another shot when this is over, even though I despise talking about my darkness. It's bad enough I know what happened. The idea of verbally reliving my past again makes me cringe, but the thought of living the rest of my life like this is far more horrifying.

Because I rarely sleep, I'm normally at the hospital long before sunrise. This particular morning, though, I have to wait for a department store to open. I've got to have new jeans. I've lost so much weight that my clothes are hanging off me. Stress destroys my appetite and makes me nauseous, so even if I eat, it's only a few bites. Last night I took off my skinny jeans by sliding them down and stepping out of them, still buttoned and zipped. While I'm waiting, I pay bills online and reply to business emails. I also email Lila and Tucker seeking their opinions about changes to my home to accommodate Mark's needs, attaching a staggering sixty-seven page file of his therapists' suggestions. I need help finding a local contractor quickly, one who does good work and won't overcharge me. I don't trust my own judgment. Unyielding stress and sleep deprivation have me functioning on autopilot, and anything requiring mental focus is a struggle.

While I'm in line at the store, I text Mark to tell him I'm running late, but there's no response. I text again to ask if he needs anything, but he still doesn't answer.

It's a shame I didn't grasp the significance of that before waltzing in unprepared.

MARK

I leap from the armored vehicle before it's come to a full stop, desperate to find her. One of our MRAPs is blackened and smoking, fully incinerated. The other is tipped over on its side in a ditch. There's no movement around either of them. I scan the interior of the burned vehicle and see four charred bodies. My stomach lurches.

Please God, no. I can't lose Charlie.

I race to the other vehicle, jumping down into the ditch. Two of my men are there, Max and Mike, gunned down on the medical aid call I sent them on. Now they lie in blood-soaked sand with unseeing eyes, their bodies riddled with bullets. I snatch the back door of the vehicle open. There are four more bloody bodies, but not Charlie. Not Lila, either. Insurgents.

Tucker grabs my shoulders from behind. "Lila? Is she –" I hear the panic in his voice and shake my head.

"They're not here."

"They're gone?" He can barely speak.

I nod my head, gesturing to the men lying behind the vehicle, my own men, men I sent to their deaths. "Max and Mike rode with them. But the girls – they aren't here."

Tucker whirls around, scanning the horizon, looking for any sign, any clue. I sink to my knees. Of the eight I sent out, six are dead, and two are missing. The two women.

They're gone.

She's gone.

And it's my fault.

I bolt upright in a panic, breathing hard, seized by intense physical and emotional pain. Spasms of phantom pain violently grip me, leaving me gasping and writhing. It's brutal. The pain meds barely take the edge off, and the frustration of everything conspiring against me piles higher and higher until I'm ready to explode.

Charlie's safe now. We found her. She's safe. Lila too.

I need Charlie.

Charlie grounds me. Reassures me. Centers me.

I'm up the rest of the night, watching for her long before daylight. She always senses when I need her. She'll be here soon.

But she isn't. Sunrise passes without her. That's not like her.

I wait, fidgeting. Another lousy breakfast comes and goes untouched. No Charlie.

Where is she?

My frustration builds, accompanied by a tightness in my chest I haven't felt in a long time.

Not in four years.

It's time for PT, but I skip it, my anxiety skyrocketing as I wait for her.

An hour later, she's still not here.

Where is she?

I'm running through scenario after scenario in my head. Where could she be? What if something's happened to her again? How can I get to her? How can I save her?

She doesn't need me.

Maybe she's with someone.

She's found someone better to spend her time with.

Someone who's not a fucking useless cripple.

Then Charlie pops in as though nothing's happened, and every drop of my anxiety morphs instantly into white-hot rage.

CHARLIE

Mark should be in PT by now, but I grab two large coffees nonetheless. It's about four hours later than my usual arrival time when I breeze in, balancing the cups carefully. But he's not in the rehab gym. He's in his chair, staring out the window, and I'm too focused on not spilling coffee to catch his mood.

"Morning, Big Guy. I brought two different kinds of coffee this morning. This one –" I raise a cup with a brown sleeve "– is a medium roast with two shots of dark chocolate. I've had it before, and it's pretty good. This one is your usual dark roast. Your choice."

"Nice of you to finally get here," he says, glowering with animosity.

Apparently, it's going to be one of those mornings. Given the way my day started – again – I should have expected it.

I sigh inwardly and let his frostiness roll off my back, setting both cups down on the table between us. "Sorry I'm late. I texted earlier to tell you I was running behind. I needed new jeans." His jaw muscles flex as he returns to staring fixedly out the window.

He's pissed. I guess he didn't see my text. I take a deep breath. *Distract him.*

"How was breakfast?"

No answer. I wait a full minute before I try again to lighten the mood.

"Someone must have gotten up on the wrong side of the bed." I lean over to kiss his cheek and feather my fingers through his hair.

Mark childishly jerks his head away, refusing to look at me. "I didn't sleep. But maybe you didn't either."

I straighten up, pretending not to notice the bite in his tone. Of course I didn't. I woke up in a sweaty panic for the umpteenth morning in a row, and my tailbone aches from spending every night perched on carpet-covered concrete, leaning against the hotel room door. But Mark doesn't need to know that. He's dealing with enough as it is.

"I never sleep well in hotels," I reply instead. "I'm sorry you didn't either. Is your leg bothering you?"

He turns his head slightly to glare at me. "You're bothering me."

Icy rage ripples just beneath his words, and it's unsettling. I keep my voice gentle, hoping to disarm him. "I didn't mean to upset you. I'm sorry."

He stares out the window and ignores me.

If I were thinking clearly, I'd go for a walk to give us each time to recalibrate. Unfortunately, I'm running on fumes. I stand in uncomfortable silence for several seconds before changing the topic. "This coffee smells fantastic." I pull the lid off the dark chocolate one and hold it out. "Want to try a sip?"

"I don't want your goddamned coffee!" Fast as lightning, he snatches the cup from my hand and hurls it past me. I gasp as hot coffee splatters all over my clothes, the walls, and the floor.

"What the hell, Mark?" The scalding liquid soaks my top and my new jeans. I quickly pluck the wet fabric away from my chest. "Dammit," I mutter. I grab paper towels and dampen them, wiping coffee off the walls and floor before attempting to salvage my clothes.

"Yeah. Make sure your *assets* are on full display." Sarcasm oozes from his words.

"What the hell is that supposed to mean? My *assets* are fully covered. I'm wearing jeans and a hoodie." I give up on my coffee-stained clothes. "What's gotten into you? You're acting like a jerk."

He snorts. "How about what's gotten into you? Or should I say, *who's* gotten into you."

I stare at him like he's sprouted a second head. "What are you talking about?"

"I assumed being stuck here with a cripple was cramping your sex life. I guess not. You did say you didn't sleep because you weren't in your own bed."

What. The. Hell.

I take a deep breath, followed by another, closing my eyes.

This is not about me.

Breathe.

I open my eyes to find him watching me with a cold expression on his hard face. His open door catches my eye, and I cross the room to close it. Mark laughs, a cruel laugh, so unlike the warm chuckle I've always known. "What? Don't want everyone hearing you're a slut?"

Sharp pain twists in my chest. I know this is his head injury talking. The personality changes, the hostility, the anger – it's a toxic sludge coursing through him, spilling out onto everyone around him. His medical team expects it. They see this stuff all the time.

But I've never seen this behavior from Mark, especially not directed at me. And calling me a slut? I panicked a few months ago because Blake ran his thumb over my cheek. I'm pretty sure sex is permanently off the table after what those bastards did to me.

I take a deep breath, returning to stand in front of him, keeping my voice even. "There's been a misunderstanding. I'm sorry I was later than usual. I was waiting for the department store to open because I needed jeans. If I'd known you'd had a bad night, I'd have postponed my errands. And I assure you I wasn't having sex. I don't have a sex life, here or anywhere else."

Contempt glints in his pale eyes. "No sex? You really think I'm a fucking idiot, don't you? I'm the one that found you screwing every goddamned one of those fuckers."

My heart pounds erratically as the room swims before my eyes. I try to take a deep breath, but breathing has become difficult. The familiar iron bands start tightening, and I force my words past numb lips. "I didn't have a choice." I look at him, pleading silently. "You know that."

He shakes his head furiously. "You went with them."

My mouth falls open. "It wasn't like they offered an invitation, Mark. We were kidnapped."

"You should have fought harder!" he roars. "You just let them take you!"

I find my voice as fury rushes over me. "I didn't *let* anyone do anything!" I yell, matching his volume and intensity, stabbing the tabletop with one finger. "I fought those bastards with everything I had. I just wasn't strong enough to stop them." I turn away for a half second before whirling back. "You know, I already blame myself for being weak. I don't need you blaming me too. Yeah, you found me getting screwed. I was strung up and unconscious. That's called rape, asshole." Shocked by my ferocity, I turn to one side, fighting to regain control of my emotions.

I sidestep reflexively at a sudden movement in the corner of my vision. Mark shoves the rolling table past me, and it crashes into the wall. The remaining coffee cup flies into the air before splattering everywhere.

I have to get out of here.

I'm picking up my shoulder bag when the door bangs open, bouncing off the wall and startling me. Stubbs strides into the room and pauses, giving me a quick once-over. I recognize that look. He's scanning me for injuries.

"You okay?"

I nod once. "I'm going out." I reach for the door handle.

"They were right! You really are a stupid cunt whore!" Mark explodes.

His coup de grâce.

The words rip through my soul. I freeze, paralyzed, unable to breathe. My purse slips off my shoulder and thuds to the floor.

I turn to meet his eyes, hoping to see remorse or shock or... something. Anything. There's emotion there, but not what I'd hoped for. Cold eyes glitter with revulsion.

"Here," Stubbs murmurs. He scoops up my purse and passes it to me. "I've got this."

I barely make it to the stairwell three doors down.

MARK

How dare Charlie just waltz in here like that?

After all I've been through, all I've been worried about, how dare she?

She's wearing jeans that fit her better.

Is she dressing up? Why?

She says she didn't sleep.

What the hell was she doing?

Suddenly I'm sure what she was doing.

What she had to be doing.

And I lose my shit.

She's shocked at first, but then she gets angry. I don't care.

How could she do that when I needed her?

I lash out again, shoving a table into a wall.

Stubbs bursts into the room and looks Charlie over like he's worried I've injured her. She turns to leave, and I deal her my deadliest blow, my ace in the hole.

"You really are a stupid cunt whore!"

All color drains from her face. She looks as shocked as if I'd slapped her. There's anguish in her eyes and defeat in her posture when she leaves. Seeing I've hurt her fills me with a perverse pleasure. After all, she clearly didn't mind hurting me this morning.

"Hey, pussy, pick on someone your own size," Stubbs demands, striding toward me, his beefy frame moving purposefully.

I look away. "Get the hell out."

Stubbs cocks his head. "Make me. Or are you just an asshole to women?"

"I'm warning you, Stubbs –"

He scoffs. "What are you gonna do, Chandler? Kick my ass with your crutch?"

"Maybe I am!" I yell, facing him.

Stubbs shrugs. "Fine. Bring it, Pretty Boy. Won't bother me a bit to beat your crippled ass." He assumes a widened stance, cracks his massive knuckles, and waits, solidly planted.

I glare at him, and he glares right back. We remain like that for long moments until finally I look away in annoyance.

"That's better." Stubbs grabs the straight-backed chair, spins it backwards, and sits down facing me.

"What the hell are you doing?" I growl.

"Waiting for your sorry ass to settle down."

"Get out."

Stubbs shakes his head. "Nope. I'm giving you ten minutes. Ten minutes to sit there and figure out what you're really mad about, because it's not Charlie."

"I said get out."

"And I said ten minutes, asshole. And no more talking."

CHAPTER SEVEN

CHARLIE

A DIMLY-LIT CONCRETE STAIRWELL is a horrible place to have a panic attack.

I manage to make it to the landing one floor below. I slide down the wall, braced by the corner, trembling uncontrollably, panting.

Breathe. Deep breaths, in and out.

But it doesn't work, because the voice inside my head is Mark's, and he's the last person I want to hear right now. I fumble in my bag with shaky hands and find my phone. I don't realize I'm crying until tears splash my screen and the images blur. I play Lila's ringtone on a loop.

"Charlie, you're safe now. No one can hurt you. Listen to my voice, Charlie. You're safe now. No one can hurt you. Pick up your phone."

I don't know how long I sit there, knees pulled to my chest, Lila's voice echoing off the walls. My teeth are chattering from the cold concrete when I can finally breathe calmly. I mop my eyes and get to my feet, brushing off dust and cobwebs. Chatty female voices drift up to me. I scurry down the stairs past their surprised stares, not stopping until I'm out in the sunshine. I pull on sunglasses and start walking to my hotel.

My phone rings. I glance down and see Mark's name.

Not a chance.

I send it to voicemail.

A few seconds later, it rings again. Mark. I send it to voicemail again. After his sixth call in rapid succession, I turn off my phone and bury it in my shoulder bag.

I rush through the hotel lobby, leaving my sunglasses on and avoiding eye contact. The solitude of my room is a relief. I catch sight of myself in the mirror above the dresser and pause.

I look awful, truly awful. It's not from the cobwebs clinging to my hair or my coffee-splattered clothes or my tear-stained face. It's the ghostly pallor and hollowed cheeks and dull eyes with craters beneath them from not sleeping.

My reflection looks every bit as broken and damaged as I feel.

I shower again to rid myself of the pain and grime of the stairwell, lingering until the water turns cold. I swipe steam off the fogged glass and, for once, face myself in the mirror, unclothed. There's no point in hiding, not after this morning.

I angle my body slightly, pulling my wet hair in front as I look over my shoulder at my back. Rope-like purple scars criss-cross my back from shoulder to hip, mingling with thinner, cord-like lavender ones. The wider scars were caused by the leather strips of their whip; the thinner ones were from the razor wire. Between and beneath my shoulder blades is a flat white scar, intricate swoops and curlicues forming letters that stretch across my back. A phrase.

That phrase.

I face forward. These scars are less vivid but certainly noticeable. My breasts sport an assortment of thin white streaks, mutilations from a rusty boning knife. A long vertical scar trails down my abdomen from my emergency surgery after my rescue, and a collection of pale pink scars mars my inner thighs. They reach higher, too.

Their mutilation wasn't just confined to the outside of my body.

I swallow hard. Discordant mauve patterns encircle my wrists, a consequence of being trussed up with barbed wire and suspended from an overhead pipe. Other scars freckle my body, but none significant enough to demand attention. My face is unscarred, though I do have a bump on the bridge of my nose and a slight ridge along my left cheekbone from fractures.

I wonder what it would be like to no longer hate my reflection. I can't even remember what my body looked like before, when I took normalcy for granted.

I've spent the last four years hiding these scars, not just from the world, but from myself. I conceal my wrists with stacked bracelets of beads and leather, only removing them to shower. You'll never catch me wearing a swimsuit or tank top or sports bra. I wear loose tops that cover everything. Outside of healthcare providers, only two people have seen my scars. Lila saw them from the beginning because she and I endured hell together, recovered together, and lived together. Mark saw my injuries when he rescued me and later, when he came to my side at Walter Reed.

He knew what the brand on my back meant before I did, but he refused to tell me. I had to force my doctor to tell me what it meant.

The same man who tried to shield me from their vile slurs called me that name today. Bellowed it, actually, to ensure I — and everyone else in the vicinity — heard it.

My hotel room is suddenly suffocating. I dress quickly in leggings and a long shirt, twist my hair up, and grab my bag, hiding my red eyes behind sunglasses.

Walking helps. I match my breathing to the cadence of my steps. Inhale for four, hold for four, exhale for four. I find myself at a park and sink onto a bench near a splashing fountain. The bubbling water sounds like a mountain stream if I close my eyes, and I can feel its mist on my skin. Carefree children play on swings and slides, and I envy their happiness as they chase each other and twirl with abandon. I watch them, unable to stop my tears. Tears for everything Mark has lost. Tears for what I've lost. Tears for damage done. Despite the warmth of the Texas spring day, I can't shake my bone-deep chill.

I abhor crying. I was never the teary type before those bastards tortured me. Now I cry so often, there are days I swear I'm going to mildew. I lift my eyes to find two women on a nearby bench, watching me cry with concerned expressions. My disgust at my weakness strengthens my resolve and squares my shoulders.

Get it together.

Trauma makes you lash out. Hurt inflicts more hurt. You know this.

Mark helped you. It's your turn to help him.

He didn't mean what he said, no matter how deeply it hurt.

And that's the thing. I know he didn't mean it. He's spent his entire life looking out for me. What happened this morning stemmed from his own emotional pain. Mark's lashing out at me because he doesn't have anyone else. And as Dr. Friedman pointed out, he feels safe enough to unleash his pent-up hurt and rage on me. He knows I'll still love him despite his horrible behavior.

That's what true friendship is. Being there even when – or maybe especially when – someone pushes you away out of hurt or fear or grief. Mark's feeling all those emotions right now.

Fear.

Pain.

Grief.

I tilt my face toward the sun, letting it warm me while I come to grips with this morning. Part of me wants to talk things out with him, but another part, a larger part, dreads facing him. This morning's evisceration was devastating, and I'm too emotionally fragile to withstand another explosion like that today. Despite my anxiety, I walk back toward the hospital, though I stall at my usual deli to fortify my nerves with food.

I'm ordering a sandwich and tea when a familiar figure struts through the door, causing the little bell above it to tinkle. Stubbs saunters over, winking at the buxom waitress. "Damn, sweetheart, you're beautiful," he says, holding her gaze. "Bring me whatever she's having." The strawberry-blond waitress looks at me, blushing furiously, and I nod with a barely-concealed grin.

"You're shameless." I shake my head as he slides into the booth. "I hope you like BLTs."

"Bacon!" he exclaims in mock horror. "What about my girlish figure?" He grins and pats his washboard stomach with one huge hand, and I smile despite my mood.

"Glad you're smiling, Green Eyes. I knew you wouldn't bail because of one tantrum."

My smile fades as I shrug halfheartedly. "He didn't mean it."

Our waitress returns with two iced teas. Stubbs winks, and she smiles shyly. When she walks away, he sighs appreciatively at the view before returning his attention to me. "That doesn't make it hurt any less when he's being an ass," he comments.

I drop my eyes. "No, it doesn't." I unwrap my straw and slide it into my glass, toying with the wrapper.

"He loves you," Stubbs announces. "You know that, right? Says you mean more to him than anyone."

I nod. "I love him, too. That's the catch. The people you love hold the power to hurt you the most."

He bobs his shaved head in agreement, pulling a toothpick from the dispenser to chew on it. "I had a nice long talk with him after you left."

I raise an eyebrow. "Really? He didn't seem particularly conversational to me."

He chuckles. "You weren't as charming as I was. I called him a pussy and threatened to beat his ass."

I can't help laughing. "It didn't occur to me. I wish it had."

Stubbs shrugs massive shoulders. "It's a guy thing." He takes a long swig of tea. "I challenged him to either put up or shut up, made him realize it wasn't me he was mad at. It wasn't you, either. When he eventually got his panties out of a twist, we got down to what was really bothering him." He tips his head. "I assume you're interested."

I nod. "I'm all ears."

Stubbs uses his toothpick to punctuate his words. "Powerlessness. Mark is used to being in control. He craves it. He coordinated missions. He'd identify a problem, find the solution, and fix it. That's how he handles things. Now his body and mind aren't responding like he wants them to. It reinforces his loss of control." Dark eyes study me. "Like when you were captured. That was outside his control. He can't handle not being in control. It makes him feel weak."

"Feeling powerless brought all that on this morning?"

He shrugs again. "Yes and no. Seeing himself as weak or vulnerable in one area makes him re-experience feelings he had back then."

"He honestly blames me for getting captured?" I squeak.

Stubbs shakes his head vehemently. "That's not what I meant. Mark can't make his body do what he wants it to. That reminds him of the powerlessness he felt when you were captured. He doesn't believe for a second it was your fault. He blames himself for sending you into an ambush. Being powerless scares him. Losing you terrified him. He carries a lot of guilt for that, and deep down, he's scared he'll lose you again. Fear breeds fear, just like hurt breeds hurt. All he needed was a trigger. You showed up later than normal, and like a wounded animal, he lashed out at you because you're safe." He grins broadly, flashing white teeth that contrast with his dark skin, and lays a huge hand on his chest. "I, however, am not safe. When I got in his face, his brain quickly reminded him he wasn't mad at me and encouraged him to regroup to avoid getting his Pretty Boy ass kicked."

I laugh in spite of myself. "I think you're secretly a big teddy bear."

He flexes one huge bicep and winks. "Part of my charm, baby." He gestures to my phone. "Have you listened to your voicemails?"

I wince. "I turned it off when he started calling. Is it bad?"

"There's at least twenty. I'd delete them, at least the first dozen or so. No one needs to hear that crap. I know I wish I hadn't." He makes a face. "At first, he was still carrying on like a little bitch. Then he got all weepy and emotional. It was like being trapped with a drunk teenage girl." He grins. "He did send one text after we talked. That's probably the only thing worth your time."

I turn my phone back on and look at Stubbs incredulously. "Twenty-three voicemails?"

He frowns. "Probably. I crammed my fingers in my ears after a while."

I swipe to my messages. Mark's sent just one brief text. "Please don't give up on me."

His simple six-word plea grabs my heart.

I return to his hospital room, bringing a peace-offering BLT. I knock lightly before entering. Mark's sitting on the bed. His left knee is bent with his leg folded under him; his caged right leg hangs off the far side. He looks exhausted and miserable, dark circles emphasizing the fatigue in his unshaven face.

"Hey, Big Guy. Okay if I come in?"

"I wasn't sure you'd come back," he says, watching me tentatively.

I breathe a huge inward sigh of relief and close the door behind me, crossing the room to place the food on his bedside table. “It’ll take a lot more than one of your hissy fits to get rid of me. Here, I brought you a BLT.”

He reaches out, lightly catching my fingertips. “Will you sit with me? I need to talk to you. Please?” I study his face, seeing vulnerability in his weary blue eyes, knowing he recognizes the anxiety in mine. I nod, and he pats the bed. “Facing me.”

I sit, watching him draw a ragged breath. “Charlie, I'm so sorry.”

I place my hand gently on his, shocked to feel it trembling. “It’s okay, Mark.”

He shakes his head adamantly. “No, it’s not. None of that was okay. I don’t even know where all that bullshit came from. I didn’t mean any of it. Stubbs made a lot of good points about feeling powerless.” His voice trails off. I wait, watching the turbulence swirling in his eyes. “I’ve been having nightmares,” he says finally. “Vivid ones.”

I’m oddly relieved. I can relate, though it saddens me to think of him reliving his injury. I wouldn’t wish night terrors on anyone. “I get it. You hear the explosion and smell the smoke and feel the pain, and it’s like it’s happening all over again.”

He shakes his head. “My nightmares aren’t about what happened to me. They’re about what happened to you.”

I gape at him, astonished.

“They’re about when I lost you. About finding the vehicles without you. About realizing you’d been taken but having no idea where, not knowing if you were dead or alive. About panicking day after day because every lead came up empty. About praying you weren’t dead, but being terrified of what they were doing to you if you were alive. I dream they still have you, and I know what they’re doing, but I can’t get to you.”

I sit in stunned silence. Mark draws a shaky breath and brushes his hand across my cheek, his eyes locking with mine. “Charlie, I swear on my life, I would go through every bit of this –” he gestures to his damaged leg – “the pain, the leg, all of it, a thousand times, to never go through losing you again. I’d do it in a heartbeat to keep you safe. And then I attack you this morning, for no goddamn reason?” He closes his eyes and tightens his jaw. “It’s like I’m pushing you away so it won’t hurt as much if I lose you again.”

“I won’t give up on you, Mark,” I vow. “You won’t lose me.”

“What I said about you fighting harder – I’m sorry. I didn’t mean it.”

I’ve never discussed what happened with anyone but my psychiatrist. Anything Mark knows is from what he saw or pieced together.

He keeps speaking. “Lila told me what they did to her and what she knew of your experience. I know you fought back. I know it cost you dearly. And I know you haven’t been with anyone.” He draws a deep breath, and his words tumble out. “I’d been watching for you for hours. I had a rough night, and

I needed you. You were later than usual, and with my nightmares and my fucked-up judgment, it sent me down a dark path. I got scared. I thought something had happened to you. When you got here and you were fine, I just – I lost my shit. The things I said… what I called you before you left…" Mark looks away, his expression tortured. "Baby Girl, I'm so sorry," he says hoarsely, his voice breaking.

Stupid cunt whore.

I drop my gaze and examine my fingers.

Those goddamn bastards branded me. *Branded* me, like a cow, with that phrase – *stupid cunt whore.* Their red-hot metal permanently seared the deceptively beautiful Arabic script into my flesh.

Stupid. Cunt. Whore.

I swallow hard against the massive lump tightening my throat. He cups my face gently in shaky hands, tilting it so I'm looking him in the eye. "Baby Girl, I'm so sorry," he repeats, his voice barely a whisper. "Please, please forgive me."

Mark's haunted expression combined with his palpable anguish and guilt rips me apart. He lashed out this morning because his own pain and fear were unbearable. *Pain causes pain. Hurt causes hurt.*

Did he hurt me? Yes.

But there's more to his eruption than a simple temper tantrum. The head injury has affected his personality – hopefully, only until his bruised brain heals. He's suffered an incredibly harrowing loss. His health, his career, his home, his men. He's hurting, scared, grieving, and angry. I was simply a convenient target when the dam burst.

I believe him when he says he's sorry. I can feel his guilt.

I can forgive this.

I slip my fingers inside the hands still holding my face and meet his light blue gaze steadily. "It's alright, Mark. I forgive you."

A choked sob escapes him as he pulls me hard against his chest and wraps his arms around me. Hot tears spill onto my neck and shoulder as his body shudders. I've not seen Mark cry since his mom died. I slide my arms around him, wishing I could erase his misery.

Several minutes pass before he leans back, wiping his eyes and clearing his throat.

"This isn't me, Charlie. I've never thrown things or ranted like a lunatic. I feel like I'm sitting in the driver's seat with someone else controlling the car. I hate it." He stares off for a moment. "I called Dr. Friedman." He takes my hands. "I asked him to come up, and we talked, really talked. I told him everything. I said I'd take anything he thought would help. He put me on a medication that's supposed to level things out, to blunt the intensity of my emotions so I don't feel so out of control. Instead of big peaks and low valleys, I should have gentle waves. I can't guarantee it will fix everything, and it might take time to get the dose right for me, but I refuse to live my life behaving the way I did this morning. You're too important to me."

I squeeze his hands. "I'm in this with you for the long haul, Mark, no matter what."

He pulls me close for another hug and kisses my forehead. "Thank you for not giving up on me," he whispers. "Love you, Baby Girl." He tugs my hand up, thumping our joined hands twice over his heart.

"Love you, too."

MARK

It's two a.m., and I've finally convinced Charlie to return to her hotel. She's not left my side all afternoon, casting fleeting looks my way when she thinks I'm not watching. I know what she's thinking. She's afraid I'm consumed with guilt.

She's right.

Eleven days.

That's how long they had her and Lila, caged like animals, tied up and starved and raped.

And in Charlie's case, tortured.

As long as I live, I'll never forget the night we found her. We'd turned the region inside out, questioned the locals, searched out every lead we could find. We kept coming up empty. I'd barely slept or eaten the whole time they were gone. I'd become obsessed. Tucker wasn't much better, but there was one difference.

I'm the one that gave the order for them to go out.

I'm the one who sent my people into a death trap.

Reports had come in of a nearby village being attacked by an I.S. group, and the villagers were requesting medical aid. I sent four medics with four soldiers. The soldiers were there in case things got dicey, watching the medics' backs and keeping the peace. Tensions run high when innocent people are wounded and dying. The soldiers also help load the wounded into the humvees to go to the field hospital if needed or call in helicopters if their injuries are critical.

But the insurgents had been watching, learning our patterns. They knew our typical response was an equal number of medics and soldiers, usually two teams of four, sent in to help the villagers. They laid in wait. They killed my men and kidnapped the women.

The morning of the eleventh day, we caught a break, a whisper that a group of men with two American women was hiding in the lower level of an abandoned mosque seventeen miles away. I strategized our plan and we moved in after nightfall, praying we were in the right place.

My men and I slipped silently into the darkened, bombed-out shell of a once-magnificent mosque. Once inside, we split into two groups of six. I led my team downstairs while Tucker and his team swiftly crossed the main level. We moved quietly, staying in the shadows. I paused at the bottom of the stairs, scoping the area ahead of us. That's when I heard the muffled pop of gunshots from Tucker and his guys upstairs.

They'd found something.

On high alert, my men and I pressed forward, fanning out. Startled insurgents began spilling out from all sides, brandishing weapons. Most never got a shot off as we cleared the area.

An urgent whisper had come from just ahead of me, to my right. "Sir! I've got one!"

One of my men was kneeling inside a makeshift cell. I'd raced over, scanning the swollen features of the woman being lowered into a sitting position. She'd been restrained facedown over a table, her legs chained to the table legs.

Lila.

Her shirt was torn and filthy, and she'd been stripped from the waist down. Her delicate face was bruised and bloodied, one eye swollen shut. She'd been gagged with a grimy rag. In one corner lay the malodorous, decomposing body of a man facedown in a pool of dark, sticky blood.

Lila gazed up at me bleakly, her expression dull. I'd squatted beside her, quickly removing the gag from her mouth. I reached into my pack for a bottle of water and poured some into her mouth. She drank ravenously, then coughed and spluttered.

"Lila? Can you hear me?"

She nodded. "Charlie," she whispered weakly. "Down at the end. On the right."

"You're safe now, Lila. We've got you," I reassured her. I glanced back at the soldier beside me. "Cover her up. And let Tucker know we've got her as soon as they've cleared the upstairs," I said in low tones, springing to my feet. As I strode out, a medic entered the cell, opening his pack and kneeling at her side.

I moved through the darkness, my eyes scanning for movement. I quietly eliminated threats as they appeared, but by the time I reached the halfway point, the rest of the lower level was silent and empty. The only sound came from a staticky radio on an empty table with two fallen chairs.

I froze outside the last room on the right, unable to breathe as my eyes absorbed the horror in front of me.

It was another makeshift cell, though this door stood open. A nude woman hung motionless, facing away, suspended by her wrists from an overhead pipe. I stared, holding my breath until I saw the slight rise and fall of her upper torso.

She's alive.

I could see every bony prominence in Charlie's outline. Her hip bones and vertebrae jutted out like sharp peaks in the dim light. She'd lost so much weight. I drew in a sharp breath as my eyes adjusted further to the darkness in her cell. Her back was raw and bloody, striped with wounds I couldn't see clearly from this distance. Darker blood stained the back and inner portions of her thighs and lower legs.

A sudden movement in the corner startled me, a man moving inside the cell. Appalled at my stupidity, I berated myself for what could easily have been a fatal mistake. It's basic training 101 – safety first. Clear the area and always be aware of your surroundings. But the bastard hadn't noticed me. He was laser-focused on his prize, oblivious to the influx of soldiers and the deaths of his comrades. He stepped behind Charlie, shoving his pants out of the way and grasping her roughly by the hips. She didn't make a sound.

Rage fired through me, and I planted two bullets in the base of his skull, shoving his falling body away from Charlie.

I turned to her and gasped as the magnitude of her injuries hit me. "Oh, God, Baby Girl."

She'd been whipped, her back torn into ribbons of raw flesh. I smelled the putrid odors of infection and charred skin. Some sort of intricate pattern had been burned into her back, and it had blistered horribly beneath and between her shoulder blades. Blood trails ran up her wrists and arms from the barbed wire gouging deep into her thin wrists. A bloodied, rusty knife nearly a foot long lay on the floor beneath her, and I suddenly realized why there was so much blood between her thighs and puddled on the floor.

My stomach clenched, and for a horrible second, I thought I might be sick.

I turned her hanging form toward me, and the sight of her beaten face shattered me. Her cheek and nose were broken and swollen, her lips dry and cracked. Her breasts had been mutilated, probably with that same rusty filet knife. She was covered in blood, both fresh and dried, and bright purple bruises from fists and boots were scattered over her abdomen and flanks. The slight rounding of her mottled belly suggested she was bleeding internally.

Dear God.

I scrambled to loosen her wrists, but the wire was wrapped too tightly. I wanted to lift her, to relieve the pressure on her shoulders and wrists, but her back was so raw and infected, I was terrified to touch her with my dusty fatigues, afraid I'd inflict more pain or damage.

I stepped out of the cell. "Jackson!" I said into my mic, my clipped voice piercing the silence.

"Yes, sir!" he answered immediately. The short medic popped out of Lila's cell with his duffel bag and jogged toward me.

"I need a sterile sheet, now," I demanded sharply. The medic promptly pulled out a package containing a sterile sheet for burn victims and started toward Charlie's cell.

"Jackson!" I barked. "Give me the sheet and find bolt cutters to get her down. Now!"

"Yes, sir!" he said, passing the sheet to me before running after the bolt cutters.

I hurried back to Charlie, pulling the sterile sheet from its package. I unfolded it and wrapped it loosely around her bloodied flesh. She struggled when I touched her back, though she was barely conscious. "It's me, Baby Girl. I've got you," I repeated over and over in a gentle voice, and she'd stilled. She whimpered as I gently lifted her, cradling her in my arms to ease the strain on her wrists and shoulders. She'd pressed her face against my chest, her eyes still closed. "I've got you, Baby Girl. I'm here."

If I live to be a hundred, I'll never forget the fear I felt when she was taken, the horror of finding her so close to death, and the heartbreak of watching her struggle to recover. I'd have done anything to take away her pain.

But today, I intentionally taunted her with what those bastards did.

With Charlie back at the hotel, I'm alone with my shame, with the memory of my horrific behavior and the brutal words I said to her. Everyone in the vicinity heard what I shouted, and those who didn't hear it for themselves have certainly heard about it. I've endured sidelong glances and stiff responses from staff all day.

I've never felt worse. Her wounded expression haunts me – her shock at my words, the devastation in her green eyes. *I* did that. I hurt her, and I meant to. Just how fucked up am I from my head injury? How much of this shit is permanent?

I need answers that aren't there yet because brain trauma takes time to heal. The doctors tell me that head injuries are like fingerprints – no two are alike. Everything hinges on which portions of my brain were affected, how much damage was sustained, and how well they heal.

Luckily, I know someone who might be able to offer some insight. Stubb's injuries were similar to mine. I text him, conscious of the late hour. "Hey man. Call or stop by tomorrow? I need to talk. Thanks for threatening to beat my ass, even though we both know you'd lose."

I snort. Not likely. Stubbs is built like a Panzer, and he's solid muscle.

My phone rings immediately. "I didn't mean to wake you," I apologize.

"You didn't. I just ended my evening with a delightful redhead."

I cringe. "Sorry I interrupted. Just stop by tomorrow."

"You're not interrupting. I was walking in my front door. I figured I ought to check on you. You're obviously confused if you think I can't beat your Pretty Boy ass."

I chuckle. "Got a minute?"

"Sure. Need me to swing by?"

"No, nothing like that," I say hastily. "I wanted to ask about your injuries. Do you feel up to that tonight? Or at all, even. If it's too painful to talk about –"

"Please," he dismisses me. "That shit doesn't bother me. What do you want to know?"

I'm floored by his nonchalance. "Oh. Uh – well, what happened?"

"Summer in the Sandbox, six years ago. Four of us were on patrol. Our sweepers missed a roadside bomb. We got hit. I was the lucky one."

Stubbs believes he's lucky because he was the one who survived, but to me, no matter how you slice it, it's a tragedy. "What kind of injuries did you have?"

I hear clinking, followed by the creak of a chair and the hiss of a twist-off cap. "I'd offer to swing by and share a beer, but they don't mix with pain meds. Let's see. Well, obviously I lost my legs. Multiple surgeries for those. Got a rod in my spine, a matching pair of titanium hips that the ladies adore, pins and screws in my right arm, skin grafts to my left thigh... What else? A bunch of broken ribs, blast lung, a skull fracture, bleeding in my brain, a broken jaw. That one was a bitch," he recalls.

"Jesus," I mutter. "How the hell did you survive?"

He laughs. "Cause I'm a badass motherfucker. Oorah! Marines, baby!" he roars, forcing me to hold the phone away from my ear.

"Your head injury. How bad was it?"

"Skull fracture. Bleeding. Burr holes. A craniotomy to open up a section of my skull."

"Shit, man."

"It's a good thing," he says confidently. "Swelling shoves your brain against your skull. That shit hurts because your skull's not soft like your belly. There's nowhere for the brain to go, and pain meds can't touch it. If they don't open your skull to relieve the pressure, you die."

His casual discussion of his near-fatal experience confounds me. "Were you always like this about your injuries?"

"Like what?"

"Like it's no big deal."

"No. It was hard for a while, but I've had a few years to gain perspective."

I shake my head in amazement, regrouping. "So after the head injury, did you have problems with mood swings or rage or depression?"

"All the above. I was a goddamn powder keg. It's a good thing I was as injured as I was, because at full strength with my attitude, I'd have killed someone."

"Seriously?"

He laughs. "What? You think a guy on peg legs can't kick ass?"

I chuckle. "You just seem so Zen now. I can't picture it."

"I'm gonna give you some advice. First of all, take the damn psych meds. Everybody fights them, but your body needs every ounce of strength to heal your injuries. Don't waste half its energy fighting the shit in your head. The second thing? Talk to the damn shrinks. I don't mean sit there pretending to listen and then blowing off what they tell you. They don't do that job for the money. They could make four times as much listening to housewives whine about their husbands not noticing them. We trust surgeons to repair our bodies. We trust PT guys to build our strength and OTs to teach us to manage in the real world. Trust the people that can help you manage the shit inside your head."

When the sun comes up, I'm still ruminating on the wisdom of his words.

CHAPTER EIGHT

CHARLIE

I'm exhausted, physically and emotionally. I take my third shower of the day, hoping to rinse away my emotions. I make a peanut butter sandwich in my beige hotel kitchenette and open my laptop. There's an email from Lila about the changes to my house to accommodate Mark. Was it really just this morning that I emailed her? It seems like an eternity ago.

Her reply leaves me speechless. She's not hiring a contractor. Most of the changes needed are things Tucker, Tom, and Lila can do, and she and Tucker insist on paying for them. The only update requiring a contractor is the shower, and Tom's friend Tyson works with a charity for disabled service members. He renovates homes to make them disability-friendly. He's redoing Mark's shower next week, and the charity is covering the cost of the shower renovation.

Lila calls before daylight, knowing I'll be up. I am, of course, thanks to yet another night terror. This time, though, the man taunting me with the whip was Mark, his blue eyes ice-cold.

It was just a dream. Mark would never hurt me.

But the realness of my dream leaves me shaken.

I force myself to pay attention to Lila, whose voice exudes worry. "You sound terrible, Charlie. Are you alright?"

"I'm okay. Yesterday was rough, but I'm fine now." I haven't been fine in a very long time, and Lila knows it, but she doesn't call me on it.

"What happened?"

"Mark's emotional roller coaster crashed."

Her voice turns gentle. “Are you okay?” Lila knows his moods have been all over the map, brooding silently one minute, loud and livid the next.

“We worked through it,” I answer, not wanting to be dishonest, but at the same time, wanting to shield him from judgment. “He lost his temper and mouthed off, I walked out, and his mentor settled him down. He called Dr. Friedman. He admitted he hated being at the mercy of his emotions and asked for help. He agreed to start medication. We had a bad morning, but the final outcome was good.” My abbreviated version makes it sound like Mark was in a bad mood and bit my head off. I suppose that's technically true, albeit significantly sterilized.

Lila can tell I’m being evasive. “Did he hurt you?”

“Mark would never lay a hand on me.”

“You know that’s not what I mean,” she probes gently, and I sigh.

“It was bad,” I finally admit. “He said some pretty hurtful things. He feels worse about it than I do, which is what pushed him to ask for help. It sucked, but it was a necessary catalyst, and if it helps him, it was worth it.”

“I’m sorry, Charlie.” Her quiet words make my eyes fill with tears again.

“I saw your email,” I say, wiping my eyes and changing the subject. “I appreciate the offer, but I can’t let you guys foot the bill for changes to my house.”

“Charlie, we love you both, so shut up.” I open my mouth to protest, but Lila ignores me and keeps talking. “I’m serious. We want to be there with Mark, but we can’t. This is something we can do to help. Deal with it.” Then she laughs. “Besides, we’ve already started.”

“What do you mean?”

“Tucker, Tom, and I met for lunch yesterday and hammered out what we needed. I placed the order at the hardware store and Tucker picked it up. We got the prep work done for our first job last night, and we start after work this evening.”

“But –” I say weakly.

“You’re too far away to fight me on this, Charlie. Is his discharge date set?”

“Maybe two or three more weeks?”

I hear her mental wheels turning. “That should be enough time. Any chance you can fly home for a couple of days before then to see if we need to adapt anything else?”

“Let me talk to Dr. Paxton. I’ll work it out and let you know. And Lila?”

“Yeah?”

“Thank you.” My words are gruff over the lump in my throat.

Her voice is gentle. “We love you guys, Charlie. Hug Mark for me.”

I shower and race to the hospital, picking up coffee on my way. Dr. Paxton meets me in the hall. “Perfect timing,” he greets me, following me into Mark’s room.

"Good morning, Mark. I just reviewed your x-rays. You're ready to have your external fixators removed."

Mark looks surprised. "So the bone is finally healing?"

Dr. Paxton nods. "That last surgery did the trick. The bones are fusing nicely."

"What does that mean for my timetable?"

He looks thoughtful. "We'll remove the fixators tomorrow morning. It's a relatively simple procedure done under sedation. You'll rest tomorrow, then we'll get you back to PT and OT the next day. My guess is we'll be discharging you in a couple of weeks." He pulls out his phone, checking his calendar. "How does two weeks from Sunday sound?"

Mark's beam is contagious. "It sounds amazing!"

Dr. Paxton laughs. "Yes, it does. You've come a long way. I'm proud of you."

He's barely out the door when Mark grabs my waist. "Two weeks," he says, his eyes alight as he pulls me against him. "I can't believe I'm getting out of here!"

I laugh at his excitement. "Did you think they were going to keep you here forever?"

"It was starting to feel like it." He scrubs his hand along his stubbled jaw. "We should celebrate."

"What do you want to do?"

"I want to play hooky," he says with a rueful grin, "but I guess I need to work my ass off in PT to make sure I'm ready."

"I'll pick up lunch and we can watch a movie," I promise. "Anything you want."

"I can't believe I'm getting out," he says, still dazed.

"Not just getting out. Going home."

"Home." He says the word, testing it. "I can't remember what that even feels like." Mark's home for the last fifteen years has been the Army. Before that, he lived with me.

"My house is just like the military, except I'm not a drill sergeant, you can sleep as late as you want, and the food is marginally better," I tease. "Now decide what you want for lunch and I'll have it waiting when you get back."

Home. The end of this nightmare is finally in sight.

MARK

I show up for my session with Dr. Friedman fifteen minutes early. I'm as surprised to see Dr. Paxton leaving the inner office as he is to see me waiting.

"Captain," he greets me. "You're here early."

"Yes, sir," I nod. "I have things I need to sort through."

He smiles. "Ted's excellent at that. The more open you are, the more he can help."

I wait for a few minutes in the outer office before Dr. Friedman ushers me into his inner sanctum. Instead of flopping on his nondescript beige couch to glare at the ceiling the way I used to, I sit in one of the two wing chairs, propping my leg on an ottoman. Dr. Friedman smiles, his steel-blue eyes crinkling a bit at the corners. His gray hair is rumpled, like he's been rubbing his hand through it. "Good morning, Mark. Tell me how things are going."

It's a good session. Ever since my blowup, I'm fully engaged in the emotional healing process. I've already read two of the books Dr. Friedman recommended. One is about neuroplasticity – essentially, rewiring your brain's automatic responses. It's like forging a new path through the woods – the more you use that path, the smoother the trail becomes. In the same way, the more you choose a new thought process or behavior, the more your brain gravitates toward it. The goal is to help me build in a delayed response. I can think logically and respond appropriately when I'm calm. When I'm not, I need to delay my emotional reaction long enough to allow reason to guide my response. The silver lining to my brain injury is that because it's actively healing, my brain is primed to more easily rewire itself.

The second book he recommended discusses the power of the mind. I was skeptical, but the more I read, the more surprised I was by the mountain of scientific evidence. Studies have consistently shown that catchy phrase, "What you think about, you bring about," is actually true. The book begins by describing the placebo effect. I'd heard stories of someone taking a sugar pill for a headache, thinking it's something stronger, and their headache disappearing. I'd always assumed they must not have had much of a headache to begin with. In actuality, their belief that the pill will work allows the brain to circumvent the pain path created by the headache. The brain is hardwired to avoid pain, and when offered another option, it often opts for an alternative path.

Far more astonishing is something called the "nocebo" effect, a term I was unfamiliar with. Basically, it's the opposite of the placebo effect. In this case, your mind creates a negative self-fulfilling prophecy. A conviction that you can't do something leads the subconscious mind to direct the body to succumb. One particular study followed an Olympic-level athlete with a spinal injury. He'd never be a competitor again, but his arms and legs were fully functional. Depression from the loss of his athleticism had him convinced he'd never walk again, and no medical expert could persuade him otherwise. He ended up confined to a wheelchair as his body responded to his beliefs. The book cited dozens of similar examples and studies to support the power of one's thoughts.

Obviously, placebo and nocebo effects don't occur one hundred percent of the time, but then again, neither does anything else. Reading these books has me carefully considering the weight of my own thoughts.

When my time comes to a close, Dr. Friedman stops me when I start to stand. "Before you leave, we need to discuss one other thing."

"Sure," I say, easing back into the chair.

"You said sometimes you wish you'd died in the Sandbox. Is that accurate? Do you truly wish you were dead?"

I hesitate. "Not if I'm thinking clearly. Charlie's lost so much already, and I think it would break her. I'm all she has left, and she's all I have. I owe it to her not to give up." I swallow before admitting the truth. "But when the phantom pains are ripping me apart, and I think about facing life without my leg, without my career, without my identity, without a plan, without anything... sometimes I think it would have been a lot easier."

He nods thoughtfully. "Yes. It would have been easier to die in the desert. It would have been easier than facing surgery after surgery, month after month in the hospital. It would have been easier than having your fiancée dump you when she found out you'd lost your legs."

Wait. What? I don't have a fiancée. And legs, plural? Is he confusing me with someone else?

"It would have been easier to die than to realize your military dreams were dead and that you had no idea what to do next, but you damn sure weren't crawling back to your father's farm in Pennsylvania after he disowned you for enlisting."

My brows pull together as I stare, confused.

"It would have been infinitely easier to die in the desert than spend three months in a bed beside your best friend, injured by the same bomb, only to watch him die from an infection after you'd made plans to start somewhere fresh together as soon as you were both well enough to leave." He pins me with an unblinking gaze, his blue eyes intense. "It would have been much, much easier to die in that desert, but it wouldn't have fulfilled your purpose, just as dying in Iraq wouldn't have fulfilled mine, Captain."

He leans forward, and I think he's going to reach his hand out to me, but instead, he grabs the ankles of both pant legs and lifts them up.

A pair of flesh-colored prosthetic legs peek out from under his dress greens.

Holy shit. My mouth falls open, and I can't stop myself. "You're an amputee?"

A faint smile curves the corners of his mouth. "I am a fifty-five-year-old Army combat veteran injured during the Gulf War in Iraq, Captain. I'm a healer, a psychiatrist who works every day with our nation's brave wounded soldiers. I'm a husband to a better woman than I deserve. I'm a father to three incredible kids, one who's pre-med, one in art school, and one who's an up-and-coming chef in one of the finest restaurants in San Antonio. I'm a creative soul who plays the sax, tinkers with the guitar, dabbles in abstract art, and secretly writes military fiction while hoping to be the next Tom Clancy. I'm a lot of things. And yes, I happen to be someone who lost both legs many years ago, but that's not who I am."

I can't stop staring, open-mouthed. "Why didn't you tell me?"

He tilts his head to one side. "Why would I?"

"Because of what I'm dealing with."

"We aren't here to talk about me. We're here to talk about you," he reminds me.

"Yeah, but I would have listened sooner if I'd known –"

He steeples his fingers. "So now that you know I'm an amputee, my words have value?"

His crisp tone startles me. "It's not that they didn't have value before," I say, flushing. "I just didn't recognize their value."

"So I was only worth listening to if you felt I had credibility?"

Shame washes over me. I dismissed everything he'd said to me for weeks because I didn't like his stance on medications. "I'm sorry. I wish I'd listened sooner."

He smiles ruefully. "Perhaps you'll pay more attention in the future."

"You can count on it," I promise.

I make my way back to my room, rocked by the revelation he's an amputee. I'd never have guessed. He's so calm, so self-assured, so settled. Maybe there's hope for me after all.

At least, there might be, if I can pull my head out of my ass and actually listen to the people trying to help me.

CHARLIE

I drag my stuffed suitcase and carry-on off the backseat and wave goodbye to the overly chatty Uber driver. I stand with my back to my house, gazing up into the clear night sky, so different from the intense artificial glow I've seen night after night in San Antonio. Hundreds of stars flicker in the silent darkness above me. The pre-dawn air is brisk, bordering on cold, and it reminds me I've forgotten my jacket in Texas.

I climb my front stairs for the first time in seventy-seven days. When I left, we were in the throes of a Colorado January, with snow and ice and bitterly cold winds. Now it's April, and though it's still chilly, the sun warms the ground during the day, and early bloomers like crocuses and daffodils are poking their heads through the soil. The mountaintops are still white; the highest peaks will have snow for several more months.

I expected my house to smell stale after nearly three months of being away, but I should have known better. When I walk in, the brightly lit interior smells of orange oil. Not only has Lila left every light in the place blazing, she's dusted.

Ever since my kidnapping, I have... quirks. I can't stand dust. It makes me feel filthy, which makes me anxious. It's why I shower at least twice a day. I can't handle darkness, either, so I have to have lights on, and if I'm alone when I first enter my home or the clinic, I turn on every light and sweep the entire building to ensure I'm safe. Lila's addressed both issues.

I drop my luggage and retrieve my handgun from the foyer table. Its familiar weight instantly calms me. I clear the house room by room, weapon raised as I scan closets, bathrooms, and corners. I'm baffled to find my office door locked and even more confused to find its furniture in an upstairs bedroom. When I'm certain I'm safe, I lower my gun and flip the safety back on.

I return to the foyer to deal with the luggage, tucking my gun into my waistband at the small of my back. I fire off a quick text to Mark to let him know I'm finally home. After unloading my suitcase directly into the washer, I go upstairs to shower. Being stranded for hours in a crowded airport with strangers invading my personal space has left me edgy.

I linger, bracing myself against the wall as steamy water courses down my body. I've been awake since my last nightmare at three o'clock Wednesday morning. It's now Friday. I'd assumed I'd be home last night, but thanks to nasty storms, I was stuck in Oklahoma. I've been awake for over forty-eight hours, and I'm feeling every minute of it.

I'd never have survived these last three months without Lila. She's managed our clinic with minimal remote assistance from me, and she really hasn't dealt with the financial aspect of our clinic in the past. She'd rather take on more clients to free me up to handle the business side. When this crisis hit, Lila took the reins, hiring another massage therapist to cover the gap left by my departure. Not only that, but she dealt with things at my house that demanded attention, like making sure my pipes didn't freeze and emptying my fridge when its contents evolved into science projects. And when I asked for help finding a contractor, she took on the work herself. Lila's my lifesaver, more sister than friend.

She's so damn strong. After Afghanistan, she recovered much faster than I did. Hell, I still haven't recovered. But she endured their hell, too, and she didn't just survive – she triumphed. Even during our captivity, the bastards gave her a wide berth, because she showed them from day one what she would do, given half a chance. She's delicate-looking, perpetually optimistic, exceptionally outgoing, and a total badass.

The same bastards that left her bruised have fucking destroyed me.

My train of thought derails as vivid images start leaking in around the edges of my mind. I try to squelch them, fighting the memories.

Don't think about them. Don't think about them. Don't –

But my exhausted state is no match for the insistent torment, and suddenly it's all I can see and hear and feel – their coarse laughter, the slicing of their whip and the broiling heat of their brand, and those eyes, those goddamned soulless black eyes.

His eyes are always my undoing.

Panic explodes like a mushroom cloud inside me, boiling up, its claws grasping and clutching inside my chest, tightening my throat.

Fucking hell.

I drop to my knees, vaguely aware of pain as they smash into the tub floor, and I gasp for air, feeling the bands closing ever tighter around my chest.

Then I hear Mark.

Breathe, Baby Girl.

Just breathe.

I've got you.

You're safe.

I squeeze my eyes shut, clinging to the voice in my head. Eventually I'm able to slow my panting. It seems like hours before I stiffly get to my feet, before I'm able to unclench my jaw and unfist my hands. I let the scalding water pound my tense neck, hammering out the knots along my shoulders.

When the water cools, I hurry to wash my hair and scrub my body. I towel off and dress before drying my hair. Despite the warm air from my blow dryer, I'm freezing. I tuck my gun snugly in its belly-band holster, catching sight of my reflection.

These past three months have taken a serious toll.

My brown hair hangs dull and listless, in desperate need of a trim. My plummeting weight makes my green eyes look much too large in my pale face, and dark circles shade the area below them like fading bruises. The clothes that fit a few weeks ago are now at least two sizes too big.

I smudge concealer beneath my tired eyes in a pointless attempt to hide the shadows from Lila. I brush my hair and twist it up in a clip before going downstairs. I need caffeine in massive quantities.

The warmth seeps through my huge white coffee mug, thawing my chilled hands as I settle on my overstuffed beige sofa and pull a crimson blanket around me. Reaching for the sheaf of paperwork, I try to focus, but my head throbs and my eyes burn. I finally surrender, huddling beneath the blanket and closing my eyes. Maybe a few minutes of rest will ease my headache.

It's still dark when Lila arrives at five-thirty. Her keys jingle in the lock, and she knocks firmly before announcing herself, calling my name when she opens the front door.

I bolt upright, throwing aside the blanket and papers as I scramble to the foyer. Lila drops her purse and a bakery box onto the table and pulls me into a long hug before studying me with her piercing violet gaze.

"You look like hell, Charlie," she says, sadness and worry tinging her voice. "You've lost weight, you're as pale as a ghost, and you look like you've not slept in days."

"Thanks. You look amazing, too," I reply glibly, but of course, she does, even at this hour. She's dressed in form-fitting jeans, a loose silk shirt that echoes her eye color perfectly, and gray suede ankle boots. It's a stark contrast to my baggy clothes and bare feet. I shrug nonchalantly. "Hospital food is terrible, and I just need a decent night's sleep. I'm fine."

Lila raises one eyebrow skeptically. "You need time to recuperate, too," she says instead. "Tara, Tom, and I have the clinic under control. When you guys come home, you're taking two weeks off to rest and eat." She smiles and lightly shakes the bakery box. "Now get that paperwork and meet me in the dining room. I brought warm raspberry danish bites."

I fetch my coffee cup and papers. "Things are already looking up if pastries are involved."

Lila chuckles as I follow her down the hall, her boots drumming a staccato rhythm on the hardwood. "Why was your flight diverted to Oklahoma for twelve hours?"

I pass her a pair of saucers, and she piles them with danishes and gathers napkins while I fill a coffee mug for her before topping off my own. "An instrument panel malfunctioned not long after takeoff, so they diverted us. As soon as we landed in Oklahoma, they grounded all flights due to severe thunderstorms and tornado warnings. Hundreds of us were jammed in the terminal like sardines. It was awful. My flight to Pueblo didn't board till after one this morning." I shudder, recalling hours unable to escape a toddler's earsplitting screams while his mother apologized profusely, explaining that flying made his ears hurt.

Lila gives me a commiserating smile. "I hate airports. Everyone's grumpy. That's why I prefer red-eye flights. Everyone's half-asleep or keeps to themselves."

"Definitely." I'm a diehard introvert. I prefer people in small doses with limited interactions, something commercial airlines don't offer. Their least-objectionable option is a red-eye flight.

When I join her at the table, I hand her the paperwork from the hospital detailing how to best set up a home for new amputees. "I haven't really looked at the work you guys did on the house," I apologize. "I did my security check, but after my shower, I crashed on the couch."

Lila tosses blond curls behind her shoulder and selects a pastry, raspberry filling oozing from slits in the top. "You look like you're dead on your feet." She knows I'd never have been able to relax enough to nap while surrounded by strangers. She wouldn't have, either.

"I've been awake for two days," I admit. I bite down and groan at the combination of flaky pastry, sweet glaze, and tart filling. "Oh my God. You're the best woman I know."

"Damn right I am. I'm freaking awesome," she laughs. "Let me bring you up to speed, and then we'll look everything over later." I nod, licking raspberry filling off my lips as she begins.

"The downstairs rooms really didn't need much. The main walking areas are clear, so Mark should be able to navigate easily. We secured all the rugs and mats with extra-grip velcro tape.

"We set up the downstairs bedroom for him," she continues. "I found a huge arched chaise so he can prop his leg up, and we swapped the standard bathroom door for one that slides on a ceiling track. I bought extra pillows and made the bed with minimal layers so he won't get tangled in the bedding.

"The biggest changes we made were in his bathroom. We installed wall-mounted shelves because they'd be easier for him to access than lower cabinets, and Tyson did an amazing job modifying the shower. We also relocated your pathetic office upstairs and repurposed the space."

I frown. "I noticed my office door was locked. And what do you mean, pathetic?" I reach for another pastry.

Lila laughs. "Your desk had three empty folders, sticky notes, and a handful of paper clips. Your credenza only had a few dust bunnies. It was merely a suggestion of an office, not a functional one."

"It functioned perfectly fine. I used my laptop at that desk. And I'm positive I had a couple of pens, too. And a green highlighter."

Lila rolls her eyes. "Well, we relocated your –" she forms air quotes – " 'office' upstairs, and transformed that space into a rehab gym. Tucker and Tom filled it with –" more air quotes – " 'necessary equipment' to help Mark regain his strength and mobility."

I finish a second danish bite and push the saucer aside. Lila studies my barely-touched pile of pastries, and I glance away, feeling the weight of her eyes. She's silent, instead reaching for the papers from Brooke.

"I thought of this," she taps the page, "keeping the most-used items within arm's reach. I put baskets in the bedroom and living room. His wall-mounted bedside shelves had space underneath for a mini fridge, so I added one." Lila ticks items off as she reads. "He's practiced with his crutches, we have wide open pathways, we added handrails in the bathroom. Oh – outlet nightlights. I didn't think of those." She scribbles on a pad she unearths from her purse before continuing. " 'Clothes that are easily removed, such as pull-on shorts and shirts.' Does he need more clothes?"

I nod. "Definitely. I only picked up a handful of shirts and shorts once he quit wearing hospital gowns. I pissed him off with non-slip socks. He refused to wear one at first because he insisted he wasn't frail or elderly." I smile. "When I pointed out that falling on his ass would keep him at Brooke longer, he shut up."

Lila continues jotting notes. "Wall-mounted hooks near the shower. I didn't think about those, either." She flips several pages before commenting, "We've done most of these other things. A shower bench, handheld shower heads, a handicap-height toilet. And we swapped out the bedroom and living room pull-switch ceiling fans for ones with remote controls."

I stare at her. "I can't believe you guys did all this. You have to let me pay you back."

"Not happening, Charlie, so shut up," she says, but her voice is gentle. "We love you guys. We'll do anything we can to help. And I owe Mark my life. So this?" she gestures around. "This is nothing."

"I get it." I owe him my life, too. No sooner has that thought crossed my mind than the memories erupt again, unwanted images forcing themselves into the forefront.

Soulless black eyes leer at me.

No. I shut my eyes tightly, fighting the fear rising in my chest.

"Breathe," Lila murmurs, her soft hand grasping mine. "You're safe now. Deep breaths."

Breathe in.

Breathe out.

I'm safe here.

No one's going to hurt me.

It takes several minutes for me to regain control. My panic attacks are always worse when I'm tired. I open my eyes and shove my chair back, desperate for a distraction. "C'mon. Let's go see your hard work."

Lila squeezes my hand before leading me to Mark's room. I've always loved this room. When I moved in, I chose the upstairs master bedroom because it was further from the entrances, giving me more time to react to intruders, but this room suits my style perfectly. Plush beige carpet cushions the hardwood underneath. White floor-length blackout curtains puddle gracefully on the floor, framing a wall of windows that provides a spectacular view of the scenic mountains. In front of them perches an enormous white arched chaise. It's easily large enough for two, casually draped with a greige faux-fur throw and piled with squashy pillows. Beside it sits a low bookcase with a few plants, a lamp, and artfully arranged books. The wall behind the bed is lined with horizontal driftwood-gray planks, creating a stunning feature wall. Bedside shelves with shallow drawers are wall-mounted on either side of the bed, and beneath one sits a new mini fridge. The bed is huge, simply dressed with a white comforter, a faux-fur blanket, and pillows. A massive dresser faces the foot of the bed, and above it hangs a large television.

It's absolutely gorgeous.

"This is perfect, Lila. He'll love this."

She shrugs. "It fits the vibe of your house." She nudges me toward the bathroom. "Check this out," she says, tugging lightly on the gray barn-style door. "It slides, so he won't need to struggle with one that swings in and out."

I reach for the wrought iron handle, and the door glides like silk along its track. "I like this."

"It's functional *and* pretty, just like me," Lila teases. "But the best part is the shower." She slides frosted glass doors open to reveal the charcoal gray enclosure. "Tyson lowered the lip to just three inches, so it'll be easy to step over, and he elevated the slope a bit to drain the water faster. And the best part is the bench." She points to a built-in tiled bench down one side of the shower. "He installed multiple handheld shower heads, handrails, and recessed lighting. We got Mark a walker for the shower because it's more stable on a wet floor than crutches, so tell him not to have a meltdown. I'm not insinuating he's frail."

I'm amazed by the tile work. "Very impressive. It looks like it was built this way originally."

She nods. "Tyson did a fantastic job. He's really nice, too. And he's single."

I whip my head toward her. "Seriously? I'm not even home and you're already trying to set me up?" I fume. "Fine. Maybe this guy will at least wait until the food arrives to be a jerk."

Guilt hits me as soon as the words leave my mouth. All Lila wants is for me to heal. She thinks – hopes – a healthy relationship will help me move forward, the way her relationship with Tucker helped her. Unfortunately, her love has blinded her to one insurmountable problem: with my plethora of issues, I'm not relationship material.

"Sorry," I mutter. "I'm just tired and cranky." I step to the other side of the bathroom, and my guilt grows as I survey all their hard work. A handicapped-accessible toilet and new handrails gleam, and reclaimed wood shelves line the wall by the sink. Lila and the guys have been busting their asses because they love us, and I'm biting her head off for an innocent comment. "Sorry," I repeat.

Lila squeezes my shoulders from behind me and presses her cheek to mine before changing the subject. "The shelves are for baskets for his personal items," she explains, pointing to empty baskets on the counter. She gestures to the wall dividing the shower from the toilet area. "We could mount hooks here for his towel and clothes. We'll pick up toiletries today." Then she smiles, rubbing her hands together. "Let's go check out your former office."

I sigh. "I'm afraid to look."

I'm pleasantly surprised by the updated space. They've painted the walls a warm grey, and the right side of the room is all floor-to-ceiling mirrors. Motivational prints line the space. The largest one, about eight feet wide, seizes my attention with its bold lime background. Emphatic charcoal lettering quotes Mohammed Ali: "The only limitations you have are the ones you place on yourself."

Despite the staggering amount of equipment, the long room still looks spacious. Lila describes each piece as she works her way around the room. "An inclining treadmill for after his prosthesis. A stability ball to rebuild his core. A leg press. Some super-fancy home gym machine with pulleys and cables and weights and bars. You can do lifts and pull-downs and probably julienne fries." She shakes her head. "The boys insist it's very important, but all their drooling makes me suspicious. And this medieval torture device," she places one hand on a thick metal post studded with multiple bars, "is, and I quote, a 'power tower'. Apparently it's for advanced core work." She continues pointing items out with one slim finger. "Weight bench and rack with dumbbells and barbells and crap." She grins. "Incidentally, this stuff should never be referred to as 'crap' in their presence. It's 'important guy stuff'." She rolls her eyes and gestures around the room. "Whatever. I run thirty miles a week and have washboard abs without any of this."

"Washboard abs," I mutter. "If I didn't adore you, I'd kill you."

Lila grins. "If it makes you feel any better, I only work out so I can eat anything I want."

"It doesn't." I actually enjoy running. It quiets my mind, something that's a real challenge for me. Having said that, I'm not running thirty miles a week or doing two hundred sit-ups a day like Lila. I'll stick to my twice-weekly runs and my Pilates.

"Speaking of eating, your fridge and cabinets are completely bare."

"I've been gone for three months. Of course there's no food in the house."

She snorts. "I cleaned out your fridge months ago. You might still have a jar of mustard, but since you don't like it, I don't understand why you have it. And you know those non-perishables you're supposed to keep on hand for blizzards, like pasta, soup, and canned goods? You had none of that, and you left during the height of blizzard season. Much like your office, your kitchen was mostly decorative. We're going grocery shopping. I'm starting a list."

I roll my eyes. "I have mustard because Tucker likes it. And how can you be this excited about shopping at the ass crack of dawn?"

My leggy blond lifesaver smiles broadly. "Because you and Mark are finally coming home. Now haul your skinny ass upstairs and lie down. I'll come get you in a few hours." I open my mouth, but Lila shakes her head. "No arguments. Besides, the stores aren't open yet. I've got plenty to keep me busy."

I know when I'm beaten, and frankly, I'm too exhausted to do anything but surrender. I hug her tightly. "Thank you, Lila. For all of it."

Lila hugs me and kisses my cheek before smacking me on the ass. "Yeah, yeah. Now go get some sleep before I kick your ass with my washboard abs." I grin and climb the stairs, falling into a thankfully dreamless sleep almost as soon as my head hits my pillow.

CHAPTER NINE

CHARLIE

MY QUICK DASH TO Cedar Ridge to ready the house for Mark passes in two whirlwind days. Lila and I replenish my kitchen, buy clothes and toiletries for Mark, and install hooks and nightlights. I spackle the bullet holes in my walls and dab new paint on them after she leaves Friday night. Saturday morning she surprises me with an unexpected trip to the salon, where she treats me to a cut, highlights, facial, and mani-pedi.

"You've not had the time or energy to take care of yourself. I'm making the time for you," she says firmly when she pulls into the salon's parking lot.

I shake my head. "I have too much to do, Lila."

"We both do. Now let's go. The longer you argue, the longer this is going to take. Besides, I have an appointment too, so unless you want to sit in the car and pout, come on."

"You know, some people might call this being pushy," I comment as we cross the parking lot.

Lila grins. "I prefer to think of this as an assertive act of kindness."

During my foot rub, I confirm with Monica that Mark is still slated for discharge tomorrow, then verify our flights. I jot final to-do lists while my toes are painted a metallic burgundy and run through mental checklists while getting my hair cut and highlighted. Once home, I hastily complete my remaining tasks, toss a handful of things into my suitcase, and race to the airport at midnight, chauffeured once again by Tucker and Lila.

Tucker smiles and Lila kisses my cheek as they send me on my way. "We'll grill steaks tomorrow night," she promises. "Tell Mark we can't wait to see him."

I'm glad I'm on another red-eye flight. There are fewer passengers, so the seat beside me is empty, and as Lila pointed out, passengers tend to keep to themselves late at night, so the flights are generally quiet.

I glance thoughtfully out the window, comparing my mood on this flight to San Antonio with the previous one. Last time I made this trek, I was a wreck, terrified Mark wouldn't survive or that I'd have to make a godawful decision I wasn't ready for. This time, I'm excited to bring him home so his real healing can begin.

The pilot's hushed voice intrudes into my thoughts. "Due to weather conditions ahead, we are adjusting course due east. We expect to land in San Antonio no more than twenty minutes later than our originally planned arrival time." A few passengers rouse slightly, but for the most part, his quiet words go unnoticed.

I stare out the window, my eyes detecting an impenetrable darkness obscuring stars to the left of the plane. If I strain, I can faintly make out the edges of sinister clouds in the pitch-black night. The dark clouds suddenly glow deep purple, illuminated by a brilliant pinkish-white flash.

Lightning.

Lightning is nature's way of exposing what hides entombed in the shadows. It arrives in tumultuous storms when opposing forces clash, twisting and writhing. It announces its presence in spring when cold and warm fronts battle for supremacy, and in summer when the sun beats down fiercely amid stifling humidity.

Lightning strikes lives, too. It struck my life, and it struck Lila's. Now it's struck Mark's.

Behind my house stands a massive angel oak tree that was struck by lightning. I was home the afternoon it happened. A late spring storm boiled up, and strong winds whipped tree branches from side to side while torrential rains lashed the house. I was making southwestern tortilla soup, planning to curl up on the couch and read. A crack like a rifle shot sounded outside, and I ducked away from the windows instinctively. Finally I realized the noise had been a lightning strike, not a gunshot. I looked outside to see smoke rising from the tree, but no flames. After the storm subsided, I examined the damage up close. Lightning had carved a gash from the upper trunk to the ground, exploding bark out of its way and leaving a trail of burnt wood behind. I was positive my beautiful angel oak would die from its wounds.

To my utter shock, my tree survived.

Bugs ate away the charred wood over the summer. The opposite side of the tree kept its green leaves until autumn, when they changed with the season. The following spring, the tree leafed out as it always had. The only visible difference was the barkless vertical scar down its trunk.

Trees die every year from lightning strikes, but mine thrives in spite of its damage. The scar is part of the tree, but it doesn't limit it, because the tree is more than just its barkless scar.

Rather than apply this insight to my own life, I consider how to use that imagery to help Mark accept his changed body. He's in worse emotional shape right now than I am, or so I tell myself. I lean back and close my eyes, and though it's not my intention, I fall asleep.

I awaken when the plane starts its uneventful descent. Tired passengers stumble down the steps and stagger into the relatively quiet airport. I take an Uber to the hotel and finish packing, eager to take Mark home. By daylight, I'm back at the hospital, ready.

After all our hurdles to get Mark well enough for release, his discharge is surprisingly uneventful. Fat packets of information regarding treatment plans, medications, physical therapy, and appointments with the VA in Pueblo are reviewed at length. An on-site pharmacy delivers his prescriptions directly to his room. Stubbs even stops by to see us off. His huge arms crush us together in a bear hug, promising to keep in touch, calling us Pretty Boy and Green Eyes. An Uber meets us outside the hospital, and after a bit of finagling, we fold Mark's lanky body into the compact car. Then it's off to the airport, and just like that, we're whisked back to Colorado and into a slightly larger Uber vehicle that shuttles us home to Cedar Ridge.

After all this time, all this pain, we're home.

Mark examines the exterior of my house appraisingly as he waits for the driver to remove my bags from the trunk. In spite of my worries, he makes it up my outside stairs without difficulty, though I maintain a firm grip on his waistband just in case. He waits patiently, looking around while I grab our luggage and clamber up the stairs.

"It's gorgeous here," he admires, gazing at the mountains. Snow covers their peaks, but in the lower elevations, trees are budding, and a fresh carpet of spring green mingles with the darker rocky mountainside. The mid-April breeze is crisp and fresh, the late afternoon sky a perfect cloudless blue. "I'll bet those are amazing to hike –" His voice breaks off and his expression tightens.

"Hey," I say encouragingly, "Dr. Paxton thinks you'll be healed enough to have your osseointegration surgery in a few months. Be patient. We'll hike them together."

He smiles automatically, but it doesn't reach his eyes. I pretend not to notice, unlocking the door. "Come on in," I say, holding it open before locking both locks and the chain behind us. "I'll give you the grand tour of the downstairs." I open the foyer table drawer and retrieve my handgun, tucking it in the back waistband of my jeans.

Mark raises an eyebrow. "Dangerous neighborhood?"

"Habit," I say lightly, then change the subject. My hand lingers near my gun, but I force myself to leave it. I'm not doing a full-security sweep. I'm not alone. Besides, I don't want Mark to know how screwed up I am. Not yet, anyway. It's not like I'll be able to hide it from him for long.

"Off here to the left is the living room," I say, leading him into the long room. In the center, two large beige sofas and a matching loveseat form a U. They face a stone fireplace topped with a chunky reclaimed-wood mantle and a wall-mounted television. Along the left by my front windows, two cream chairs flank a low bookcase. On the opposite side of the room is the wide doorway to the kitchen with a rustic desk to the right. Crimson throw blankets add splashes of color, as do sprawling green plants that have only survived my absence due to Lila's tender care. "The sofas recline, and Lila's made sure anything you can possibly need is within reach. She even put in mini fridges." I point below an end table and grin at his raised eyebrow. "At last count, I saw three. Apparently, she's extremely concerned about your hydration."

He looks around. "Gas fireplace?"

I nod. "I'm too lazy to build a real fire most nights. I do have a firepit for the patio, and both gas and charcoal grills, but in here, gas is easier." I point to the basket on the end table. "It even has a remote, in case you're kicking back watching TV one night thinking, 'God, if only there were a fire to go with my beer from the mini fridge while I watch football'."

Mark studies the fireplace wall and the ceilings. "The rockwork and exposed beams are nice." His eyes halt on my freshly patched and painted bullet holes. The hardware store had assured me the paint was an exact match for the color I'd bought before, but it's lighter, making the wall appear freckled. I should have just painted the whole damn wall. I keep moving, hoping to distract him.

"The kitchen and dining room are through here. I'm a decent cook, mostly because I enjoy eating. Lila's a much better cook than I am. But there's always stuff for sandwiches or soups or pasta if I'm feeling lazy."

"You know I can cook, right? I'm not here for you to wait on me. I just need time to get things sorted out."

"I didn't bring you home out of pity like some stray dog. You're my person, Mark. You can stay forever if you want to."

He studies me. "I appreciate this. You've been... much more than I deserve, Charlie." Emotions boil in his pale blue eyes.

"Quit thanking me," I say firmly. "You and I take care of each other. We have ever since that day when you stopped Corbin Holmes from bullying me. It's what we do."

Uncomfortable with his gratitude, I turn away to focus on the kitchen. White cabinets line my kitchen, and wide hardwood planks cover the floors.

Vibrant blood-red pendant lights hang above a wooden island with black leather bar chairs, their lights reflecting off my sleek black granite countertops. Despite its contrasting colors, the room feels warm and inviting.

His gaze follows as I point out specific cabinets. “Plates, bowls, and glasses are there. Silverware is in that drawer. Snacks are there, coffee stuff is above the coffeepot, and liquor is in that cupboard.” I point past the dining table at the far end of the room. “The patio is through the sliding doors, and the stuff for the grills and firepit is stored inside the benches if you want to sit under the stars with a fire.

“This way,” I direct him out a doorway at the far end of the room, back into the hall. We pause at the door to my repurposed office, and I tap the door lightly with one newly-manicured nail. “This is Tucker’s big surprise. He and Tom – a good friend and your new physical therapist – did this, and it’s ‘important guy stuff’ ” – I form air quotes like Lila had – “so I’ll let him unveil this. He’s very proud of it, so be sure to act impressed.”

Mark trails behind me, balancing on his crutches as I stop again. “Here’s a half bath for the downstairs,” I say, opening the door to expose a small but functional neutral-toned bathroom. “Down this hall is the washer and dryer, and the glass door at the end leads across the breezeway to our clinic. That’s where you’ll be doing physical therapy and getting your massage and hydrotherapy treatments.”

I lead him back to the entry where we started, stopping at the door beside the foyer table and bench. “And this is your room.” I open the door and step aside. Mark enters, looking around. I cross the large room and open the drapes, exposing the magnificent floor-to-ceiling mountain view. The sun is beginning its descent, scattering its first hints of rosy color across the snow-capped peaks.

Mark nods approvingly, taking in the pale neutral walls, the driftwood-gray planked wall at the head of the bed, and the reclaimed wood furniture. “This is really nice, Charlie.”

I tug the pewter-colored sliding barn door aside to reveal the bathroom. “Tom knows a guy who remodels homes for wounded veterans. He modified the bathroom. There’s a shower bench and handrails, and everything is set up so you won’t have to lean over on crutches. Lila found that huge chaise so you can relax and put your leg up, and she stuck another mini fridge under your bedside shelf. It’s already stocked with water, soda, and beer. And I picked you up more clothes. They’re washed and put away. We can go shopping for anything else you want.”

I look at him, noticing for the first time the tightness around his eyes and the tension in his jaw. “You’re hurting, aren’t you? You’ve been up all day. Your leg’s probably swollen. Why don’t you rest for a while? It should be a couple of hours before Lila and Tucker get here.”

Mark studies me for a long moment. “I know you said no more thank you’s, but I owe you so much, Baby Girl. I can’t ever thank you enough for this. For everything.” He smiles. “I'd hug you, but if I fall over, you’ll make me wear that damn non-slip sock again.”

I laugh and step closer, careful not to bump his crutches, wrapping my arms snugly around his waist. He hugs me tightly with his left arm, leaning on his right crutch. “Don’t worry,” I tease, “it’s carpeted in here, so no non-slip sock required.” I stand on tiptoe to kiss his soft stubble and grin. “Unless you fall on your ass.”

He chuckles and kisses my forehead. “I’ll change clothes and then I’m going to check out that chaise. I’ll yell if I need help,” he adds when I open my mouth.

I relent. “Fine. Your clothes are mostly in the top drawers so you don't have to lean over. I’ll close your door, but I’ll have my phone if you need me. Do you need anything for pain?"

He shakes his head. "I'm going to elevate it and see if that helps."

I nod. "Call me if you need me," I reiterate, closing the door.

I start a load of laundry from our suitcase before carrying my toiletries upstairs. I catch a glimpse of myself in the mirror. It’s not flattering. My hair looks good thanks to Lila’s mandated cut and highlights, but my pale face draws attention to the huge shadows beneath my eyes.

All seems quiet downstairs, so I race through a shower, anxious to rid myself of the grimy feeling being around strangers gives me. Afterwards, I dig through my closet and find black leggings and a sweater that matches my eyes. I apply makeup to conceal my exhaustion and add my favorite gold earrings.

Not great, but it’s definitely an improvement.

I listen briefly at Mark’s door, but his room is silent. Hopefully, he’s dozed off. I wander into the living room and flop on the couch, leaning my head back. I close my eyes, empty my mind, and feel my body relax into the cushions.

We’re finally home.

MARK

Charlie's upstairs. She must be showering, because I hear water running. Lila said she showers multiple times a day. She can't stand to feel dirty after being held captive in squalid conditions.

I rummage through the dresser drawers and find clothes, changing into a soft black shirt and dark gray sweats that I safety-pin up to accommodate my missing limb. I sink into the plush chaise with a bottle of water and stare at the breathtaking mountain view, seeing none of it.

I'm home.

And I feel more like giving up now than I ever have.

I lie there, my ruined leg propped up, stuffed like a sausage into a compression stocking from my upper thigh to its weirdly rounded tip. Supposedly, the stocking will reshape my residual limb and compress my burns to minimize scarring. Given the multitude of scars on that leg, it's an exercise in futility. I rub my eyes as they suddenly sting. Despair so intense I can scarcely breathe floods my soul.

I'm a useless goddamn cripple.

I'm such a fucking idiot. I believed the hype they fed me at Brooke, swallowed it hook, line, and sinker. I convinced myself that by pushing harder, working my ass off, and doing everything they said, I could beat the odds. Not grow back a limb, obviously, but be – well, better off than *this*. This is living in a room in Charlie's house, dependent on help from others, barely more than a damn invalid. From now on, friends and strangers alike will see me as a cripple first and a man second. That's all I am now – a cripple. There's no possible way a woman could ever see me as attractive or masculine or virile again. Hell, I can't even stand without using crutches. My whole life, I've been strong, capable, and confident. Now I'm damaged goods. I can't hide the fact I'm missing half a limb, like some jacked-up starfish.

I wasn't conceited before the explosion – at least, I don't think I was – but I knew I was good-looking. Light blue eyes, thick sandy hair with a hint of curl, and tall, with broad shoulders and a tapered waist, giving me that enviable V-shape. I was athletic and formidable, a natural leader, an alpha male – all advantageous traits for my military career. I've enjoyed my share of women over the years while carefully sidestepping long-term entanglements.

I stare into the burgeoning sunset and snort. What good are blue eyes and broad shoulders when I'm half a man? At thirty-five, I thought I'd still have time to play the field. I figured I'd eventually settle down once I got out of the Army, maybe even have a family someday. Instead I'm missing a leg, covered in scars and wobbly as a newborn foal. I can't approach a woman like this.

I no longer have strength or athleticism to get by on, and I sure as hell can't rely on my looks with this fucked-up body. The only career I've ever known was blown to hell, and leadership skills are useless with no one to lead. I lost everything because of that damn IED.

Dark thoughts return to rear their ugly heads, whispering enticingly.

That explosion could have killed me. It killed Rivers. He was right next to me. Thomas, Varnes, Carswell, and Dillon – they all died.

Maybe I'd be better off dead, too.

Instead of automatically dismissing the thought, I allow myself to consider it.

Giving up.

Giving in.

Letting go.

The idea seduces me.

No more pain.

No more misery.

No more self-loathing.

No more uselessness.

Just... quiet.

Nothingness.

Peace.

It sounds good.

But after a brief moment, I shove the idea from my mind. I can't do that to Charlie. She's lost too much already. All we have left is each other.

But rejecting that choice comes at a steep price. Without the option of death as a path to freedom, my only alternative is being trapped in this misery forever. The likelihood of years or even decades condemned to unending, hopeless torment crushes my heart in an invisible fist.

I close my eyes and throw my arm over my face, praying Lila and Tucker run out of gas or forget to come by. I just want to be alone.

The thought has literally no sooner crossed my mind than I hear the rumble of a diesel engine.

Fuck.

CHAPTER TEN

CHARLIE

I've no sooner melted into unconsciousness than the growl of Tucker's big truck rouses me. I stagger to my feet and meet them at the door. "Sorry we're early," Tucker apologizes, "but Lila practically knocked me down in her excitement to get to Mark." He carries a covered platter and a large bowl to the kitchen. "If I weren't so secure, I'd be jealous."

Tucker is one of my favorite people. He's tall, over six feet, with broad shoulders, golden brown hair that curls against his wishes, and dark blue eyes that are usually twinkling with mischief. He's sweet, loyal, and completely dedicated to taking care of the people he loves. It was his idea to install the camera in my foyer to transmit to his and Lila's laptops and phones so they could help with my night terrors. He's also a goofball, guaranteed to liven up any situation.

Lila follows him, unloading canvas bags on the island. She pulls scrubbed potatoes from one and places them on a baking pan before sliding them into the oven. She glances over her shoulder, pulling an assortment of containers from another bag. "I cooked bacon for the potatoes and salad and made red wine vinaigrette. The garlic bread is ready to bake, and the steaks are marinating. Tucker, put the salad in the refrigerator and the steaks on the counter to come to room temperature," she directs before turning excitedly to me. "Where is he?"

I grin. "Lying down. Let me see if he's awake."

"I've got this," Tucker insists, heading down the hall.

"If he's asleep, don't you dare wake him," Lila scolds.

"I've waited long enough to see him. His ass is mine."

I hurry in front of Tucker and block his path. "He was in a lot of pain. Let me check on him before you barge in there braying like a donkey."

Tucker looks offended. "What makes you think I'd do that?"

I roll my eyes. "History. Now wait outside." I knock softly and peek around the door. "Mark?"

He's lying on the chaise, his left arm covering his eyes. I slip inside and close the door behind me.

"Hey, Big Guy. You awake?" He sighs heavily but doesn't move his arm. I cross the room to kneel by the chaise, placing my hand on his shoulder.

"I was hoping they wouldn't come by right as they pulled up," he murmurs.

"Are you still hurting? I can tell them you aren't up to a visit. I'll keep them company for a while and they can come back another day."

"It doesn't matter. I'll still be a goddamn useless cripple no matter what day they show up."

I gasp in shock. "Mark! That's not true!"

From behind me, Tucker shoves the door open and stops before bellowing through cupped hands. "Chand-ler!" Then he beelines straight to Mark.

"Tucker!" Lila chides, scurrying in right behind him.

"Keep laying there like Sleeping Beauty and I swear to God, I'll kiss you right on that pretty mouth of yours," Tucker announces, rounding the foot of the bed and stopping at the chaise. "Now get your lazy ass up here so my wife can hug you."

His words aren't issued as a request.

Tucker grabs Mark's hand, easily hoisting him to a sitting position. As I watch Mark's expression change, I smile. A visit from Tucker and Lila is exactly what he needs.

Mark swings his left leg around and reaches for his crutches, then slowly maneuvers to a standing position. Tucker pulls him into a tight hug. "Glad you're home, brother," he says gruffly, thumping his back as he holds onto him longer than necessary.

"Yeah, well, keep those bristly walrus lips to yourself," Mark mutters, and I chuckle.

Lila is right behind Tucker, impatiently waiting her turn before pushing him out of her way. She gives Mark a long hug and a quick kiss. "You look good," she says, holding his face between her hands and kissing him again despite Tucker's vehement protests in the background. "I'm so glad you're home. This is where you belong." Tears shine in her violet eyes.

Mark kisses her delicate cheek and returns her hug. "It's good to see you." I hear his surprised undertone and smile.

"Alright, enough mushy shit," Tucker declares. "We hanging out in here?"

Mark shakes his head. "I've spent enough time in bed to last a lifetime. Lead the way. I'm right behind you."

We relocate to the living room. Mark reclines on one sofa and the rest of us gather around him. I pour red wine and we unwind, conversation flowing as easily between us as it always has. Mark studies Lila and Tucker nervously before gradually relaxing, and I realize he's been waiting for them to stare at his leg or ask questions.

But no one does. We discuss random, everyday things. We bring him up to speed on local life: the town of Cedar Ridge; Tucker's three brothers, Joey, Ethan, and Shepherd; Lila's farm animal obsession; and Tucker and Lila's jobs as a gym owner/ personal trainer and a wellness clinic co-owner/ massage therapist. Nothing exotic, just ordinary, everyday topics.

It's wonderful, and I know Mark feels it, even if he isn't aware of it. During his time at Brooke, everyone constantly asked how he was feeling. It was necessary in order to care for him, but it was also an inescapable reminder of his brokenness. An evening of listening to Tucker describe his younger brothers' escapades and Lila explain why she named her goats after supermodels (including accidentally naming one after Tom's ex-wife, Chele) is doing wonders for him. He actually looks like he feels – well, happy.

I haven't seen him look like that since before his injury.

After about forty-five minutes, Lila and I break away to finish dinner preparations. I light the grill, basking in the cool dusk air as sparks shoot skyward from the charcoal.

It's going to be okay.

He's home.

MARK

The light-hearted living room conversation puts me at ease, and the red wine relaxes me even more. No one has stared at my hideous half-leg or asked how I feel. It's really good not to have my injuries be the center of attention. Instead, I'm listening to Lila's stories about life on the homestead, as she calls it. She has goats. Lots of goats. And horses.

I'm intrigued by this disclosure. Lila looks like she belongs in a sequined gown on a runway, not mucking out stalls. The fact she named her goats after supermodels from the nineties makes me laugh out loud. There's Kate Moss, an angular Nubian goat; Chele, a dark and exotic beauty; Cindy Crawford, who has a facial marking reminiscent of that famous mole; Carol Alt, a lithe beauty with piercing blue eyes; and Heidi Klum, a goat whose breed I can't recall, but it's German. I listen in utter fascination. Even with her colorful stories, I still can't picture Lila with goats any more than I can envision the Pope making twenty-dollar bills rain at a strip club.

When Lila and Charlie excuse themselves to finish dinner, Tucker leads me to the room Charlie pointed out. It's a rehab weight room filled with shiny new equipment.

"Check this out," Tucker announces proudly. He starts extolling the virtues and features of each apparatus at length, but my eyes halt on the massive lime green sign that boldly proclaims, "The only limitations you have are the ones you place on yourself."

Tucker follows my gaze to the motivational print. "Pull up a spot on the weight bench. I've got some things to talk to you about." After I'm seated, Tucker sits on the floor facing me.

"Look, I hate this shit happened to you. You sure as hell don't deserve it. But you oughtta know up front, you'll get zero pity from me."

Hot anger rushes over me. "I don't want your fucking pity –"

"Do your damn deep breathing and let me finish," Tucker cuts me off, his gaze steady. His reaction startles me enough for me to get a grip, and I nod. "What that means is that because I'm your trainer and your friend, I'm going to push you hard, because that's what you need even if it's not always what you want. There'll be days where you're convinced I'm a complete asshole. Tough shit. That's how this goes. Joey hated me when he first came home because I told him losing the use of his legs didn't mean a damn thing in the bigger picture," he says, referring to his younger brother.

His callous words stun me. His youngest brother, Joey, returned from Afghanistan paralyzed from the waist down, and Tucker said losing the use of his legs meant *nothing*? Where the hell does he get off?

He keeps talking despite my appalled expression. "God, my mom was pissed off about that for weeks. But I pushed him to his limit, and now, instead of moaning about not being able to do something, he figures out how to do pretty much whatever he wants. He's driving, he's got his own place, he cooks – not great, but he's not gonna starve. He's dating a cute redhead. But when he first came home, he was convinced his life was over, that his injury made him less of a man. Bullshit. Stuff like what he went through, what you're going through – hardship emphasizes someone's true strength. Joey's a stubborn-ass fighter, and so are you. Just know there's gonna be days you'll hate me, and that's good, because later on, you'll be glad I pushed you."

"How did Joey learn to cope with his disabilities?"

"We worked on upper body strength and flexibility, and we problem-solved how to navigate his surroundings. Anything he wanted to do, we talked out ways to approach it. We took his strengths and built on them."

I can't stop my words from rushing out. "What about the other part? About seeing himself as less of a man?"

Tucker studies me. "I figured you'd have a similar reaction. You two are a lot alike. Physical abilities came easily for you. But being a man isn't about physical shit, Mark. It's not how far you can run or how much you can bench press. It's what's here." He thumps his chest. "We've both known guys with muscle, but no character, no inner strength. That's what defines you."

It's all I can do not to openly scoff.

Tucker accurately reads my dismissive expression and goes straight for my jugular. "Lila says those bastards bragged about how mutilating Charlie made her less of a woman. So you tell me. Does it make her less of a woman because a bunch of assholes brutalized her?"

My blood freezes, followed by a surge of blistering rage. "Charlie endured hell and fought her way back. Lila too. Those fuckers didn't lessen who they are. They didn't have that power."

"Then why would your battle wounds make you less of a man?" Tucker counters, and I falter, having waltzed right into his trap. "Charlie told us about your mentor – what's his name?"

"Stubbs," I answer, reluctantly smiling when I think of his big grin and bigger personality.

"Lost both his legs, right? Built like a Mack truck? Struts around on his prosthetics, ballsy as hell. Is he less of a man because of his injuries?"

I shake my head grudgingly. "He's one of the toughest guys I've ever met," I admit. "Threatened to kick my ass once, and I'm pretty sure he could do it."

"So even though Stubbs isn't less of a man after losing both his legs, you're writing yourself off because you lost one?"

"It's more than that, Tuck," I say slowly. "I don't know what I'm supposed to do. I've lost my leg. I've lost my career. Everything I thought I could do after the military – maybe coaching or something – it was based around me having two legs. What the hell am I supposed to do now?"

"You're a natural leader, Mark, and that has nothing to do with legs. People need someone to guide them. You can be whatever you want to be – motivational speaker, teacher, coach." He reads my disbelief and points to the wall. "That's right, a coach. Stop putting limitations on yourself. Figure out what you want. We'll help you make it happen."

Warmth floods my chest, and my voice is gruff when I can speak. "Thanks, Tucker."

He grins. "I'll remind you of that when I'm pushing your ass till you cry like a little girl."

"I can still kick your ass, you know."

Tucker snorts. "In your dreams, Princess."

I glance around for something to throw at him, but settle for flipping him off instead. He winks and blows me a kiss. "You're pretty, Chandler, but not that pretty."

I narrow my eyes. "I told you earlier, weirdo, keep your bristly lips to yourself."

He laughs, about to make another smartass remark, but a knock at the door interrupts Tucker's obnoxious behavior. "Dinner's ready," Lila says, poking her head around the door frame.

"Thank God," I mutter, and Tucker grins.

I reach for my crutches and follow Lila to the dining room. Charlie has placed a soft stool beside an end chair so I can prop up my leg. The four of us relax around the table, and I find myself enjoying the camaraderie and comfort of good food and good friends.

Charlie leans over once to quietly ask if I need anything for pain while Lila and Tucker are squabbling good-naturedly about her goats. I shake my head.

Today has been another emotional roller coaster. A few hours ago, I was at the end of my rope. Now I'm looking at the people who mean the most to me, and I have hope that I just might get past this and maybe even be stronger in the long run.

Dr. Friedman said strength is knowing when to ask for help and being willing to accept it. He was right.

Time to figure out what the hell I want.

CHARLIE

Phantom pain is a bizarre phenomenon. Over the past two months, I've devoured every scrap of research and anecdotal information I can find. Phantom pain is extremely intense and quite real, even though it feels like it originates in amputated body parts. Although the limb is gone, the mind is convinced it's there because the spinal cord continues sending frantic signals from damaged nerves just above the amputation. The mind and body translate those signals into severe pain. Essentially, the brain and spinal cord get trapped in an endless loop, and the only way to stop the pain is to interrupt the loop. Pain meds block the pain receptors in the brain, but they can't break the loop, so the pain returns when the meds wear off.

I've exhausted every resource, determined to find a way to help Mark, and I'm hopeful I've found something. I'm planning to test it the next time they strike.

Mark's worst episodes always seem to follow strenuous days when he's most fatigued, and today has been long and exhausting. He's been up all day, unable to elevate his leg while traveling and unwilling to take any medication while Tucker and Lila were here. I'm positive his phantom pains will hit tonight.

Mark's gone to lie down. I've changed into sweatpants and a loose shirt, and I'm wiping down the kitchen when I hear his anguished groan. I'd expected the pain, but not with such immediate intensity. I dash down the hall, stopping at his door. I hear his gasps and rush in without bothering to knock. He's gritting his teeth and gripping the comforter, his breath coming in tight bursts. I'm at his side in a heartbeat. "Phantom pain again?"

He nods, his eyes squeezed shut. I place my hand against his clenched jaw. "I want to try something different, to see if it will help." He nods tersely. I grab a long folding mirror and a bottle of muscle-relaxing massage oil from the closet.

"I need you to help me. We're going to slide your upper body to the right and position your legs toward the left, okay? I'm setting up a mirror on the right side of the bed." I slip an arm beneath his shoulders to shift him. He's still gritting his teeth, and another groan escapes his lips as he moves. I cross to the other side of the bed. "I'm shifting your legs," I caution, and a guttural moan escapes him when I reposition them.

"Did you take your pain medicine?" He shakes his head, unable to speak. I snag a bottle of water and two tablets before helping him sit up enough to swallow.

"I'm propping you up with pillows so you can see my mirror." I assess him as I arrange extra pillows. His jaw is tight, his skin pale. Beads of sweat dot his face, and his breathing is rapid and shallow. I move to the foot of the bed, adjusting the mirror's angle as I scuttle back and forth to see what Mark will see when he looks at it. I need the reflection of his left lower leg visible exactly where he would have previously seen his now-missing right lower leg.

When I have the mirror situated, I rub his left shin to get his attention. "I need you to show me on your left leg exactly where you feel pain in your right leg."

Mark opens pain-filled eyes and raises his head. "What?"

"I've been researching phantom pain," I explain. "I'm going to combine massage with something called mirror therapy. You're going to show me where your right leg hurts, and I'm going to rub that area on your left leg."

His brows draw closer in utter confusion. "What?" he repeats.

"Mirror therapy uses an image of your healthy leg to trick your brain into thinking you aren't hurting. Show me on your left leg where you feel pain in your right leg."

"The place my right leg hurts is spread all over a road in Afghanistan," he growls through clenched teeth.

"C'mon, work with me," I encourage him. "Let's give this a shot. Your right lower leg hurts. Front or back?"

Mark stares like I've lost my mind. "I don't have a right lower leg. This is ridiculous."

"Yeah, well, your pain looks pretty damn real, so let's see if we can persuade your brain the relief is real. Is the pain in the front or back of your right leg?"

He regards me for a long moment, and I meet his skeptical gaze with stubborn determination. I see it in his eyes when he finally surrenders. "Both. All through the shin and calf."

I squirt massage oil into my palms to warm it. "Okay, Mark, I want you to look in the mirror and watch what I'm doing. We're going to convince your brain that I'm massaging the pain out of your right leg."

He shakes his head. "This is crazy."

"What's crazy is deciding this won't work before you even try," I say firmly. "Maybe it will, maybe it won't, but there's only one way to find out. There's a decent amount of evidence supporting mirror therapy, so I say we give it a shot." I pause for a moment. "Unless you have a better idea?" When he remains silent, I push on. "Look at the mirror. Do you see the reflection where your right leg would be?"

He studies my face, then glances at the mirror. Reaching behind his head, he readjusts his pillow, settles back, and nods reluctantly.

"Good. I want you to watch that reflection while you tell yourself you're looking at your right leg. I need you to convince yourself I'm massaging the pain out of your right leg. Really think about it. Imagine what it feels like. If it's easier, you can close your eyes, but you need to look at the mirror sometimes to reassure your brain I'm working on your right leg. Okay?"

I wait until he nods again, his eyes locked on the mirror.

I slide one oiled hand under his left calf and begin to gently knead the muscles there while my other hand finds the taut muscles in his shin. "Think about how your right leg is relaxing," I say quietly after a couple of minutes. "Focus on how your pain is diminishing."

I massage in silence, observing over several minutes the perceptible changes in Mark's body. His fists gradually unclench and his jaw relaxes. The tension slowly leaves his shoulders. His breathing grows more even and his face softens.

It's working.

Holy shit, it's actually working.

I continue rubbing, working into his deep muscle tissue.

"Tell me how you feel," I say about twenty minutes later, still massaging his left leg.

"I don't understand," he says, bewildered. "How did you do that?"

I smile. "Well, it doesn't work every time, and it won't work for every person. The nerves for both your right leg and left leg branch off your spinal cord in the same general area. By making your brain think your right leg was being massaged while I stimulated nerves in your left leg, we interrupted the pain loop trapping your brain and spinal cord." I gently release his leg and put the mirror away. "Studies suggest it can not only disrupt a current pain path, but prevent new ones from forming. We're going to make this a nightly routine." I return to sit beside him again.

Mark grabs my hand, a desperate edge to his voice. "Baby Girl, I can't tell you how much this means. The phantom pain has been hell. You've got to tell them about this at Brooke."

"They're the ones who pointed me to the research, but they've not had much success," I admit. "People are skeptical, and you have to really commit for it to be effective. Let's face it, if it had been anyone but me, I'm not sure you would have tried as hard." I squeeze his fingers and lean over to kiss his cheek. "How about a hot shower? I'll set up what you need and stay within earshot."

His expression turns wistful when I mention a hot shower. "It sounds wonderful."

I turn toward the bathroom. "I'll put everything where you can get to it."

Mark gathers some clothes, then joins me. I've already placed shower gel, shampoo, and a washcloth on the shower bench and hung a soft bath towel on a hook. I turn on the water to warm up.

"There are more hooks for your clothes, and the walker is right here for the shower." He rolls his eyes. "No arguments," I say sternly. "If you fall and screw up your femur, you'll be right back at Brooke, explaining your pigheadedness to Rick."

I know he's silently conceding I'm right because he frowns but says nothing. I barely suppress a victorious smile. "Do you need help?"

"It's a shower. I've taken them before."

I cock an eyebrow at him. "Sit down to dress and undress so you don't have balance issues. If you need help getting into the shower, I'll be nearby. Yell if you need me."

"Thanks, Charlie."

I linger in his room, listening to be sure he's alright. There's the rustling of clothes, followed by the scuffing of the walker over the tile. I smile. It may be under duress, but he's cooperating. I finish tidying the kitchen, fold his freshly washed laundry, and check all the door locks again. When I return with his clean clothes, the shower is off, and I hear him moving around. I'm putting his clothes in the dresser drawers in neat stacks when he slides the bathroom door open.

He glances over. "You know I can do that, right?"

I shrug. "It gave me something to do. Do you need anything? A snack or something to drink?"

He grins. "I'm good. Lila made sure I have easy access to refreshments."

I chuckle. "If you need me, you can yell or text or call. I'll be up for a while." I wait until he's back in bed before heading to his door. "Good night, Big Guy. Love you."

"Love you, too, Baby Girl. Good night."

CHAPTER ELEVEN

MARK

I'M LYING IN BED hours later, still marveling at Charlie's ability to relieve my pain with brain tricks and mirrors. Maybe it works on the same principles I've been reading about – neural paths and neuroplasticity, or maybe placebos and the power of the mind. When I hear an odd noise, I sit up, straining to identify it.

It's a cross between a growl and a curse, like a werewolf with PMS. Charlie must be watching a movie.

I don't hear any background music or dialogue, though.

"Charlie?"

She doesn't answer. I pause and wait, listening, but there's nothing else.

I guess it's just the television.

CHARLIE

Loud boots echo sharply on the stone floors, moving closer. A metal door clangs open behind me, then slams shut. Grating voices outside the cell utter crude comments and laugh as a pair of rough hands grabs my hips.

No!

The foul stench of body odor hits me. A zipper scrapes behind me as he drags me backwards.

No!

I pull my right knee forward before driving my heel upward behind me, connecting with his exposed groin. I hear a man's deep groan. My body swings, unviolated for this round but still suspended in midair. The barbed wire bites deeper into my wrists with every sway of my body.

I hear the door again. Someone else is coming.

They never stop coming.

Fucking bastards!

No no no no no NO NO!

MARK

I've just decided it must have been the television when I hear it again. This time it sounds like someone snarling "No!" right outside my door.

Is that... Charlie?

I hear it a third time. "No!" It's a fierce, feral growl, and it's definitely Charlie. *Shit!*

I spring up, grabbing my crutches and hauling myself awkwardly across the room. I reach the door and grab the handle, shoving as I turn, but nothing happens. Frustrated, I jiggle it and shove again, harder this time. Still nothing. *Fuck!* My lagging brain prods me until I realize I need to pull the door, not push, and my damn crutch is in the way. Cursing, I lunge left and jerk it open.

A gun blasts twice from the left, just outside the door. Bullets strike the wall to my right, exactly where my head would have been if I'd rushed straight into the hall. The drywall explodes in a cloud of dust as bits shower to the floor. I drop to a crouch, scanning my immediate area for any weapon I can use.

There's a single sneaker – mine – and a glass bowl of driftwood pieces and pinecones on a table.

Wonderful.

I snag the shoe and quietly empty the bowl's contents on the carpet. The bowl is heavy enough to buy me a second or two. I can hurl it at the intruder's head and tackle him while he's distracted. If I'm lucky, I might avoid getting shot in the process.

"Charlie?" I call.

No answer.

Please be okay, Baby Girl, please.

"Charlie? Can you hear me?" I rise to a standing position, bracing myself against the door frame. I throw the shoe across the hall into the living room, where it smacks the wall and thuds to the floor. I expect gunfire in that direction as I prepare to hurl myself at her attacker.

Instead, I hear... Lila? But her voice sounds canned. Soothing, repeating itself. Then another sound reaches me.

Charlie. Sobbing.

I dart my head around the corner to chance a glance at the intruder, but the only person in the foyer is Charlie.

Kneeling on the floor.

Gripping her gun.

Her hands are over her ears, and she's rocking, her bony form wracked with sobs.

What the hell? *Charlie* almost shot me?

I let go of the bowl, and it thunks into the thick carpet. "Baby Girl?"

"Charlie?" It's Lila's voice again, but it's different from the tinny sound I still hear echoing around the foyer. "Charlie, you're safe. Put your gun down, Charlie."

Charlie continues to rock and cry.

"Mark, are you okay? Mark?"

I frown at the sound of Tucker's voice. What the hell is going on? Where are they?

"Charlie, you're safe. Put down the gun," Lila says again, and this time, Charlie releases the gun from her right hand. It clatters to the floor beside her.

I ease into the foyer, utterly confused. Charlie's wrapped her arms around her head, knees now drawn to her chest, still sobbing, moaning "No, no, no," over and over.

I lower my crutches carefully as I sink to the floor beside her. "Baby Girl? I'm here. You're safe." I speak softly, not touching her. I just sit beside her, repeating myself.

"Thank God." I hear Tucker breathe a sigh of relief, and this time I follow the sound of his voice to the ceiling. There's a camera and speaker there I didn't notice earlier.

Why do Lila and Tucker have a camera feed to Charlie's foyer?

"We're headed over, Mark," Lila says. "We're only five minutes away. If you can unchain the front door, it'll help. If not, we've got bolt cutters in the truck."

Bolt cutters?

And why don't they sound shocked? Has this happened before?

The tin-can-Lila voice continues, and eventually it dawns on me it's coming from Charlie's phone. I find it on the floor and silence it. Charlie gives no indication she's aware of my presence, continuing to rock and moan, arms locked around her head.

I have no fucking idea what to do or how to help. I simply recite the same things over and over, telling her I'm here and that she's safe. I don't touch her or get too close. I do push her gun beneath the foyer table, though.

It's not even three minutes later when I hear Tucker's big truck sling gravel as he slams to a stop. I open the door, and they sprint up the steps two at a time. Lila's wearing yoga pants and a baggy shirt, her jacket inside out. Tucker's in shorts, a tee shirt, and running shoes. He hasn't bothered with a jacket or socks.

"I've got this," Lila says decisively, pushing past me. "Tucker, take Mark into the other room." She drops to the floor beside Charlie and slips a hand under her chin, murmuring in her ear.

Tucker squeezes my shoulder. "Head back to your room. I'm grabbing a couple of beers. We need to talk."

I lock the front door, hesitating. Lila speaks in a soothing tone, stroking Charlie's face with her thumbs. I watch, transfixed, as she convinces Charlie to lower her arms.

Charlie looks directly at me, and the raw pain in her startling green eyes hits me squarely in the chest, so hard I nearly stagger under the weight of her anguish. Lila cups her cheeks. "Look at me, Charlie." Her voice is gentle. "Are you with me?"

Tucker appears in the hallway, beers in hand. "C'mon, Mark," he says in a low voice. "She's in good hands, I promise."

I don't want to leave her.

But Tucker nudges me, so I amble forward after another uncertain glance at Charlie. He follows, closing my door. I perch on the edge of the bed, adrenaline rocketing through my veins. He sits cross-legged on the floor, twisting open a beer and passing it to me before opening his own. I wait impatiently as he rubs his hand over his face, then takes a deep breath.

"Charlie has night terrors, Mark."

I try to reconcile his words with what just happened. "She had a flashback?"

He half-shakes his head. "Not exactly. Flashbacks happen when people are awake, and there's usually a trigger, like a sound or smell. Night terrors are a cross between nightmares and flashbacks. There's not necessarily a trigger, and she's usually disoriented when she wakes up."

I swallow hard. "So her night terrors, they're about the bastards that took her."

There's a brief silence. "Charlie relives what they did to her, Mark." He's quiet for a moment before adding, "Everything they did to her."

Jesus Christ.

Chills run down my spine, and it's hard for me to breathe as images I've tried to repress surge forth. I stare at Tucker, remembering in excruciating detail the night we rescued Lila and Charlie. Lila was in bad shape – beaten, bloodied, and raped. Those assholes were brutal to her.

But to Charlie? They were barbaric.

Those savage bastards tortured her. Carved her up with a rusty knife. Burned their filth into her flesh. Strung her up like an animal waiting to be gutted. All that, on top of the beatings and rapes and God only knows what else.

I almost lost her twice, once because I fucked up, and a second time from infection from the shit they did to her.

I close my eyes, horror settling in the pit of my stomach. I fight the urge to vomit.

Charlie's reliving what those fuckers did all over again.

"Every night?" My voice is hoarse.

Tucker shakes his head. "Not every night. At least, not before she went to San Antonio. I don't know about now."

My eyes land on him. "Why didn't you tell me?"

My accusatory tone doesn't offend him. "There's nothing you could have done from halfway around the world except worry or get yourself killed by being distracted. Charlie needed you to come home alive, not in a body bag. Lila and I help her as much as she'll let us."

Though part of me knows he's right, my scowl persists. "Does she sleep-walk? How did she make it down the stairs from her room?"

Tucker shakes his head. "She won't sleep upstairs. Most nights, she barely sleeps at all. She stays on the bench outside your door. She feels safest there because she can monitor the front door, both entry points in the kitchen, and the hall entrance. She has a blanket and pillow and keeps her gun with her, safety off. If she even thinks anything moves, she shoots."

I recall the spotted paint on the living room wall nearest the kitchen, where there's both a sliding glass door and a side entrance. It's the most vulnerable area in her home, which is likely why she faces it. I bet those splotches are patched bullet holes. "She shoots the walls?"

"I've completely reframed her living room wall and hallway with solid 6x6 posts. They're heavy enough to stop the bullets. I replace the drywall a few times a year."

Jesus Christ. I drag my hand through my hair.

"What did she do while she was in Texas?"

"I sent her a pair of tactical batons heavy enough to break bones. She couldn't take her gun."

"I wonder how she slept."

"Probably like she used to here, with her back against the door. That's why Lila bought her that bench. But Charlie never slept more than a couple of hours a night at the hotel. She didn't feel safe. She's looked exhausted for a while, and she's lost weight. She does that when she's struggling."

My face burns with shame when I recall the accusations I hurled at her a couple of weeks ago, when she was late because she had to buy jeans, and she said she didn't sleep well in hotels.

God, I was an asshole.

And not just that one time, either. I've been a jerk the whole time. She's been losing weight, not sleeping, struggling to survive, and I've been too self-absorbed to even notice. She slapped on a fake smile for my benefit, and I was too busy being a dick to see her distress. The shit that happened to me pales in comparison to the hell she went through.

The hell she's still going through.

"She never told me," I mumble. "All this time, all these weeks in a hospital room with nothing for us to do but sit and talk, and she never said one word."

Tucker sighs heavily. "Charlie's ashamed of her PTSD. She didn't want to worry you, and she wouldn't let us tell you. I'd planned to tell you tomorrow anyway. I didn't think anything would happen her first night back. I thought she'd be too tired to dream. That happens sometimes."

Well, that plan nearly got me shot in the head.

I keep that thought to myself and focus on Charlie. "So the camera in the ceiling, that's so you can keep an eye on her?"

He nods. "It feeds to my laptop in our room. If she cries out or fires her gun, it triggers an alarm. Lila calls her and we talk with her through the phone and the two-way speaker. Once she's reoriented, she puts down her gun, and Lila calms her down. Usually we can do it from our house, but sometimes we have to come over. Depends how bad it is." His blue eyes are troubled as he raises his beer bottle to his lips and looks away.

He's remembering a bad episode. Maybe more than one.

"What about her psychiatrist?"

He shakes his head. "Charlie stopped going to Dr. Martin after about a year. Her night terrors had stopped. When they came back, she decided she was too broken to be fixed."

We're both quiet for a few moments. "Did Lila have night terrors?"

Tucker sucks in a sharp breath as a pained shadow passes over his face.

"I don't want to pry," I say hastily. "I just wondered how you both knew exactly what to do for Charlie tonight."

"We've had a lot of practice," he says darkly. "She's had them from the beginning. Lila's started when I came home. When we –" he breaks off, and I suddenly understand. Tucker and Lila were engaged before she was taken. Their intimate relationship must have triggered hers.

"So how did Lila move past them?"

"Dr. Martin had us see someone who specializes in intimate relationships."

"You both went?"

He nods. "She taught me how to help her, what things to watch out for when we – uh – well, how to rebuild positive associations for her." His eyes grow immeasurably sad. "The first time I came up behind her and wrapped my arms around her waist, she had a full-blown panic attack." He gestures toward the hallway with his beer bottle. "Exactly like what you saw earlier, except she broke a glass and damn near shivved me with the shards."

"Those goddamned bastards," I growl. Fucking sadistic assholes, ruining lives, hurting women and getting off on it. Death was too good for them.

Tucker's jaw hardens. "If I'd known then what I know now, I wouldn't have killed them quickly."

It's silent until he gets to his feet. "C'mon. Let's pack you a bag."

My head jerks back. "For what?"

"You can stay with us."

I shake my head. "I'm not going anywhere."

"You can't stay here. She nearly shot you in the head."

I cross my arms, unmoving from my spot on the bed.

"Fine, I'll pack your stuff," he mutters, opening the closet.

"Pack anything you want, but I'm not leaving Charlie."

Tucker whirls around. "What happens if next time she doesn't miss? Be reasonable."

"I won't leave her, Tucker."

"Mark –"

"It's my fault she's like this, Tucker!" I explode, stabbing my fingers into my chest. "Mine! I sent them into that trap. I made that call, the wrong call. I won't desert her because of the damage my actions caused."

He sighs wearily. "Mark, if she shoots you, it will destroy her."

"She won't." My voice is quiet, exuding a certainty I don't feel. But it doesn't matter. I won't leave her when she needs me, no matter what.

I won't abandon Charlie.

CHARLIE

I hear the door again. Someone else is coming. They never stop coming.

Fucking bastards! No more!

No no no no no NO NO!

Gunfire. Two shots ring out.

The pale beige walls of the foyer slowly come into focus. I'm panting, kneeling on the floor, facing – oh fuck – why am I facing the open door to Mark's room?

Oh God no, please no! What have I done?

Did I shoot him?

No no no no no!

I hear distant voices. Lila. Tucker. And wailing. Someone is wailing. Not in the distance. Here. I drop my gun and cover my ears with my hands.

Make it stop! Make it stop!

"Charlie?" The voice is so far away. It sounds like Mark, but it can't be.

It's not Mark. It's in my head again. He's dead. He's dead. I killed him. He's dead. I want to die. Just let me die.

"Charlie? You're okay. You're safe. We're all safe."

Lila's voice. Soft hands touch my face. Her gentle voice is beside my ear.

"I shot him!"

The wailing noise is coming from me.

"No, Charlie. Mark's fine. He's safe. You didn't shoot him. You shot the wall. You just shot the wall. Everyone's okay."

"I shot him."

Lila's fingers cup my face. "No one's hurt. Tucker and I are here. Mark is fine. Everything's fine. Open your eyes, Charlie. Mark's fine."

"I shot him."

"No, Charlie. It's okay. I promise. Everyone's safe. Mark's right here. Open your eyes."

Please don't be dead. Please don't be dead. Please don't be dead.

I open my eyes. Lila kneels beside me, her eyes anxious.

I look up. Mark's there, leaning on his crutches. His light blue eyes zero in on me. He's pale and shaken, but very much alive. Not bleeding. Not dead.

I didn't shoot him.

Not this time.

Oh, fuck.

Not this time.

But what about next time?

Tucker appears and ushers Mark into his room, closing the door, and I fall apart. Lila wraps her arms around me and rides out the storm.

It's a bad one.

"I need to be locked up, Lila." My breath hitches in a half-sob.

"No, you don't, Charlie," she says firmly, brushing my damp hair out of my eyes.

"What if I'd killed him?"

"You didn't."

"I could have, though." I point at the holes in the wall, exactly at the level of Mark's head.

Lila takes a deep breath. "Yeah. You could have."

"I need help, Lila. When it was just me, it was bad enough, but I'm a danger to others. You need to make them commit me."

She shakes her head. "Involuntary commitment is for people who are dangerous to themselves or others but refuse to believe it. That's not you. You're asking for help."

"I need help."

"That's my point. You want help. You don't need to be committed. You just need help."

I point to the wall again. "I'm dangerous, Lila."

"Only because of your gun," she says quietly. "Without your gun, you're not."

Oh.

The bottom drops out of my stomach as I realize she's right.

Without my gun, I won't be safe. I'll be a victim again.

But Mark will be safe.

"Do you think Dr. Martin will still see me?"

"I'm sure she will, Charlie."

"I need to call her. In the morning. I need to call her but it's too late tonight. Don't let me forget to call her," I babble uncontrollably.

"We'll call her in the morning, together. I'll go with you if you want me to."

"You should go. You can tell her to commit me."

Lila stands up and pulls me to my feet. "Nobody's getting committed. You need help for your PTSD, Charlie, that's all."

I laugh, and even to my ears, it sounds hollow. "Yeah, I need help. I almost shot my best friend in the head because of these goddamn night terrors. I definitely need help."

Lila leads me to the kitchen and pushes me onto a bar chair, then reaches into an upper cabinet. She grabs a bottle and a couple of glasses before pouring a hefty amount of bourbon into one. "Here. Down the hatch."

I take it from her and toss it back. She refills it, and I down it as well. It burns my throat, but I know it will settle my nerves in a few minutes.

Lila sits down and pours herself a drink too, though hers is smaller and she nurses hers rather than gulping it down all at once.

"I wish I were as strong as you," I blurt.

Lila's head twists toward me. "What?"

"You're strong. I wish I were strong like you."

Lila shakes her head. "Charlie, you are strong."

My voice is hoarse as tears fill my eyes. "I don't feel strong."

"Trust me, you are." She pauses a minute before smiling softly. "Do you know what you do when you have night terrors, Charlie?"

"Destroy something else in my house?"

She chuckles. "No. Well, yes, but that's not what I meant. When your dreams start, you don't cry or cower. You come up fighting, Charlie, each and every time. You growl and hit and kick and yeah, sometimes you fire your gun. But you fight, every single time. You never give up. Those fuckers wounded you, but you weren't a victim, and you're not just a survivor, either." She smiles. "You're a badass."

I appreciate Lila's words and the loyalty behind them. They aren't accurate, but her sincerity is palpable. I lean against her, and she rubs my back until the bourbon numbs my pain.

CHAPTER TWELVE

MARK

It's nearly an hour later when Lila knocks and leans around my door frame. I've been going crazy with worry, but her face is calm. "We're going home, but I'll be over early. Charlie and I are going to call Dr. Martin first thing and see when she can work her in."

Tucker scrambles to his feet, and I reach for my crutches. "Can I see her?"

Lila smiles. "She'll feel better when she sees you. Stay put. I'll get her."

"Lila? Thank you. You too, Tucker. I didn't know..." My voice trails off. "Thank you."

She smiles softly again, and Tucker squeezes my shoulder. "See you tomorrow, brother."

I hear Lila and Tucker leave, followed by the click of the deadbolt. Charlie's huge green eyes peek anxiously around the door. She looks terrified.

"Hey, Baby Girl. Are you okay?"

She starts to cry and rushes to me. I catch her and hold her against my chest. "I'm so sorry," she sobs, and her cries tear at my heart.

"It's okay, Charlie. Everything's fine."

"Nothing's fine. I nearly shot you in the head."

I wave dismissively, keeping my tone light. "Expert marksman, my ass. You missed at close range. You're out of practice."

Yeah. I got shot at by a certified expert marksman at close range.

If I hadn't struggled with the door, tonight would have turned out very differently.

My offhand remark catches her off guard, and she chuckles through her tears. When she does, I smell bourbon. That's probably a good thing.

I reach beneath her chin and tilt her face up. "Why didn't you tell me what you were going through?"

She drops her gaze, her words barely audible. "I didn't want you to know." She covers her face with her hands, and I feel her trembling.

"Why wouldn't you want me to know you were struggling?"

She laughs, but it comes out as a strangled cry, muffled by her hands. "Why would I want anyone to know what a fucked-up, broken disaster I am?"

I gently tug her hands away from her face and wait for her to look at me. "Because I'm not just anyone, Charlie. I love you, and I want to help."

She shakes her head sadly. "I think I'm beyond help."

"Do you feel up to talking?"

She shrugs. "Pretty sure I won't be sleeping."

I scoot up to the head of the bed. "Want something to drink? I have a full complement of beverages in my shiny new mini-fridge."

She smiles faintly. "You get comfortable. I'll get the drinks." She opens the fridge. "Water, beer, or soda?"

"Water's fine."

She pulls out two bottles and passes one to me, then clambers onto the bed. We sit side by side against the headboard. She's agreed to talk, but she doesn't speak, so I break the silence. "How about I start by telling you what I know, and you can fill in the gaps?"

She nods.

"You have night terrors. Sometimes when you go to sleep, you get trapped in your past and have trouble waking up. When you do, it takes time to reorient yourself, and in that period when you're not fully aware of your surroundings, you've been known to fire your handgun, and that happened tonight." I glance down. "How am I doing?"

"Accurate, but understated. It's not just 'sometimes' anymore."

"How often does it happen?"

She drops her head, her posture ringing with defeat. "Every night."

Shit.

I slide my arm around her bony shoulders, troubled by her too-thin frame. She nestles closer into my side, her head against my shoulder.

"Tell me about your gun."

She doesn't lift her head. "Taurus nine mil, fifteen in the clip and one in the chamber." She pauses. "I guess it's thirteen in the clip and one in the chamber now."

I nudge the side of her head with my chin. "Not what I meant."

She glances up. "What did you mean?"

"As soon as we walked in the house, you got your gun. Do you always carry it?"

She nods. "I have my concealed carry permit."

I smile. "I'm not talking about when you're in public with strangers. I meant the rest of the time, when you're somewhere you're comfortable being. Do you always keep your gun on you?"

She nods. "It stays in my desk at work, but aside from that, I'm virtually always armed." She lifts the hem of her tee shirt, revealing a soft spandex holster, though it's currently empty. "But I'm never comfortable, no matter where I am."

Even awake, she's held captive by her past.

"Do you sleep with your gun?"

She falters. "That's complicated."

I smile, trying to inject a bit of levity. "It's a yes or no question."

"I don't sleep much. I can't. I have to monitor the entrances."

Tucker was right. She's hypervigilant.

My voice is intentionally gentle. "Why?"

She swallows hard and looks down at her hands, shifting her golden brown hair forward to hide her face. "I can't be a victim again, Mark. I won't. Not ever again."

Her anguish washes over me, a tidal wave of fear and hurt and anger. "So you don't sleep in your room."

"No. I stay on the bench outside your door. I can see where the back door leads into the kitchen from the opening in the living room, and I can see the hallway where someone would approach if they came in through the sliding glass doors. I can also watch the front door and the opening of the clinic hallway, all from that spot. I spend every night there, but I rarely get more than a couple hours of sleep, and –" she hesitates "– and if I do, it's fragmented. I wake up a lot to check and make sure no one snuck in when I dozed off."

Damn.

Charlie can't escape her fear, so she's always on alert, prepared to fight.

I watch her face. "What happened tonight?"

She draws a ragged breath, looking down at her hands. "I had a – an episode. A dream. They came to my cell again. I fought one of them off, and then I heard more of them rattling my cell door. I remember believing they'd never stop coming. I remember being angry and telling them no. And then I heard the gunfire. It snaps me out of it," she confesses. "The sound of the gun, I mean. Even with all the shit they did to me, they never used a gun. The gunfire triggers my brain to recognize what I'm seeing isn't really happening, and I wake up. Or come around. Whatever."

Everything clicks into place. The "No!" I heard was Charlie fighting off her attackers in her dream. Rattling my door handle because I was too agitated to open it properly made her think more of them were coming for her, and she fired her weapon in an attempt to kill her attacker. A chill runs down my spine as I realize exactly how close I came to dying tonight.

I redirect my thoughts. "So you only feel safe when you're armed."

She nods. "But I'm no longer safe around anyone else if I am, at least not at night. I'm relatively fine in the daytime, as long as nothing weird happens."

Her choice of words catches my attention. "Define 'relatively fine'."

"One day last year, a delivery guy walked right into the house. I came into the hall and there he was. He said he'd announced himself, but I was in the living room, and the TV wasn't on. I'd have heard him knock or call out. I pulled my gun and pointed it at his head. He backed out of the house and called the police, and as soon as he was outside, I had a full-blown panic attack. The police sided with me because he was big and I was obviously terrified." She pauses. "I came really close to shooting him. The officer came back later to talk to me about PTSD and invite me to a support group meeting. He had served, too, and he thought it might help."

"Did you go?"

She shakes her head. "No. I still have his card, though. Just in case."

I shift topics, sticking to safer ground. "How did you manage in Texas without your gun?"

"Tucker sent me tactical batons, and I spent every night against the hotel room door."

"You slept against the door." She nods. "For three months." Another nod. "To be there for me." She nods again.

Jesus.

I examine her sad eyes and tear-stained face. "We're both a mess, Baby Girl."

She laughs shakily. "I guess we are."

We sit in silence for a few minutes while I turn things over in my head.

Charlie only feels safe when she's armed. Having said that, we have to at least keep her gun out of reach at night. The only way that can happen is if she feels safe. Protected.

I've just found my purpose.

"I have a proposition." She glances at me, curious. "What would you think about staying with me at night?"

I expect her to look wary, but she doesn't. She merely tilts her head to one side, an unspoken question in her eyes.

"I think we can help each other, Charlie."

"How?"

"You relieved my phantom pain. That's something nobody has done, not with any amount of medication. Once it starts, it usually happens multiple times that same night. If you're with me, you could help me with the mirror if I need it." Her expression is unfathomable. "You can have the bed. I'll take the chaise. I don't want you to be uncomfortable."

She glances sideways. "The chaise looks comfortable."

I shake my head. "I don't want you uncomfortable being too close to me. I'd take the chaise and let you have the bed."

Charlie frowns. "The bed's for you. It's softer and roomier. And I'm not uncomfortable with you. I'm curled up in bed with you right now," she points out.

"Then if you're willing, you can take the other half of the bed. You can trust me, Charlie. I would never –"

She flashes me an annoyed look. "Don't be a dumbass. Of course I trust you. But I'd worry about hurting your leg if we slept in the same bed."

"I won't be asleep." Her eyes flick to mine. "I said we could help each other. You need to let me help you in return. I'll stay awake while you sleep. Leave your gun with me. I'll keep you safe, and you'll help me when I need you. We're both broken, but we can help each other."

"But when will you sleep? You need rest."

I shrug. "I'm a night owl, and I don't need much sleep. When you wake up, we'll have breakfast together and I'll sleep in the daytime."

Charlie frowns. "What are you going to do all night? Watch me sleep?"

I laugh. "I don't know. Read. Watch a movie. Think profound thoughts. Write poems about your snoring. The possibilities are endless."

She swats me. "I don't snore."

I grin. "All women say that."

She hesitates, and I watch her struggle to accept help.

"Every soldier comes home with scars, Charlie, every single one. Some scars are visible. Some aren't. There's no shame in it."

She looks away, and I can hear her silent disagreement. "Yeah, well, not everybody has night terrors and shoots up their house."

"Not everybody, no, but some do. Let me help you. Please, Charlie. You've helped me so much. Will you trust me to keep you safe?"

She shouldn't. I'm the reason for the hell she went through.

She meets my eyes without wavering. "I trust you, Mark. I always have." She looks down. "I don't know where my gun ended up, or I'd give it to you."

"If no one's picked it up, I slid it beneath the foyer table earlier."

She pads across the room, squatting by the table outside the bedroom door. She returns a moment later, engaging the safety and holding it muzzle down before passing it to me. I place it on the bedside table.

Charlie climbs onto the bed next to me, curling against my side, and I wrap my arms around her. "Thank you for giving me a purpose."

She looks up at me, her brow furrowed. "Thank you for being here for me. Again," she adds.

I kiss the top of her head. "Alright, Baby Girl, which side of the bed do you want?"

"I need to face the door," she answers immediately.

I nod. "Then I'll be on your right, and my right leg should be out of harm's way if you wake up kicking or fighting."

"Are you sure about this?"

"I'm positive," I say firmly. I'll do anything to help her get past this.

I'm rewarded with her tentative smile. "I'll go get my pillow."

Much later, Charlie is sound asleep beside me, her back pressed tightly to my side as she faces the door. Even with me standing guard, she's determined no one will sneak up on her.

Today has been a day full of firsts.

I was outside a hospital for the first time since January.

I got on an airplane and used public transportation for the first time as an amputee.

I came home to stay with Charlie.

I faced Tucker and Lila in person with my injuries.

For the first time, I have hope my phantom pains aren't insurmountable.

I got shot at by my best friend. That's a first I could do without.

And I learned Charlie's still trapped in hell.

The thought of what she relives every night makes me nauseous. I hate that she's ashamed of having night terrors, loathe that she sees herself as weak. Jesus, after what those fuckers did to her, how could she *not* have nightmares?

Charlie's coping method has always been to ignore her pain and pretend it doesn't exist. She tells herself it doesn't matter, that it's not important, to forget it. She repeats this mantra until her subconscious dulls the pain and suppresses the memories. But an event this significant isn't something she can bury, especially not with constant reminders each time she looks in a mirror. It's been four years, but that doesn't make it any less traumatic. Some damages can't be hidden. She's got to acknowledge and deal with what happened.

Maybe the nightmares are her mind's way of demanding that she does.

There's a lot I don't understand about trauma and PTSD. I reach for my tablet on the bedside table and start scouring the internet. Charlie found a way to ease my pain when all the doctors at BAMC couldn't. My new purpose is finding a way to help Charlie with hers.

CHARLIE

Mark's physical therapy starts the day after he comes home. When I walk him over for his first appointment, he looks around our lobby with interest. He's heard Lila and I discuss our clinic a lot these past few months, but this is the first time he's seen it.

The majority of our clients have endured a military-related trauma or injury. Because of this, Lila and I intentionally designed the space to exude a sense of tranquility, using soft neutral colors with crisp white and matte silver accents. Our artwork consists of huge nature photographs taken by Tucker's famous photographer brother. Lush green forest paths, bubbling streams filled with mossy rocks, starry midnight skies, and calm mountain sunrises grace our walls. I have some of these same prints hanging in my own home.

"Let me show you around," I offer, leading him down a hall to the right and opening a door. "This is one of our massage rooms. The tables are electric, so we can lower them for our wheelchair-bound clients, then raise them to a comfortable working height."

Mark examines the room. The rockwork along one wall, the floors, and the cabinetry echo the interior of my home, another space designed to be calm and peaceful. Soft lighting keeps the room soothing, and a tabletop fountain trickles while meditative music flows from an unseen source. His eyes travel over the serene space. "Nice."

"We have four rooms like this."

He glances over. "I thought it was just you and Lila."

"Lila had to hire another therapist when I flew to Texas for three months, and when we built this place, Lila insisted we plan for the future we want. Apparently, her future includes four massage therapists." I grin and open a door directly across the hall, and he follows me inside. This room's design is similar to the massage room, with one rock feature wall and soft lighting. A large whirlpool tub occupies most of the space. A bench perches alongside the tub, providing easier transfers for wheelchair-bound clients. In the corner is an open shower stall for rinsing off the mineral soak afterwards. "This is one of our hydrotherapy rooms. We use these in conjunction with PT. Tom works his clients pretty hard, and then they receive hydrotherapy and massage to prevent muscle spasms," I explain.

Mark nods. He's endured numerous challenging PT sessions followed by late night spasms.

We walk back through the lobby and past the reception desk where I point out the communal kitchen, bathrooms, Lila's office, and my office.

"I'm down here on the right," I say, leading him into my normally soothing space. My jaw drops as I glance around. The usual serenity of the room is jarred by precarious stacks of paper obscuring my desk, credenza, coffee table, and sofa. It's even piled on and behind the sofa.

My inner OCD organizer nearly faints at the sight. I wince as Mark raises an eyebrow. "Lila doesn't usually deal with the paperwork, so I'll assume this is her filing system. I'll sort it out." From the look of things, it's going to take several days and a couple of bottles of wine.

Large bottles.

We return to the lobby, veering left into a huge open area as large as all the other rooms combined. "This is our rehab gym. Tom's office area is in that corner," I point to the far left, "and this seating area is for family conferences. The rest of this space is for equipment and treatment." Mark's familiar with most of what he sees here. BAMC's rehab gym is gigantic. We have much of the same equipment, just in smaller quantities.

I direct Mark to the seating area. "We're starting with a group planning session. Tom wants us to complement each other's therapies, so Tucker and Lila will be joining us for this since we're all working with you." I glance up just as they stroll in, hand in hand. Tucker's clearly just left the gym. His light brown hair is still damp from a shower and he's wearing shorts and a tee shirt emblazoned with his business logo. Lila's dressed in our standard khakis and a loose white shirt. Her curls are pulled up in a loose twist, though a few blond tendrils have escaped.

I flush, feeling Tucker's gaze. Lila came by this morning and we called Dr. Martin. My appointment is first thing tomorrow. This is the first time Tucker's seen me since I nearly shot Mark.

He seems completely unfazed, winking at me as usual. "Hey, Charlie." Then he lightly punches Mark's shoulder. "I still can't believe you're here."

Mark grins. "That's right, baby. I'm your dream come true."

Tucker rolls his eyes. "Don't flatter yourself."

Tom appears with a stack of papers. "Hey, guys, sorry I'm late. My conference call ran long," he apologizes. I watch Mark size Tom up. Tom stands a couple of inches shorter than Mark, but his chest and shoulders are even wider than Mark's, and he's as solid as a bulldog. His eyes and smile are warm, though his nose has a couple of distinctive crooks. I see Mark's gaze stop there, probably trying to gauge whether the breaks were acquired in a bar fight or a boxing ring. "Everybody grab a seat and we'll get started. Anybody want water?"

"I'll grab it." I collect several bottles from the corner fridge and pass them around as we all settle into the comfortable grey chairs.

Tom plops the pile of papers down on a table, then leans over and sticks out his hand. "Hey, Mark. Tom Edwards. It's great to finally meet you. I've heard about you for years. Everything the ladies said was complimentary. Tucker, not so much." He grins.

Mark shrugs. "Never trust the opinion of a petty, jealous man."

Tucker snorts, and Mark grins.

"We're taking a team approach to help you achieve your recovery goals. My job is to work with you on exercises and techniques to improve mobility and strength. Tucker will focus on rebuilding muscle. Lila and Charlie will help with massage, hydrotherapy, and home exercises. I've gone through your records from Brooke," Tom gestures toward the papers on the table, "and I just spoke with Rick, your lead therapist. He shared his input on where he thought we should focus, but I'm more interested in your personal goals, because if our goals don't align, we won't be successful."

Mark answers immediately. "I want my leg strong enough for osseointegration. I want to get my permanent prosthesis and look and walk like a normal guy."

Tom raises an eyebrow at the word "normal", but lets it slide. It's not uncommon to hear similar statements from new amputees. Instead, he claps his hands together. "Alright. You want to walk, let's make it happen. Come over to a table and we'll discuss how we get you there. Today, we create the plan. Your work starts tomorrow."

Mark looks slightly overwhelmed by the time the hour is up. Just the sheer number of colorful belts, resistance bands, straps, and carabiners is a lot to take in. Tom has planned several series of exercises to strengthen his core, straighten his thigh, and build his quads. He's also scheduled for upper body massages and hydrotherapy. Then there's the at-home plan: Pilates with Lila twice a week and weight training with Tom and Tucker three days a week. I'll handle nightly mirror massages for his phantom pain and any post-workout strains, and Mark is responsible for "tummy time" four times a day, lying on his stomach to stretch and lengthen his thigh muscles.

"It's going to be a lot of work," Tom cautions Mark.

Mark shakes his head. "I don't care. I'll do whatever it takes."

"So will we," Tucker promises.

I recognize the set of Mark's jaw, the look in his eyes. He's focused. Determined. And for the first time since his injuries, he looks hopeful.

It's all going to be okay.

It's got to.

CHAPTER THIRTEEN

CHARLIE

Lila insists on accompanying me to Dr. Martin's the morning of my appointment. "I'm just your chauffeur and moral support. I won't intrude."

"You might as well come in. It's not like you haven't had a front-row seat to my shitshow."

She scowls. "It's not a shitshow."

She follows me into the office under protest. "Look, Lila, you actually see what happens. I only know my side of things. Giving her more information can only help."

"Well, we're not having you committed, so don't even start that shit again," she mutters.

Having Mark beside me, knowing he's watching over me, is helping. I had another nightmare last night. I was in the cell again, bound and powerless. The cell door banged open with a metallic crash, and my entire body tensed. When I heard Mark's voice soothing me, I knew I was safe. I woke up just enough to recognize my surroundings before drifting back off to sleep.

Maybe he and I really can help each other heal.

Dr. Linda Martin is a petite blonde with warm brown eyes and a pleasant contralto voice. Today she's wearing gold stilettos that put her barely at my eye level, and I'm only five four. She ushers us into her office, a cozy room with peaceful blues and warm wood tones. Linda's the one who encouraged me to promote inner tranquility by styling my surroundings to encourage serenity.

Lila and I sit on the plush cream sofa while Linda perches in a matching chair across from us. Her fitted deep blue dress says poised professional, but her stilettos scream something else entirely. She smiles warmly. "It's good to see you again, Charlie."

"Thank you for working me in so quickly."

She nods. "It sounds like things have been difficult."

And with that tiny bit of encouragement, I'm off and running. I admit to the return of my night terrors, initially once or twice a week. I describe the progression in my anxiety, requiring me to be armed to feel safe. I explain my need to remain on the bench at night and how my night terrors have morphed into a daily occurrence. I tell her about the camera Lila and Tucker installed and the custom-made ringtone they use to help bring me out of the nightmares and calm me down.

She turns to Lila. "How long do her episodes seem to last?"

She presses her lips together, thinking. "It varies. A lot of times, we're asleep when it starts, so we don't realize there's a problem until she's fully engaged. But when I can't sleep, I watch her. I can always tell when it's starting because she follows the same pattern every time."

"What does she do?"

"She starts by looking back over her left shoulder."

My mouth goes dry. That's where the door to my cell was. Behind me and to my left, so I couldn't see who was approaching.

"Then she twitches her shoulders. Sometimes it's her entire upper body. Well, except for her arms. It's like they're detached from her torso."

They'd lashed my wrists together above my head, suspending me, making my shoulders feel like they were on fire. The only way to move my arms was by thrashing my entire body. My chest grows tight.

"She starts kicking. Cursing, growling, yelling. After a while, she'll move her arms, punching or shoving at someone who isn't there. Eventually, she'll raise her gun and fire it in whichever direction she believes her attacker is coming from."

I close my eyes, breathing deeply, willing myself to relax. *I'm safe now. No one can hurt me.*

"Has she always fired her gun?"

"Not at first. It's gotten a lot more intense lately, though." She glances worriedly at me. "Sorry."

I shake my head. "Don't apologize. I want you to tell her. You see what I do when I'm at my worst, so if I need to be committed to protect Mark, let's do it."

Linda gives me a questioning glance. "I remember we discussed your friendship with Mark in prior sessions. Why would he need protection?"

"Because he's living with me. He was badly injured in Afghanistan and just got out of the hospital a few days ago. I had an episode my first night back, and he overheard me. When he came to check on me, I nearly shot him in the head." My eyes fill with tears. "That's why I'm here. I'd never forgive myself if –" My throat tightens in fear.

Lila squeezes my hand, and it helps me find my voice. "We talked about it afterwards, and he suggested I give my gun to him at night and let him keep watch so I can feel safe. He insists he sleeps fine in the daytime. It's only been two nights, but I think it's helping. I've had the dreams, but when they start, he talks to me, and both times, it's stopped them."

She turns to Lila, her expression pensive. "Do her episodes often occur at the same time?"

Lila nods. "Almost always between three-thirty and four. Once in a while it starts earlier if she's had a bad day or she's more stressed than usual."

Linda shifts her attention back to me. "I'd like to try a two-step approach to break your cycle of night terrors. First, I'd like to prescribe something to help you sleep. The second thing I want to try is called 'anticipatory awakening'. Essentially, we disrupt your sleep pattern by waking you up for a few minutes shortly before you'd normally experience the nightmares. Have Mark wake you around three o'clock. You need to be awake enough to talk to him for a few minutes. Sit up and have a glass of water or walk around. Engage your mind. After that, lie back down. The sleeping tablet should let you fall back asleep, but because we've reset your internal clock, we can hopefully stave off the nightmares."

I stare. "You don't think I need to be committed?" Beside me, Lila huffs in exasperation.

Linda chuckles, her laughter as rich as her voice. "No, Charlie, you don't need to be committed. I don't believe you're likely to hurt yourself or anyone else."

My eyes widen as my voice rises an octave. "Weren't you listening? I almost shot Mark in the head. How am I not a danger to everyone around me?"

Linda's tone turns serious. "You aren't a danger because you recognized the potential for a bad outcome and took steps to prevent that. You chose to relinquish your weapon and embrace vulnerability to protect Mark."

I frown. "'Embracing vulnerability' is an overstatement. I'm not embracing it, but I won't risk Mark's safety."

"Fine," she agrees, "embracing may be overstating things, but you're intentionally choosing to be vulnerable at a deeply personal cost. That speaks volumes. You're prioritizing his safety over your feelings of security."

I study her dubiously. "You're sure?"

She smiles again. "I'm positive. You don't need to be committed. We just need to help you work through your trauma. You're a strong woman, Charlie. You can face this."

Lila and Linda are sincere when they tell me I'm strong.

I just wish I were half as strong as everyone says I am.

MARK

Charlie and I settle into a comfortable routine over the next couple of weeks. Every morning, her alarm goes off and I put down whatever I'm doing to say good morning. She goes upstairs and brushes her teeth while I start the coffee. We eat breakfast together, and then she goes to work and I sleep until one or one thirty.

Every weekday at three, I go to the clinic and work with Tom for an hour, strengthening my body in preparation for osseointegration surgery. I follow PT with a soak in the whirlpool and an upper body massage. After that, I tackle more exercise. On Tuesdays and Thursdays, Lila and I do Pilates in the living room. Lila banished Tucker from watching our sessions unless he's an active participant because he made fun of the poses. After the first week, I was convinced she was torturing me just to prove that they weren't "wimpy girl workouts". They're every bit as taxing as anything I do with Tucker and Tom, focusing on muscle groups I'm unaccustomed to working. On Mondays, Wednesdays, and Fridays, I do strength training with the guys. The combination is effective. I'm rebuilding muscle and getting stronger faster than I expected.

I can't wait to have this surgery so I can look normal again.

Working out with Tucker and Tom at the house is fun and challenging. When Tucker's exercises need to be modified for my injuries, Tom adapts them to work with my body instead of against it. I really like Tom. He's not military, but he'd have done well in the service. He's a natural leader and a genuinely nice guy, coaching boxing at a center for disadvantaged youth and fostering dogs for the local animal rescue.

While we work out, Lila and Charlie chat and make dinner. Some days, Maya comes over after school, and she and Tom join us for dinner. Maya's astonishingly outgoing and comfortable around adults for someone so young. I was initially nervous around her, worried she'd be freaked out by my leg. Maya proved Lila's right – I know absolutely nothing about women, young or old. My missing leg didn't make the least bit of difference to her. I found this out when she told me all about Eddie, her three-legged cat.

"He lost a leg, and he's fine. You'll be fine, too," she said, her springy curls bouncing as she nodded. Then she'd grinned. "If you want, we can let Bella chase you to build up your speed. It did wonders for Eddie." Lila and Charlie dissolved in giggles at the image of me racing on my crutches to escape an overgrown, slobbering puppy.

Dinners when we're all together are always an event. Lila's an incredible cook whose love language is food. When it's just Charlie and me, we keep it low key. She's a good cook, and I can hold my own, but we stick to simple meals with enough leftovers for lunch the following day. We spend every evening together. We cook together (unless it's a Lila day), clean up together, watch movies and have snacks together, even fold laundry together. Even bedtime has a routine. Charlie showers upstairs and hands over her gun when she returns. After her mirror massage magic, she goes to sleep with her back against my side. It's very domestic, and I enjoy it more than I'd ever thought possible.

Our arrangement seems to be benefiting both of us. My phantom pains have diminished considerably, and her nightmares have gotten better. I've started doing as her psychiatrist suggested and waking her up a little after three. She gets out of bed, drinks a glass of water, and talks with me about random things for a couple of minutes before going back to sleep. Occasionally her nightmares start earlier, but now I know what to watch for – twitching, fluttering eye movements, or upper body spasms. If that starts, I speak to her in a low voice, saying the same things over and over: "I'm here, Baby Girl. You're safe. I've got you." Once the tension leaves her body, I'll stroke her hair until she falls back to sleep.

This arrangement is working out better than either of us anticipated. She's keeping my phantom pain at bay, and I'm staving off her night terrors. I'm so glad I have Charlie. I don't know what I'd do without her.

CHARLIE

Things are going incredibly well, for the first time in a really long time.

Mark is amazing. I was terrified to relinquish my gun, even to him, but I'm glad I did. Knowing he's protecting me has given me a sense of security I've not felt since I was taken. Every night, he wakes me up to talk about something innocuous for a few minutes, and then I go back to sleep. Most of the time now, I don't have nightmares. The few I do have are flashes of images, like movie clips, not the fully-immersed experiences I'd been having. When they hit, his voice reaches for me, pulling me back to the present.

Mark makes me feel safe. He always has. As a result, I'm getting the best sleep I've had in years. My appetite has returned, and I'm regaining the weight I'd lost. My overwhelming feelings of stress have disappeared.

I even see differences in our moods. We're both more relaxed, more positive. In my case, it's because I'm sleeping better, having fewer nightmares, and spending time with Mark. He grounds me. He always has. For Mark, I'm not sure how much is from his antidepressant and how much is from being with friends, but he's more like the old Mark. He laughs more, and he's relaxed.

He was right. We're helping each other heal.

Our clinic is humming along. It took me the better part of a week to figure out Lila's piling – I mean, filing – system and get everything straightened out, but I managed. Once I had things put back together, Lila sheepishly asked me to teach her my organizational system. We both hope it won't be necessary for either of us to leave like that again, but emergencies happen, and this experience has taught us that we need to be prepared.

Tara, the massage therapist Lila hired in my absence, is an absolute godsend. She's fifty but looks no more than thirty-five, with long auburn hair and dark brown eyes. She's been divorced for three years and has a son who lives nearby and a newlywed daughter living in California. Tara's ex was extremely wealthy, and after twenty-two years of marriage, the judge felt she'd earned half of what her husband had made plus large alimony payments, especially since he left her after impregnating his twenty-year-old assistant. Tara only works because she likes taking care of people. She's a hugger who can coax a smile out of even our most curmudgeonly clients. She brings in cakes to celebrate their birthdays, brews their favorite coffees and teas as they arrive, and even adjusts the music in her massage room to their requests. She's amazing, and she fits our clinic to a tee.

A couple of weeks after we've come home, I'm behind the front desk when Blake saunters into the clinic carrying two paper cups. His blue eyes find me immediately. His shaggy blond hair has that messy-surfer look, and he's dressed in soft jeans and a white shirt with the sleeves rolled up. He's long and lean, muscled yet graceful. His lips curve in a slow smile. "Every time I see you, you're even more beautiful than before." He holds out one of the cups. "I thought you might like a coffee. Medium roast with double dark chocolate."

That's... surprising. "Thank you." I take a sip from the cup he passes me, and it's sinfully sweet and smooth, not unlike Blake himself. Maybe that's the point. "It's delicious."

He smiles again, but it's not his usual wickedly-flirtatious grin, and his eyes hold mine. "I'm glad you like it."

Something's different about him, but I can't put my finger on it. "You're here early this morning. Is something wrong?"

He shakes his head. "I got some unexpected good news. Thought I'd tell Tom in person."

"Maya forgot her homework on the coffee table. He'll be here soon."

He nods and leans on the counter, openly admiring me. I awkwardly shuffle papers on the desk, wishing someone would come in or the phone would ring. Maybe I could "accidentally" set off the alarm system for a distraction. His intense scrutiny is unnerving.

He takes a deep breath. "I missed you when you were in Texas, Charlie." His voice is quiet, his tone sincere. I glance at his face, and there's no trace of a smile.

He's not blithely flirting.

He's serious?

Surely not.

I respond with the first thing that pops into my head. "Why?"

He smiles slowly. "Seeing you is always the highlight of my day. Having you gone for three months was like losing my sunlight."

Losing his sunlight?

And just like that, with one cheesy comment, we're back on familiar territory, and the tension leaves my shoulders. Blake is like the American male version of Pepé Le Pew, persistently flirtatious but essentially harmless.

"I have a proposition for you." His voice is rich, like warm honey.

"I'm sure you do," I mutter, and he grins.

"A perfectly innocent proposition," he clarifies.

I raise one eyebrow. "Do tell."

"Let me be your next Winner versus Whiner date."

My mouth falls open. "How do you know about those?"

He chuckles. "Tom and Lila were bickering about them one day. He was giving her a hard time about the guys she's picked for you."

Fantastic.

I take a deep breath. "Those dinners aren't about finding Mr. Right. I really don't do well with dating. I'm just trying to get comfortable being around guys again."

"So have dinner with me. You'll be more comfortable with someone you know, right?"

Not necessarily.

He smiles. "And I've learned what not to do, so I won't screw up again."

What. The. Hell.

"What do you mean, you've learned what not to do?" My words come out sharper than I'd intended.

His eyes widen as he realizes he's said too much. I stand, glaring, hands on my hips. What exactly did Tom and Lila tell him?

If I weren't so annoyed, the always-suave Blake stumbling over his own words would be comical. His face reddens. "I – well – I didn't know that you didn't – you know, not to touch you. And Tom – well, he's really protective of you. Said you're like his sister and if I ever upset you like that again, he'd beat my ass even worse."

My mouth falls open. "Beat your ass? And what do you mean, worse? You two fought?"

He shakes his head. "We always spar after practice with the kids, but we don't try to hurt each other." He laughs. "You missed it. It was right before you left for Texas. He broke my damn nose. That's my third time." He traces his finger along the bridge of his nose, and now that he's mentioned it, I can see the difference. "I had two black eyes for a week. The kids thought it was great." He rolls his eyes but grins. "We used it to reinforce the importance of protecting your face and keeping your guard up." He scrolls through pictures on his phone before passing it to me.

He isn't exaggerating. Two purple circles bloom brilliantly around his eyes. I bite my lip to hide my smile. "You look like a panda."

He laughs. "I did," he agrees before turning serious. "I never would have touched your face if I'd known it would upset you. I'd never hurt you." He pauses. "Think about it, okay? One dinner. It doesn't even have to be on a Wednesday."

I study him. He seems genuinely interested, although Blake finds most women interesting. Still, he's a decent guy, and he's aware that Tom will inflict bodily injury if he mistreats me, something I find equally endearing and appalling.

Maybe.

"I'll consider it."

His eyes twinkle, and he winks. "You know where I am when you're ready."

I raise one eyebrow. "Confident, aren't you?"

"I've based my entire career around positive thinking." He pushes off the counter as the door opens.

"Hey, Charlie. Is this guy bothering you?" Tom grins, jerking his head toward Blake.

I smile. "Not today. He bribed me with coffee. Did you get Maya's homework there in time?"

He shakes his head. "She'd already gone to class, but one of the ladies in the office offered to run it down to her."

I'm sure she did. Tom's single again. His relationship with Whitney fizzled out shortly after I left for Texas, something that delighted both Maya and Lila. His next girlfriend, a flight attendant, lasted barely two months. Tom ended things with Stella when, after canceling on dinner with him and Maya for the fourth time, she revealed she'd rather have bamboo shoved under her nails than be around kids. After that, Tom swore off dating for the foreseeable future.

"I'm great, too, by the way, thanks for asking," Blake interrupts.

Tom sighs. "Good morning, Blake. You're early." Then he grins. "I'm surprised you're up this early after your four-day weekend with Sandi."

I blink. He's just coming off a four-day weekend with a woman named Sandi, and he's trying to score a date with me?

Total. Player.

And to think I almost believed him.

"Change of plans," Blake says smoothly, not looking in my direction. "Sandi and I were on different wavelengths. We aren't seeing each other anymore."

Tom's brows lift at that news, making me wonder how long Blake had been seeing her. Tom glances over and recognizes my irritation, though I can tell he's not sure what's annoying me. "What's up? Class doesn't start for another eight hours."

"I have big news. Thought you'd want to hear it from me."

Tom's immediately interested. "What kind of news?"

Blake smirks. "Maybe I should wait. After all, class doesn't start for another eight hours."

Tom grins mischievously in my direction. "Did I ever show you the pictures of Blake drunk off his ass at last year's Fourth of July festival?"

"Fine, asshole," Blake mutters. "I got a call. The boys get to participate in the regional boxing tournament next month. The officials weren't going to allow it because they aren't affiliated with a specific school," he explains to me.

Tom's face lights up, and I smile. "That's fantastic! They'll be so excited."

Tom looks at me. "They were crushed when we told them the committee said they couldn't compete. I didn't tell them I was appealing the decision, so this will be a big surprise. We have a couple of kids I think will do really well. They're great at reading their opponents, and they're fast. You should come by and watch sometime. The boys love to show off." He glances out of the corner of his eye. "Some boys never outgrow that."

I snort. "Like you have."

Tom grins. "I never claimed I had."

"Good thing."

I spend all day turning things over in my mind. Despite Tom's untimely revelation of his breakup, Blake's a nice guy. He's good-looking, owns his own business, and goes out of his way to compliment me. He's a life coach, so he actually believes those bubbly sentiments on motivational posters. He's exactly the kind of man single women long for, and apparently, he's back on the market, although, to be fair, I never had any inkling he was seeing someone.

He's a decent guy. So why am I so resistant to one measly dinner with him when I've willingly gone out with so many Whiners?

The problem isn't Blake. It's me.

"I don't get it, Lila," I say later, trying to make sense of things. "I've tried dating since what happened – well, not since we got back from Texas, but still, I've tried, and it's been a colossal waste of time. I've felt absolutely nothing with anyone I've gone out with. Nothing positive, anyway," I amend. She and I are alone at the front desk. Our last client has just left, Tom is at the youth center, and Mark's in the whirlpool.

"Your heart hasn't really been in it, and that's okay. Right now, the goal is just to get you comfortable around men."

I snort. "That's gone well."

Lila shrugs. "I picked simple ones to start you with. It's like riding a horse. You don't start a nervous rider on a feisty stallion – you start her on the old gray mare."

I laugh. "You've been sending me on dates with old gray mares?"

Lila grins. "Absolutely. You needed to get your feet wet with some entry level guys. We could try someone more advanced."

I hesitate. "Blake wants to be one of the Winners versus Whiners."

She cocks her head to one side. "Really?"

I repeat our conversation and include Tom's inadvertent outing of Blake's recent breakup. I'm surprised when Lila shrugs. "So have dinner with him."

I frown. "I don't know. Blake had been acting like he'd been harboring this interest in me for months, and I fell for it until Tom asked him about the woman he'd been seeing. Besides, when things don't work out with guys I never have to see again, it's no big deal. But if things went sideways with Blake?" I shake my head. "He's already seen one of my panic attacks. I couldn't face him if it happened again."

"It's one dinner, in public. Trust me, he'd be on his best behavior."

"I know. It's just –" I break off, not sure what to say.

Lila gently covers my hand with her own. "You think you're too damaged," she says quietly, her words settling in my gut like lead.

She's right.

My reluctance isn't merely about Blake's reputation as a womanizer. It's about me, about opening up with someone I already know.

I was reticent and reserved before the attack. Now I keep people at a distance on purpose. I'm too messed up to let people outside of my inner circle see the real me.

"You're afraid of intimacy, and your body and mind have absorbed that fear. I get it," Lila continues, squeezing my hand. "If I hadn't already loved Tucker and known him as well as I did, our relationship wouldn't have survived. It was hard for both of us, not just me. I knew I could trust him, but it took a long time for us to work through things." Lila hesitates. "We went to a sex therapist, a woman Linda recommended. I could give you her name."

An extremely unladylike snort escapes me. "Lila, I'm not having sex. A sex therapist is the last thing I need."

Lila shakes her head. "She's more of an intimacy specialist. There's more to having sex than just the act itself."

I raise one skeptical brow.

"Seriously, Charlie. Sex begins long before any clothes come off. Your mind is powerful. True intimacy begins in your mind, and most of it is about allowing yourself to be vulnerable." She pulls out her phone and starts typing, and my phone beeps with Lila's message. "Her name is Willow. She's very easy to talk to. That's her name and number. Just think about it."

I'm frustrated when I get home after work, cooking dinner in silence as my mood darkens. It's bad enough what those bastards did when they had me. Do they really get to ruin my future, too?

Depression weighs on me like a wet blanket. Maybe this is as recovered as I get to be. A basically functional adult, as long as (a) it's daylight, (b) I'm armed, and (c) you ignore my panic at interacting with any man besides Mark, Tucker, or Tom.

I try to hide it, but I know the truth. I know what I am.

Broken.

Shattered, like a windshield after a car accident, spider-webbed into hundreds of shards. Fractured into splintered bits and pieces that can never be put back together again.

God, I hate being so fucked up.

CHAPTER FOURTEEN

MARK

SOMETHING'S UP WITH CHARLIE after work. I keep trying to strike up a conversation, but all I get are one-word answers. It continues all through dinner. I try to draw her out, but I'm getting nowhere.

After watching her pick at her food the entire meal, I can't stand it any longer. "Are you going to tell me what's bothering you, or are we going to keep pretending you're fine?"

Charlie shakes her head. "Sorry, I'm just tired."

"Bullshit. You've spent fifteen minutes pushing that same bite of chicken around."

She shakes her head again. "I'm working through some stuff in my head. I'm sorry. I'll be more present."

I frown. "I'm not asking you to be more present. I'm asking what's wrong. Maybe I can help."

She looks up, and the sadness in her eyes startles me. "I'm not sure this is fixable."

I wait patiently, but she just sits there, staring at her plate. I finally speak when it becomes clear she doesn't intend to. "I can sit here all night, and I know where you sleep, so spit it out. What's on your mind? "

She looks at me uncertainly. "I'm not sure this is something I can discuss with you."

Charlie and I talk about anything and everything, so I can't imagine what could make her this uncomfortable. I try to lighten the mood.

"Is this about menstrual cycles? Because I know a surprising amount. It's part of leading a platoon that includes women of childbearing age. I can even discuss feminine hygiene products. There's some you can launch like a rocket, and some that have wings like a jet." I smile broadly and puff out my chest. "Not to brag, but I do have a working knowledge of these things."

My teasing works, and she laughs. "No, it's not about my cycle, but it's delightful to know I can come to you with those issues."

I smile. And wait. And wait some more.

She's still not talking.

"You know, it's easier to help when you actually share what's bothering you."

She bites her lip.

I gesture toward my room. "I have a drawer full of socks. We could turn them into puppets if it would help."

"You just won't give up," she mutters. "Alright, but when this gets awkward, remember, I tried to spare you."

Finally. I grin and lean back. "Duly noted."

"Ok, ever since – what happened – I've had trust issues." I nod. "Lila's been encouraging me to date, to not let my fear control me. I joined a dating website, and she'd pick guys for me to go out with."

"How'd that go?"

She laughs without humor. "Awful. A couple of guys immediately said they weren't interested in someone with that much baggage. More than one called me 'damaged goods'. A few assured me they could 'fix me'. One offered to take me straight back to his place to remind me how great sex could be, to get me over my 'hang-ups'. I went out with at least twenty different men, and they all sucked in varying degrees."

I'm instantly pissed. They didn't want to deal with her "baggage"? They called her "damaged goods"? They offered to "fix her", like she's the problem? Who the hell has Lila been setting her up with? No decent guy would say shit like that if they knew even half what she's been through.

I suppress my temper. Getting mad won't help her. Instead, I shrug like it's no big deal. "There's plenty of fish in the sea. You just ended up with a bunch of slimy eels."

She laughs. "That's basically what Lila said, but she used horse references and the term 'old gray mares'."

I study her thoughtfully. "How much of your past are you sharing? If they're talking about 'baggage' and 'fixing you', it sounds like you're putting a lot out there."

She nods. "I tell them. Not graphically, but I let them know I was kidnapped and raped and have intimacy issues."

She might not be giving them details, but she's certainly sharing more than I would have expected. "Are you sure that's first date material?"

Her answering nod is quick and firm. "I learned the hard way. The first time I went out with a guy, I didn't tell him anything. I thought it was too personal to share with someone I'd just met. Things were going well. He seemed nice, and he was easy to talk to. We were having a good time, so we went for a walk after dinner. Then he pulled me into an alley and pressed me against the wall to kiss me." Her face falls. "He thought he was being romantic. I pulled my gun on him and had a panic attack."

"I'm guessing that killed the mood," I murmur. Having a panic attack and threatening to shoot her date? Not good.

But maybe there's more to it. Maybe in telling them her history, she's sending the message that getting to know her won't be easy, protecting herself by subconsciously pushing them away.

Or maybe I'm reading too much into it. Maybe she's simply weeding out the obvious losers.

I wisely keep my Dr. Phil moment to myself. "You're giving these guys a lot of heavy information right off the bat. It might unintentionally imply that getting to know you will take a lot of work. Someone who's just met you hasn't had time to see you're worth the effort. Men who know you are more likely to want to gain your trust."

"I hadn't thought about it like that," she admits. "I didn't want to waste my time with guys who were only looking for a hookup."

"I understand. Just maybe wait and see how things are going. Better yet, skip the websites and go out with someone you know, someone you're attracted to."

Her demeanor changes immediately, her expression changing to one of defeat. "The thing is, Mark, I just..." She bows her head and looks ashamed. "I think I'm too broken for any of it. It's not just that I'm afraid of physical contact. It's like... I see a good-looking guy, and my brain recognizes he's attractive, but that's all. There's no sparks, no desire, no passion. It's like that part of me is dead." Her eyes fill with tears. "Those bastards took so much, and even though they're dead, they still keep winning."

I lean across the table and take her hands. "Look at me, Charlie." I wait until her sad eyes look up. "They don't get to win. You're too much of a fighter to let them."

Tears trickle down her face, and she drops her gaze. "All I've done the last four years is fight, Mark, and I'm so tired. I'm not sure this fight's worth the effort." Her voice is barely a whisper.

I jostle her hands to get her attention. "Listen to me. You're a fighter. You fought your way back after the shit they did. You fought your fears when you slept on a bench with your gun every night because you refused to be a victim. I know you're tired of fighting. We all get tired. But when one of us is too tired to fight, the other one holds us up until we're strong enough to fight again.

One of these days, you'll find the guy you're meant to be with, and he'll know you're worth the effort, and you'll have a beautiful life together." I squeeze her hands. "You can't give up yet. It's not even halftime, Baby Girl."

She bolts around the table, and I wrap my arms around her. "Thank you," she whispers.

I dry her tears and kiss the top of her head. "I meant every word of it."

She sits beside me, snuggling into my chest. "So you think the dating app is a bad idea?"

I shake my head. "I said you might be better off with someone you already know."

She tilts her head back and looks up at me. "Blake wants to be one of my Wednesday Winner versus Whiner dates."

An image of Tom's overly-friendly assistant coach pops into my head, followed by a brief flash of irritation. "What did you tell him?"

"That I didn't do well with dating."

My tone is wry. "So you immediately shot him down?"

"Not exactly." She leans her head against me again. "I said I'd think about it."

"Do you like Blake?" I ask curiously, resting my cheek on her hair.

She pauses. "He's nice. Good-looking. Single, though he's kind of a man-whore. There was a time I'd have had dinner with him without a second thought. But that part of me feels dead now. There's nothing about him that makes me feel... passionate. There's nothing about anyone that makes me feel that way anymore."

This is what Charlie didn't want to discuss. I can tell she's mortified; heat radiates from her face as she buries it in my chest to avoid looking at me. I ignore it, knowing if I tell her to relax, it will only embarrass her.

I keep my tone casual. "Maybe it's like riding a bike. Once you get more comfortable with someone, it'll come back to you."

"Maybe." I hear her skepticism.

"You said he's nice. You know him, and he thinks you're worth getting to know better."

She purses her lips. "He saw me have a panic attack once. He was flirting, and he brushed his hand across my cheek, and I – well, Tom came in and realized what was happening and talked me through it." She sighs. "So Blake's seen a glimpse of the shitshow." Then she chuckles. "Tom broke his nose for upsetting me, even though he didn't do it on purpose. He gave him two black eyes and said I was like his sister, and if he ever upset me again, he'd beat his ass even worse."

I make a mental note to thank Tom for looking out for her. "So Blake's seen you have a panic attack, and he still wants to have dinner with you. That should count for something, right?"

She wavers for a second. “Maybe,” she says again.

“If you think he might be your type, even if you don’t feel passionate, you can still test the waters. Have dinner. Or meet for a cup of coffee, if that would be easier. Or hell, tell him you aren’t interested. Just because Blake’s interested doesn’t mean you’re required to say yes. Don’t go out with anyone you’re not comfortable with. Coffee and conversation are relatively harmless, though, right?”

She hesitates. “I guess.”

I laugh aloud. “You might want to show a little more enthusiasm with your dates.”

She wraps her arms around me more tightly. “Thank you.”

I kiss her hair. “See, this wasn’t so bad. Two mature adults, talking about passion and relationships. No awkwardness.”

“I was fine until you suggested sock puppets," she mutters.

I laugh again. “It got you talking, didn’t it?”

She leans back and eyes me, all tension gone, replaced with an impish grin. “It did indeed. Now, I’d like to talk to you about my menstrual cycle.”

CHARLIE

By the time I get to work Wednesday morning, Lila's already told Tom about Blake asking me to dinner. I glare at the two of them when I walk in and find them discussing it in the communal kitchen over coffee.

"Really? You just spill the details of my personal life, just like that?" I flop down at the table and reach for her coffee cup, stealing a sip.

Lila rolls her eyes. "Please. How many mornings have we discussed your Whiners? Tom's almost as invested as I am. Besides, he knows Blake better than either of us. Don't you think you should get his opinion?"

Her point is annoyingly valid. I turn to Tom. "Well?"

"Well, what?"

I tilt my head. "Aren't you the one who wanted to vet my dates? Here's your chance."

He takes a deep breath, contemplating.

"The fact you're taking so long isn't exactly a ringing endorsement," Lila says dryly.

He shoots her a look. "After some of your selections, I think one of us should take the time to consider every angle."

She frowns. "I choose them based on their profiles. I can't help it if they deliberately skew things in their favor."

"That's why the app is a bad idea," Tom counters, turning to me. "Blake's been hounding me for months to encourage you to have dinner with him. I've refused because I don't want to get involved. Honestly, though, after hearing about some of the guys you've been out with? You could do a lot worse than Blake. Besides, it's just one dinner."

"I'm considering it," I admit. "But what's the deal with that four-day weekend you mentioned?"

Tom purses his lips. "I asked him about that yesterday. They'd been seeing each other for six or eight weeks. He said she was getting too serious, and he broke things off because he couldn't envision the future she wanted them to have."

"I wonder what she was picturing," Lila muses.

"He gave me the impression she wanted something permanent."

"After less than two months? That's kind of fast." I shake my head. No wonder he ended things.

He nods. "That's what he said."

"I can't fault him for that."

Tom studies my face. "So you're considering having dinner with him?"

I frown. "I don't know. He's way out of my league."

Lila's head whips toward me. "Excuse me?"

"You know," I say, reddening. "Good-looking, smooth, flirty." A little too smooth, actually. I don't want to be one more woman who falls for his lines.

Tom puts down his coffee. "He's a flirt, I'll give you that, but that 'out of your league' business is a crock of shit. If anything, it's the other way around." I scoff, and Tom frowns. "I'm serious, Charlie. Quit selling yourself short."

"Tom's right," Lila agrees. "You don't see yourself the way others do."

"Fine. I'll think about it." I get to my feet, uncomfortable with this turn in conversation. "I need to restock my massage room. I'm low on towels." Lila raises an eyebrow, knowing I refilled them yesterday, but she lets me leave without commenting.

Being a massage therapist provides a lot of mental downtime. Most clients don't talk during their massages, preferring to drift off in silent relaxation. This can be good or bad, depending on my state of mind. Today I spend hours obsessing over whether or not to invite Blake to dinner.

After an entire day of waffling, I decide I'm not ready for someone of Blake's caliber. He can have any woman he wants, and he knows it. I may be tired of old gray mares, but I'm not up to dating a thoroughbred. He's too flirtatious for me to be comfortable with one on one, and the entire point is for me to become comfortable again. I catch Lila at work the next morning.

"I'm not quite ready for dinner with Blake yet," I tell her.

She raises one delicate brow. "Don't tell me this is more bullshit about him being out of your league again."

I frown. "Not exactly. It's more like he's too much of a jump from the old-gray-mare league for me."

"So you're willing to start seeing guys again, just not Blake," she clarifies. I nod reluctantly. "Does this mean you're ready for me to check the dating app?"

I sigh heavily. "Line them up. It doesn't have to be just Wednesdays."

I'm a glutton for punishment.

The next few weeks consist of one comically bad date after another. There's Donovan, who was perfectly nice if you didn't mind the five drinks he consumed during dinner, not counting the one in his hand when I arrived. Then there was Michael, who clearly wasn't thirty-five and whose toupee kept slipping while he tried to surreptitiously slide it back into place. Paul never stopped talking long enough for me to get a word in edgewise. Quinn never spoke at all except to give one or two-word answers to my questions. Dylan wore half a gallon of cheap cologne and complained about the price of everything. Jay spent so much time talking about his ex-girlfriend Amy that I felt like I knew her by the time the check finally came. Vinnie seemed to be a cardboard copy of a movie mobster, from his slicked-back hair to the overly-heavy Jersey accent to talking with his hands. I half expected him to rush into the kitchen of the (naturally) Italian restaurant to offer to slice their garlic with a razor blade. I did have a nice time with Tyson, the guy who redid the shower for Mark, but he's got too much drama in his life already to add mine to his pile. (My words, not his.) His ex-wife is stalking him, he's raising their three kids, all of whom are under the age of ten, and his brief fling from the summer he was seventeen just dropped his previously-undisclosed teenage daughter on his doorstep so she could elope with her much-younger contractor who doesn't want kids.

I never felt a single spark, not even with Tyson, whom I genuinely liked. They were all handsome, decent guys, but I may as well have been conducting a research project.

"I don't know why I even bother," I tell Tom and Lila over our usual Whiner doughnuts and coffee. Given my track record, we've dropped the "Winner" portion of the name. I describe my far-too-long evening with Alex, who prefers to be called Axel and is trying to launch his grunge band. He takes the "grunge" part very seriously, having arrived in torn jeans and dirty flannel, reeking of body odor. "The waiter thought he was homeless and offered him a free takeout meal. It was mortifying explaining that he's not homeless, he's my date."

Tom turns to me. "Blake's still hounding me to tell you to have dinner with him."

I sigh. "I'll think about it. He can't be any worse than the guys I've been out with lately."

By Friday morning, I've decided. Not dinner, but drinks, and not in the evening, but during the day over the weekend. I text him, erasing and rewriting my words repeatedly before finally forcing myself to hit send before I lose my nerve. My text is nothing short of sheer poetry.

"Do you have plans tomorrow afternoon? Thought maybe we could meet for a drink."

Blake answers immediately. "Are you trying to get me drunk?"

I blush, uncertain how to respond. Before I can decide, another text lands. "You won't need me drunk to take advantage of me. In fact, I'd prefer to be sober."

Now I really don't know what to say.

He's just flirting, like always. This is how he is. It's fine. Breathe.

My phone rings. It's Blake. "Hello?"

"Good morning, Beautiful." His voice is deep and husky.

I chuckle. "You can't see me. For all you know, I might look like a swamp witch."

"Not possible," he purrs. His tone causes an echoing twitch in my stomach. Butterflies?

That's new.

I force myself to focus as he continues. "I actually have plans tomorrow with my eight-year-old nieces. A double feature at the movies, pizza, the whole nine yards. But I'm free Sunday if you want to go to the Memorial Day festival with me and share hotdogs and beer and carnival rides." He hesitates. "Or I'm free tonight."

Mark's voice echoes in my head. *Test the waters.*

My heart beats faster, but not in a bad way. "How about Duffey's at eight tonight?"

I can almost hear him smile through the phone. "I'll be there."

MARK

I'm in the kitchen when Charlie comes home from work Friday smiling, the first genuine smile I've seen in days. She must have decided to have dinner with Blake. As the thought crosses my mind, a flash of irritation pops up again, then evaporates. It's the same irritation I felt when we first discussed her having dinner with him.

"You're smiling," I say, ignoring it. "Good day?"

"I've decided to try one more attempt at a Winner, but I'm going off-app." She grins.

"Dinner with Blake?"

She shakes her head. "I asked him out for drinks tonight at Duffey's."

I smile in approval. "You asked him out? Way to kick ass."

"I'm testing the waters. If it doesn't work out, it's just drinks."

I drop a kiss on her head. "I'm proud of you, Baby Girl." She beams.

When she's upstairs getting ready, I try to analyze what it is about Blake that irks me. It makes no sense. I love Charlie and I want her to be happy, and I've not reacted like this to anyone else she's had dinner with. Maybe it's because I know him, unlike any of the other doorknobs she's gone out with. I don't think so, though. It's something about Blake himself.

I spend hours turning it over in my head after she leaves, searching for why this particular guy grates on my nerves.

He seems nice enough, though I can't help rolling my eyes at how he flatters every female he encounters. I see him at the clinic when he needs to chat with Tom. He's always friendly, not just with me, but with everyone. He volunteers with at-risk kids, and he's a life coach, encouraging people to achieve their dreams. Physically, he's good-looking, strong, and athletic.

Fuck.

That's it. That's what's bothering me.

Blake is what I used to be – good-looking, strong, and athletic.

Now?

Now, I'm scarred, battered, and broken. He's a visual reminder of what I was before I lost everything.

My problem isn't Blake.

The problem is me.

CHAPTER FIFTEEN

CHARLIE

"I HOPE YOU HAVEN'T been waiting long," I apologize when I finally make my way to Blake at the bar. "I had trouble finding a parking place."

"Not long at all," he says, leaning closer so he doesn't have to shout over the rumble of other voices. His cologne has a pleasant woodsy smell. His black pants and the crisp steel blue dress shirt the same color as his eyes both look expensive, but the undone top button and rolled-up sleeves say casual. His eyes rake over me, a smile curving his lips as he moves closer to my ear. "You're breathtaking," he says, his warm breath tickling my neck.

"Thanks," I say, suddenly shy. "You look nice, too." I'm wearing a simple batik patterned maxi dress in autumn colors and a pair of strappy gold sandals that show off my burgundy pedicure. My hair is styled in loose waves, and I'm wearing my favorite gold earrings. I inhale the scent of his cologne again before realizing he's watching. I bite my lip, embarrassed at being caught. He gives me another slow smile, and an unfamiliar sensation ripples through my belly.

The bartender takes our order, and the raucous group behind us relocates to a table for twelve. The noise dies down just as he returns with our drinks. Conversation with Blake flows easily, presumably because we know each other and because I suspect he's keeping things intentionally light. We talk about our first jobs – my first official job was the military, though I babysat in high school; he waited tables dressed as a pirate, complete with a puffy shirt and an eyepatch. It's so out of character for the smooth-talking guy in front of me, I can't help but laugh. He talks at length about his twin nieces, Addison and Avery, sharing stories and pictures of them. They clearly have him wrapped around their little fingers, and it makes him seem more approachable. By the end of my second drink, I'm more relaxed. I switch to water – I never have more than two drinks unless I'm at home – and we discuss favorite foods, travel destinations, movies, and books. Things are going far better than I'd expected.

"Would you like something to eat?" he asks, and before I know it, we've ordered burgers and moved to a quieter table upstairs.

"Do you mind if I ask you something?" His gaze is curious. My spine tenses as I reach for my water.

"Okay."

"You're beautiful, smart, funny, successful – how are you still single?"

Everything in me screeches to a halt. Telling him the truth isn't an option, at least, not the full truth. I scramble for a benign answer. "I have trust issues," I finally say. "They add an extra degree of difficulty to dating."

He nods, his expression thoughtful.

I don't want him to continue probing, so I tip my head at him. "What about you? You're a handsome, charismatic guy. How are you still single?"

His eyes cloud before he smiles without humor. "You aren't the only one with trust issues." He leans forward, resting his elbows on the table. "I was married briefly. We got married young," he admits, "but I loved her. I thought that was enough." He shakes his head, and his blond hair falls over his eyes. "It was enough for me, but not her. She started seeing someone on the side and left me for him. It was a hard lesson to learn."

"And now you avoid commitments," I surmise, remembering Tom saying Blake had ended things with Sandi because she wanted something more permanent.

He shrugs, staring off with unseeing eyes. "I'm not averse to commitment, but it's easier to keep things casual. The majority of the time, love is nothing but pain."

His bleak outlook surprises me for someone who's based his career around positivity. Then again, who am I to judge? Most days, I slap on a fake smile for the rest of the world, too. But it's a shame his marriage left such deep scars. "I'm sorry, Blake. You deserved better."

"Thanks," he says quietly, his voice rough.

"Your turn to ask me something," I say, anxious to move to a lighter topic.

He smiles at my obvious reprieve. "What do you enjoy in your spare time?"

"I'm pretty boring. I hang out with my friends. I read. I journal. Watch a lot of movies, listen to lots of music. I run. I torture plants under the guise of gardening. I love being in the woods."

The woods are my happy place, magical and healing. The solitude and peace I find there quiets the cacophony inside my head.

"What kind of music do you like?"

I shrug. "Anything from the last fifty years is fair game."

His face lights up. "Who are the last three artists you've listened to?"

I pull out my phone and open my streaming service, scanning my recently-played titles. I laugh when I see them. "Proof of my eclecticism. James Taylor, Eminem, and Katy Perry. And the two before that are AC/DC and Bruno Mars."

He grins, ticking them off his fingers. "Let's see. Smooth and easy. Angry pounding. Girl-power ballads. Guitar-centric screeching, and R&B? That's quite the range."

"Sometimes I choose music to match my mood. Other times, I use it to alter it."

"What mood is Eminem for?"

I grin. "Usually burning off frustration. That, or I need to be productive."

He raises his eyebrows. "Eminem inspires productivity?"

"Matching my rhythm to his cadence helps me get a lot done. That's the same reason he's on my running playlist."

"I love playing music," he says, his voice and eyes softening. "It transcends all barriers. People can come from completely different cultures, speak completely different languages, and be in completely different social circles, yet one exquisite piece of music can touch them all."

His attitude is pure reverence. "You must play very well."

He nods. "Piano and guitar. Drums as well, but piano and guitar are my favorites."

"I can lose myself listening to piano music or an acoustic guitar for hours."

He nods. "Lost in music is one of my favorite places to be."

"I'd love to hear you play."

He smiles slowly. "Anytime, Beautiful."

There's an emotional weight to his words that makes me uncomfortable, and I redirect the conversation. "What else do you like to do?"

"Work out. Box. Spend time in nature. Hang out with my sister and my nieces. Listen to motivational seminars. Listen to music."

"Do you dance?"

His eyes twinkle with laughter. "Are you asking if I go clubbing? Not since my early twenties. A guy my age with a bunch of barely-legal girls grinding on him is creepy."

I laugh. "Not clubbing. Just dancing in general. Lila insists there are only two kinds of men – men who dance, and men who are too chicken to."

"I love slow dancing," he murmurs, his gaze intensifying. "A dimly lit room, holding a woman close as her body moves against mine. Slow dancing is foreplay with clothes on."

My smile fades. The seductive turn in conversation makes my heart accelerate, and not in a good way. I swallow hard as an invisible door slams shut.

His expression turns guilty. "I'm sorry. I didn't mean to make you uncomfortable."

I shake my head and glance away. "I'm fine," I say automatically, but the warm atmosphere between us has chilled noticeably.

I'm glad the waitress chooses that moment to bring our burgers, because discussion drops to a minimum as we eat and listen to the music. My tension gradually returns to a manageable level. When we resume talking, it's merely surface level chit chat, nothing personal or provocative.

The obvious halt to any meaningful conversation is both a relief and a disappointment. I'd been having a good time until things turned suggestive. As soon as anything hinting of sexuality came up, everything soured, including my mood.

Maybe my sexual side isn't merely dormant. Maybe it's as scarred and ruined as the rest of me. I'm starting to think my gut feeling is right – that desire and arousal are no longer an option. The slightest sexual insinuation triggers my fear response. Deep gloom saturates my spirit.

The waitress clears away our plates and offers refills, but when I glance at my watch, it's nearly midnight. "I didn't realize it was so late. I should go."

Blake stands and tosses a handful of bills onto the table. "Come on, Beautiful. I'll walk you to your car."

We walk side by side through the humid night until we reach the furniture store parking lot where I found a space. He waits as I unlock my door and toss my purse inside. I turn to him.

"Thank you for a nice evening." I smile despite my discouragement.

His gaze holds mine. "I enjoyed getting to know you better."

My smile fades as I study him, trying to gauge whether he's going to try to kiss me.

I'm caught off guard by the octopus tentacles of anxiety clenching my heart, slamming it inside my chest. The sudden intensity startles me. Iron bands squeeze my chest like a massive python, and I'm left fighting to breathe.

Dammit! Not now!

I pant, gulping in air, but I can't get enough. My entire body grows rigid. I clench my fists and widen my stance as though preparing to fight off attackers, but my vision goes dark. I'm fucking helpless, at the mercy of anyone who walks by, all because of my damn fears.

Then I hear Mark's voice in my head.

Breathe.

Slow and deep.

You're okay, Baby Girl. Just breathe.

With tremendous effort, I drop my head and roll my shoulders. I slow my breaths, deepening them, fighting to regain control. I'm still way too emotional when metal squeaks to my right.

My eyes fly open. Blake has stepped back, putting my car door between us and opening it further to give me space. His arms rest casually atop the door, his hands in plain view. His body is at ease, though his eyes are troubled. His mouth moves, but I'm concentrating so hard on breathing that I miss his words. "What?"

"Please don't be afraid."

I shut my eyes, trying to calm myself, but when he keeps talking, I open them again.

"I won't hurt you. You don't need to be afraid of me." His voice is gentle, like he's trying to soothe a frightened rabbit.

Or in my case, a train wreck in the midst of a panic attack.

A lump forms in my throat, too large to swallow around. "I'm sorry," I whisper, glancing away. I should never have agreed to this. It was easier with the old gray mules. I would never even have considered being alone with any of them in a deserted parking lot at midnight.

"Don't be sorry. I had a good time tonight. I think you did, too." He speaks slowly, calmly.

I nod cautiously. I *was* having a good time... until he mentioned foreplay.

He tips his head and smiles. "Maybe we can do this again sometime."

I'm shocked to feel myself nodding in agreement.

His smile widens as he opens the car door further. "I hope so. Good night, Charlie."

"Good night, Blake."

My eyes linger on him for another second before I get inside. He closes my door and waits until I start my engine before strolling casually away.

Hot tears of frustration flow unchecked as I drive too fast down mostly empty streets. *What the hell?* One minute I'm smiling and saying I had a nice time. He smiled and said he enjoyed getting to know me. A second later, I have a meltdown, even though he didn't *do* anything.

Fuck.

No matter how many crappy dates I've been on, none of them have brought me to tears. Tonight, I sob the entire time I'm barreling back to the safety of my house.

I just want to live in the moment like everyone else, without fear, without panic, without hang-ups. But wishing I were normal doesn't change a damn thing, and I'm starting to think my damage runs too deep to be repaired.

I pull into my driveway behind Tucker's enormous truck. *Damn.* I was hoping to sneak upstairs.

I check my eyes in the rearview mirror. They're red, but thanks to my waterproof mascara, I don't have inky trails down my cheeks. I can fake my way through this. I'll just keep my distance. I press my icy hands against my face, then plaster on my best smile and go inside.

Mark and Tucker are in the living room, beer bottles and a pizza box on the coffee table. They're watching an MMA match with the TV cranked up. I wave from the hallway when they both glance up. Tucker reaches for the remote and lowers the volume to a dull roar.

"Look at you. Grown-up clothes and everything," he says admiringly.

"Thanks, Tucker. Nice shirt." I gesture to his pizza-stained gray tee. "Is Lila here?"

He shakes his head. "She said something about peace and quiet and sent me on a playdate."

I adopt a teasing tone. "Heaven forbid I interrupt your date night. I'm going upstairs. You guys have fun." I feel Mark's eyes, but I wave again and scoot upstairs like everything's fine.

I change my clothes and sink into the recliner in the corner of my bedroom. Part of me wants to call Lila, while the other part knows exactly what she'll say. She'll encourage me to go see that sex therapist she and Tucker went to.

Like I need a sex therapist. I can't even handle the possibility of a goodnight kiss.

But something Lila said nags at me.

Intimacy begins in the mind.

I sit alone, pondering that concept.

Sex and intimacy don't necessarily go hand in hand. You can have sex with another person without ever being truly intimate. People do it all the time. Intimacy implies emotional closeness.

What happened to me, though it involved sexual acts, was about power and humiliation, control and pain. There was no intimacy whatsoever.

So if intimacy wasn't part of what happened, why does it scare me? Why are sex and intimacy so entangled in my mind? And why does the thought of a simple goodnight kiss make my anxiety level skyrocket?

I drop my head. I'm so fucking tired. Tired in my heart. Tired in my soul.

Tired of crying.

Tired of being afraid.

Tired of being alone.

Tired of being too afraid to not be alone.

Tired of feeling too damaged to allow anyone in.

Tired of *being* damaged.

A heaviness falls over me, so heavy I can't even cry. I was never the crying type until the kidnapping. I'd occasionally shed a few tears, but rarely over relationships. My tears were reserved for serious losses, like losing my or

Mark's parents or fellow soldiers. But ever since what happened, I've been a mess, and I loathe it.

My life is controlled by fear now, whereas before, I was... well, not quite fearless, but close. The Me from five years ago would be sorely disappointed in the Me I've become. I'm essentially the photo negative of the woman I used to be. My confidence, my hope, my trust, my strength, my happiness – they're gone. They were destroyed in a cell deep in the desert, ripped away brutality by brutality.

The worst part is that even after death, those bastards still torment me. I may have been rescued from their cell four years ago, but I'm still a captive. My prison is just less visible now.

No matter what Mark or Lila or Tucker say, I've finally accepted it. The bastards won.

And I lost me.

MARK

Charlie comes downstairs just after Tucker leaves. I can tell by her posture something's wrong. I noticed it when she came home, when I got the distinct impression she was avoiding me. I scrutinize her. Her eyes aren't red, but there's a definite sadness about her.

I'm already sitting in bed reading with the covers turned down when she silently pads into the room, dressed in her usual shorts and tee shirt. "You okay, Baby Girl?"

"I'm fine. I just have a headache."

I pretend not to see through her lie. "Need an aspirin?"

She shakes her head. "I just want to go to sleep and forget today ever happened."

Something happened on her date. She was in a decent mood when she left. I don't push. She'll tell me when she's ready. Then I'll decide whether or not to kick Blake's ass.

"Lila called me while you were upstairs. She wants to go on an overnight girls' trip tomorrow. Shopping and restaurants and stuff."

Her mouth turns up in a faint smile. "You two have a great time."

I smile wryly. "Not me, smartass. She tried your phone, but you must have been in the shower."

"What will you do if I leave?"

I shrug. "Hang out with Tucker. He's so thrilled not to have to go shopping, I could probably get him to agree to anything."

"Text her and tell her to send me the details." She doesn't look excited by the prospect, but then, Charlie's never really been into shopping.

She retrieves the mirror and massage oil and settles down to work her magic. I'm still amazed that something as simple as an optical illusion can relieve my phantom pain, but there's no doubt it's helped. Tonight, though, Charlie's distress flows through her fingertips. She works my muscles intensely, almost painfully, and I'm secretly relieved when she finishes.

She climbs into bed and curls up against me, but instead of facing the door as usual, she burrows her head into my shoulder.

I glance down at her. "Wanna talk about it?"

There's a long pause. "Not tonight," she says finally.

I kiss the top of her head. "Whenever you're ready, you know where to find me. Can I do anything?"

"Can we just stay like this for a while?"

I tug the covers up and wrap my arm around her. "For as long as you want."

She falls asleep like that, her head on my left shoulder and her left hand on my chest, leaving me wondering what the hell went wrong on her date with Blake.

CHARLIE

I awaken at seven as usual, despite being awake until after two. Lila will be here before nine, giving me just enough time to shower, dress, and throw a few things into my carry-on. Lila's a marathon shopper. My role is to follow along and occasionally offer an opinion.

I'm wolfing down coffee and toast when she arrives. She's dressed in form-fitting jeans and a flowy periwinkle top that makes her eyes even more luminous. Perfect blond curls spill over her shoulders. Meanwhile, I'm wearing comfortable jeans, a soft coral tee, and running shoes. She frowns at me. "Why are you eating? You know we're going to brunch."

"It's toast. I can make room."

Lila has today and tomorrow's outlet shopping already mapped out. Apparently, she "needs" dresses, shoes, and decor for her newly finished basement. She also has a burning desire for mimosas over brunch and Mexican food for dinner. I'm merely a prop in her endeavor.

I pull my sunglasses down and rest my head against the headrest while she zips through the curvy mountain roads in the bright sunlight, singing along with the radio. I doze off and wake up to her saying my name. I stir and blink tired eyes.

"Wake up, Sleepyhead. I'm starving."

Brunch at Magnolia Cafe is a shopping-trip tradition. Every time Lila drags me on what I've nicknamed her Acquisition Expeditions, I fortify myself with mid-morning mimosas. Consolation for my aching feet will occur tonight with bottomless margaritas and tacos.

Lila's halfway through her honey-crunch waffles and sausage when she looks at me nervously. "I went off the pill January first," she blurts.

It takes a minute for her words to sink in. "You're pregnant?" I'm startled, but only because Lila hasn't mentioned wanting a baby, and she usually keeps me in the loop, especially on something so monumental.

She shakes her head. "No. Not yet. But maybe soon. At least, I hope so. We're trying."

Her words imply enthusiasm, but her tone and expression seem distressed, and I don't understand the disconnect. "That's good, right?" I ask cautiously.

She nods, reaching for her mimosa but not taking a drink. Her eyes never leave my face.

"Then why do you look like it's a bad thing?"

She swallows. "I wasn't sure what you'd think."

"I think you guys will be amazing parents."

"That's not what I mean."

I can't figure out why she's so troubled. "What am I missing?"

She bites her lip. "I wasn't sure how you'd feel if I got pregnant."

"Thrilled," I answer, still confused.

Lila reaches across the table and takes my hands. "I don't want to hurt you by getting pregnant when you can't."

Oh.

Something deep inside me twists painfully, but I shove it down, shaking my head.

"I would never be upset at you for starting a family, Lila. I think it's wonderful. This is life-changing for you and Tucker. I'm happy for you."

That's one thousand percent true. If Lila and Tucker want babies, I hope they have an entire houseful. They deserve kids, and I would never hold it against them. Just because motherhood is one more thing those bastards stole from me, I could never be upset at Lila for having a baby.

"Well, it's not life-changing yet," she says, looking down. "We've been trying for five months and nothing's happened."

I shake my head. "That's not very long. Besides, it's been a rough year. I wouldn't worry."

"I'm not worried. Not yet, anyway. I've started tracking my ovulation dates. That way, I know when our best window of opportunity is."

I grin. Lila's a planner through and through. "Poor Tucker, being called upon for stud services on a schedule."

She laughs. "Yeah, it's a real burden for him. I'm pretty sure he's been penciling in extra days." She turns serious again. "Are you positive you're okay with this?"

I squeeze her hand. "I promise you, Lila, I'm completely okay with it."

"Good, because I might want to look at maternity clothes and baby furniture."

"Hoping to inspire a hormone surge?" I tease.

She shakes her head. "Plan for the future you want, right? Besides, the maternity clothes on clearance now will be perfect for this winter if I get pregnant."

It's a long day. After I finish my BLT omelet and draw strength from a second mimosa, we start at one end of the outlet strip and work our way down. Lila focuses mostly on dresses. "Wrap dresses can conceal a baby bump, and depending upon the cut and the fabric, they can work in late pregnancy, too," she says when I raise an eyebrow at her armload of clothing.

I grin. "Like you'd try to hide a baby bump."

She sniffs delicately. "I might."

Store after store, purchase after purchase, we shop our way down the strip. "You have to get something," Lila scolds when it's late afternoon and I still haven't bought anything.

"I'm only here for decorative purposes."

"At least get one outfit," she urges me. Then she assumes an innocent look. "Something you could wear out with Blake."

I'd been expecting her to bring him up. "Subtle."

She shrugs. "You're always upfront with your stories about the Whiners, but you've not said a peep about last night."

"I'll make you a deal. I'll buy something if we can put off talking about him until I've had a margarita."

"Deal." She grins triumphantly because she knows I'd have told her anyway, and now I'm forced to participate. Lila flips through rack after rack of clothes while I let her fill my arms with garments. When she's finally satisfied, we go to the dressing room, where I model outfit after outfit while she purses her lips and fusses. She eventually whittles it down to three options.

"Choose from these dresses," she says when I return in my own clothes. She's already hung the rejects on a return rack. The first is a deep red print dress fitted at the waist before flaring out in a full skirt that hits my calves but is split to the thigh. The second dress is the exact green of my eyes, a wrap dress with butterfly sleeves and a lightly ruffled skirt. Her final selection is a teal ruched sleeveless sheath that hugs my body and lands mid thigh.

I truly couldn't care less. It's not that I don't like the clothes – they're perfectly fine. It's just that this is far more her arena than mine. I spend ninety percent of my time in work clothes, jeans and tee shirts, or sleepwear. Lila's the one that's always perfectly put together.

"Which one do you like best?" I ask instead.

"I think you should buy all three of them."

I sigh. "You would buy all three, but I'm not you. If you had to choose the one that looked best on me, which would you pick?"

She studies each dress carefully, holding them against me one at a time. "The green one looks best with your eyes, but the other two really draw attention to your legs."

Problem solved. I have no desire to draw attention to my anything. I hang the red and teal dresses on the return rack before turning toward the register.

"I'm just going to try this one thing on while you pay," she says, slipping into the dressing room with a miniscule white dress that doesn't contain a handkerchief's worth of fabric.

"I'm pretty sure that won't hide a baby bump," I tease.

She laughs. "Nope, but it might help me get one."

When Lila finally decides she's had enough shopping for today, we check into the hotel. She's reserved adjoining rooms for us. I long to shower because I've been around people all day, but since we're going right back out to dinner, I settle for freshening up and changing clothes. We meet in the lobby for our Uber since we're both planning on drinking margaritas tonight.

We're halfway through our appetizer nachos when she raises an eyebrow at me. "So. Blake."

I sigh. "Really? Over appetizers?"

She lifts her margarita. "Why not? It's an upgrade from doughnuts and coffee."

"I'm not drunk enough to have this conversation yet."

Her eyes turn sad. "That bad?"

Lila's convinced a relationship with the right person will help me heal. As a result, every failed date leaves me feeling like I've let her down. But last night, I had an epiphany. I realized it doesn't matter who I go out with. There's no "right guy" for me. I'd fail with Prince Charming, because the problem isn't the guy. The problem is me and my U-Haul of emotional baggage.

"It started off well enough. He was easier to talk to because I knew him. But then he made a comment about foreplay, and..." I shrug.

She takes a sip of her margarita, her gaze lingering.

I take a deep breath. "One innuendo, and all relaxed conversation came to a screeching halt. It was awkwardly quiet after that. Then he walked me to my car, and everything went to shit."

"What happened?"

I shake my head. "It was a dark parking lot with no one around. He said he'd enjoyed the evening. I was trying to decide if he was going to go for a goodnight kiss." I sigh. "Next thing I knew, I was in a full-blown panic attack. It was awful."

"Did you pull your gun?"

I shake my head. "I'd put my purse in the car already. But I looked like a fool. Again," I add, remembering that this is the second panic attack he's witnessed.

Lila frowns. "No, you didn't."

"You weren't there. I couldn't breathe, couldn't move. It took two or three minutes for me to calm down. When I opened my eyes, he was standing on the opposite side of the car door." She looks perplexed, so I explain, "He put the door between us, trying to give me space. He was talking to me like I was a frightened animal." I'm silent for a minute. "I can't do this anymore, Lila. I'm done."

"What do you mean, done?"

"I'm so tired, Lila," I say quietly, my voice breaking. "No matter how much effort I put in, it always ends up the same. Insanity is doing the same thing over and over, hoping for a different outcome. That's what this is. I need a break. No more blind dates, okay?"

I expect her usual pep talk, but instead, she just nods.

When I'm alone in the hotel room later, I consider her reaction.

Maybe she was just being supportive, agreeing to what I said I wanted.

Or maybe she can see the truth: that those bastards in Afghanistan got exactly what they'd intended – to destroy me.

Remembering them reminds me of her worry that I'd be upset if she got pregnant.

Alone, I can admit the truth.

I am upset, but not at her. *Never* at her. She and Tucker deserve to have as many babies as they want.

I'm upset because it's one more way those fuckers won.

They mutilated my womanhood – both externally and internally – with a rusty knife. They raped me with their filthy bodies, grimy metal pipes, and broken glass bottles.

Around the clock.

For eleven days.

I was critically ill when Mark rescued me. The field hospital pumped me full of antibiotics and repaired my lacerated vagina and cervix as best as they could, but the damage was done. Mark held my hand when the doctor at Walter Reed delivered the news.

I'll never be able to conceive.

My womb is like the rest of me – permanently scarred and irreparably damaged.

I spend the rest of the night depleting the room's minibar, trying to numb my pain.

CHAPTER SIXTEEN

MARK

SATURDAY EVENING IS, HANDS-DOWN, one of the weirdest nights of my life.

Tucker and I head to a local sports bar since we're fending for ourselves. The place is packed, full of braying laughter and boisterous cheers. Huge TVs line the walls, and if not for the closed captions, I wouldn't have the faintest idea what the announcers were discussing. We find a table in the back and I take a seat, leaning my crutches against the wall while Tucker wends his way to the crowded bar to get a couple of beers.

I'm looking at my phone when a woman I've never met slides into the seat across from me. She's wearing a strappy red top with her cleavage popping out. Her jeans are so tight, they look like they're airbrushed on. She tosses her blond hair over her shoulder and points to my crutches.

"What happened?"

I blink, startled by her bold inquiry. No hello, no "My name is", nothing.

She raises one over-plucked brow. "Sports injury? Car accident? What?"

I feel like I'm in an alternate universe. I know I haven't been to a bar in a while, but have things really changed this much?

Her uninvited interrogation irks me, and my response comes out clipped. "War wound."

The irritation in my voice goes right over her head. She peers up at me through spider-like fake lashes, her garish red lips pouting. "Want me to kiss it better?"

Is this her idea of flirting? Maybe she thinks this is sexy.

It's not.

I glance toward the bar, wondering if Tucker is somehow behind this. Maybe it's a prank. But he's not looking my way. He's still trying to catch the attention of the harried bartender.

I look back at the blonde. "This isn't the kind of injury you can fix with a kiss."

Long red nails scrape over my forearm, and she leans closer, thrusting her ample breasts in my direction in case they've somehow gone unnoticed. "Are you sure? I'm quite good."

"Unless you can regrow my leg, I'm not interested."

She pales noticeably. "You're missing a leg?"

"Explosions tend to cause that sort of thing." When she shrinks away from me, my temper flares. "Don't worry. It's not contagious."

The blonde rapidly withdraws her scarlet claws and scrambles to her feet. "It was nice to meet you. Uh, thank you for your service." She makes a beeline straight for the exit. At her retreat, my momentary flash of temper recedes, leaving discouragement in its wake.

Tucker tips his head in her direction when he returns. "Who's the blonde?"

"I thought maybe she was one of your pranks."

He laughs. "Nope. I don't know her."

I reach for the beer and drain half of it. "She offered to kiss my war wound and make it better until she found out I'm an amputee. Then she couldn't escape fast enough." I set my bottle down a little too hard, and it sloshes onto the tabletop.

Tucker makes a face. "You're better off. You'd probably catch something antibiotics can't cure."

I smile automatically, but it doesn't reach my eyes. Like I needed a reminder that a missing leg is a massive turnoff. I never had trouble getting a woman before, back when I was whole.

But that was before.

Before I was damaged. Scarred. Broken.

I don't realize I've sighed out loud until Tucker raps on the tabletop. "Quit with the pity party, Chandler. So some slutty chick is too shallow to see you for who you really are. Big deal. There are a lot of assholes in this world, and if you're smart, you'll avoid them."

I drag one hand over my whiskers. "You're right. She just caught me off guard."

Tucker grins. "Of course I'm right." He turns to the closest screen, becoming absorbed in a pair of featherweights pummeling each other in a boxing ring. I try to watch too, but regrets still occupy my mind, useless wishes that my life had turned out differently.

That I wasn't half a man now.

A couple of beers later, I've calmed down. Yeah, some woman bailed after finding out about my leg, but it's not like I was interested in her. She approached me. I'd been wishing she would disappear before she flipped out and ran off. She saved me the trouble of asking her to leave.

Things take another turn the next time Tucker heads to the bar. He hasn't even waded through the crowd to the bar before another blonde slides into his seat, her gaze roaming over me like I'm on tonight's menu. Her green eyes remind me of Charlie's. She's dressed in a skintight black dress and skyscraper heels.

"I'm Champagne," she says, her voice husky. Champagne sounds like a stripper's name, and her outfit certainly supports that theory.

"Mark," I reply, smiling blandly. Her cloying perfume assaults my nostrils, and I change my mind. Her eyes are nothing like Charlie's. Charlie would never apply makeup with a trowel.

'Forgive me, but I couldn't help noticing your right leg."

My missing leg.

Seriously?

"You're an amputee, right?"

My tone is sharp. "Yes, Champagne. I lost my leg in Afghanistan."

Her pupils dilate and her breathing quickens. "That is so fucking hot."

My jaw drops.

I whirl around to locate Tucker. He's got to be behind this. But once again, he's talking to the bartender, not looking my way.

"I'm a stump bunny."

"I – a what?"

"A stump bunny. You know. Amputations turn me on. Like, really turn me on." Her voice has a sudden urgency.

This is a thing?

Apparently she's not kidding. She's practically panting, right there at the table. She reaches both hands across the table and wraps them around my forearm. "Wanna get out of here?"

What. The. Fuck.

I'm looking around for the hidden camera when Tucker reappears, glancing from me to Champagne and back.

"Champagne, this is Tucker. Tucker, Champagne. Champagne was just leaving," I say firmly.

"Maybe I could give you a ride," she offers throatily. Tucker snorts with laughter, and she glares at him. "A ride home."

"Sorry, Sugar, he's going home with me tonight," Tucker says in an extremely effeminate voice. He sets our beers down and squeezes my shoulder, leaving his hand to stake his claim.

I want to crawl under the table.

Champagne looks from me to Tucker and back again. I smile weakly. She unearths a card from her ample bosom and slides it across the table to me. "Call me if you change your mind."

She's barely ten feet away when Tucker starts laughing. "If you could see your face."

"I'm never coming to this fucking bar again," I mutter. He only laughs harder as he slides back into his chair.

"Shut up, Tucker. It's not that funny."

He grins broadly. "You've been hit on twice tonight, and I'm your best offer. That's fucking hysterical."

"Have you ever heard of a stump bunny?"

"A what?"

I shake my head in disbelief. "Champagne has an amputation fetish."

He winks. "I'm more of an ass man, myself. Now finish your beer so I can take you home, Soldier."

This time when he laughs, I laugh too.

CHARLIE

Sunday finds me trailing through stores after Lila, thinking. Yesterday, I told her I was done with dating, but my emotions have cooled enough to allow me to be objective. I initially enjoyed my evening with Blake. Until his comment about foreplay, that was the most promising date I've been on since I moved to Cedar Ridge. The downward spiral that culminated in my panic attack stemmed from his provocative statement.

What I need is to figure out how to stop reacting to non-threatening flirtation. Just because a guy mentions sex or foreplay doesn't make him a threat. After a full day of self-examination, I decide to visit Lila's sex therapist. Doing the same thing over and over hasn't worked for me. It's time to try something new. I place a call to her first thing Monday morning, startled when she offers me an appointment for Wednesday afternoon.

Willow Entwein works out of her home a few miles north of Cedar Ridge. I pull up about ten minutes early. I've imagined an older hippie-type woman with long graying waves dressed like a flower child. When a tall siren opens the door, I'm shocked. Willow has rich hazel eyes and dark curls that hang to her waist, and she's wearing a black wrap dress with a plunging neckline.

"Wow," I say awkwardly. "I feel very underdressed." I gesture to my khaki cargo pants and flowing white top. I drove here straight from my last appointment, not wanting to arouse curiosity by stopping to change because I've not told anyone about today's visit.

"You must be Charlie. Please come in." Her voice flows like warm brandy, and everything about her oozes sexuality. She runway-walks down a long hall wearing (what else?) black stilettos, leading me to a sunny room with a pair of overstuffed plush chairs and a comfortable sofa. Colorful art and rugs add life to the space, and plants sprawl happily across a bookshelf below the window. "Take a seat wherever you feel comfortable."

I choose one of the squashy red chairs, and Willow takes the other, facing me. It's silent until she smiles. "Perhaps you could start by telling me what brings you here today."

I take a deep breath, wondering where to begin. "My friend Lila recommended you. Lila Maxwell," I add. "She and I were medics together in Afghanistan. We were kidnapped for eleven days. They – " I stop to compose myself, staring at my hands. "I was beaten. Restrained. Whipped. Branded. Mutilated. Raped repeatedly. More men and more times than I can count." Memories of rough hands, soured bodies, and fetid breath overwhelm me. The familiar band tightens around my chest. My hands dig into the arms of the chair, and I squeeze my eyes shut.

Breathe.

You're safe now. They can't hurt you.

Just breathe.

It takes me a couple of minutes to regain control. I open my eyes to find Willow watching me closely. She passes me a box of tissues. I hadn't realized I was crying.

Again.

Fuck.

I blot my eyes and take a deep breath. "This happened about four years ago. I'd ended a casual relationship not long before that. I've not been in a relationship since then." I sigh heavily. "I can't let anyone get close to me. If it wasn't someone I trusted before, like Lila or Mark, I have a hard time letting them in. I'm friends with Lila's husband Tucker, but we were friends before. I have a co-worker, Tom, who's become a friend, but I've never told him what happened. I've been on several dates, but I have too much baggage for most men to deal with."

I pause. "Last week, I went out with a nice guy who was interested, even though he knows I'm a disaster. I had a good time, but I got uncomfortable when he made an offhand comment about foreplay. When he walked me to my car, I had a panic attack at the thought he might try to kiss me. I hate being like this." I pause for a moment before I quietly finish. "I feel like I'm too broken to move forward, and I'm sick of being imprisoned by my fear."

"Does Nice Guy have a name?"

I smile. "Blake. His name is Blake."

"See what you did there?" Willow asks, pointing with one French-manicured nail. My brow wrinkles in confusion. "You thought about him when I asked his name. You looked to the side, accessed your memory bank, and smiled. That smile was a subconscious reaction."

"I'm not sure I understand your point."

Totally untrue. I'm positive I don't understand her point.

She smiles. "Your mind has classified Blake as a good memory, a pleasant experience. Your subconscious has already decided he's safe."

"Then why did I freak out when I thought he might kiss me?"

Willow studies me. "Do you panic with any male touch?"

I nod. "Everyone except Mark. I don't panic with him."

"Tell me about Mark."

How do I explain our relationship to someone who likely won't understand?

"Mark is the person I'm closest to. We grew up together, joined the Army together, were in the same platoon for several years before – you know. He led the mission to rescue me. He literally saved my life. He was badly injured earlier this year and spent months in a military hospital. Now he's home with me, recovering. He's just – he's my person, and I'm his."

"You said you grew up together. Are you related?"

"Not by blood. After his dad committed suicide, my parents became his guardians."

"So you lived in the same house?"

"He moved in with us when he was fifteen."

"So you're best friends?" Willow clarifies.

"Yes."

I watch her face. I recognize her skeptical look. She believes Mark and I are more than friends. I've never understood why people find it so hard to believe honest, platonic friendships can't exist between men and women.

She tilts her head. "You're able to be affectionate with Mark?"

I nod.

"If he were to suddenly hug you, would you panic?"

I make a face. "No."

"If he were to kiss you, how would you react?"

I narrow my gaze. "I'm comfortable with Mark. We know each other inside and out. We trust each other. We've been best friends for almost twenty-five years. He helped me survive the worst period of my life, and I'm helping him through his. We're close. We're affectionate. We hug, we kiss each other's cheeks, we lean on each other when we watch movies. But there's nothing sexual or romantic about our relationship."

Sensing my annoyance, Willow shifts the subject. "How well do you know Blake?"

"Not well," I admit. "He's an acquaintance. But Tom knows him pretty well, and he'd have said something if going out with Blake was a bad idea."

"Tom is the other male friend you mentioned?"

"Yes. He works with me, and he's very protective of me."

"You became friends after your trauma?"

I nod.

"And you spend time with him?"

I nod again. "Five days a week at work, plus he works out with Tucker and Mark at my house three afternoons a week, and I have dinner with him and his daughter at least once a week."

"Would you say Tom has built your trust over time?"

"Yes. I feel safe with him. Our friendship is like a sibling relationship."

"Can you be affectionate with Tom like you can with Mark?"

I shake my head. "I haven't been affectionate with any male besides Mark since I came back." I pause. "I've been trying to get used to touch again. A few weeks ago, I let him pull me to my feet, but as soon as I was standing, I jerked my hand free. It was too much."

"So you trust Tom, but you have difficulty being affectionate with him."

"I trust him, but not as much as I trust Mark."

"You've spent years with Mark," Willow points out. "Given time, do you believe Tom could reach a higher level of trust with you?"

"Yes."

"What about Blake?"

I shrug. "I don't know. He's nice, but I had a meltdown at the thought of a kiss."

Willow uncrosses and recrosses her legs to the other side, revealing shapely calves. She leans back in her chair before continuing in her sultry voice. "Intimacy begins in your mind. It starts with emotional connection. Both people in any healthy relationship have to allow themselves to be vulnerable for emotional connections to form. As those connections grow, they lead to intimacy. And I'm not just talking about romantic relationships," she adds. "This applies to friendships as well. Part of the reason you're closest to Mark and Lila is that you've shared emotionally raw moments. You and Lila have a shared trauma, and you experienced vulnerability and healing together. You've let Mark inside your pain, and he's let you into his. You lack that deeper trust and connection with Tucker and Tom because even though you're friends, you haven't let yourself be vulnerable with either of them. If you want to deepen a relationship with someone, you have to be willing to bare your soul, to go below the surface."

Her words ring with truth. "I don't like being vulnerable," I confess.

"Of course not. You were brutalized because you were physically vulnerable, and as a result, your mind and your body have gone into lockdown mode for self-protection. Your subconscious fear of pain keeps you from giving most people access to your feelings. You have a choice to make. You can wall yourself off to stay safe from emotional harm, or you can open yourself to others. Both options carry risks. Keeping everyone at arm's length causes its own emotional pain, and opening yourself up to the wrong person can lead to harm. But you can choose to be intentionally open and vulnerable, a little at a time, with someone who might be worthy. It might be your Nice Guy. Or it might not."

"I get what you're saying about emotional connections," I say slowly, "and I think I'd be willing to open up more to people I trust. But the biggest reason I'm here is because I don't want to have another panic attack if I go out with Blake again."

"It's all interconnected." She waves her hand breezily. "There are other things you can do. Visualization, desensitization techniques. I can make recommendations, if you like."

"That's why I'm here." I hear the exasperation in my tone.

"Alright," Willow replies with a hint of amusement. "I'll give you homework. First, consider talking to Tom or Tucker about being more physical."

"More physical? What does that mean? And how does that help if I see Blake again?"

Not that he's asked.

Not that I blame him.

She continues as though I'd never spoken. "When I say physical, I don't mean sexually. I mean affectionately. Touching hands. Sitting with an arm around you. Hugging. Leaning against each other. This particular task," she taps her knee for emphasis, "involves you being vulnerable enough to talk about your fear in advance, and it will allow you to experience positive male touch with someone you trust. You've let your past convince your mind that touch between a man and a woman means pain. You have to change your inner dialogue. As you become more comfortable being affectionate with Tucker and Tom, you'll find it easier with Blake, if you should choose to pursue that avenue. A romantic relationship would presumably lead to more physical intimacy than with Tom or Tucker. That's why I suggest starting with a male friend to get your feet wet, so to speak.

"Your other piece of homework," she continues, "is optional, but I highly recommend it. I want you to develop a sexual fantasy." My eyes widen. "It could be about Blake, or the produce guy at the grocery store, or someone you'd never actually have an encounter with. This is a mental story you write, and you can move at whatever speed you're comfortable with. If it becomes uncomfortable, back up to where you're comfortable. This is about incremental progress, gradually easing yourself into the idea of sexual intimacy. Immerse yourself fully in your fantasy. Imagine what's being said, who's doing what to whom, how it feels. Pay attention to sounds, scents, and sensations." My face burns. "Your goal is to create a positive view of sexual intimacy. And if your biggest fear right now is panicking during a kiss, start by visualizing kissing. Light kissing, French kissing, deep kissing. Lots of kissing."

I drive home, my mind a jumbled mess. I didn't schedule a follow-up appointment, because until I've put her suggestions into practice, there's not much point. I suppose I need to figure out how to be more open with Tom and Tucker, but I'm not sure how to even start.

When I get home, Tucker's truck and Tom's SUV are in the driveway.

I forgot today was a workout day. I really wanted time to process everything Willow and I talked about. "Be open," I mutter.

Loud music blasts from the weight room. I drop my bag on the foyer bench and peek inside. Lila's running on the treadmill with her back to me. Mark is doing crunches while Tucker braces him, and Tom is bench-pressing an obscene amount of weights in the corner. I wave as Mark looks up, then point upstairs, and he nods.

I'm halfway up the stairs when my phone signals a text. It's Blake.

"Are you free Saturday? Addison and Avery are spending the night, so we're having Chinese takeout and watching movies. Thought maybe you'd like to join us."

My stomach shocks me with a tiny flip, something I haven't felt in years. That's good, right? And he's asked me to dinner again, this time with chaperones, so I'm less likely to panic.

Maybe he really did have a decent time.

"Figured I'd scared you off."

His reply is immediate. "I enjoy a good challenge."

"Chinese food feels like a bribe..." I type.

"Did I mention I live near a cupcake shop?"

I smile. "I'm free. With or without cupcakes."

"Cupcakes make everything better. See you Saturday night."

Baby steps.

When I'm showering before bed, I think about my visit with Willow. She's right. Thinking about Blake again makes me smile, something a guy hasn't elicited from me in a long time. Maybe I really can move forward.

But opening up to Tom and Tucker? I don't even know where to begin.

I should probably start with just one of them. Dip a toe into the icy pond of intentional vulnerability instead of diving in headfirst.

I think I'll start with Tom. I usually end up at his house on Friday nights anyway.

A thought pops unbidden into my mind. *You should tell him what happened in Afghanistan.*

All of it.

I spend longer than usual massaging Mark's legs. Increased workouts to strengthen his right thigh have left the muscles tight, so I spend several minutes working on it before setting up his mirror. Combining mirror therapy with massage has been extremely effective. He's gotten so good at visualizing his lower leg, he only needs an occasional glance at the mirror.

I'm lost in the massage, my thoughts drifting like lazy clouds, when it occurs to me that the concept of mirror therapy isn't that different from Willow's suggestions. The process is different, but the goal is the same: to stop the pain by changing the way the mind interprets physical touch.

Massaging Mark's left leg while he visualizes the agony in his right leg easing has broken the pain loop between his brain and nerves. If Willow's right, then accepting affectionate touch and – God help me, creating sexual fantasies – should break my mental reflex that equates male touch to pain.

I'm still mulling this over when I finish.

"I feel guilty," Mark comments. "You're always massaging me, and I don't reciprocate."

I grin. "You're more than welcome to."

He scoots up in the bed. "What do you want? I'm no expert, but I'll do my best."

I answer without hesitation. "My hands. They ache when I schedule clients too close together without a break." Today I did four fifty-minute massages in a row to ensure I could make it to Willow's on time.

"I can handle that. Do you want me to use the oil?"

I nod and pass him the bottle. "A little goes a long way." I put away the mirror and sit facing him, holding out my hand. I watch as he squirts oil in his palm, then begins to rub, starting with the thick pad at the base of my thumb. "Mmmm. That's where I usually hurt most."

"Tell me if you want something different. This is your area of expertise."

"That feels incredible." I relax into his firm touch.

He watches me while he works. "Can I ask you something?"

"Of course."

"You've been uncomfortable around men ever since what happened."

I grin up at his serious expression. "That's not a question. That's a statement. Perhaps you need a grammar refresher."

He rolls his eyes. "I wasn't finished. I was leading up to my question. If you're uncomfortable with men and touch, why choose massage therapy? It's based entirely on physical contact."

My jaw drops. How have I never once seen the irony in spending my days with my hands all over male clients, while simultaneously being terrified for a man to touch me?

That's certainly something to discuss with Linda.

I pause, thinking. "I have a positive association with massage. When Lila and I started seeing Linda, she recommended following our sessions with a massage to help release tension from dealing with trauma. We got them at the massage school. Students have to perform massages for a certain number of hours to get their license, so they offer them inexpensively. And it did help," I add. "I carry my tension in my neck and shoulders, and when I'd skip the massage, I had neck pain and headaches. Lila and I saw what a difference it made when we were trying to recover, and we knew we could help other struggling veterans."

"Is it difficult for you to work with male clients?" From his controlled expression, I can tell he's referring to their nudity.

"Not usually, because I feel like I'm the one in control. Our clients are referred to us by the VA or their family physician, so most of them treat us as medical professionals. Plus, our 'welcome to the practice' paperwork states that inappropriate behavior won't be tolerated. We've only had a couple of men push the boundaries."

Mark moves his attention to the bony base of my thumb, his long fingers gently probing and working out the soreness in the joint, and I sigh. "That feels wonderful."

He smiles. "I've been taking notes."

He works in silence for several minutes before reaching for my other hand and carefully kneading the base of each finger. "So how are things with Blake?" His tone is casual, but I know he's asking because of my bad mood after my date Friday night.

I take a deep breath. "We're having dinner again Saturday."

He beams. "A second date? You actually had a Winner? I'm proud of you."

I laugh. "Well, we're having takeout and watching a movie with his nieces, so we'll be fully chaperoned. I'm not sure that's cause for celebration."

He shakes his head. "Progress is always worth celebrating."

"I'm not sure I'm making progress, but I'm trying."

"That right there," he tips his head instead of pointing because his hands are massaging mine, "that's the progress I'm talking about. A few weeks ago, you weren't even sure it was worth it to try dating. Now you're giving it a chance. That's progress, Charlie. Even if things don't go anywhere with him, you –" he emphasizes, "are making progress."

I smile shyly. "I guess."

When I return after brushing my teeth, Mark is already in bed with his tablet. He's got the covers turned down for me, and my handgun sits on his bedside table. I crawl in beside him, looking up at his face. "Are you sure you don't mind staying awake every night?"

"I'm positive," he says firmly. "I sleep perfectly fine in the daytime, and I wouldn't sleep at all knowing you were on that bench. Besides, I like having you close in case I need you."

I study his stubborn expression. "If you get tired of it, promise you'll tell me."

He nods. "I promise."

I watch him another moment, then roll to my side facing the door, wriggling closer until my back nestles into his side. "Love you, Big Guy," I say, closing my eyes.

"Love you too, Baby Girl."

CHAPTER SEVENTEEN

MARK

IT'S NOT LONG BEFORE Charlie's breathing becomes even. When I'm sure she's asleep, I stuff another pillow under my head and tuck an earbud into one ear, then start a movie on my tablet.

The movie's nearly finished when Charlie starts twitching erratically. I glance over. She's tensing her arms, pulling them to her chest defensively and snapping her head from side to side.

I sit up quickly and toss my tablet aside. I look at the clock, worried I've missed her wake-up time, but it's not even two.

"No," she mutters. Her words quickly become more forceful. "No. No!"

Charlie begins struggling in earnest, kicking the comforter off the bed. Her eyes are open but unfocused, and she's not registering her surroundings. I roll toward her. "Charlie," I say in a loud but gentle voice. "You're safe, Charlie. No one's going to hurt you. You're safe." I repeat myself close to her ear, but she's still not with me. I touch her shoulder as I say her name again.

In a flash, she throws her elbow back, catching me in the face as she growls curses. My head jerks back, and I rub my cheek. I'd forgotten how much elbows hurt. I avoid her elbow and wrap her in a secure bear hug so I can safely wake her, but restraining her only increases her agitation. With her arms immobilized, she arches her head backwards, aiming for my face. I tuck my head between her shoulder blades to protect my nose. I continue repeating her name, telling her she's safe, but it isn't helping.

Despite my firm grip on her upper body, I can't control her thrashing legs. In the past, I'd have wrapped my right leg around both of hers to hold her until I could wake her, but thanks to some asshole over in the Sandbox, I'm missing half of it. I attempt anyway, but she easily wriggles free and slams her heel back into the center of my healing thigh bone. I groan in pain and move my leg out of range.

I don't know what to do. Charlie isn't snapping out of it. She's not responding to my voice, and this bear hug isn't doing a damn thing to help. If anything, it's making her fight harder.

Should I release her and call Lila? Is there time? It'll take them several minutes to get dressed and drive over. Is it safe for this to keep going that long?

Fuck. I've got to wake her up.

After another minute of unsuccessful grappling and saying her name, I reach a horrible conclusion.

I have to turn her onto her stomach and pin her.

I don't want to. I feel sick for even considering it. Charlie is fighting, believing those bastards are trying to rape her again. Holding her down with my body is probably the worst thing I could do, but I have no idea how else to subdue her long enough to wake her and free her from her hell.

I close my eyes, hating myself as I lift her and roll her onto her stomach. She growls, "No!" followed by a series of expletives, fighting harder. I wrap both her legs in my left one and pin her upper arms at her sides. I bury my face between her shoulders as she continues trying to headbutt me. I use my weight to restrain her, repeating her name, telling her she's safe, that I'm here.

Only when I switch to calling her "Baby Girl" does her struggling noticeably diminish.

"Baby Girl, it's me," I say, and her screaming stops as her body stills. "It's me, Baby Girl. You're safe. No one's going to hurt you," I repeat, moving close, speaking into her ear. The fight leaves her, turning to wracking sobs. I roll off her immediately, and my heart throbs, echoing her anguish.

I turn her to face me. "Baby Girl?"

She puts her hands over her face, crying. I gently pull them down, needing to see her eyes to make sure she's fully present. The devastation in her expression rips me apart. "You're safe, Baby Girl," I murmur. "I've got you."

Charlie launches herself at my chest, sobbing harder than I've seen since they summoned me to Walter Reed. I tuck her face into my shoulder and hug her, stroking her hair.

I'm listed as Charlie's sole family member on all of her Army paperwork through a loophole formed when her parents became my legal guardians. It's the same loophole that allows her to be listed as my next of kin even though we're not related. Following her rescue, Charlie went into a catatonic state. She didn't speak, didn't eat, didn't do anything except stare into space. She rarely slept. When she did, she awoke with violent nightmares, screaming until they sedated her. The lead psychiatrist called Colonel Sherman to request I be flown stateside. If I couldn't get through to her, he'd recommend she be moved to a psychiatric facility for long term – and possibly permanent – care.

No pressure.

Colonel Sherman agreed without hesitating. Despite the differences in our ranks, he'd become our friend over the years. He was devastated by what happened to Charlie and Lila. He flew me out within the hour, and I arrived at Walter Reed shortly after midnight, unshaven, still dressed in fatigues. The nurse cautioned me that Charlie probably wouldn't respond, but allowed my visit anyway while someone kept watch from the doorway, ready to sedate her if things went poorly.

I'd quietly entered the dimly lit room. Charlie lay in the bed, eyes open but vacant, a frail figure motionless under spotless sheets. I stood at the foot of her bed and spoke to her, calling her name, but she didn't respond. Fear shot through me when I thought she didn't recognize me anymore. After a moment, I sat down on the edge of her bed and said, "Baby Girl, it's me. I'm here."

And I reached her.

She'd turned toward the sound of my voice, her sad eyes locking on my face. "Hey, Baby Girl." She'd burst into tears before crawling onto my lap to lay her head against my chest. I'd scooped her up and carried her to a recliner in the corner, cradling her on my lap like a child while she cried. The nurse tucked a blanket around us and quietly left the room. We stayed there until her psychiatrist arrived the following morning.

I was always the one who could reach her. I suppose the reverse is true as well.

I hold her close now as she trembles, letting her cry against my chest while I rub her back and press my cheek against her silky hair. It's a long time until she calms, and even longer before she speaks. "I'm sorry," she whispers finally.

I tilt her tear-stained face up. "You have nothing to be sorry for."

She glimpses my cheek and gasps, sitting up. "Oh my God. Did I do that?"

"I'm fine," I insist, sitting up as well. "I'm more worried about you."

She looks down. "I'm glad you had my gun."

I am too. She'd have shot me for sure, and this time, she wouldn't have missed. "Do you want to talk about it?"

She laughs sadly. "There's not much to talk about. Just reliving my own personal hell. I see them, smell them, feel them. It's like it's happening all over again."

She leans into me again, and I hug her tightly. "I'm sorry you're going through this."

She sighs. "It's a lot better than it was, thanks to you."

I hesitate. "I think I made it worse with the bear hug. I'm sorry."

She shakes her head again. "You were trying to help. Calling me Baby Girl made me realize it wasn't actually happening now."

We sit there for long moments before I speak again. "You haven't had a night terror that intense since the first night I got here. Did something change? Do I need to adjust the wake-up time?"

She's quiet for a moment. "I went to see a different therapist yesterday. I talked about things and it got a little too real. I had a panic attack in her office. I guess it stirred everything up."

I glance down in surprise. "I didn't know you were going to see someone else."

"I'm sorry. I should have told you."

I shake my head. "You don't have to tell me. I just didn't realize you'd changed doctors."

"I'm not leaving Linda. This woman focuses on teaching people to be more open, to foster emotional connection. I thought it might help me become comfortable around men. Maybe help me be less broken." She sighs deeply. "It didn't work out so great tonight."

"Can I do anything?"

She hesitates. "Really bad episodes leave me drained. Linda says intense crying makes the brain release endorphins to numb the pain. Even though I'm exhausted, I'm still anxious." She looks away when she says the word "anxious", like it's something shameful. "Would it be okay if you held me till I fall asleep, so I feel safe? Is that alright?"

I kiss the top of her head. "Of course it is." Hell, all this shit's my fault anyway. Her and Lila's kidnapping, her night terrors, making things worse tonight by manhandling her. Helping her feel safe so she can fall asleep is the least I can do. I'd give anything to undo the pain I've caused her.

We straighten the comforter and retrieve the fallen pillows, and I move to the center of the bed. Charlie reaches out and lightly touches my right cheekbone. It feels swollen and tender. I wonder how bad my thigh will look in the morning from her kick.

"I'm sorry I punched you," she murmurs.

"I grabbed you, so you were justified. Besides, you didn't punch me. You threw an elbow. Very nicely, I might add. You haven't lost your touch." Charlie was always skilled at hand-to-hand combat, and she knows sharp elbows often inflict more damage than blunt fists.

She winces. "Do you want some ice?"

"Nope. It looks worse than it feels. I'm fine." I lay down. "Come here."

She curls into me, nestling her head into my shoulder and laying her hand on my chest. I fold my arms around her, holding her close as I pull the covers up.

"You've called me Baby Girl for a really long time," she says out of the blue.

"Since you were fourteen and I was sixteen."

"You remember that?"

"I do."

"That's been...." She makes a face, counting in her head, but with her fatigue, it takes longer than usual. "Nineteen years."

I nod. "We've been together a long time."

"Why did you start calling me Baby Girl?"

I smile. "I can't tell you. It's a secret."

She raises her head. "What?"

"It's classified. I could tell you, but I'd have to kill you."

"What a load of crap," she mutters, laying her head back down on my shoulder.

I laugh. "Sometimes it's better for things to remain a mystery."

"I'm pretty sure this isn't one of those things."

I chuckle. "Good night, Baby Girl."

"Good night, Big Guy." There's a pause. "Thank you."

I kiss her head. "Any time."

I'm shocked by how quickly she falls asleep again. I figured she'd be awake for hours. Apparently, those endorphins are quite effective. Once her breathing is steady, I reach for my phone and draft a text to send at a more reasonable hour. I need advice from Lila and Tucker about waking Charlie up when she's trapped in a bad episode. They took care of her while I was still in Afghanistan. Maybe they can guide me in the right direction.

Charlie awakens a couple of hours later, long before her usual wake-up time. "My head is killing me," she mumbles, rubbing her neck at the base of her skull.

"Want some aspirin?" When she nods, I pass her a water bottle and a couple of tablets, which she quickly downs.

"Thanks."

I remember what she said last night. "How about I rub your neck and shoulders?"

"Really?"

I nod. "Roll onto your stomach." I wait for her to turn over, then move her thick hair to one side and slip my hands beneath the back of her tee shirt. My jaw clenches and my stomach knots as my fingers slide over the thickly textured scars along her back and shoulders.

Those fucking bastards.

Her muscles are as taut as steel cables. I start at her shoulder blades and gradually work up to her neck. I massage for a long time, feeling the tension in her muscles ease as my fingers unravel each tight knot. I work until her neck and shoulders are fully relaxed, then move to the base of her skull, finding more tense areas and kneading them into submission.

"Do you want a job?" Her voice is muffled. "Because I'll hire you in a flat second. Not for the clinic. Just for me."

I chuckle. "You can't afford me. I'm easy, but I'm not cheap. Did that help?"

She nods. "My head still hurts, but my neck feels much better."

"Try to go back to sleep. When is your first massage?"

"Not until ten. I can sleep a little later this morning."

I wait while she settles facing the door, then curl behind her while she dozes again. I smile when she drags my arm around her waist in her sleep.

Charlie sits up sleepily when her alarm goes off. I watch her stretch. "How are you feeling this morning?"

"Like a bird made a nest in my mouth and stuffed my head full of feathers. I'm going upstairs to brush my teeth," she mumbles.

"There are extra toothbrushes in my bathroom," I remind her. "Why don't you just start brushing your teeth down here?"

"Sold." She stumbles into the bathroom, reappearing a few moments later, pulling her hair away from her face.

"How's your headache?"

"Better. I just need a big dose of caffeine."

I smile. "I already started the coffee."

"You're a beautiful, brilliant man. Just for that, I'm making you toast. With jelly," she adds, flashing me a perfect but sleepy smile.

When she goes upstairs, I send the text I drafted last night. I don't know anything about full-blown night terrors except (now) what not to do. I need guidance so I can help Charlie with her pain as much as she's helped with mine.

CHARLIE

Thursday is ridiculously long. Not only am I tired from last night's episode, I've also somehow scheduled four fifty-minute, back-to-back (to-back-to-back) massages for the second day in a row. When my last one leaves at two, I flop into a chair at the table in the communal kitchen, rubbing my throbbing right hand with my aching left one.

Tom breezes into the kitchen, whistling as he heads for the refrigerator and pulls out a bottle of water. He sits down beside me and takes a long drink, then gives me a quizzical look.

"What are you doing?"

"My hands hurt. I overbooked myself."

"Want me to rub them?" he offers.

I hear Willow answer in my head. *Be open to affectionate touch.*

Just what I need. More voices in my head.

It's okay. This is Tom. I can do this.

I need to do this.

"That would be great." It would have sounded convincing if my voice hadn't broken.

Surprise shoots across his face, quickly replaced with his usual smile. He scoots his chair closer, leaning forward. "Which one do you want me to start with?"

Fear slithers through me, but I squelch it down. "My right one," I say, holding it out. Tom moves slowly, gently taking it in his bear-paw-sized hands before rubbing the pad at the base of my thumb. It feels so good, I groan.

He releases my hand immediately. "Did I hurt you?"

I shake my head. "It's a good hurt." He resumes the firm pressure, his huge fingers working in slow circles.

We sit in silence for a few moments before I hesitantly speak. "I talked to my therapist about how tired I am of being afraid to be touched."

Tom glances up but keeps massaging. "How'd that go?"

"She suggested I turn to a guy I trust and allow myself to be vulnerable with him. You know, simple touch. Affection." I swallow hard. "Maybe talk about hard things."

"Maybe let someone rub your hands?" he asks quietly.

My face grows hot. "When you say it out loud, it sounds really –"

"It sounds brave."

"Stupid. It sounds really stupid," I mutter.

"You're taking steps to break free from your fear. They don't have to be giant steps. Every step, big or small, moves you forward. That's not stupid. It's courageous. I'm honored to help."

I glance up. "Why?"

"Because it means you trust me, and trust isn't something you bestow easily."

My eyes soften. "I've always known I could trust you, but knowing it and controlling my reflexes are two very different things. She said I need to retrain my brain to remember that touch isn't always bad. She encouraged me to face my fear of vulnerability with someone I trust. I don't want to impose, though."

He laughs. "I can't imagine massaging your hands becoming an imposition, Charlie." He squeezes my fingers, one at a time, working the muscles in the pads. "It's Italian night again tomorrow at Casa di Edwards. The girls are either making lasagna or having me order pizza. They haven't decided yet." He shrugs. "But Maya and Skyler said you – and I'm quoting here – 'totally have to come'." He grins. "Are you free?"

"For Italian food? Obviously. What can I bring?"

"Just yourself."

"I'll bring dessert," I promise.

Friday evening, I show up at Tom's with a carrot cake. I knock, but there's no answer. I hear voices around back, so I let myself in and leave the cake in the kitchen. The stove is cold and empty. Apparently the girls opted for pizza.

"Knock, knock," I call, opening the back door and stepping onto the porch.

Maya and Skyler scramble to their feet. "Charlie!"

"Crap," Tom mutters. "We're not even cooking and I'm running late."

"Hello to you, too," I grin. "How can you be late?"

"I was going to walk Bella and then call in our order."

I shrug. "So let's walk her."

He glances at my feet. "Can you walk in those?"

I look down as well. "I haven't fallen down yet," I say cautiously. I'm wearing dark jeans and a cream sleeveless blouse with a tropical green and orange scarf, and my strappy gold sandals sport a two-inch heel.

He laughs. "Sorry. I'm used to women who buy 'cute shoes' they can't walk in."

I scoff, recalling Whitney's too-tight-to-walk-in dresses and sky-high stilettos. "That's because you're dating the wrong women. Cute or not, I'm not wasting money on non-functional footwear."

He grins. "Let me get Bella's leash."

I drop to my knees as the huge red dog bounds up the stairs toward me. She nearly bowls me over in her excitement before covering me in slobbery kisses. Tom reappears from just inside the house and playfully grabs her muzzle.

"Bella, sit." She stops playing and does as commanded. "Lay down," he says, and again, she immediately obeys. He clips her leash onto her collar.

"Such a good girl," I croon, and she licks my hand.

"If she'd quit knocking people down, I'd be a lot happier."

Maya and Skyler stay behind while Tom and I walk Bella. She trots happily along, ears flopping as she excitedly investigates every scent.

"You've fostered a lot of animals. What made you keep Bella and Eddie?"

He shakes his head. "Bella was small, maybe four months old, abandoned in an old warehouse. Somebody had chained her to a leaky pipe and left her there."

Like me. Despite the warm evening, a shiver runs down my spine.

"She was just skin and bones when a construction crew found her. She'd ground her teeth down to the gum line chewing on rocks and bricks because she was so hungry. When I fostered her, I fell in love. I couldn't give her up. They had to remove all of her teeth, so she's like the snow monster in that kids' Christmas movie – scary-looking, but harmless."

I frown. "She's not scary. She's beautiful." Bella turns back, thumping her tail and pushing her face into my palms as though she knows what I'm saying. I rub her jowls. "And sweet."

"She is beautiful," he agrees. "True fighters always are."

"That's why you named her Bella?"

"Technically, her name is Bellissimo Guerriero. It's Italian for 'Beautiful Warrior'. But yeah, we call her Bella." He shrugs. "I know. You can say it. I'm sappy."

I grin. "What about Eddie?" Eddie is their friendly black and white cat who's surprisingly athletic despite his disability. He can run faster and corner better with three legs than most cats can with four.

"He lost his leg in a trap, and no one wanted a three-legged cat. He looked miserable at the animal rescue center, so I brought him home to give him some normalcy. He fit in perfectly with us and bonded with Bella immediately."

I chuckle. "So your dog is 'Beautiful Warrior', but you named your cat Eddie Edwards?"

"Eddie is short for Edward. He's Edward Edwards."

A small giggle escapes me. "Bella and Edward? You named your pets Bella and Edward?" He glances over, not grasping the significance. "Who named him Edward?"

"Maya. Why?"

I stop walking, laughing out loud.

He stops, too. "Are you going to let me in on this joke?"

"Seriously? Bella and Edward?"

I see his mental wheels struggling to turn, but he's still not catching on. "I know Maya made you watch the movies. I had to endure your endless complaints."

He smacks his forehead the second it hits him. "Oh, God," he groans. "They're named after emo vampires? I'm gonna kill Maya. Jesus. That's just what every burly boxer wants, pets named after teenage – Oh my God." He rubs his hand through his hair in frustration.

I can't stop laughing. "You planted that seed when you named Bella. And I wouldn't call you burly. Lumberjacks are burly. You don't have enough facial hair or flannel to be a lumberjack."

"Do you prefer the term 'manly'? Would I qualify as a manly boxer?"

I try to stifle my giggles. "I can't believe you didn't catch on. You didn't think it was weird she wanted to name a cat Edward Edwards?"

"She's ten. I was happy she didn't want to call him Mr. Fuzzy Boots." He drags a hand over his jaw. "I have to change his name."

I shake my head. "Nope. You agreed, and he knows his name. Just because you didn't recognize Maya's intent doesn't mean you can change it now."

He purses his lips. "A nickname. I'll come up with a nickname."

The sun is dipping behind the nearby rocky peaks when we return. "The girls want pizza. Let me call in the order and we'll start the movie," he suggests.

"Sounds good. Do we know what the movie is?"

He shakes his head. "They had it narrowed down to three options. One has a princess and singing animals, one's a teenage girl band, and one's a superhero movie."

I bite my lip. "I'm not sure what to hope for."

"I'm rooting for superheroes."

The girls have disappeared upstairs, and I pause by his mantle, admiring the family photos stretching from one end to the other. There's one of a young Tom beside another young girl with dark hair, both perched on the edge of a pool, laughing. Another photo is of a woman, her husband, and four kids ranging from their late teens to roughly Maya's age. This must be Tom's sister, Tracy, and her family. Maya spends weekends with her cousins about once a month, and I've heard a lot of tales that I'm relatively certain neither Tom nor Tracy are aware of. Nothing dangerous, of course, but nothing either of them would endorse.

There are lots of pictures of Maya at various ages – a tiny sleeping infant curled against Tom's broad chest while he smiles proudly; a chubby-cheeked, tawny-complected toddler clad in nothing but a diaper, dragging a large stuffed bear while pointing at something outside the frame; Maya with Skyler, both of them five or six years old, with huge gap-toothed smiles, dressed in matching fluorescent pink bathing suits. There are also pictures of

Maya and Skyler at a butterfly exhibit a couple of years ago, each with dozens of butterflies lining their outstretched arms.

Heaviness falls over me, compressing my chest. I'll never have a daughter of my own. The reminder's been hovering around the outer edges of my mind since Lila told me she and Tucker were trying to conceive.

It's nothing new. You've known this for years. Let it go.

I force my attention back to the photos on the mantle. There's a new one that's been added since the last time I studied these. Maya's dressed in a winter parka with a faux-fur-lined hood. Huge snowflakes dot the photo. Maya stands beside a tall, lithe beauty with flawless chestnut skin, golden topaz eyes, and the same copper-highlighted curls as Maya.

Her mom, Chele, supermodel and Tom's ex-wife. Like Prince or Cher, she goes by a single name, and it's pronounced "shell"... and just like a seashell, she's beautiful on the outside, but empty where her heart should be.

I don't have much use for Chele. I don't give a crap about her money or success or fame. What I do care about is that she likes the title of motherhood far more than actually being a mother. Tom flies Maya to New York to see her mom two or three times a year. That's their only interaction, because Chele refuses to come to Colorado. It's apparently far too uncivilized here for her to grace Maya with her presence. She never calls, never emails, never sends birthday gifts, never remembers anything of significance. Despite that, just last year, she gave an interview in which she discussed the struggles of juggling motherhood with her career, giving the interviewer the impression she was a single mom, raising her daughter all alone.

Lila swears it wasn't her, and given the pain it caused Maya, I believe her, but someone went on several online entertainment forums and "enlightened" the media to the actual role Chele plays in her daughter's life. At that point, it became a scandal, and Chele's agent blamed the interviewer for twisting her words and misrepresenting her. The whole thing turned into a debacle, and while Chele came out of it fine in the end, it hurt Maya deeply.

That's why I don't care for Chele. She has an amazing daughter, but she only wants her when it's convenient. Meanwhile, my longing for an unscarred life with a loving husband and a houseful of kids and animals and chaos is unattainable, thanks to a bunch of assholes in the Afghan desert.

Tom, Maya, Skyler, and I spend the evening piled around his cozy living room, eating cheese-laden pizzas and salads. Tom ordered my favorite – Hawaiian – for the two of us to share, along with pepperoni for the girls. Tom is the only person I know who'll eat Hawaiian pizza with me. He orders it whenever we have pizza after finding out that I love it but never order it because Tucker, Lila, and Mark hate it. The girls choose the teen pop group on stage in London for our evening entertainment. Maya and Skyler occasionally put down their food to sing or dance while Bella enthusiastically joins in, howling and bouncing excitedly. I smile at Tom, who shrugs.

"It could be worse." We're beside each other on the sofa. I'd grinned and caught his eye when I sat down, deliberately resting my leg against his. He'd smiled and nodded. "Impressive."

I've been sitting that way for twenty minutes, and aside from an initial spiral of anxiety, I haven't panicked once.

"It could definitely be worse," I agree. "At least it's only an hour and a half."

When the concert finally ends, the girls go upstairs to Maya's room. "Make sure you leave your bedroom door unlocked," Tom calls after them. He gathers the dishes and I help him clean up. When we finish, he whistles for Bella. She scampers into the kitchen, skidding across the tiles. He glances over. "Want to sit outside? It's supposed to be nice tonight."

"Sure." I follow him as he holds the door open for Bella, who dashes down the porch steps and into his fenced-in backyard. He grabs a blanket from a shelf by the back door, then sits on his top porch step. I sit next to him, gazing up at the twinkling stars caught in the quiet interlude between sunset and night. The mountain air is cool but not cold, and the breeze gently whispers through the trees. Neither of us speaks, content to enjoy the peace.

In the silence, I hear Willow's voice in my head again. *You trust Tom. You can choose to be vulnerable with him.*

I've thought about it since my appointment. About telling Tom the dark, shameful truth about what happened in Afghanistan. About lowering the walls I use to keep people out. About inviting him deeper into my shitshow of a life.

I trust Tom, but the thought of exposing the whole truth of how screwed up I am terrifies me. I've erected my walls to protect myself from pain.

The problem is, those walls are also holding me back. In the long run, those protective walls are hurting me and my relationships with the people I trust.

My heart hammers in my chest. This is going to suck.

No, it's not.

I'm strong.

I'm a fighter.

I survived everything they did to me. Talking about it is nothing by comparison.

I'm not sure who that inner voice is, but I appreciate her encouragement.

I take a deep breath.

Fuck it. Bring on the awkwardness.

CHAPTER EIGHTEEN

CHARLIE

I LOOK OVER AT Tom, his eyes on the stars waking up to share their light. I swallow hard, forcing myself to speak before I lose my nerve. "I've been thinking about something my therapist said."

Tom unfolds the blanket and tucks it around my shoulders. "What's that?"

I weigh my words before replying slowly and deliberately. "She said intimacy between two people, not just romantic intimacy, but also closeness between friends, when you really know someone – it all starts when they allow themselves to be vulnerable. I've been very guarded with everyone since I moved to Cedar Ridge, physically and emotionally. I don't want to live like that anymore. I want to allow certain people to get closer. And that starts with me opening up." I glance over to find him watching me intently. "I was thinking about telling you what happened to me in Afghanistan." I look down at the steps.

I watch as Tom slowly reaches toward my hand. He holds his hand in front of mine, palm down and fingers spread, waiting to see if I'll take it.

I can do this.

I can trust him.

He's safe.

I take a deep breath and slide my hand into his. My small hand disappears beneath his huge one before he loosely laces our fingers together. I tense automatically but sit in the moment, not pulling away, reminding myself I can trust him until I relax into the warmth of his hand.

"You don't need to tell me anything you aren't ready to." His gentle voice breaks the silence. "Don't feel pressured to open up to me just because she told you to. This is something you should only do if you want to, and it should be on your timetable, not someone else's."

Tom telling me to do what's best for me rather than pushing me to bare my secrets strengthens my conviction that opening up to him is the right thing to do. "I've thought about it. I trust you, and I don't want you to be one of the people I keep at arm's length anymore. I want to let you in." I glance over nervously. "If that's okay, I mean."

He rests our joined hands lightly on my thigh, my hand on my own leg. "Of course it is."

I realize our arms are touching from shoulder to hand. I scan my emotions, amazed to find I'm not bothered. Not by that, anyway. I'm too afraid of how his view of me will change when he hears my story.

I draw a slow breath, trying to quell my nerves. "You already know the four of us were stationed together. One afternoon, a call came in. Insurgents had attacked a nearby village, and the locals needed medical attention. I.S. groups would sometimes attack villages near military posts because they viewed the villagers as American sympathizers. We took two medical trucks to go help. Both trucks had two soldiers up front and two medics in the back. The soldiers would protect us while we worked. We'd treat locals on site for minor injuries and load the seriously wounded in the truck and head for the field hospital, or if they were critically injured, we'd call a chopper.

"But this time was different. The insurgents had laid a trap. It's like the 'double wave' effect you see sometimes with suicide bombers. The goal of the first wave is to cause mass casualties, like hitting a crowded market or a village. The second wave of bombers attacks when first responders arrive. It instills more terror if people believe help can't get to them. That was their goal – to make the villagers fall in line while also ambushing us. Two for the price of one."

I have to stop for a moment. This is where it gets hard to talk about. Tom waits patiently, rubbing his thumb lightly over mine.

"Lila and I were in the back of the second truck. Max and Mike were our soldiers up front. We were almost at the village when I heard the shriek of an RPG just before it hit the first truck and killed everyone inside. Mike swerved to miss the explosion, and we flipped into a ditch. Lila and I got thrown around. She was knocked unconscious. I was injured, but I knew I had to get to my feet. I heard Max and Mike outside the truck. Mike stood guard while Max crawled in to help me with Lila." I close my eyes, remembering in excruciating detail my throbbing head, the blood in my eyes, and the harsh smell of the black smoke choking me, making it hard to see.

Tom squeezes my hand gently. I open my eyes. My breathing has picked up as the familiar bands tighten around my chest, but I need to do this, to talk about this. I take several deep breaths and steel myself against the pain.

I can do this.

I've already done this.

All I'm doing now is telling the story.

They can't hurt me now.

I swallow hard. "I heard gunshots, and we knew they'd shot Mike. Max burst out of the truck and started firing. I saw him fall when they shot him. I dragged Lila into the corner, knelt in front of her, and pulled my gun. I knew they were coming for us. They climbed into the truck to get us, and I just – I started picking them off, one by one. They kept coming, like a swarm of ants, but I didn't stop, and I didn't miss. I dropped four of them where they stood and hit five more. Those five died before we got to where they kept us. I fired every bullet I had and was trying to free Lila's gun when they got to me. I don't remember anything else until I woke up in the cell."

I'm not sure Tom's even breathing, but I can't bring myself to look at him after what I've just told him about calmly killing one man after another without so much as a drop of remorse.

"They were fascinated with Lila's blond hair and violet eyes. They'd never seen a woman like her. They underestimated her because she's beautiful, but she's a badass. You know that saying, 'It's not the size of the dog in the fight, it's the size of the fight in the dog'? That's Lila. The first man that tried to rape her bled to death in her cell. After that, they tied her down. Me, though..."

This is the part of the story I've dreaded most. I pause, swallowing against the growing lump in my throat. My heart slams against my ribs, and my eyes burn as I fight not to cry.

"They were furious with me – more than furious. They were enraged because I killed their men. It's a massive dishonor to die at the hands of a woman, especially an American infidel. The men I killed were banned from entering paradise, according to their beliefs." I drop my head and clench my jaw. Tom releases my hand and gently puts his arm around my shoulders, tucking me against him. I tense at first, but soon lean into him, hoping to draw strength from him.

Those fucking bastards. I'm glad they're dead, every last one of them. I hope every single one of them rots in hell because of what they did to people trying to save the lives of wounded innocents.

My jaw is still tight, and my fists are clenched. I breathe slowly, deeply.

They can't hurt me. I'm safe now.

All I'm doing is sharing information. Debriefing.

They can't hurt me, not ever again.

I unfist my hands and lift the wrist closest to him, moving it into the glow of the porch light.

"They wrapped my wrists with barbed wire and hung me by my arms from a pipe in the ceiling. The wire cut all the way to my bones." I move my stacked bracelets aside to expose the circumferential scars I keep covered. "They stripped me to humiliate me. They shredded my back and hips with a homemade whip of leather strips and razor wire. They had a metal brand with the words 'stupid cunt whore' in Arabic, and they branded me with it across my back." I look down again. "They hit me. Kicked me. Broke my cheekbone and my nose, some ribs and my tailbone. I had internal bleeding." I stop, staring blankly into the darkened sky. "They used a rusty boning knife on me. Mutilated my breasts and –" A strangled sound escapes me. I take another deep breath. "And internally. They made sure I can't have children, though they'd never planned for me to survive. And they raped me, not just with their bodies, but with bottles and pipes and anything else they could find. I have more scars than I can count, Tom, and not just physically."

I stop when I feel tears trickle down my face. When I move to dry them, Tom gently brushes them away with his thumb. I lean my head on his shoulder.

"Eleven days," I say quietly. "They had us for eleven days and nights before Mark led the rescue team. If he and Tucker and the others hadn't found us when they did, we wouldn't have survived much longer, maybe a couple of days." I hesitate. "For a long time, I wished I'd died there. The fear, the nightmares, the depression... It's a lot to deal with, and God knows, I've not done very well. I drank pretty heavily at first," I admit, "but alcohol was only a temporary way to numb things, and when I sobered up, the pain was still there. I saw a psychiatrist, and she helped, but not as much as I'd hoped."

When I continue, my voice is barely a whisper. "You know I have panic attacks. What you don't know is that I also have night terrors, where I wake up screaming and fighting because I believe it's happening all over again. I've woken up disoriented and shot holes in my walls because I believed they were attacking me again.

"I'm not telling you this to freak you out or push you away. I'm saying it because –" I falter momentarily. "Because I'm a train wreck, and you have a young, impressionable daughter. You deserve to know who I really am, so you can decide if you want Maya hanging out with someone who's done the things I've done. And I'm telling you because even if you don't see me the same way anymore, I wanted you to know the real me, the one I hide from almost everyone else."

Tom sits quietly with me. I'm trembling under the thin blanket, but my chill has nothing to do with the temperature. Finally, he leans over and presses a featherlight kiss to my temple. His voice is as soft as velvet when he speaks. "I'm so sorry for what you've been through, Charlie." Then he wraps both arms around me loosely, so I won't feel trapped.

I don't feel afraid or trapped. It's comforting. I hug him back, tighter than he's hugging me, and when I turn my face into his chest, he rubs my back, resting his cheek on my head. We stay like that until Bella bolts up the steps, pushing her face between us to drop a slobbery yellow ball in Tom's lap.

I chuckle and move one arm, but stay where I am, still leaning into him. Tom throws the ball for Bella, and she bounds after it, chasing it under a bush and hurling herself beneath it to retrieve it. He wraps his arm around me again.

"You're not a train wreck, Charlie," he says into the silence.

I laugh sadly. "Trust me, I am."

He shakes his head. "You're not. You're an incredibly strong woman."

My voice sounds small, even to me. "I don't feel strong at all."

"Strength and courage aren't feelings. Strength is pushing on when you don't think you can, and courage is being afraid to do something and doing it anyway. Look at everything you've accomplished these last two days. You let me rub your hands. You took my hand. You're leaning on me. You're letting me comfort you. Those are all firsts, and that's just the physical part. The emotional part? Opening up? That's the hardest part, the scariest part, and you did it. You chose to be vulnerable, to bare your pain and bring your demons into the light. That's strength. That's courage."

Tom looks down at me. "I absolutely want Maya to have you as an influence. You and Lila are two of the few positive female role models in her life. And as far as whether I see you differently now? Yes, I do."

My heart drops.

Of course he does. How could he not? I gunned down nine men and I shoot holes in my walls.

I'd expected it, and I understand, but his words still sting. I move to pull away, but he tips my chin up until I look at him.

"I see you differently because you let me see who you really are." He smiles, trying to lighten my mood. "You're like Bella. A beautiful warrior."

My eyes fill with tears again, but for once, they aren't sad tears. Tom accepts me, even with my past. He doesn't think I'm a train wreck. And he's comfortable with me being around Maya, even after hearing my shameful secrets.

He stands up, reaching down and tugging me to my feet, whistling for Bella. "You're shivering. Come back inside, and I'll tell you about my own demons."

Tom leads me back into the living room. I sit down on the couch, removing the blanket from my shoulders and folding it neatly. Bella flops in front of the fireplace as Tom chooses a framed photo from the mantle and joins me. The picture is one I'd admired earlier.

"I grew up a little north of here, closer to the peaks. There were three of us kids. You've heard me talk about my older sister, Tracy, and her four kids. I was the middle child. And I had a baby sister named Dana."

Had. Past tense. A sudden sadness fills my chest.

"Dana and I were close growing up. Tracy's five years older, so there was enough of a gap that I was her annoying little brother. Dana and I were only a couple of years apart, and we were inseparable. She was my baby sister, and I was her protector, from the playground up through high school. Nobody messed with Dana because they knew they'd have to answer to me.

"When I left for college in New York, Dana took it hard. She was a junior when I left, but I flew home for long weekends and school breaks every chance I got. My mom took this picture of us during spring break her senior year." He hands the picture to me.

A beautiful girl laughs, leaning against a much younger Tom who's also laughing. Both are deeply tanned and fit, sitting with their legs submerged in a crystal blue swimming pool. Her long brown hair spills over her shoulders to her bright orange bikini top, and Tom is shirtless, wearing blue swim trunks. They look happy and carefree. Dana has Tom's mischievous smile and twinkling eyes. "She's beautiful," I say softly.

"Three days before her prom, I flew her out to New York for the royal treatment – manicure, pedicure, facial, cut and color, spa time. I wanted her to feel like a princess. I took her to some of my favorite spots. We had a great time." His smile fades as he looks down.

"Dana had started seeing a guy I didn't know. He was new to the area. I'd heard from friends that he wasn't the nice guy she thought he was. Before she flew home, I told her to be careful, but she laughed and said she was fine, that I needed to relax."

He stops talking. I know where this is going, and without a second thought, I lay my hand on his forearm.

"He raped her the night of the prom. Drugged her and raped her. He was rough. Hurt her pretty badly. She went to the police, but even with the drugs in her system, he said it was consensual, and with no witnesses, it was he-said, she-said. He'd taken pictures of her and passed them around. My dad called." He pauses again. "I flew home, found the guy. I mouthed off enough to get him to throw the first punch, then broke his jaw and some facial bones and left him unconscious. I called the police myself. The officer that came knew what had happened to Dana, so when witnesses said the other guy threw the first punch, he called it self-defense. The guy spent eight weeks with his jaw wired shut, eating through a straw. But it wasn't enough."

He drops his head, elbows on his knees as he stares, tangled in tragic memories. "Dana never recovered," he says finally. "I called her every day, but she became a shadow of the girl she'd been. She withdrew from everyone, quit hanging out with her friends, stopped talking to my parents. I had classes over the summer, but I had a two-week break coming up, and I kept telling myself that when I got home, I could get through to her. I could help her."

He sits silently for a full minute. I know what he's going to say, and it breaks my heart for both of them – for the girl who couldn't bear the pain, and for the older brother who blames himself for something that wasn't his fault.

His voice breaks. "She killed herself. Left a letter, went into the woods, and shot herself. I wasn't there to protect her, and I wasn't there to help her pick up the pieces."

Tom's jaw is tight, his eyes bright with tears. Without hesitating, I pull him into a hug. He grips me tightly, but it doesn't frighten me. I rub his back, offering the only consolation I can.

After several minutes, I lean back slightly. He releases me immediately, thinking the contact has been too much for me, but I shake my head and hold his gaze. Tom is consumed with undeserved guilt. I place my hands on either side of his face, rubbing my palms through the soft stubble of his short beard.

"It wasn't your fault." A wall comes down behind his eyes as he automatically dismisses my words, and I give his head a tiny shake. "Listen to me. You aren't to blame. The bastard that hurt her is. Even if you'd been here, she'd have gone to the prom with him. You couldn't be with her every moment. He was a coward. Cowards lie in wait, too afraid to strike when there's risk to themselves. Even if you'd been here afterwards, Dana is the only one who could have decided if she wanted to keep fighting. For some people, the pain is unbearable."

"I could have helped her," he insists. "I could have carried some of the load."

"Not if she wasn't willing to share it. Some pain is just too heavy to share."

He closes his eyes, his expression anguished. "I let her down. She needed me, and I wasn't there. And I miss her. God, I miss her." His breathing picks up speed. He's on the verge of breaking down, but he's fighting it.

I remove my hands from his face and pull him close again, hugging him tightly, not the least bit afraid. He buries his face in my neck. I run my fingers through his soft hair, stroking his head like a child. After a long time, his shoulders relax as he regains control of his emotions. When he finally raises his head, I gently press a kiss to his cheek.

Tom catches my chin between his thumb and forefinger. "What was that for?"

"To remind you that you're not alone."

"Thank you," he says. He lightly kisses my forehead and moves back, studying my face in the lamplight before speaking.

"Dana would have been thirty-two now. Maybe married, maybe with a couple of little ones. She never got the chance to heal. She hurt too badly to try. You're trying. You're opening up, even though it terrifies you." His eyes linger on my face. "You remind me of her in a lot of ways. Maybe that's why I'm so protective of you." He frowns. "Especially with some of these dates Lila's sent you on."

"I had drinks with Blake last Friday."

He nods. "I heard."

"I'm having dinner with him and his nieces again tomorrow."

His expression becomes suddenly guarded. "Be careful with him, okay?"

My eyes flash to his, startled. "Why?"

"Nothing like that. He won't lay a hand on you," he says quickly. "He's hot-tempered when he's embarrassed, but that shouldn't be an issue with you. A few weeks ago, he lost his shit after a guy at the gym kicked his ass while sparring. What I meant was – well, Blake is nice, but he isn't the relationship type, and he never lacks for female company."

I relax a little. "He told me he has trust issues and avoids commitments because of his failed marriage. The bit about his hot temper surprises me because he seems so Zen," I admit. "But I'm not looking for a relationship, so I'm glad he doesn't want one, either. This is merely a minor adjustment to the Winners versus Whiners. For the first time, I've agreed to a second date. I'm not planning on doing anything but getting comfortable being around a guy again."

He smiles. "You've done exceptionally well tonight. I'm impressed. You should be, too."

I smile, too. "I am, actually. Physical contact, emotional vulnerability. Who knew a therapist might actually know what she was talking about?"

Tom lightly squeezes my fingertips, and I don't flinch or panic. "Thank you for trusting me."

I laugh. "Letting you see my train wreck of a life probably isn't something you should thank me for."

He shakes his head. "You're not a train wreck, Charlie. You're a fighter, and I'll fight alongside you anytime. I'll do anything to protect my family, bloodborne or chosen." Tom referring to me as family brings me to tears again, and he hugs me again before I leave.

I consider the wisdom of Willow's words on my short drive home. Intimacy begins with an emotional connection.

I've been more open and intentionally intimate with Tom than with anyone since my trauma. I didn't need to tell Lila – she lived it with me – or Mark, because he saw it when he rescued me.

Tonight was different. I invited Tom in, sharing things I've tried to bury, and he didn't pull away. On the contrary, he offered to wade into the trenches beside me. Then he shared his own pain, allowing me access to a part of himself he keeps tucked away.

It's truly intimate. Not romantically, but in a soul-baring kind of way.

This was what Willow was talking about. Because I was willing to be vulnerable and let Tom in, we connected on a deeper level.

A smile crosses my face as I pull into the driveway. I leaned against Tom. I consoled him and let him console me. I hugged him. I kissed his cheek.

I showed physical affection and didn't panic.

Maybe there is something to this intimacy business after all.

CHAPTER NINETEEN

MARK

TUCKER SHOWS UP SHORTLY after Charlie leaves for dinner with Tom and Maya. He'd texted me earlier to ask if he could stop by. When I meet him at the door, he's carrying his laptop. I tip my head at it as he closes the door behind him. "What's with the computer?"

"You asked us about dealing with night terrors," he answers, leading the way into the living room. "I figured I'd field this one since I've dealt with them with both Lila and Charlie."

We sit down on the couch. I explain what happened last night with Charlie while he opens the camera program on his laptop. He winces when I get to the part about holding her arms and shakes his head vehemently when I describe rolling her onto her stomach and pinning her down.

"If it happens again, don't touch her. Move away so you can't even accidentally make contact. In that moment, anyone who touches her is her attacker."

My spirit sinks as I remember how poorly she reacted to my touch. "I know that now. At the time, all I could think about was waking her up."

"Lila would become more... defensive, I guess, although that's not the most accurate way to describe it. With her night terrors, she'd bolt awake in a panic and sort of fold in on herself. If I touched her, she'd turn ferocious, but as long as I didn't come near her, she didn't. I'd talk to her calmly and reassure her until she woke up enough to realize where she was. Her flashbacks were different. She was awake, but she wasn't present. In her mind, she was still in that cell, fighting to free herself. All I could do was back off and talk to her until she was with me again."

"What did you say to snap her out of it?"

He shakes his head. "It's not about what you say. Your words won't register, but your voice and your tone will. In that moment, she believes you're the bastards who attacked her. When it sinks in that you're not yelling, that you're speaking gently and not touching her, her mind will pause and reassess. Hearing your voice will draw her back to the present. Touching her will have the opposite effect." He glances at my face. "Is that how you got that bruise?"

I nod. "Charlie threw an elbow when I put my hand on her shoulder."

"Remember how I said as long as I didn't touch Lila, she'd go into defensive mode?" He waits for me to nod again. "Not Charlie. She immediately goes on the attack." His hand hovers over the touchpad of his laptop. "You up to seeing footage of her on the bench?"

"Having a night terror? I guess so. I saw her have one last night."

"Brace yourself," he warns me, then presses play. I watch the scene play out before me. It starts with Charlie asleep on the bench. Her knees are pulled to her chest, gun loosely gripped in her right hand, her head on her knees. Within seconds, her head snaps up, scanning the area with unseeing eyes. Her feet drop to the floor. Her shoulders twitch erratically. "She's only moving her shoulders because she believes her arms are still tied above her head," Tucker says quietly.

My stomach lurches as I keep watching. Her upper body spasms intensely before her whole body explodes into movement, kicking, thrashing, punching empty space. Tucker adjusts the volume so I can hear her snarled profanities. My chest tightens as she fights to free herself from long-dead assailants. She slides smoothly off the bench into a crouched stance facing the living room, her gun firmly held in both hands as she stares down the barrel. A flash erupts from the muzzle as she fires three times in rapid succession. Her spine stiffens at the noise, and she pants as her head sweeps the room from side to side. "The gunfire usually breaks through her terrors," he mutters.

I lift my gaze to his troubled blue eyes. "Usually?"

He sighs heavily. "Sometimes we'd have to come over."

I look back at the screen, envisioning Tucker and Lila entering the home of an armed sharpshooter trapped in the throes of a night terror. "And do what?"

He shakes his head. "We have kevlar vests and helmets. I'd unlock her door and cut the chain with bolt cutters."

"And go inside? With her like that?" Jesus. Talk about a recipe for disaster.

He shakes his head. "We'd stand on either side of her front door and talk to her from outside until she knew where she was. Then Lila would calm her down."

I close my eyes. I never knew. I was half a world away, with my best friend reliving brutal horrors night after night, and I never knew.

"I wish you'd told me." My voice is quiet, but there's no accusation in my words. "I understand why you didn't, but I wish I'd known."

"You couldn't have helped from where you were, and Charlie needed you to come home alive. She was barely hanging on as it was. Losing you would have destroyed her."

My eyes return to the screen. Charlie's sitting on her backside now, knees bent, gun on the floor beside her. She's still breathing hard, but she's talking to the camera in the ceiling. The pain in her expression guts me. Tucker closes the program. "You said Lila had flashbacks and night terrors. Does Charlie have flashbacks, too?"

He shakes his head. "Not that I've ever seen. And Lila's were mostly when I would touch her, when I first came home. She hasn't had them in a while now."

I draw a slow breath. "So I stay out of reach and talk to her? That's all I can do?"

Tucker nods. "You'll feel completely and utterly helpless. Suck it up. It's not about you. It's about getting through to Charlie without escalating her fear. Until she realizes where she is and that she's safe, touching her will only make things worse."

It's late when Charlie gets in. I'm prone on the living room floor having "tummy time", as we now refer to it, stretching and straightening my thigh. I roll to my side and look up when she pauses beside me. "Hey, Baby Girl. How was your evening?"

"Different," she muses, "but good."

"You're smiling."

"I am. I'm going up to shower and change. Do you need anything before I head upstairs?"

"I'm good, thanks." I turn onto my stomach again as she jogs upstairs.

When I'm done, I grab a bottle of water and stretch out on the sofa. I can't erase the images I saw on Tucker's laptop from my mind. Until I came home, Charlie relived what those bastards did every time she'd close her eyes. Knowing I'm beside her, knowing I'll protect her with my life, has allowed her to mostly move past that. The magnitude of her trust in me leaves me awed.

I only wish I deserved it.

After several minutes, Charlie comes downstairs and stops in the kitchen. She joins me moments later with iced tea. I'm surprised when she curls against my side and leans her head on my shoulder. "Got a minute?"

I look down at her anxious expression. "What's up?"

She sits up, then bites her lip. "I need to talk to you about tonight, but I have to back up a couple of days first."

I nod, curious.

"I told you I'd seen a new therapist. She's actually an intimacy counselor slash sex therapist. Lila recommended her."

A sex therapist? That's the last thing I'd have expected her to say, considering the way she panics around men. Then I recall our discussion last night. "This is the therapist who encouraged you to be open and vulnerable?"

She nods. "Her name is Willow. I made the appointment because –" she falters "– because at the end of my date with Blake, the thought of a goodnight kiss sent me into a full-blown panic, even though he wasn't even within two feet of me. And I'm tired of freaking out for no reason, so I called her."

So that's what was troubling her after her date. I study her face. "What did you think of her?"

"She made some good points. She said all intimacy, whether between friends or partners, starts with emotional connections. The only way to form real connections is to share your authentic self with someone else."

I nod. "Makes sense."

"Right. And in my case, the only two people I'm ever intentionally vulnerable with are you and Lila. Even with Tucker, I sort of keep my guard up. I'm not afraid of him," she says hastily, "but he and I aren't as close as you and I are, or Lila and I are. It's like I have one tight inner circle that's you, and slightly further out is Lila's circle, and the next circle would be Tucker, and then Tom, and then a lot further out would be Blake and other people. And instead of bringing people closer, I keep them out."

I nod. "You've been hurt, so you don't open yourself up emotionally, and that limits your connections."

"Exactly. And even though I went to see her to stop freaking out about physical contact, she said what I really needed was to forge emotional connections. She also suggested I open up more with males I do trust, specifically Tucker and Tom, and trying some affectionate touch with them. You know, things like hugs or – hell, just basic human contact. She said it would help me see male touch in a positive light, which would help me stop panicking with Blake."

I nod again. "That's reasonable."

She's silent. I remember this was her prelude to whatever was on her mind when she came downstairs. After another minute, I take the plunge. "What happened tonight, Charlie?"

She sighs. "It's the whole 'open and vulnerable' thing. I decided to bare my whole shitshow of a life for Tom to see. He's been a good friend, and I'm tired of shutting him out. It wasn't exactly that I thought he'd think less of me. But talking about it... it makes *me* think less of me. Anyway, I told him about Afghanistan. Everything. The initial attack. Picking them off. What they did. Why they hated me. How it fucked me up. How I drank. How I still struggle with night terrors and panic attacks and discharging my weapon."

Emotions play across her face as I watch her talk – dejection, resignation, and disgust – and I'm saddened to realize the one she's most disgusted with is herself, not with the barbaric assholes who got off on rape and torture, or with me, the one to blame for the whole thing.

"How did Tom react?"

"Pretty well. He put his arm around me while I talked, and I didn't freak out. He said I wasn't a train wreck," she laughs sadly, "which is sweet but untrue. He called me strong, which doesn't feel true at all." She hesitates. "He said he did see me differently, because I let him see the real me. He called me a warrior and a positive role model for Maya. And he opened up, too. He told me about his baby sister who committed suicide after being raped." My stomach fists. "He said I remind him of her, and that's partly why he's so protective." She smiles weakly. "I even hugged him of my own volition."

"Those are all good things, Charlie." Her earlier distress seems out of place with the progress she's describing.

Her face falls, and she stares down at her hands. "I know. But when I talked about Afghanistan with Willow the other day –" She breaks off.

Understanding dawns. "You're afraid it's going to be another bad night."

Her voice is barely a whisper. "Terrified."

I lift her chin until she looks at me, her emerald eyes clouded with fear. "I talked to Tucker to learn how to help with your night terrors. I'll stay beside you, but I won't touch you, and I'll call you Baby Girl until you come out of it. And if you need me to, I'll hold you all night afterwards and rub your neck and shoulders. Whatever you need me to do, I'll do it, Charlie. You're not alone."

She nods, still unable to speak, but she hugs me. When she finally leans back, I scrutinize her, wondering whether to ask about something I've never understood. "Can I ask you a question?"

"Of course."

"You said you explained to Tom why they hated you. You specifically, as opposed to Lila. What did you mean?"

Surprise flits across her face. "You know all this."

I shake my head. "I know they took you and Lila and killed the others, but that's all I know, at least until I saw what they did to you two." I pause. "If it's too hard to talk about, forget I asked. I don't want to make your dreams worse tonight."

She shrugs. "My demons have already been unearthed today, so it can't make things any worse." She takes a deep breath. "When the RPG hit the first truck, Mike swerved and our vehicle flipped. Lila and I were tossed around in the back of the truck. She hit her head pretty hard." She grimaces, remembering. "I thought at first that she'd been killed because she was unconscious and her neck was at such an awful angle. I could hear Mike and Max, and I yelled for them to help me with her. Max climbed inside with me while Mike stood guard. When they shot Mike, Max charged out, and I saw him fall, too. I knew they'd kill us, so I pushed Lila into the corner behind me and pulled my gun. When they started climbing in, I picked them off like fish in a barrel. I shot nine of them." Her voice is low, and I have to work to hear her. "I dropped four where they stood. The other five died before we got to their hideout. I hit center mass on every shot. I fired every bullet I had, but they just kept coming. I'd lost my extra magazine when our vehicle rolled. I was trying to get Lila's gun free when they rushed me, and then everything went black."

She pauses, gathering her thoughts. I watch her closely, but she doesn't look upset. She seems detached, maybe because she's already pictured it once tonight.

"Lila came around before I did. They looked at her and saw an insignificant little blond plaything. They threw her in a cell with a blood-stained wooden table with iron rings along its edges. The first asshole that went into her cell was a huge bearded man. When he came in alone and locked the door, she thought he was there to intimidate her into answering his questions. Instead, he shoved her to her knees. Then he dropped his pants and grabbed her face." She looks down. "Well, you can imagine what he wanted."

Fury rises in my chest as I remember the night we rescued them, when I saw what the two women who mean so much to me went through at the hands of those cruel bastards.

"But Lila's one hundred percent badass. She didn't panic. She batted those big violet eyes, gave him her best come-hither smile, and moved toward him instead of struggling. He was so excited, he let go of her face." Charlie smiles without humor. "She bit down and didn't let go until she'd torn it off and spit it on the floor. When he collapsed, she latched onto his neck like a wolf and ripped his throat out before the others finished fumbling with the keys. They were horrified by the tiny blonde baring her bloody teeth, daring them to try next. It took five men to shackle her facedown on that table, and even after she was restrained, they never went into her cell alone again.

"I was a different story, though. When I regained consciousness, I was already strung up. They were livid. The I.S. claims it's dishonorable to be killed by a woman, especially an American infidel. They say men won't get into paradise if that's how they die. And this American infidel –" she taps her chest "– killed nine of their men and denied them their virgin-filled paradise. That's why I was whipped and branded and mutilated, and Lila wasn't. They felt the man she killed had shown weakness in falling for her deception."

I'm speechless, both at Lila's tenacity and Charlie's strength.

I should have pieced it together from the scene. Charlie's right – all the bodies we found were shot center mass. Even under tremendous pressure, her aim never wavered. And I'd never understood why the insurgents had left their fallen men when there'd been ample time to retrieve them. Most Muslims are devoted to respectful care of their dead. Were those men left behind because they died at the hand of an American woman?

I study her green eyes. They're somber, but calm. "You never told me any of this."

She shrugs. "I assumed you knew."

I shake my head. "We found four of their bodies at the truck, and Lila said she remembered hearing you fire your gun, but that's all. I didn't know you shielded her. I didn't know you were the one who shot those men. And I never understood why you were tortured in ways Lila wasn't. Now I do. It was because of your strength."

Her eyebrows pull together in confusion. "What?"

"Your strength. Your spirit. Your fight. You never backed down. That's why they hated you. They couldn't break you. You think those bastards took everything from you. You believe you're weak." I tip her chin up to look me in the eye. "Charlie, you're the strongest person I know."

Her mouth falls open. "I don't know what to say," she mumbles.

"Just file it away and remind yourself of it when you need to hear it." I lift her hand and kiss her knuckles. "Come on. Let's get ready for bed."

I watch her put away the mirror after she finishes my massage. "I have another question, Baby Girl." She glances over. "I've been researching night terrors, and they recommend relaxing bedtime routines, things like music or massage or yoga. Want to give it a try?"

She grins. "You want to do yoga with me?"

I chuckle. "I'll try it if you want me to, but I doubt it'll go well. I meant you could put on some soothing music, and I'll give you a back rub."

Her eyes fly to mine. "You'd give me a back rub?"

"Not if it would make you uncomfortable," I say hastily. "I just thought –"

She shakes her head. "That's not it. It's just – won't my scars bother you?"

I scowl. "It won't bother me to rub your back any more than it bothers you to massage my leg because some bastard blew half of it off. They're both battle wounds."

She hesitates. "They're very... textured."

I start to remind her that I rubbed her shoulders a couple of nights ago, but don't. I don't want her to not ask in the future because of her worry that I might be bothered by her scars. "Does it hurt when they're touched?" I ask instead.

"No."

"So you're telling me they're textured just to warn me?"

"I guess."

I frown. "Then quit being stupid."

"I just don't want you caught off guard. They're a lot to take in." Her face reddens.

I think about how she always keeps her back covered. She's ashamed of her scars. I keep my voice gentle. "Charlie, I saw your wounds when they were raw, and I was there when they were healing. Your scars won't bother me."

She finally nods and picks up her phone, finding something that sounds like bamboo wind chimes and trickling water. I reach for the bottle of oil. "Turn around," she says, reaching for the hem of her shirt. I comply and hear the rustle of fabric. The bed shifts as she lays down. "Okay."

She pulls a hair tie from her wrist, securing her hair out of the way. I squirt massage oil into my hands and warm it between my palms as I study her bare back.

Fucking savages.

Thick purple ropes and jagged, thin lavender stripes mar her entire back and dip below the waistband of her shorts. Across the middle of her back is that goddamn brand, flat and pale, a collection of artistic dips and wide swirls that might be pretty — if they weren't burned into her flesh.

Stupid cunt whore. They branded her with their vile slurs, forever emblazoning their lies on her soft skin.

I remember my tantrum in San Antonio and once again feel sick. I'd give anything to take that back. To take every second of it back.

Most of all, I'd like to take back my mindless agreement to send two medical teams to help those villagers. Every bit of the hell she's been through is my fault for dropping my guard.

I place oiled hands on her back and start to massage in long strokes, working from the small of her back to her neck and shoulders. Within a minute, she's relaxing into my touch.

"Visualize something relaxing."

"I don't know what to visualize," she mutters.

"Lying on a beach, listening to the rain, whatever. Hell, I don't know. Just pick something."

She snickers. "Some visualization coach you are."

"Just shut up and picture something relaxing," I grumble, untangling her tightly knotted neck and shoulder muscles. Within a few minutes, I'd swear she's melted into the bed. I haven't seen her this relaxed in years.

I'm anything but relaxed, though. I'm still processing her earlier revelations. It's always troubled me that Charlie's treatment at the hands of her captors was markedly different from Lila's. Not that they weren't awful to Lila as well – obviously, they were – it's just that they did particularly horrific things to Charlie that they didn't do to Lila. It never made sense, not that most of what those fuckers did made sense. It's impossible to rationalize that level of intentional brutality. Lila told me once that she didn't understand why they did things to Charlie that they never did to her. She'd started crying then, saying she felt guilty for being grateful that they hadn't, even after she'd killed the first man who'd tried to assault her.

I didn't know until tonight how Lila had killed him. I hadn't asked at the time because she was so upset.

Nine. Charlie killed *nine* of those fuckers, crouched in the corner of an overturned vehicle, protecting Lila's life with her own. If she hadn't lost her extra magazine when the humvee flipped, she might have doubled that number. Yet she sees herself as weak? Charlie's the strongest person I know, a warrior through and through.

After about twenty minutes, I finish her back rub with several long, smooth strokes. "I'll turn around while you get dressed."

"I'm not sure I can move," she mumbles.

I chuckle and turn away. "I can just pull the comforter over you and let you sleep if you want." I feel the bed shift as she sits up. "What did you visualize?"

"My stream in the woods. I'm dressed," she adds, climbing under the covers.

I turn around and wait for her to get settled before sliding in beside her. "Feeling relaxed?"

"More than I have in years. Thank you." She scoots against me and faces the door.

I kiss her hair and wrap one arm around her waist. "Anything for you, Baby Girl."

I'll do anything to make up for the shit my actions have put her through.

CHARLIE

I hear them long before I see them – angry male voices rapidly approaching from behind. The sound snaps me into consciousness. I strain to catch their words. There's three voices, or maybe four. It's hard to tell because their heated words overlap and tumble over each other. I try to move, to get away, but I can't. My fogged brain becomes aware of sharp pain in my shoulders and wrists. I look up, finding twisted barbed wire digging into my wrists, suspending me from a pipe in the ceiling with my feet off the ground. I struggle to free myself, but it's futile.

I hear a roar of fury from one of them.

He's coming for me.

There's venom in his tone, and I'm the murderous infidel.

The metal door of my cell bangs open a split second before a booted foot slams into my lower back, sending pain shooting through my tailbone and down my legs. I bite my lip to keep from crying out. I breathe slowly through my mouth.

No fear. No tears. Game face on.

Fucking cowards. I won't let them win. I won't give them the satisfaction of breaking me, no matter what.

My nude body swings from the force of the kick. Rough hands grab and hold me as a short man moves in front of me. He's angry, like a bitter chihuahua that's been kicked its whole life. That's what I name him in my head – the Chihuahua, small and mean to conceal his own cowardice. His soulless dark eyes glitter with hate. He glares before forcefully backhanding me.

I taste blood.

Without hesitation, I spit on him. Bloody spittle splatters across his cheek. He narrows his eyes, wiping it off with his sleeve, then punches me in the face. There's a crunch of breaking bone, and blood pours from my nose.

He begins screaming, gesturing wildly. His anger seems overly personal. One of the bastards I killed must have been a friend or family member.

He's here for revenge. He wants to hurt me.

He wants to make it slow.

Fuck that. I'd rather die quickly than die a slow, torturous death.

I just need to goad him into it.

Bracing myself for another punch, I meet his eyes, smiling through bloody teeth. "He died whimpering like a coward," I declare, laughing condescendingly.

One of the men behind me must understand English, because he rattles off something to the man in front of me. The Chihuahua turns apoplectic, his face reddening. He bellows down the hall and a man enters, handing him something coiled. The Chihuahua moves in front of me and lifts it, fanning it out for me to see. My eyes widen involuntarily as I realize he's holding a whip. It's no Indiana Jones bullwhip, either. This one is handmade, with a duct-tape grip and numerous tails of metal and glass-studded leather strips and strands of razor wire. Horror washes over me.

I raise my eyes to his face and find him watching me closely. He's waiting to see my terror, hoping I'll beg.

Dream on, you cowardly little bitch.

Lightning fast, I spit on him again. He wipes his face again and laughs cruelly, then steps behind me, out of sight.

The first fiery slash of the whip takes my breath away as it slices my back and hips. After the initial shock, I try to steel myself, but his lashes come one on top of the next, like lightning bolts in a fierce thunderstorm. The intense pain makes me nauseous. I'm panting like a thoroughbred, but I refuse to cry out, clenching my teeth till my jaws ache.

He whips me until his arms grow tired. I can hear him breathing hard behind me. My blood flows in rivers down my back and legs. I hear it drip onto the stone floor.

The Chihuahua steps around in front of me again, his eyes locked with mine. He watches my expression eagerly as he leers at me and unbuttons his pants.

Of course. The pain of the whip was merely foreplay for him. He's going to rape me, and he wants me to know it. He wants to see my fear.

Fucking bastard.

Despite the searing pain in my back and hips, my anger boils. When the Chihuahua shoves his pants down, I look at his groin and snicker. If my hands weren't tied, I'd point and laugh. That's alright. My obvious implication transcends any language barriers.

His face darkens as his visage turns savage. He rushes forward to strike me again. In his fury, he forgets the importance of situational awareness.

When the Chihuahua's almost in front of me, I draw back my right leg and jam my heel hard into his naked crotch. I connect so forcefully with my target that he skids backwards, tumbling ass-first to the floor before groaning and clutching himself.

I laugh derisively as I watch him rolling on the ground, then spit a third time in his direction, though it doesn't land anywhere near him. It doesn't matter. It's the principle. My actions are going to cost me dearly, but I don't give a fuck.

He takes several minutes to get to his feet. When he does, he beats me until I lose consciousness. The last thing I hear is him taunting me.

When I resurface, I wish I hadn't, because each of them takes his turn with me. I hear their raucous laughter, smell their soured bodies, feel their rough hands gripping my raw, bloody hips. My breathing quickens and I struggle, kicking and writhing, but it's no use. There are too many of them. I'm growling swear words through gritted teeth as I try to fight them off.

I'll fight till my dying breath before I let these fuckers break me.

"Baby Girl, you're okay. You're safe," comes a voice.

The voice doesn't fit with what's happening, and I cease fighting for a second.

"Baby Girl, you're with me. I've got you. You're safe."

It's a familiar voice. Someone good.

I shake my head and hear him again. "Baby Girl, it's okay. You're safe."

Sudden thoughts worm their way through my haze.

Mark is talking to me.

He's here with me.

This isn't happening now.

I'm safe.

The room around me suddenly comes into view. I'm not imprisoned in their cell. I'm in Mark's room. He's cross-legged on the bed, facing me. I'm squatting, backed against the headboard. My fists are clenched, and I'm breathing hard.

Mark watches me carefully, his light blue eyes anxious and tinged with sadness. "You with me, Baby Girl?" he asks as I glance around, scanning my surroundings again.

I'm safe.

After a moment, I nod. Mark opens his arms, and I go to him, burying my face in his chest, still panting.

"I'm sorry, Baby Girl," he says softly, rubbing my back.

"I remembered specifics this time, from the day I was taken," I mutter. "Details."

"What can I do to help?"

I sit there for a minute, slowing my breathing and waiting for my heart to stop its furious pounding, but I can't stop thinking about what I've just dreamed.

No. Not dreamed.

Remembered.

I *fought back* against those bastards.

I wasn't weak. I fought back.

All this time, I've believed I was weak. A victim.

But I wasn't. I was a *fighter*.

I smile against his chest as tears of pride fill my eyes. I choke out words over the lump in my throat. "I fought back, Mark. I fought them. I never gave in."

"Of course you fought," he says with conviction. "You're a warrior."

"I fought them," I repeat. "Maybe – maybe I didn't remember before because I was trying so hard to forget." I swallow hard. "I was strong," I whisper.

He slips a hand under my chin, tilting my face to meet his gaze. "You still are, Charlie."

"All these years, I've blamed myself for not being strong enough. But I – I was fierce, Mark. They overpowered me, but they never broke me."

"No, Baby Girl, they didn't. They may have outmuscled you, but you have a strength they never had."

Chills run up my spine, and the hair on my arms stands on end, but not from fear – from my sudden clarity. It's like I'm watching a movie in my head, seeing myself through someone else's eyes.

I didn't go quietly when they attacked us in the truck – I fought, killing them one at a time from a completely defensive position.

When they had me tied up, expecting me to be fearful and submissive, I fought with my words and my attitude and whatever I could manage with my restrained body.

And when they battered and wounded me, I still fought, refusing to submit, letting my fury rule my reactions.

Even in my worst night terrors, when I end up shooting holes in the walls, I'm fighting them.

I tuck my head back into Mark's chest and smile softly.

I may be a train wreck, but those bastards didn't beat me.

CHAPTER TWENTY

CHARLIE

It's late when I wake up and grab my phone. "Crap." I sit up rapidly. It's after nine-thirty.

"Relax." Mark is resting on the chaise. "I turned off your alarm. It's Saturday, and you needed the sleep."

I stretch. "Has anyone ever told you that you're too damn nice?" I get up and head toward his bathroom.

"It's embroidered on a pair of boxers Tucker gave me."

I'm too groggy to decide if he's teasing. It does sound like something Tucker would do. I lean around the door, toothbrush in hand. "Tell me you're lying." He just laughs.

We share coffee and cinnamon rolls. Mark doesn't mention last night, but I can tell he's relieved I'm okay this morning, and he hugs me before going to bed.

I spend my morning alternating between streaming TV shows and doing quiet chores – laundry, dusting, scrubbing bathrooms, watering plants. I'll vacuum and clean Mark's bathroom after he wakes up. I'm elbow deep in the refrigerator when my phone rings.

It's Blake. A frisson of nervous anticipation runs through me. I'm seeing him later.

Or maybe not. Maybe he's reconsidered.

"Hey," I answer, slightly breathless from dashing across the kitchen.

"Hi, Beautiful. Did I catch you at a bad time?"

"You caught me at the perfect time. I was cleaning out my fridge, playing 'Name That Leftover'."

"That does sound thrilling." His teasing tone is encouraging. Maybe he's not calling to cancel.

"Listen, the girls want to go play mini-golf. I thought I'd see if you were interested in a cutthroat competition before Chinese food. Of course, if you're having too much fun with your leftovers, I understand." Humor oozes through his mellow voice.

I'm still surprised he wants to see me again after my panic attack in the parking lot. *Test the waters.* It's mini-golf with his nieces. It's safe. "I think I can tear myself away from this."

"Pick you up in an hour?"

I smile. "I'll be ready."

I take a quick shower, throw on my robe and quickly style my hair. I apply makeup carefully, spending extra time on my eyes since they're my best feature. I flip through my closet, finally deciding on dark wash jeans and a loose mauve top that's fitted across my hips, along with a cream and beige scarf. I add cascading gold earrings and beige suede flats just as he pulls in.

He's early.

I scribble a note for Mark and meet Blake on the porch as he bounds up my stairs. "Sorry I'm early. The girls were rushing me." His eyes travel down my body and back to my face. "So beautiful," he murmurs. His tone makes me shiver.

"I can't take the credit. Lila gave me this top. I've been looking for a reason to wear it."

"Forget the clothes. It's you that's beautiful," he says in a low voice, and my shiver turns into a sizzle of excitement.

Excitement is definitely new.

My face heats. "Thank you." I let my eyes boldly rove over him the same way his traveled over me. He's in jeans and a soft blue-gray shirt that hugs his defined chest and arms. I realize he's watching me admire his physique, but I don't look away from his warm gaze. "You look good, too. Really good."

He chuckles. "Jeans and a tee shirt?"

I echo his own words back at him. "Forget the clothes. It's you that looks good."

Blake's eyes darken as he takes one step closer. He looks like he wants to kiss me. My throat tightens reflexively. My body freezes.

Dammit.

But he doesn't kiss me; he stops in his tracks, leaving me both relieved and... disappointed?

The relief makes perfect sense, given my plethora of issues. But *disappointed?* I panicked the other night when I thought he might kiss me. Now I'm disappointed he didn't try? What the hell?

Blake offers his hand palm up, giving me the option of taking it. "Ready?"

You'll be with eight-year-old girls.

You can do this.

You did this with Tom yesterday. It's just a palm and five fingers.

I tentatively take his hand. "Ready."

It would have been more convincing if my voice hadn't wavered, but if he noticed, he doesn't comment. Instead, he smiles broadly as his long fingers close over mine, firm but not too tight as he leads me to his truck.

"Hi, Charlie," one of the girls calls from the backseat.

"Charlie, this is Avery," he points to the one behind the driver's seat, then to the other, "and this is Addison." Both girls have blond hair hanging down their backs and steel-blue eyes just like their uncle's. They're dressed in jeans and matching pink tee shirts, identical right down to their pink and white sneakers.

I smile as I climb inside. "Nice to meet you. Blake said you were twins, but I didn't realize you'd be identical. What's the secret to telling you two apart?"

They both giggle.

Blake grins. "I bought them necklaces," he says, moving one girl's hair aside to reveal a leather necklace with a wire-wrapped pale pink stone. "Addy's is rose quartz. Avery's is turquoise."

I wink at the girls. "How do you know they don't switch necklaces?"

"I –" he stops, staring between them. "Crap," he mutters, and the girls giggle again.

The girl behind the driver's seat leans forward and motions to me. "I'm Avery. Addison always wears pink nail polish to match her necklace. It's her favorite color," she whispers.

Addison. Pink. I file that tidbit away for later. "Thanks."

Blake still looks unsettled when I straighten.

"I'm glad you're coming today," Avery says.

"I'm glad you invited me. I was cleaning out the refrigerator." They laugh as I wrinkle my nose.

"This will be way more fun," Addison insists.

The mini-golf course is fifteen minutes away, and conversation is minimal since Blake has let the girls select the music. Angsty emo music is the soundtrack today. He smiles apologetically, but I grin and shrug. I'm used to it from spending time with Maya and Skyler. When he reaches for my hand again, I don't flinch. Instead, I place our joined hands on my lap, my own hand resting on my thigh.

I smile. Being affectionate with Tom does make holding hands with Blake less scary. Still, my opposing emotional reactions when I thought he was going to kiss me have me baffled. Relief and disappointment? Shouldn't I just feel one or the other? My confusion consumes me for the rest of the drive.

We have a blast playing mini-golf. Avery and I play for fun, but Blake and Addison are extremely competitive, trash-talking each other at every turn. Addison wins by a single stroke after Blake mysteriously struggles on the last hole. I cock an eyebrow at him when the girls aren't watching.

"I just couldn't get past that windmill," he winks. We return to the arcade, where he challenges them to several rounds of video games, this time losing to Avery at the last second. No wonder they adore him. The man intentionally boosts every female's confidence.

We stop at the cupcake shop near his house to pick up dessert. The dark-haired beauty at the counter flirts with Blake nonstop, and he doesn't discourage it. My jealousy flares as I watch their teasing rapport, but not because of any imagined claim I have on Blake. I'm envious of her, of how flirting comes so naturally to her. I'd give anything to be that comfortable around men.

Blake's house is like many in this area, craftsman-style with warm woodwork throughout. He leads me inside, and the girls race past me to go upstairs and change. The walls in his entry are cream-colored and lined with wooden shelves filled with unique pieces. Blake takes the cupcakes to the kitchen while I examine the items on his shelves. One entire section is dedicated to hammered metal bowls of assorted sizes, some with wooden mallets that resemble pestles.

"Tibetan singing bowls," he offers from the doorway, then enters. He takes one down, and I note the intricate pattern on the inside of the bowl. He strikes the bowl with the mallet, producing a smooth tone that reverberates through the entry. He follows by rubbing the wood against the rim of the bowl in a circular motion, producing a higher pitch that makes my eardrums feel all quivery. "The wavelength of the vibrations affects the same part of the brain where soothing music triggers relaxation. These bowls are used to help people achieve a meditative state."

Interspersed among the bowls are strings of beads from various semi-precious stones. I reach for a beautiful strand near me made of pale green stones flecked with darker forest green, but stop myself before touching them. "Prayer beads," Blake says. "Those are made of aventurine. Each strand has one hundred and eight beads. Some forms of meditation combine breathing and recitations. The beads let them keep track." He tips his head. "You can touch them."

"I didn't want to be disrespectful."

"You can touch anything you want to, Beautiful," he purrs. His rakish grin makes his meaning clear. "In fact, I strongly encourage it."

The air whooshes from my lungs, and I spiral from comfortable to panicky in the space of a single heartbeat. I take one slow deep breath and step away from him, moving toward a hanging display of metal gongs, painfully aware of his gaze. I realize too late I've boxed myself into the corner of his foyer. My spine stiffens as my eyes flash to the front door.

Blake's eyes haven't left me. Without a word, he steps forward and away, deliberately opening a space between us to create a clear exit path for me.

Rather than calming me, his actions ignite a deep frustration. He's walking on eggshells, constantly assessing my labile emotional state and adjusting course, trying not to inadvertently set me off. Watching it unfold in real time reinforces what I already knew. Normal women don't have panic attacks in parking lots or scope out escape routes for dinner with a hot guy and his twin nieces. Blake deserves someone he can be himself with.

"I bought that gong after a meditation retreat in Thailand," he says, inclining his head toward the gong closest to me. His tone is nonchalant, but his eyes remain alert as he tries to redirect my attention. "Gongs are another form of therapeutic sound. That particular retreat focused on music as a path to achieving inner harmony."

I breathe slowly, attempting to slow my pounding heart, forcing myself not to edge closer to the door.

God, I wish I weren't so fucked up.

Just get through today and you can end this dating nonsense.

I take another deep breath. "That sounds interesting." It's a lousy reply, but at least I'm talking instead of shutting down.

He nods. "Music is part of our souls. You said you sometimes use music to alter your mood. That's the basis of sound meditation. Different sound waves affect different kinds of brain waves. Altering your brain waves has the power to change your mood, moving you from a hyperalert state to a calm one."

I take one step backwards without moving closer to the door, focusing on the conversation. "I've tried meditating, but I can't do the whole 'quiet your mind' thing. My brain won't shut up."

He grins. "Sure it will. When do you feel peaceful? Where's your happy place?"

"The woods. Next to a stream, sitting under a tree, surrounded by green in every direction."

He nods. "Try meditating next time you're in the woods. Or try it in a quiet room while listening to nature sounds. They have hundreds of looped nature audio tracks online. Water sounds are particularly calming. Find one that sounds like your stream and close your eyes. Imagine being there, and focus on the sounds. Everything else will slowly slip away."

My stress level is decreasing as he speaks, and I breathe as he watches cautiously.

"I'm sorry for making you uncomfortable again," he says suddenly. "It wasn't my intent."

I shrug. "I apologize for being so sensitive."

He studies me carefully. "Maybe someday you'll feel comfortable enough to tell me what happened. Why you're skittish around me."

"It's not just you." I look down at the warm wood flooring, the planks wide and comfortably worn from years of use. "It's men in general. I'm working on it."

I hear thudding sounds above my head just before Avery and Addison scamper down the stairs and stop beside us. They're still dressed identically, this time in denim shorts and hot pink shirts. One of them tugs on Blake's hand. "We changed and washed up. How long until dinner? I'm hungry." I study her fingernails. They're unpainted. Avery.

Blake's eyes remain riveted on me. "Go find a movie, and when everyone decides what they want to eat, I'll call in the takeout order."

A heated discussion ensues between the girls over sweet and sour chicken versus sweet sticky ribs. When they've gone into the living room to pick a movie, I take a deep breath. "Maybe I should go."

He tilts his head. "Please stay. I'll try not to say the wrong thing again."

I shake my head. "That's not it. You shouldn't have to weigh every word you say before it comes out of your mouth."

He snorts. "People do that all the time."

"They shouldn't have to."

He raises an eyebrow. "That's how society functions. Men don't call their bosses idiots. Women don't tell each other if an outfit looks terrible on them." He studies me. "The girl at the cupcake shop irritated me. She could see you were there with me. For all she knew, we were a married couple there with our daughters, but she kept flirting. Rather than tell her she was being rude, I laughed and changed the subject."

He changed the subject? "I wasn't listening," I admitted. "Once she started hitting on you, I tuned out."

His brows pull together. "Why?"

"Because she's more your type. Personality-wise, at least. Someone who's comfortable with innuendos and double entendres."

Someone not like me.

I don't say it, but he hears my implication. He steps toward me, then stops, rubbing his hand through his hair, making it stick up. "I don't flirt with other women when I'm on a date, Charlie. I may have earned my reputation as a player, but I respect the woman I'm with. Watching what I say to avoid upsetting you doesn't mean I'm not being myself. It means I'm trying to respect your boundaries." He watches me, his eyes softening. "Please stay for dinner."

Something in his steel-blue eyes sets off a herd of butterflies in my stomach.

Butterflies are definitely new.

I nod. "Alright." He smiles slowly, watching me beneath long lashes. My butterflies spiral wildly under his warm gaze.

Dinner is low key. The four of us pile into Blake's cozy living room with its overstuffed sofas and warm wood furniture. We use chopsticks and eat from the containers while watching an animated movie about dogs plotting to rescue their stray friends from the villainous dogcatcher.

"It's not as bad as some movies they've picked." He tilts his head closer when he speaks.

"I've suffered through far worse with Maya," I agree. We're sunken into the plush sofa, my upper arm resting against his warm, muscular one.

And I'm not anxious.

I'm so pleased with my progress, I feel playful. I frown, staring past him. When he turns to see what I'm looking at, I swipe a snow pea from his container with my chopsticks. He looks back just in time to see me putting it in my mouth.

He grins. "So that's how it's going to be?"

I deliberately crunch the crisp vegetable. "Tastes better stolen," I say impishly, licking sauce from my lips. "Besides, it's your fault. I love meat and green stuff with brown sauce. You tempted me."

His gaze lingers on my mouth, and my heart pounds erratically. "You find me tempting?" His voice is low as he leans closer, then stops, testing my reaction.

He's close enough for me to smell his cologne, close enough to feel his warm breath on my skin. Warm eyes hold my gaze. I bite my lip, and my heart gallops, but I'm not afraid. Not exactly.

A sexy grin spreads lazily across his face, making it hard for me to think. "There's a penalty for stealing, you know."

I wonder briefly what sort of penalty he has in mind, thankful he can't hear my hammering heart. When he leans even closer, I stop breathing altogether.

While he holds my gaze, distracting me, he steals a broccoli floret from my container and pops it into his mouth, grinning.

Relief and disappointment battle again as he sits back without ever touching me. Apparently, my body and mind can't agree on what they want.

I sigh and concede defeat on the stolen food front. "Well played."

He winks. "I play to win."

It's only later, when I'm showering, that I can untangle my ball of messy emotions.

There's fear, but not of Blake himself. I may not trust him completely, but I'm not afraid of him doing anything to me. My fear is just a reflex, a habit I need to break.

There's also a growing attraction. That's encouraging. I haven't felt attracted to anyone since what happened to me.

And there's disappointment.

Despite my progress, I'm disappointed with myself. Now that I'm away from the situation, I can admit that deep down, I wanted Blake to kiss me, but I succumbed to fear. Granted, it's not like he tried and I pulled away or panicked, but I could have leaned forward and kissed him. I didn't, though. I let my fears rule my behavior.

Willow's instructions rattle around in my head.

Be affectionate with Tom and Tucker to become more comfortable with Blake. And fantasize about kissing Blake so I don't panic when it hopefully gets to that point.

Wait – *hopefully*? I'm so startled I knock over my shampoo bottle.

I'm looking forward to kissing Blake.

Warmth floods my chest, and I smile. Baby steps.

MARK

Charlie's in a better mood than after her date with Blake last week, but something's still not right. Something about seeing him always leaves her rattled.

She flops beside me on the sofa, her head on my lap as she faces the television. I mute the baseball game I'd had on in the background. "Wanna talk about it?"

"Talk about what?"

"Whatever's bothering you." She opens her mouth to deny it, but I shake my head. "Don't even try. If you don't want to tell me, fine, but don't pretend nothing's wrong."

She frowns, exhaling heavily. "Fine. I'm frustrated. All this dating crap takes so much effort. I just wish I weren't so messed up."

I smile gently. "Be patient with yourself. You'll get there."

She plucks at the beige fabric of the couch. "I'm tired of being patient."

"You're making progress, and it's getting easier to be affectionate, right?"

"I guess." She still looks discouraged.

"If Lila were the one struggling, you'd tell her to give herself as much time as she needed. You wouldn't rush her. Cut yourself the same slack you'd give her."

She rolls onto her back, gazing up at me and pursing her lips. "You know, you're pretty smart for a guy."

I wink. "That's me. Pretty and smart."

She chuckles and shakes her head. "Totally not what I said."

I tweak a lock of her damp hair. "Seriously, quit worrying about things not lining up with some timetable in your head. Focus on your victories."

"Fine, if you'll stop quoting fortune cookies at me." Then she scoots up and kisses my cheek. "Thanks, Mark."

I press my lips to her forehead. "My brilliance is always available for a nominal fee."

I'm at the rehab gym a few days later, working on my core, when Blake enters. He scans the area, presumably searching for Tom. I nod once, not breaking my pace. "Tom's already gone home for the day. He had to pick Maya up from school. Skyler's home sick."

He nods. "Thanks."

But instead of leaving, he strolls around the gym. I watch as he aimlessly meanders, hands stuffed in his pants pockets. His shoulders flex beneath his blue tee shirt as he paces. I'm the only one here, and while he and I are cordial, we aren't friends. He's a friend of Tom's that I've chatted with a few times. It doesn't take a rocket scientist to figure out what he's lingering around to talk about.

Or more accurately, whom.

Sure enough, a few minutes later, he sits down on the padded table adjacent to mine.

I stop doing my ab crunches and unclip the carabiners that connect resistance bands to a belt around my waist before sitting up to face him. "Something on your mind?"

He rests his arms on his legs, leaning forward and staring at the ground. "I'm hoping you can tell me what I need to know about Charlie."

I wait for him to meet my gaze, to see the seriousness of my response. "The most important thing you need to know is that if you hurt her, I'll mop the floor with you."

He raises both hands in surrender. "First Tom, now you. I don't want to hurt her. That's why I'm here. I need –" He closes his eyes for a second. "Look, I know she's been through something bad. I touched her cheek a few months ago and she had a panic attack. I didn't know not to touch her. She had another one the first time we went out, even though I put a lot of effort into making sure I kept my distance. I still have no idea what happened or where the boundaries are. I don't want to scare her or accidentally do something I shouldn't. I was hoping –" He stops again, pinching the bridge of his nose before jumping up. "Never mind. Sorry to bother you."

I sigh. "Sit down, Blake." His eyes are cautious, but he eases back down. "Look, I don't know what to tell you as far as boundary lines go. That's something you'll have to discuss with Charlie. She's trying to open up, be more relaxed with people, but only she can tell you what she's okay with."

"By 'relaxed with people', you mean with guys?"

I shake my head. "With everyone. Charlie's very guarded, and she keeps almost everyone at arm's length. When someone asks a personal question, she redirects the conversation, usually without them noticing. She stays detached to protect herself. Most people never know what's going on with her below the surface. She hides behind a teasing, cheerful façade. Sometimes, even Lila and I struggle to get her to open up. She's working at letting people in, people she trusts, but she doesn't trust easily, because to her, vulnerability means pain. Getting involved with her won't be easy, but if you think she's too much work, you're dead wrong."

He sits silently, pinching his lower lip between his thumb and forefinger. I keep talking. "Charlie's an incredible woman. She's worth every ounce of effort it takes. The question is whether you're worth hers." Annoyance flits across his sculpted features, but I ignore it. "Because make no mistake, letting someone get close is extremely difficult for her. Things you'd do automatically, like hugging someone or taking their hand or talking about personal things – those things require her to fight all of her instincts."

Blake purses his lips. "Will you tell me what happened to her?"

I hesitate. "Details are hers to share, not mine, but I know she started her 'Winner versus Whiner' dates by sharing basic information. She wanted to head off any preconceived notions about where the date might lead. I'll tell you the basics, but nothing more." He nods, looking entirely too eager, like he's about to hear juicy gossip. I barely manage to conceal my irritation.

"When we were in Afghanistan, Charlie was kidnapped by insurgents." I leave Lila out of it. Her story is her business, not Blake's. "They had her for eleven days before we found her. They'd raped her and –" I break off, sickened by memories of the night I found her, of discovering what they'd done. "They brutalized her. That's why she struggles."

He looks at me, his expression unreadable. "She panics at physical contact, but not with you. Why?"

"Charlie and I've been best friends for almost twenty-five years. Her family took me in when my dad died, and since her parents died, it's just been the two of us. I'd die for her, and she knows it." I don't mention that I've killed for her, though if he considers what I've told him, it should be obvious.

"It's good she has someone she trusts." He pauses. "Do you think she's capable of trusting someone else?"

I nod. "She didn't know Tom until after she moved here, and she trusts him. She can trust someone new if you can prove to her you're worthy."

He studies me with somber eyes. "What should I do if she has another panic attack?"

"Don't touch her," I say immediately. "Just keep telling her to take deep breaths and remind her she's safe, that no one's going to hurt her. She has PTSD, and unexpected or unwanted touch can trigger her. Give her space and remind her to breathe and she'll calm down. If you need help, call me. Or call Lila and Tucker. They're good at calming her down over the phone."

He's silent for a long moment. "She's got to move past her past."

My temper flares. "She's working on it, but this isn't like getting passed over for a promotion or not fulfilling your life goals before you turn thirty, Life Coach."

His expression tightens when I mock his self-imposed job title. "I'm not saying it is. Obviously, Charlie had a very traumatic experience. I'm just saying she can't grab her future while she's clinging to her past."

I growl without intending to, and his eyes widen. "Clinging to her past? After what those bastards did, you think –" I glare at him. "Her past imprisons her. She's not clinging to it, she's trying to escape it. You think she can just flip a switch and forget? It's assholes like you who make her think she's damaged beyond repair."

"I'm not trying to sound callous. I like Charlie. I want to help her, not hurt her. I was trying to find out what I needed to know."

I stand and reach for my crutches. He gets up, too, realizing he's gone too far. I move purposefully toward him, and he backs up. "I told you, if you hurt her, I'll fucking wipe the floor with your ass. That's what you need to know."

He scurries out of the rehab gym, nearly knocking Lila over in his haste. "Sorry," he apologizes with a backward glance in my direction.

"Chasing the boxing coach out of the building? That's new." Lila stares pensively after his retreating form. "Blake's left a string of broken hearts in his wake. I'm glad Charlie's felt secure enough to go out with someone more than once, but I don't think he'll be as patient as she needs someone to be." She cocks her head. "You don't like him much, do you?"

"He said Charlie should get over what happened to her." Her eyes flash dangerously. "And she's come home upset each time she's gone out with him."

She shakes her head. "He has no idea how much hell will rain down on him if he hurts her." Then she grins. "I've never heard you threaten anyone she went out with before."

I frown. "I didn't worry about her then like I do now."

Maybe if I had, none of the shit she's been through would have ever happened.

CHAPTER TWENTY-ONE

CHARLIE

"I don't get it. I panic at physical contact, and I was relieved Blake didn't try to kiss me, but I was also disappointed. It doesn't make sense. Shouldn't I just feel one or the other?"

It's late Friday, and I'm in Linda's soothing blue office, tucked into her plush sofa with my shoes kicked off and legs folded beneath me. She's in the wingback chair, her spiked gold heels on the floor and her knees drawn up, rumpling her black pantsuit with its leopard print blouse peeking out of the prim jacket. We're working through my (lengthy) list of issues. We've talked about the improvement of my night terrors with Mark's help. I've brought up what Willow and I discussed, including my recent affectionate touch with Tom. I've told her about sharing my past with him, and him sharing his pain about his sister with me. Now we've moved on to whatever this is with Blake. Seeing him, I guess, though our encounters have mostly been chaperoned, either by his nieces or my coworkers. Three times this week, he's brought me lunch at the clinic.

"Why should you be limited to one emotion?" Linda smiles. "Life is complicated. Why shouldn't feelings be?"

"Shouldn't I either want him to kiss me or not want him to?"

"How would you have felt six months ago?"

"I would have freaked out."

She nods. "Progress isn't instantaneous or linear. It's a process. Think about your life six months ago. You were still in combat mode. You had severe night terrors, and you were extremely uncomfortable around men in social settings. Compare that to today. You haven't fired your weapon since the first night Mark moved in. You relinquish your gun every evening, entrusting your safety to someone else. You sleep in the same room as a trusted male friend. You're seeing someone. You're choosing intentional vulnerability." She smiles gently. "Healing takes time. The fact that part of you wants Blake to kiss you means your inner self is trying to break free from fear. I believe in the near future, you won't feel conflicted. Celebrate your progress, Charlie. You've grown tremendously these past couple of months."

"Because of Mark."

She shakes her head. "Because of you."

"Being around him makes me stronger," I insist.

"He encourages you, but your strength is your own, and you should acknowledge it."

I sigh. "So what do I do about these conflicted feelings?"

"What do you want to do?"

I cock my head. "You know that's a cliche, right? Psychiatrists turning everything back into a question?"

She smiles. "Why do you think they're cliches?"

I fight the urge to stick out my tongue. "Fine. I guess I go with my gut. But I'm more comfortable actually being affectionate with Tom than with thinking about kissing Blake."

"You trust Tom," she points out.

"So I need to work on building trust with Blake." I sigh. "You know, life would be a lot easier if I were like everyone else. Normal, I mean. Without all these issues."

Linda studies me before walking to her bookcase. "I bought this on my trip to Japan last year," she says, picking up a black saucer and crossing the room to me. "Have you ever heard of kintsugi?"

I shake my head, and she hands the saucer to me. It's stunning – a rich, glossy black with veins of gold running through it. I trace the smooth surface with my fingertips, mesmerized.

"Kintsugi means 'mended with gold'. When a piece of pottery breaks, rather than discard it, they clean the pieces and glue them back together. Once it's repaired, they trace the repair lines with gold and apply several coats of lacquer. They accentuate the cracks, rather than hide them."

I glance up at her, seeing the parallels, but wanting her to continue.

"A flawless black saucer lacks the character of this repaired piece. The beauty comes from the fact that it was broken and repaired with intent and care. Only by being broken first can its true beauty be seen."

"It's a beautiful piece," I agree, reluctantly handing it back to her, "but I'm not even close to being repaired."

"Not true," she counters. "We were just discussing your progress."

"Progress isn't perfection."

"No one's perfect, Charlie, so get that notion out of your head."

"I have no illusions about being perfect. I'd just like to be able to extend trust to the guy I've been seeing."

"Have you two discussed your trauma?"

I hesitate. "No. He just knows something bad happened."

"Shouldn't you at least give him a general idea?"

I sigh again. "I don't want him to see me differently."

She tilts her head. "If he's going to see you differently, shouldn't you know sooner rather than later?"

I frown. "It's very difficult for me to cling to my iron-clad reasoning when you constantly use logic to destroy it," I mutter.

She grins. "That's one of the perks of my job."

I'm Linda's last appointment of the day, and when we finish, it's five-thirty. I text Tom from my car. "Do you have ice cream?"

"Probably. Hang on." There's a thirty-second pause before he answers. "Yes. Butter pecan, chocolate, and birthday cake with weird sprinkly things."

I laugh out loud and send several laughing emojis. "Sprinkles? LOL. Wait till I tell Lila. AND TUCKER."

He sends back a frowny emoji. "Maya's, NOT mine."

I chuckle again. "Stopping to pick up dessert. Need anything?"

"Not unless you want wine."

I send a thumbs up, followed by, "See you shortly."

It's pasta night at his house again. He's ordered family-sized pans of spaghetti bolognese and chicken alfredo, garlic bread, and salad. I purchase an apple galette from the bakery and, on a whim, pick up white and red wine.

I park on the street behind a familiar minivan. Skyler and her mom are talking to Tom outside. Skyler is jumping up and down excitedly. When I get out of my car, she dashes toward me.

"Guess what, Charlie? Mom's friend gave her four tickets to the Vibe concert tonight in Pueblo. We came to see if Maya and Tom want to go." She's bouncing on the balls of her feet. Her red hair is caught in a side braid, and she's wearing a black shirt with The Vibe in fluorescent pink letters. Horizontal slits in the shirt reveal a painfully bright pink tank top underneath.

"That sounds fun. You'll have a great time." I hope my voice doesn't sound as deflated as I feel. I'd been looking forward to an evening with Tom and Maya, but the girls will enjoy the concert. Tom? Not so much. He groans every time the girls play their music, which in his opinion, is entirely too often.

Skyler's mom turns and waves, her mouth forming a slight "o" when she sees the bakery box and wine. I struggle to remember her name. It's something hip. Paxton? Peyton? I know it starts with a P. Whatever it is, she's dressed in black leather pants and a plunging hot pink shirt that clashes against her strawberry blond tresses.

"I should have called. I didn't realize you had plans," she's telling Tom as I approach.

"Hey," I greet Tom. "Skyler told me. We can reschedule. I understand."

"I've already ordered dinner," he says smoothly, taking the bakery box from me. I start to tell him I'll stay and accept the delivery so he can go, but his expression stops me. He turns to Skyler's mom. "I'm sorry, Parker. But perhaps you wouldn't mind if Maya went along? I know she'd be thrilled."

Parker. I knew it was something like that.

She tries and fails to hide her disappointment. "Of course." She plasters on a smile and turns to Skyler. "Run upstairs and get Maya. I'll be in the car." Skyler sprints inside, and I hear her sneakers pounding up the stairs as she calls Maya's name.

"You're welcome to wait inside," Tom offers.

She shakes her head, still smiling. "It's okay. I need to make a call." She tosses her hand up again in a small wave. "You guys have a good time," she says wistfully.

Tom holds the door, and I carry the wine into the kitchen. He follows, putting the apple galette on the counter. "Seriously, Tom, if you want to go, you should go. She's clearly into you. We can do this anytime."

He shakes his head. "That's a horrible idea."

"Why?"

He looks at me like I've lost my mind. "She's not my type."

I gesture vaguely in her direction. "You saw her, right? Strawberry blond hair, flawless skin, big blue eyes, curves in all the right places. How is she not your type?"

He chuckles. "I didn't say she wasn't attractive. She is. She's also very –" he pauses, searching for the right word. "She's the female equivalent of a barnacle."

I raise an eyebrow. "A barnacle?"

"She attaches quickly," he explains. "She inserts her own subtext into situations and reads things that aren't there. Plus, she's Skyler's mom. Our daughters are best friends. If we went out even once, the girls would get overly excited, and Parker would feed into that excitement instead of tempering it. When things didn't work out, it would be awkward for Skyler and Maya. It's not worth it."

I smile. "You've given this a lot of thought."

He sighs. "She's been dropping hints for a while."

"So that's why you insisted on staying with me. Dinner, dessert, wine. To imply your interests lie elsewhere."

"I'd have stayed anyway. You're much more fun."

I sniff in mock annoyance. "I feel used. If there weren't pasta, you'd be in a lot of trouble."

He grins his boyish grin, eyes twinkling. "I'm sorry."

I snort. "Nice try. You're just lucky I'm a sucker for Italian food."

Feet thunder down the stairs, and Maya runs in and grabs me around the waist. "Charlie!" she squeals. I plant a noisy kiss on her cheek as Skyler comes in.

"Sounds like you're gonna have fun."

"I wish you guys could come," she complains. Her black shirt has The Vibe emblazoned across it, too.

"Sorry, kiddo, not enough tickets for all of us," Tom says. "Do you have your phone?"

"Yes, and it's charged."

He reaches for his wallet and hands her some bills. "Stay together and be safe." He hugs and kisses both girls. "Text me when you get there and when you head home. Have a good time."

"We will," Skyler says, skipping out the door.

"Bye, Dad!" Maya calls, banging the screen door on her way out.

After Parker's minivan pulls away, Tom turns to me. "Well, I guess it's just us. What do you want to do?"

"I don't care. Music? Movie? Whatever."

He nods before holding out his hand. "Want to go sit on the couch and listen to music?"

I take his outstretched hand, and he grins. "Nicely done."

"You make it easy," I admit.

"How so?"

"I never feel pressured with you."

His fingers tighten around mine. "Is Blake pressuring you?"

"No," I say hastily. "I pressure myself. To be normal."

He frowns. "You are normal."

I laugh. "I'm a lot of things, but normal will never be one of them."

"Just because some women are more comfortable being physically expressive doesn't mean you're not normal. And it's not like you don't have a damn good reason for being cautious." Ferocity flickers briefly across his face. "If Blake's pressuring you –"

"He's not. I promise," I insist.

I trail behind him to the living room. He releases my hand at the couch and picks up a remote. He's scrolling through streaming music services when there's a knock at the door. "Pick something," he says, passing me the remote. I scan playlists, selecting one with an assortment of R&B, soul, and contemporary pop.

"No Eminem tonight?" he teases as he carries the food to the kitchen.

I laugh. He knows Eminem is my go-to for sour moods. I follow him, sniffing the delightful smells wafting from the takeout bag. "Who needs Eminem when there's pasta and garlic bread?"

The food is amazing. I eat until I'm full and on my third glass of wine, warm and relaxed. I kick off my shoes and snuggle deeper into the sofa. Tom chuckles. "Comfy?"

"Very."

He clears our plates, and I hear splashing as he runs water over them. A familiar song starts playing. I turn up the volume and jump up. Tom returns to find me rolling my hips to the music.

His mouth quirks up in a smile. "Feeling the wine?"

I just grin and keep dancing. He pulls the coffee table aside, opening up the center of the room. I raise an eyebrow. "Worried I'll lose my balance?"

"Just giving you room."

"Not going to dance with me?"

"I prefer slow dancing." He sits on the arm of a recliner, watching in amusement.

"Please," I scoff. "Slow dancing is just hugging and swaying. Anybody can do that."

He chuckles. "We can't all be Shakira."

I shimmy my hips in response and he grins. I twist and bob my way through three songs before a slow song starts. Tom stands and holds out his hand. "Feeling brave?"

There are six feet between us, but all the air is suddenly sucked out of the room.

Slow dancing.

Chest to chest, hip to hip, upper bodies entangled.

My automatic tension pisses me off. This is *Tom*. He's safe. I've spent all evening alone with him, side by side, our arms touching, even having a third glass of wine because I know he'd never hurt me.

He lowers his hand. "It's okay, Charlie."

"Just gimme a minute." My breathing picks up speed as my heart pounds, but it only makes me more determined. "Talk."

Chocolate brown eyes flicker uncertainly to mine.

"Talk to me about dancing." My words sound like a plea.

Dammit.

His gaze softens. "If we were dancing, I would hold your hand in mine right here," he closes his left hand over his heart, "and put my right hand on your hip. And we would stand close and move together with the music."

Breathe.

Tom is safe.

Like a drowning woman, I drag in a deep gulp of air before stepping toward him. He meets me halfway. I slip my fingers inside his. He curls his massive hand loosely around mine and tucks it against his chest, smiling. He stands patiently, his stance wide, his body relaxed. I pause, heart pounding, then take his right hand and place it on my hip.

"You're doing great." His sincerity startles me because I'm still pissed at myself. "Now you decide where to put your other hand."

I stare at my left hand before stepping closer, skimming my hand up his chest to the top of his shoulder and leaning my head against his broad chest. In my bare feet, I barely reach his shoulder. I'm close enough to smell his soapy scent, and I pray my trembling escapes his notice.

No such luck.

"Please don't be afraid of me, Charlie," he says quietly. "I'd never hurt you."

I look up, meeting his eyes steadily. "If I were afraid of you, I wouldn't be doing this."

He smiles and slowly sways with the music. I join in and find myself relaxing within a couple of minutes. Some of it is the wine, I'm sure, but most of it is Tom.

Two songs later, his chest rumbles under my cheek. He's chuckling. I realize I've absently begun tracing the muscles of his shoulder with my fingertips.

"You've melted," he teases, gesturing down our bodies with our joined hands.

It's true. I'm leaning into him, chest to chest, hip to hip, thigh to thigh, and I'm not the least bit anxious. "I told you I wasn't afraid of you. You make me feel safe."

He kisses my forehead. "You're always safe with me."

Two more slow songs play before the playlist changes back to something faster paced. I sigh when I step out of the warm circle of his arms.

He grins at my reluctance. "That's definitely progress."

I hide my smile. "You're warm and cuddly, like a bear." I point to his huge hands. "You've even got the paws for it."

He laughs out loud and tugs a lock of my hair. "C'mon. I want some of that dessert."

"Good. I need a picture of you eating sprinkle ice cream for blackmailing purposes."

I'm walking in my front door, smiling at my success, when my phone buzzes with a text from Blake. "Any interest in dinner for two tomorrow?"

Something in my stomach flutters. "No nieces this weekend?"

"Nope. They're at their grandparents' house."

I think back to my discussion with Linda. *Build trust with Blake.* "Sounds nice."

"Pick you up at six?"

"I'll be ready."

"Sleep well, Beautiful."

When I drift off to sleep, I'm picturing his slow, sexy grin.

MARK

Charlie's said she's going out with Blake again tomorrow night. It'll be her first time going out with him since I gave him some basic information about her past.

Maybe I shouldn't have said anything to him the other day in the gym. Maybe that's crossing a line Charlie wouldn't have wanted crossed.

Then I shake my head. I only gave him the same short version she gave dozens of other douchebags on those ridiculous Wednesday Whiner outings Lila engineered. Well, that plus his own personal health and safety warning.

There's just something about him that doesn't sit right with me.

My initial objection to Charlie going out with Blake stemmed from my own issues. He reminded me of how I was prior to the explosion, when I was strong and athletic and whole. Blake was an unintentional reminder that I'll never again be what I once was.

My objections now have nothing to do with how I feel about myself and everything to do with how he acted in the rehab gym the other day. The way he so flippantly declared she needed to get past her past, to quit clinging to it, has chafed at me like sandpaper in my boxers for days. That dumbass doesn't have a clue, and I'm afraid he's going to end up hurting Charlie.

The way he said Tom's already warned him against hurting her tells me that Tom sees something that gives him pause as well. Maybe he's being overprotective, but I don't think so.

I realize my fists are clenched just thinking about Blake.

I meant what I said.

He'd better not hurt my Baby Girl.

CHARLIE

I'm spritzing on perfume when Blake pulls into the driveway Saturday night. "I'll let him in," Mark calls. I check my reflection in the mirror. My red wrap dress with butterfly sleeves fits perfectly now that I've regained some weight. I insert earrings to match my gold lariat necklace and finger my loose waves one last time. As I'm slipping into my heels, I hear Mark open the front door. I grab my purse, feeling the reassuring weight of my handgun inside.

Blake looks up as I'm descending the stairs, and his eyes darken. "You look beautiful," he says in his warm-honey purr. Something sizzles low in my belly at his tone. Black pants sit low on his hips, and his white dress shirt is open at the throat. His blond hair is artfully messy, and his gray-blue eyes smolder.

"Thank you. You look nice yourself." I glance over to tell Mark good night, but I'm startled by the tightness of his jaw.

Something happened before I came downstairs.

I stop beside him, laying a hand on his forearm, waiting until his pale blue eyes meet mine. "I'll see you later."

He nods his head. "Have a good time," he replies, then stares meaningfully at Blake.

I wait until we're in his truck before turning to Blake. "What's up with you and Mark?"

"What do you mean?"

"I could cut the tension with a knife. What's going on?"

He shakes his head. "Nothing. You just have some very protective friends."

I groan. "Seriously? Mark too?"

He grins. "And Tom. And Tucker. And Lila. You have very loyal, caring friends."

"Of the four of them, you should be most frightened of –"

He starts the truck. "I know. Mark, because you've been best friends for forever."

I laugh. "Actually, I was going to say Lila."

His eyebrows vanish beneath his hairline as he whips around. "Sweet little Lila?"

I laugh again. "Don't be fooled by her blond curls and big violet eyes. The guys throw punches. Lila would rip out your throat without ever batting an eye."

After a moment of stunned silence, he pulls out of my driveway. "I made reservations at a steakhouse, if that's alright."

"It sounds delicious."

The ride is quiet but short, the silence broken only by the radio, but it's a comfortable silence, at least for me. For all I know, he's picturing a trim blonde shredding his throat.

When we get to the restaurant, Blake shuts off the motor. "Stay put," he says, hopping out of the truck. He comes around and opens my door. "Let me help you," he says, offering his hand.

No panic.

I smile and take his hand, stepping down onto the running board and then the ground as his warm fingers close over mine. He keeps a loose grip on them as we walk into the restaurant. A perky blond hostess stands behind a small counter. "Blake," she purrs.

I glance up in time to see him wink at her. "Hi, Talia. We have a reservation for two." She looks down at the book in front of her, a faint blush tinging her lovely features.

I try to ignore my building irritation. He's eye candy. Of course women flirt with him.

Except he winked at her.

I don't have any claim on Blake, so it shouldn't annoy me.

But it does.

It's disrespectful to wink at other women when you're on a date. Just the other day, he told me he makes it a point to respect the woman he's with.

The blond hostess leads us to our table. I try not to notice her perfect figure and the extra shimmy she's adding to her walk. Blake releases my fingers, instead placing his hand lightly on the small of my back as we follow her to a corner booth. I tense slightly but rein it in.

"I went out with her older sister a few times," Blake volunteers after she's left and we're seated. "Talia was about fifteen at the time, and she had a crush on me. It drove her sister nuts because Talia had no qualms about flirting with me right in front of her sister."

My irritation drops to a low simmer, but it doesn't disappear. "How old was her sister?"

He thinks back. "It was about seven years ago. I would have been twenty-five. Tasha was twenty-two. She was one of the first girls I dated after my marriage ended, so I was gun shy. We didn't date very long."

I can excuse Talia's behavior, but Blake's wink? That gives me pause.

The corner of the restaurant where we're seated is quiet and cozy. Our window overlooks a peaceful lake encircled by a paved walking path. Benches are spaced every few yards with bird feeders near them. Two fat squirrels squabble over sunflower seeds at the feeder nearest us, and we both laugh as we watch them wrestle.

Dinner is wonderful. The red wine has hints of blackberry, and the same flavors are echoed in the mouthwatering blackberry vinaigrette on my salad.

The steak is well-seasoned and cooked to perfection. Conversation is light, mostly revolving around Blake's nieces and their escapades. He doesn't make a single flirtatious remark, and despite the sketchy start to our dinner, I'm more relaxed than I've ever been around him.

The server has cleared away our plates and refilled our glasses when it happens. Blake looks at me, his eyes suddenly intense. "What happened to you, Charlie?"

I'm completely caught off guard by his borderline-accusatory tone. "What?"

He takes a deep breath, refining his question to make it a bit more palatable. "I'm hoping you might tell me what happened that's left you so uncomfortable with men. Will you tell me about it? I'd like to understand, so I know a little more about your boundaries and what to expect."

My throat tightens, and I swallow convulsively.

I know he needs to know, if for no other reason than to determine whether or not this path we're taking is worth continuing down. Besides, Linda's right. If my past – and present – are more than he can handle, better to find out now.

But not here. Not in a noisy restaurant surrounded by curious onlookers. The thought of anyone overhearing and staring in fascination makes me queasy.

I nod once, resignation sinking my spirit. "I'll tell you. Not here, though." I stare out the window into the growing darkness at the well-lit walking path. "There."

"By the lake?"

I remember discussing Afghanistan with Tom and being able to look at the stars instead of his face. The darkness helped me feel less exposed, and the night air had soothed my ragged soul. "It's easier to talk about in the dark."

There's no more chitchat, just awkward silence and a growing knot in my stomach. I wish I'd foregone that delicious dinner and had a second glass of wine, or better yet, a stiff drink. All too soon, I find myself outside, taking his offered hand for what feels like the final time, setting off down the path. We walk silently as he waits for me to bare my soul.

I wonder if I'm imagining his eagerness. Probably. He doesn't look excited, merely curious. But it doesn't matter. Once I tell him, one way or another, everything changes.

I tug him toward a bench facing the water, and when I sit, he sits next to me, close enough that I feel the heat of him all down the left side of my body, though he doesn't actually make contact. The street light is close enough to shine on our backs, but far enough away so I can see the stars. I focus all of my attention on them as I talk. I detach from the pain of my memories, instead noting each flicker, each twinkle in the dark sky above me.

Just like with Tom, I tell him all of it – the kidnapping, how long they had me, and what they did. I show him my wrists, just as I did with Tom. It's easier to talk about this time, maybe because in the past two weeks, I've shared these details with three other people, and definitely because I never meet his eyes, focusing only on the stars. But unlike with Tom or Mark, there's no comforting touch, no one to draw strength from. Blake remains silent.

He offers no sympathy, no pity, no reassurances, no support.

Yet despite his total silence, I plunge ahead with my biggest bravery test of all, not just for me, but for Blake, too. I'm not just taking a baby step – I'm leaping off the damn cliff. I need to know if he's going to bother sticking around.

Deep breath.

I glance over at him before reaching back between my shoulders and grasping the zipper of my dress. The rasping sound as I unzip it to my waist is loud, louder than the splashing from the fountain out in the lake, noisier than the songs of the tree frogs in the dark. I fold the fabric vee open, baring my back to him. The night air chills my exposed skin. I glance sideways. Blake's face is completely devoid of expression.

"Give me your right hand." He does, and I reach behind me, pressing it palm-side-down against my back. "Touch them. My scars." His eyes widen. "I'm serious. You wanted to know what happened. Feel. Better yet, there's a streetlight – take a good look."

I'm terrified on the inside, but my exterior is calm, and I sweep my hair out of the way and shift my back toward him, letting the light hit my exposed flesh.

Light fingers skate over my skin, tracing the scars. I close my eyes as his other hand pushes the fabric aside for a closer look. I'm trembling now, not because I fear his touch, but because I'm scared to death of how he'll react.

His sharp intake of breath as his fingers move lower makes me wince. He's found the top part of the brand. His thumb traces the flat white scar.

He gulps audibly. Then he snatches his hands away and zips my dress back up. I turn to face him, bracing myself for his reaction.

He looks horrified. Appalled.

This was a mistake. A massive, disastrous mistake.

I shoot to my feet and grab my purse. "I'd like you to drive me home, please." I don't wait for his answer, striding in the direction of his truck. I hear him follow, his long legs easily catching me. I stop long enough to yank off my heels, then march ahead, barefoot. He unlocks my door with his key fob, and I clamber inside without waiting. He climbs in and closes his door, sitting in the darkness without speaking. He makes no move to start his truck.

I can't just sit here. I'm dangerously close to ugly-crying, and I refuse to do it in front of him.

"Forget it. I'll call an Uber," I say stiffly, pulling my phone from my purse. He shakes his head and starts the motor.

He never says a single word.

Not. One. Damn. Word.

The ride home is short, presumably because he can't escape fast enough. I know I can't. The truck isn't even fully stopped when I fling the door open and jump down. The gravel bites into my bare feet, but I don't care. I slam his door closed and run up my stairs. My keys are already in my hand, and I unlock the door and close it quickly, leaning against it. Only when I'm inside do I hear him pull away.

Mark doesn't come out to greet me. I poke my head into his room and hear his shower running. I take my handgun out of my purse and place it on his bedside table with my phone, then go upstairs to my own shower.

Not a word. Not one single goddamn word.

Just a loud gasp before he snatched his hand away from my scars like they'd burned him, racing to get me home, to be rid of someone so horrifyingly repulsive.

Blake's reaction reinforces what I've known all along.

I'm too damaged for anyone else, physically and emotionally.

I push my face under the streaming water, too discouraged to even cry.

CHAPTER TWENTY-TWO

CHARLIE

Mark's waiting when I pad barefoot down the stairs much later. His damp hair curls at his nape, and he's wearing a gray Army shirt and shorts. "You're home early."

"Things ended sooner than expected." Literally.

"Your phone's been blowing up. Lila called me when you didn't pick up. She and Tucker are coming over."

I sigh. "I really don't want to see anyone tonight."

"She said that's what you would say and to tell you they're coming anyway."

There's a distinct downside to living five minutes from them at times like this. Before we're even done speaking, Tucker's knocking, and I sigh loudly.

"Can we do this tomorrow?" I call through the door.

"You know I have a key," he reminds me.

I unlock it, standing aside. "I'm changing my locks." Tucker's blue eyes look both furious and worried, and Lila's share the same expression.

"I'm going to your liquor cabinet," he announces. "Who else wants a drink?"

Startled, I look at Mark, who motions for me to follow as both Tucker and Lila stalk to the kitchen. Tucker retrieves rum and scotch. Lila takes fruit punch from the refrigerator and fills glasses with ice. We end up at the dining room table where Tucker pours scotch for himself and Mark and rum for Lila and me. Both Tucker and Lila are visibly seething, though I'm not sure why. I reach for the fruit punch.

"Anybody wanna tell me what's up?" I ask.

"Tom called," Lila says.

That's all she says, even though I keep waiting for more. "And?" I finally probe.

"Blake went to see him." I wait for her to elaborate. "He told Tom what happened tonight."

I close my eyes. As if his private reaction wasn't mortifying enough, Blake's ensured all my friends know exactly what happened. It's a twofer – two for the price of one, both private and public humiliation.

"What did Tom do?" Mark asks, and his words surprise me. Not what did Tom say, but what did he d

Shit. As protective as Tom is, I can guess. "Does Blake have two black eyes again?"

Tucker shakes his head. "As soon as he told Tom, he threw his hands up to protect his face. Tom dropped him with a punch to the solar plexus and then the jaw."

"Pussy," Mark mutters. When I glance at him, he clarifies, "Blake should have just taken the punch. He knew he had it coming."

"No one should have anything coming to them!" I splutter. "You guys can't go around punching people just because my feelings get hurt."

"Watch me," both men say in unison, and I sigh.

"We're going to have a serious discussion later about the use of the word 'pussy' as an insult," Lila announces, glaring at each of them before turning to me. "Are you okay?"

I shrug. "I've been down this road before, telling guys and watching them disengage." I open the fruit punch and add it to my rum.

"But unlike with the Whiners, you didn't gloss over what happened. You told him details." She hesitates. "And you showed him."

I pause, my glass halfway to my lips. "Yeah. I did."

Tucker's eyebrows pull together. "Why?"

I set down the glass. "If he was going to freak out, I needed to know. Besides, I'm trying to let myself be more vulnerable. Open up."

"With people you trust," Mark says quietly. "You trusted him?"

"I trusted him not to try anything physical. This was a test. For both of us, not just for him," I add. He's still frowning. "I talked about it with Linda yesterday."

"And her advice was to show him your scars?" Tucker's disbelief is evident.

I shake my head. "She told me it was better to find out now if he would see me differently once he found out." I drain my glass. "And now I know."

Tucker shakes his head. "He wasn't worthy of you, Charlie."

"There's only one way to find out, Tucker, and I didn't need to get attached if this wasn't going to pan out."

"I'm guessing he didn't handle it well."

I sigh heavily. "He gasped and jerked his hand away. He never said a single word, not one. But he looked at me like –" I take a deep breath and meet Tucker's eyes. "Like I was a monster." A lump builds in my throat, but I won't cry, not over Blake.

Tucker places one hand on mine, squeezing slightly. It's the first time he's touched me since I was taken, and though I'm startled, I'm not afraid. His expression is fierce. "The only monsters were the ones we put down." He looks away. "Goddamned bastards," he growls.

My heart swells with affection for Tucker. I love him like a brother, and I want to let him past my protective walls the way Willow encouraged me to, but I don't know how. He's already part of my daily life, and he's definitely seen the worst of me.

Almost.

I've never let Tucker see my scars. The only people who've ever seen them, aside from the medical professionals, are Lila and Mark. And Blake, though clearly, that didn't go well.

Tucker's right. Blake wasn't worthy.

But he is.

I meet Tucker's deep blue eyes in a burst of determination. "Stand up."

"What?"

I move to stand in front of him. "Stand up. I'm done hiding from someone I trust with my life." When he stands, I turn away. He and Mark look confused, but Lila gives me a small smile of encouragement.

I draw a deep breath, then lift the hem of my shirt all the way to my neck, baring my back to him while keeping my front covered. My hands stay on my shoulders, tightly gripping the fabric. "I never should have hidden the shameful stuff from you, Tucker." I swallow hard, and my eyes burn. "It was never that I didn't trust you. It's just... I hate my scars, and I hide them, trying to pretend I'm not... broken." I can barely speak over the lump in my throat.

I hear Tucker's heavy sigh, so different from Blake's appalled gasp. His large hands cover mine, loosening my grip to let my shirt fall back into place. He steps closer, pressing his cheek to the top of my head as his arms loosely surround me. It's comforting, not frightening, and I turn and throw my arms around his neck. His big arms fold me into his chest. "You're not broken," he says against my hair.

I laugh out loud at his preposterous statement. "You of all people should know how screwed up I am. You're the one who installed the camera. How many times have you two had to intervene in my night terrors?"

Tucker releases me, and we take our seats. "We installed that camera and intervened when we needed to because you're determined to kill whoever's coming for you." Then he frowns. "And don't call your scars shameful. They're nothing to be ashamed of."

Lila's violet gaze is steady. "Charlie, you've got to stop defining yourself by your scars."

I can't keep the frustration out of my voice. "I don't have any other choice."

Her tone turns firm. "Yes, you do. You didn't have a choice when they hurt you, but how you see yourself is up to you. You're more than your scars."

I shake my head. "How I got them may be in the past, but they're always with me, Lila, always. For the rest of my life, I'll have tangible reminders of the shit they did. I can repress the memories, bury them, and in time, I might not think about what they did. But the physical scars will never fade. I see them every time I change clothes, every time I shower, and so will everyone else. My scars will always be an issue."

Mark looks at me, his ice-blue eyes blazing. "So what if you have scars? They're part of you, but they don't define you. No one who gives a damn about you will view them as anything but proof of your strength. And the people who don't? Who cares what they think? And if Blake was too stupid to see that, fuck him. You can do a hell of a lot better anyway."

Lila looks up from her phone. "Tom's asking if you need him to come over. His sister can take Maya for the night."

I smile. "Tell him thanks, but I'm okay. And thank him for defending me, even though punching Blake wasn't necessary."

Tucker says, "Totally necessary," at the same time Mark says, "Yes, it was."

I look at each of them in turn. "Blake got one thing right. He said I had loyal friends."

"Damn right," Tucker says, scowling at the mention of Blake's name.

Lila searches my face. "So what now?"

"No more Winner versus Whiners. I've had my fill."

"So there's no possibility of redemption for Blake?"

I raise one eyebrow. "After tonight? Not a chance. Besides, he made it clear he's no longer interested."

Mark crosses his arms. "I wouldn't be so sure of that."

"Why?"

"His truck pulled in a few minutes ago."

There's stunned silence before Lila goes to look out the window. "That's Blake all right."

Tucker frowns. "Want me to deal with him?"

I shake my head. "Nope. He can sit there until his tires rot for all I care."

Lila looks surprised. "You aren't going to talk to him?"

I shrug. "He didn't say anything when it mattered. He doesn't need to waste my time now."

You could hear a pin drop. Tucker's the one who breaks the silence. "Well, we've determined that Blake's an ass and Charlie's a badass. What's next?"

The tension dissipates and everyone laughs. We eventually decide to move to the living room and watch a stand-up comedian. I nurse a couple more drinks, enough to take the edge off but not enough to get buzzed.

When Tucker and Lila leave a couple of hours later, Blake is still outside, leaning against his truck. He catches sight of me briefly before I close the door. I leave it cracked, curious what Tucker and Lila will say to him.

"Can I just talk to her?"

Tucker's voice is decisive. "Nope." I picture him standing with his arms crossed and feet planted, the way I've seen him a thousand times when he's determined.

"I need to explain."

"She's not interested in anything you have to say."

Blake appeals to Lila, hoping she'll take his side. "Please. I know I messed up."

"I warned you, Blake. Go home before I rip you to shreds right here."

"I can explain, Lila," he pleads. "I didn't know what to say. I didn't want to say the wrong thing, and I knew not to hug her. But the longer the silence got, the worse it was, and by the time I knew what I wanted to say, it was too late."

Gravel crunches as Tucker's voice cuts across the driveway. "Leave."

When I hear their car doors close, I lock up and go to Mark's room. He's waiting. "Want me to get rid of him?"

I shake my head. "He'll leave eventually. I just want to forget today ever happened."

I lie down beside him, and he pulls me close, his arm around my waist. "I'm proud of you."

I turn my head to look back at him over my shoulder. "Why?"

"Because you fought your fears and took risks. You bared yourself literally and emotionally to Blake, and despite his reaction, you still chose to be vulnerable with Tucker."

"I should have let Tucker in years ago."

"I think it meant more now, after what happened today."

I hope so, for Tucker's sake. I fall asleep, pondering that thought.

MARK

It's two am. Charlie's sleeping, her mouth forming a perfect "o". I've been listening since Tucker and Lila left, and I've still not heard Blake's truck start.

I ease out of bed, noiselessly pulling a sneaker on my left foot. I slip out of the room and peek out the window. He's laying on the hood of his truck, his arm over his eyes.

I quietly open the front door and make my way down the steps. He gets up immediately, sliding to the ground and waiting as I approach. The night air is cool and damp as I hobble toward him, my crutches crunching in the gravel as I consider whether or not to beat his ass.

Not yet, I decide. I want to hear what he has to say first. I study his face, noting the bruise along his right jaw and making a mental note to compliment Tom on a solid hit.

"You gonna punch me too?" he asks, shoving his hands into his front pockets.

I'm not sure if he thinks a one-legged guy on crutches can't flatten him or if he knows he deserves it. I'm good either way. "Undecided. Why are you here?"

"I just want to talk to her. I need to explain."

"Go ahead." His eyes fly to mine. "Let's hear this amazing explanation you have for making her feel like a repulsive monster."

His spine stiffens. "Jesus. That's not it. That's not it at all."

"As explanations go, that one needs a lot of work." I survey him, taking in his defeated posture and downturned mouth.

He lifts a hand and runs it through his shaggy blond hair, brushing it out of his eyes. "I wasn't expecting what she said, what she showed me. You didn't tell me they tortured and mutilated her." His accusing tone rings in the quiet night.

I cock my head. "I told you I'd only give you the basics. You knew they kidnapped her. You knew they had her for eleven days, eleven goddamn days. What did you think they did, throw her a party? I told you she was raped. I told you they brutalized her. The rest wasn't mine to tell. Charlie only shares that information with people she trusts not to see her differently." I stare at him. "Clearly, she overestimated you."

He blanches under my glare. "I was shocked, okay? I didn't know people actually behaved so savagely. I mean, branding? Who does that? You hear stories on the news, but you assume they're sensationalizing things. You don't think that stuff happens to real people. People you know." He pauses. "When she showed me her back, I was horrified by what they'd done to her. I didn't know what to say. I wanted to hug her, but I knew not to touch her.

Saying I was sorry didn't seem right. She saw my face and asked me to take her home. I kept trying to find the right thing to say, but the longer the silence went on, the worse I felt. I handled it badly, and I need to apologize."

"So that's why you're here? To relieve your guilt?"

"It's not about me feeling guilty. I want to tell her I'm sorry for how I made her feel."

"You're right. This isn't about you. Charlie's asleep, and I'm not waking her up for your sorry ass."

"I'll wait, then."

I look at him skeptically. "All night?"

"All weekend, if I have to. I need to make this right."

I purse my lips. "She's fine. We've got this. Take your guilty conscience and leave."

"I don't want to leave. I want her to give me another chance."

"To do what? Twist the knife a little more?"

"I like Charlie," he says, his expression bleak. "I just want a chance to tell her I'm sorry."

"And if she tells you to leave?"

He stands taller. "If I explain things, I don't think she will."

"If she tells you to leave, you're done. No harassing her or trying to change her mind."

He sighs. "In the morning, let her know I'm here. She's blocked my number."

I shrug. "Maybe that's your answer." I turn back to the house. When I close the door, he's back on the hood of his truck, leaning against the damp windshield.

CHARLIE

My night is restless, plagued by repeated dreams of Tucker, Lila, Tom, and Mark staring in horror at my scars, which are growing and wrapping around my entire body like huge purple vines. Several times I hear Mark murmuring against my ear, and I drag his arm around my waist until I fall asleep again.

I sleep late and wake up alone. I smell coffee and bacon, though, and that gets me out of bed. Bacon makes everything better. I brush my teeth and run a comb through my hair before going to the kitchen. Mark is flipping pancakes and scrambling eggs from a barstool in front of the stove.

"I was going to wake you if the smell of food didn't," he greets me.

"What's all this?"

"Most people call it breakfast."

"You're making pancakes?"

He grins. "They are considered a traditional breakfast food in many cultures."

I shake my head, retrieving plates and forks, butter and syrup, mugs and juice glasses. "This is a lot of food. Are Tucker and Lila coming over?"

"Not unless you have plans I don't know about." He pulls the last pancake from the pan and passes me a platter of them, then scoops eggs into a serving bowl.

I pour juice and coffee for us and sit across from him. I fall on the pancakes and bacon like a starving woman, and he chuckles.

"Hungry?"

I nod. "I'm still not sure why you made so much food. I mean, some of it we can reheat tomorrow, but eggs? It looks like you cooked the whole dozen."

"I thought Blake might want breakfast."

My fork slips from my hand and clatters to the floor. "Blake's coming over?"

"Blake never left," he corrects me.

"He's here?"

He nods. "Say the word and I'll get rid of him."

I open my mouth, then close it, frowning instead. "Why is he here?"

"To apologize."

I scoff. "He just needs to relieve his guilt."

"That's what I said."

My gaze narrows. "You talked to him? When?"

"After you fell asleep last night."

I tilt my head. "What did he say?"

"That he handled it badly. That he wants to make it right. And I think –" he looks at me, his expression carefully neutral "– I think he's hoping this isn't the end of things."

I'm speechless.

Mark passes me his unused fork. I take it, unable to do more than stare at it.

"It's your call. I can go tell him to get the hell out, or I can invite him in for breakfast."

My stomach is in knots. I don't understand. Blake was horrified when he heard – and saw – what happened to me, but he spent all night in my driveway, waiting to apologize?

Maybe Tom hit him in the head a little too hard.

Mark reaches over, pushing my plate toward me. "Eat. Cold eggs are gross."

I spear a bite of pancakes, then lay the fork down. "I just don't get it."

"I can't explain his behavior. Just keep in mind, people who haven't been exposed to military life can be naïve to the atrocities in other parts of the world. Stonings, beheadings, and dismemberments are mainstream punishments in some places, but here, they're unthinkable."

I stare at his impenetrable pale blue eyes. "So I should give him another chance?"

He shakes his head. "I'm not saying that at all. I'm your enforcer. You want him gone, he's gone. You want him in here, I'll get him. You want to give it a few days and think it over, I'll give him the message. You want me to beat his ass, I'm all over it. I'll do whatever you want, Charlie. This is entirely up to you."

"What would you do?"

"If it were me?" I nod, and he grins. "I'd have cold-cocked him last night and gotten an Uber home. But that's me. You're nicer than I am."

I laugh. "I pulled a gun on the first guy I went out with after I came back," I remind him. "I'm not sure 'nice' applies to me."

"I didn't call you nice. I said you were nicer than I am. Big difference."

I stick my tongue out at him, and he grins again. "Fine," I sigh. "He can come in for breakfast. I want you to stay, though. And if he's not okay with talking to me with an audience, he doesn't need to bother coming in."

Mark nods and heads down the hall. I get up and collect a plate, silverware, and a coffee mug, putting them on the other side of Mark instead of beside me. I pick my dirty fork up off the floor and set out a fresh one for Mark, since he gave me his. I hear the front door open and close, male voices, and two sets of steps approaching.

Blake's still in the same clothing he wore last night, though his shirt is damp and smudged and the sleeves are rolled up. He walks to the table without his usual grace, instead moving awkwardly and shuffling from foot to foot.

I pick up my fork and take a bite of pancakes. “Have some breakfast,” I offer. Mark sits down and starts eating. Blake perches on the chair beside him but makes no move toward the food.

Mark and I continue eating while Blake sits in silence. Mark finally pushes the serving bowl of eggs toward him. “Eat, talk, or leave.”

Blake’s jaw tightens before he reaches for the bowl. His pissy attitude toward Mark doesn't improve his standing with me, but I hold my tongue.

He helps himself to eggs and bacon before pausing, his fork in midair. “I didn’t know what to say,” he says, his eyes finding mine. “I knew something bad had happened, but I had no idea how bad. I couldn’t think of anything to say that didn’t sound trite, and the longer the silence went on, the worse it got. I still don’t have the right words. I’m not sure what the look on my face was.” He stares at the table. “I’m guessing I looked disgusted, and I was. What they did to you makes me sick. But I don’t see you as a monster. You were just a victim.”

Mark presses his lips together and hardens his jaw at the same time my hackles rise.

I’m not ‘just a victim’. I’m a survivor.

No, I’m more than a survivor. I’m a warrior.

Those assholes may have outmuscled me, but I was stronger than they were.

“I’m sorry, Charlie. I’m sorry I handled things so poorly and made you feel bad about yourself. You’re still beautiful to me, even with your scars. Please forgive me.”

I’m “still” beautiful.

To him.

Even with my scars.

His words grate on me like nails on a chalkboard. It’s like he’s deigning to look past my hideous outer shell to focus on my inner beauty, like he’s taking one for the team because of what I went through. It reeks of condescension. I do believe he didn’t intentionally hurt me last night, and I can forgive that, but I won’t make the same mistake again.

“I forgive you, Blake.”

He relaxes his tense posture, and the three of us eat in silence. There’s no cozy chit chat. Mark looks annoyed, and I have nothing else to say. I offer Blake coffee when I realize I forgot to get him some. He shakes his head. “I’m going to go home and get a few hours of sleep,” he says, stifling a yawn. “Would you like to have dinner tonight? Maybe go to the movies?”

“No, Blake. We’re finished.”

“But I thought –”

I push back from the table and stand. "You see me as a victim. Those bastards did horrible things to me, but I'm not a victim. I fought like a fucking wildcat the entire time. That's why I have so many scars. I'm a survivor, but more than that, I'm a warrior. And frankly, I deserve someone who doesn't patronize me by insisting he can still see me as beautiful, even if I'm scarred. I deserve someone who doesn't feel the need to reassure me that he doesn't see me as a monster." Blake's mouth falls open. "Stay away from my clinic. You aren't a client. If you need to talk to Tom, call him."

"But Charlie –" he splutters.

I meet his eyes determinedly. "Goodbye, Blake."

Mark stands and glares at Blake. When he doesn't get up immediately, he pokes Blake's foot with one crutch. "You heard her. You can leave now, or you can leave bleeding. Your choice."

Blake's face reddens. "Fine. But –"

"Don't forget what I told you, Blake." Mark's voice is soft but laced with warning. Blake shoves his chair back and storms from the room, slamming my front door on his way out so hard that it rattles. Gravel clatters against my porch as he speeds out of the driveway.

"Sorry," I say in the sudden silence.

Mark stares after him. "Me too. I really wanted to pound the hell out of him."

I chuckle, coming over to wrap my arms around his waist. He shifts his crutches aside and kisses the top of my head. "What's that for?"

"For being my enforcer, among other things. Thanks."

He slips one arm around my shoulders and squeezes tightly. "Anytime, Baby Girl. Anytime."

CHAPTER TWENTY-THREE

CHARLIE

I PASS THE MORNING cleaning the house and listening to Eminem via earbuds so as not to disturb Mark. I throw all of my energy into scrubbing fiendishly, working up a sweat. I climb into the shower just before noon, having burned off enough energy to settle my nerves. I even channel my inner Linda and pat myself on the back for telling Blake I'm entitled to someone who will treat me the way I deserve.

My mood shifts when I get out of the shower to find a missed call and a voicemail from an unfamiliar number.

My stomach clenches when I play the message.

Blake's called from a different phone since I blocked his number last night. He's also drunk off his ass. His words are slurred, and his normally smooth cadence is disjointed.

That all pales in comparison to his words.

"I can't believe I thought you were hot. You're so fucking high and mighty. I offered to overlook your fucking scars. I mean, Jesus. Your back looks like something out of a horror movie. And you think you deserve better?" He laughs, a thin cruel laugh that eviscerates me. "Gorgeous women throw themselves at me, and you think you're too good for me? You just missed the best chance you'll ever have. No, you missed the only chance you'll ever have. Nobody should have to look at that shit, but I was willing to for you. You'll never find anybody better. All those guys you labeled as losers? Whiners? They weren't the problem. You are. You and your scars. You're too fucked up for anyone to want, Charlie, so get used to being alone."

The phone slips from my hands and tumbles to the floor. Blake's just voiced my deepest beliefs and fears.

That I look like something out of a horror movie.

That I need to get used to being alone.

That no one will ever want someone who's as scarred as I am, inside and outside.

I remember the night in Tom's kitchen months ago, when Maya hugged me after asking if we could always be close.

I remember my sudden, desperate longing, my pointless dream for a home full of love and kids and puppies who don't know their own strength.

For three-legged cats and science projects and messy faces.

For a man who loves me and doesn't see or treat me like I'm broken.

Blake's right. It's never going to happen for me.

I'm shaking all over, pain welling up inside me like a tidal wave. It takes a minute to realize the sounds I'm hearing are my own harsh sobs.

I go downstairs to the liquor cabinet to numb my pain the only way I know how.

MARK

It's mid-afternoon when I wake up. The faint scent of bacon still hangs in the air. Charlie sent me to bed shortly after I strongly encouraged Blake to leave under his own power. She said she'd clean the kitchen – something about needing to burn off her frustrations.

After I wash my face and brush my teeth, it dawns on me that the house is strangely quiet. Normally on weekends, I wake up to the sounds of the washer or vacuum. I don't hear anything, though, not even the television.

I glance at the bedside table. Charlie's gun isn't there. It was there when I fell asleep.

Maybe she had errands to run. God, I hope that's all it is. I hope she's not more bothered by the Blake thing than she let on.

I pause with my hand on my bedroom door, suddenly remembering my first night here. "Charlie?" I call as I open the door. I don't step out, waiting to hear her voice. I'd prefer not to get shot at again.

"In here," comes a muffled reply. Something about her voice sounds off. I follow it into the living room and survey the scene in front of me. A bottle of rum perches precariously on the edge of the coffee table beside a half-dozen empty pineapple juice cans and her handgun.

This can't be good.

"Everything okay?" I ask cautiously.

Her head pops over the back of the sofa as she sits up, clutching a mostly empty glass of clear liquid and melting ice cubes. "Oh, yeah. I'm peachy." Her words slur and her eyes are bleary. Judging by her blotchy face, she's been crying.

That fucking asshole.

I thought she was doing alright when Blake left this morning, but I guess it's caught up to her. I ease down beside her, leaning my crutches on the end table. "I see you've been in the rum," I comment casually, noting the nearly-full bottle of rum from last night is almost empty. I point to her glass. "How many of those have you had?"

"One for every juice. And, and then a couple more when I ran out of juice. And maybe another one, but I'm not sure. Or two." She looks at me, her eyes slightly unfocused. "You look nice." She reaches over and awkwardly pats my black tee shirt.

She's had a *lot* of rum. "Are you okay, Charlie?"

"Whaddaya mean?"

"I thought you were alright when I went to bed, but now you're drunk. Did something happen?" I smile gently, speaking slowly so she can keep up.

She sighs and flops her head beside my leg, liquid sloshing from her glass. I pull it from her loose fingers and set it on the coffee table, pushing the rum bottle away from the edge while I'm at it. "You have such a nice face," Charlie says, staring at me upside down.

I chuckle. "I haven't seen you this drunk since high school."

She points at me. "You haven't. But I used to drink a lot. You know, after. But I stopped."

"What made you start drinking today?"

She swallows hard and looks away. "All I wanted was a normal life. You know, with a husband and kids and dogs and bake sales. But that's never gonna happen. Not for someone like me." Tears fill her eyes. "That fucker's right, even though he's an asshole."

I blink, trying to make sense of her tangled ramble. "Blake?" I'm fairly certain he's the asshole in question.

She nods adamantly. "Fucker," she repeats.

"Is this still about last night? I thought you settled things this morning."

She fumbles for a long time on the couch, rooting around, squirming, until finally she unearths her phone from between the cushions.

"Voicemail," she mutters.

"You want me to play a voicemail?"

She nods, turning her face away. I hit play with the speakerphone on. She starts sobbing halfway through his tirade.

Fiery rage tears through me as I listen to his drunken rampage. *That motherfucker.* I'm going to rip his goddamn head off. I look down to find my hands fisted, ready to beat the shit out of him. It's all I can do not to storm out and find his sorry ass.

Then I glance at the shattered woman beside me, crying her eyes out. I pull her onto my lap and cradle her against my chest.

"Ignore him," I growl. "He's just mouthing off because his pride is wounded."

"He didn't say anything I didn't already know."

I'm going to fucking kill him.

I turn her tearstained face to mine. "Listen to me," I say firmly. "He's just an angry drunk running his mouth. He's not used to being put in his place. Blake's a player. He's the one who walks away from a woman, not the other way around. His ego couldn't handle being called out this morning. He's hurting you to make himself feel better. None of that bullshit he said is true, Charlie, not one word."

But she's too drunk to listen to reason.

She shakes her head, tears streaming down her face as she stumbles over her words. "I'll always be alone. He's right. I'm too fucked up. Scars on my body. Scars in my mind. A scarred monster. I don't get a happily-ever-after."

I want to find Blake, rip his spine out, and beat him to a pulp with it. Instead, I nestle Charlie deeper into my chest and stroke her hair. "You're wrong, Baby Girl. He's the monster." She turns her face into my shoulder, crying until she falls asleep.

When she wakes several hours later, it's dark. She's still on my lap, though I've shifted her so her head's on a throw pillow with her legs curled next to me. Without warning, she claps her hand over her mouth and bolts for the bathroom across the hall, barely making it in time to throw up everything she's eaten today and then some.

I join her a moment later, dropping my crutches and leaning against the sink for balance as I pull her hair back and secure it with a hair tie lying on the counter. I grab a clean face cloth, soaking it with cool water and wringing it out before draping it across the back of her neck. I rub her shoulders while she kneels there, her stomach still heaving, but nothing left to throw up.

Eventually her stomach settles and she sits back on the floor, closing the toilet lid and resting her head against it after flushing. She takes the washcloth from her neck and wipes her face.

"How do you feel?"

Her voice is hoarse. "Like there's an army of jackhammers in my head."

"How's your stomach?"

"Empty, so we're safe." She slides back to lean against the wall. "Sit," she says, gesturing to the closed toilet.

I balance against the sink and sit down. "When you're feeling better, we need to get some water into you, and maybe some food. Later," I add when she raises an eyebrow.

She pulls up her knees and lays her head on them, her face turned away. "You wanna hear something stupid?" Her tone is subdued. "I felt bad for Blake after he left this morning."

I scowl. "Why?"

"I felt like I'd been too harsh. I thought maybe he didn't realize calling me a victim was insulting, or that emphasizing that *he* still saw me as beautiful –" her voice breaks "– that he didn't mean it to be condescending or patronizing. I thought maybe it was an extension of last night, like he still didn't know what to say and he was grasping at straws. Even so, I was proud of myself for standing up for what I deserved."

"You should be proud. You were right."

She shakes her head. "I'd like to think I deserve a happily-ever-after, but there's a lot of truth in his words, even if I don't want to admit it."

I shake my head fiercely. "No, there's not. He's a mean drunk who lashed out like a little bitch when you injured his pride. He's a life coach, okay? A control freak. He's used to telling people what to do and having them do exactly what he says. He sat outside last night planning how this was going to go. When you didn't fall in line with his expectations, it pissed him off, and he showed his true colors. He's an asshole, Charlie. Don't let him get inside your head."

She lifts her head, and her bleak expression makes my heart ache. "He didn't say anything I haven't believed for a long time."

"Just because you feel something's true doesn't mean it is, Charlie. You're wrong about yourself."

This isn't a battle I'm going to win tonight. It's going to take a lot more than one conversation in a half bathroom to show Charlie her value. I study her carefully. "So what happens now?"

Green eyes hold mine for a split second before her expression fades. "Nothing. I move on."

I recognize the emotional detachment in her eyes. It's the coping mechanism she always turns to when things are painful. She tells herself it doesn't matter and buries her hurt. Eventually, the pain resurfaces and has to be dealt with. I don't push the issue, though. She's not up to it tonight.

I plant my left leg firmly and brace my left hand against the wall, then reach my right one out to her. "Let me help you up." She grips my hand and I hoist her to her feet. She leans down and collects my crutches, then waits while I stand.

"You always take care of me," she murmurs.

"We take care of each other, remember?" I rub my thumb over her cheek.

She looks down at her shirt. "I'm going to shower and brush my teeth. Wanna watch a movie when I get back?"

I nod. "I'll make something mild for dinner."

While she's upstairs, I record the asshole's voicemail onto my phone. I'm unquestionably going to beat Blake's ass, but not tonight. Tonight is about taking care of Charlie. I call Lila and give her the Cliff's-notes version of events. She's appalled and furious. "I can be there in five minutes."

"I've got this. I just wanted you to know."

"Fucking asshole," she mutters. "I think she's only got two clients tomorrow. Two of her regulars have doctor's appointments. Tell her to stay home. Tara and I will cover them."

My next order of business is dinner. Charlie needs something light. I search the cabinets and freezer, deciding to make homemade chicken soup and sandwiches. I pull shredded rotisserie chicken from the freezer, collect some vegetables and broth, and drag a barstool to the other side of the island to work closer to the stove. I dice carrots, onions, and garlic and let them caramelize. When they're soft, I add the chicken and broth, turning the heat high. I lean on my crutches while scouring the cabinets, finally locating noodles and adding those with frozen green beans and a healthy amount of sea salt and black pepper. When the soup bubbles, I drop the heat to low. I hear her shower cut off while I'm gathering what I need for turkey sandwiches, tearing leaf lettuce and slicing tomato. I leave the turkey in the fridge and the lettuce and tomato covered until she feels like eating. Finally, I fill a pitcher with ice water and wait for Charlie.

It's not long before I hear bare feet padding downstairs. She's dressed in her usual shorts and loose shirt. Her eyes are red and puffy, her face pale. She stops in the living room, and I hear the clinking of glass and crumpling of cans. She joins me in the kitchen, setting the rum bottle on the counter before taking the juice cans to her recycle bin. She shudders as she empties her glass in the sink and the smell hits her. "Easy," I caution, watching her fighting nausea.

"Never again," she mutters, and I chuckle.

"Fine. Never again before one pm," she amends, then sniffs the air curiously. "Something smells good." She lifts the lid on the pot and stirs the soup, inhaling. "Oh, wow."

"It can hold until you're able to eat. There's stuff for turkey sandwiches too. Let's start with water, and when you're feeling better, we'll try something stronger."

She puts the lid back on the pot and comes to lean against my side. "Thank you."

I grin down at her, slipping my arm around her. "It's just soup."

"No, it's you letting me cry on your shoulder, listening to my drunk ramblings, holding my hair when I was puking, and yes, soup and a movie."

"Remember when I first got out of the hospital and I kept thanking you, and you told me to quit because you and I take care of each other?" She nods. "Quit thanking me. This is what we do." I kiss her damp hair. "Can you grab our water glasses? I'd do it, but they'll be half empty by the time I get in there."

She grabs the glasses and pitcher and follows me to the living room. "I need to see when you can take me to the VA in Pueblo," I say over my shoulder. "I need X-rays and a CT scan of my leg next month. If everything looks good, I may be able to have surgery in late August."

Her face lights up. "That's just a little over two months away!"

I grin. "Yep. I might actually be walking on my own before Christmas."

"That's wonderful!"

"Don't get excited yet. My femur has to be healed enough for the surgery," I caution her.

"So after you have the CT scan and X-rays, then what?"

"If my femur is healed enough for weight bearing, they'll measure how much of my tibia remains and create a custom implant based on my bone structure. They attach the implant directly to the bone, and a plastic surgeon will reshape the soft tissue. I'll stay a few days in the hospital, and I should progress to weight bearing with about twenty pounds of pressure within the first few days after surgery." I point to a thick book I've been working my way through. "There's a ton of information on the process if you're interested."

"I'll read it. I've seen the after-effects in clients, but I don't know a lot about the implantation process. Schedule the appointment and I'll get Tara to cover for me." She rubs her forehead, then opens a bottle of aspirin. She tosses back two tablets and downs a full glass of water.

"Maybe you should slow down a little," I suggest.

"My stomach's better. I need my head to stop pounding."

"Alright. Pick a movie," I say. She grabs the remote and scans the streaming channels, skipping everything with even a hint of sex or romance.

A stand-up comedy special seems to help. She leans against me as we laugh. We pause halfway through for sandwiches and soup, returning to eat on the couch so we can continue watching the comedian.

Charlie tastes the soup and smiles, looking surprised. "This is really good."

"Your mom taught me her recipe."

"Seriously?" Her eyes widen.

I nod. "She wanted to be sure I could cook if I were living alone. I think she was afraid I would starve or go broke eating fast food all the time, so most of the stuff I know how to cook, I learned from her."

She smiles softly. "That's pretty cool." She gets a nostalgic look on her face at the same time memories start springing to my mind. They're just everyday memories – nothing particularly special. Family dinners with Charlie and her parents, her dad helping me pick out my first car, her mom kissing my forehead and tousling my hair after I broke up with my first girlfriend. But my favorite memories center around spending every afternoon helping a young, beautiful Charlie with algebra, and the following year, with chemistry.

Charlie gets to her feet and retrieves a large photo album from the bookcase.

"A trip down memory lane?"

She grins. "Why not?"

We sit with our heads close together as she flips through the pages. She pauses on a picture of me with my mom after her cancer diagnosis. She's wearing a pink scarf around her head and gazing at me with such deep love, it pains me to look at her expression. I run my finger across the picture, unable to stop myself. I miss my mom, even after all these years.

"Do you have a copy of this?"

I shake my head. I don't trust myself to speak.

"I'll get you one," she promises.

We keep flipping through photos, landing on one of Charlie and me at her kitchen table working on algebra. I grin as I examine it. She's wearing a strappy pink tank top with lace around the top, and I'm in a black tee shirt. My hair was longer then, and hers hung to the small of her back. Though the picture doesn't show it, I know she's wearing short denim shorts that barely reached the top of her thighs. We sit side by side, books open in front of us. I'd been trying to show her how to solve a problem, but she kept distracting me. The look on my face is one of pure adoration, but neither Charlie nor her parents ever had a clue how I felt about her.

It was better that way.

I smile down at her. "I've always loved this picture. It's my favorite one of us."

That's when I started calling her Baby Girl.

"Really? My favorite is the one Tucker took when I first showed up on base." She flips a few pages over. We're both wearing gray combat fatigues. She'd been on base for just a couple of hours and was headed to the mess tent when I saw her up ahead. I'd cupped my hands around my mouth and yelled, "Baby Girl!" She'd turned, her eyes honing in on me instantly, and she'd taken off running toward me. I'd met her halfway and scooped her up and spun her around. She'd wrapped her legs around my waist and kissed my face and hugged me tighter than I've ever been hugged, then pulled back to hold my face between her hands and just look at me. Tucker had snapped a photo at that exact moment, with the two of us looking at each other, elation on both our faces.

"I love that one, too. I was so glad to see you. I thought you'd be safer with me." I pause as guilt floods over me. "Guess I was wrong on that count."

She shakes her head. "No matter what, Mark, I'm always better with you than without you. Always."

I pull her toward me and kiss the top of her head.

Me too, Baby Girl. Me too.

CHAPTER TWENTY-FOUR

MARK

MONDAY AFTERNOON, I HEAD to the clinic for rehab. Lila's helping a blond guy in a wheelchair navigate the front door when I arrive. She smiles but doesn't speak. Charlie's at the front desk on the phone, having refused to take the day off despite Lila's "assertive encouragement". She tucks her hair behind her ear as she types on the computer. "I have those records," she says, glancing up. "I can fax them to you if you'll send me a signed records release." I study her when she looks back at the screen. Her face is pale, with deep circles beneath her eyes. As I'm watching, she absently rubs her right temple. I frown. She should have stayed home.

I start toward the entrance to the rehab gym. As I do, something catches my peripheral vision. I look over my shoulder and spot a large black truck pulling into the parking lot.

No.

Surely he wouldn't be that stupid.

Turns out, he *is* that stupid. I'm flabbergasted to see Blake hop out and saunter toward the clinic.

Hot anger washes over me as my eyes flash to Charlie. She hasn't seen him yet. Lila has, though, and she looks worriedly at me. "I've got this," I mutter, pushing past her and hauling myself rapidly across the gravel parking lot. He looks up, his eyes suddenly cautious at my approach. I launch myself through the air when I'm close enough to take him down, flinging my crutches aside. Our bodies connect, and I ride him to the ground. He lands beneath me with a thud, and the air whooshes from his lungs as his startled eyes meet mine. I straddle him as he wrestles, trying to free himself, but I knocked the wind out of him when I tackled him. Fueled by the memory of Charlie's anguish and self-loathing, I land two solid punches before he gets his hands up to protect his face. My third hit is a body blow that elicits a deep groan from him. I hear Lila yelling behind me, but I don't stop. I bring both fists down on the hands covering his face, smashing them into his nose. Blood spurts from between his fingers. I pound them again.

Huge arms heave me upright. I struggle, trying to wrench free, but Tom keeps me off balance, dragging me backwards so I can't get my leg beneath me. When I stop fighting him, he slings me aside, roughly propping me against someone's car. "What the hell's gotten into you?"

I glare past him. Blake's gotten to his knees, blood streaming from his nose and mouth. "Ask that fucker what he did yesterday." Tom whips around to stare at Blake. I glower at him. "Don't you ever come near Charlie again."

Tom immediately releases me and hauls Blake to his feet by his bloody shirt. "What did you do to her?" he demands, shaking him.

Lila forces herself between them, her small hands on Tom's chest, shoving him backwards. "Not here," she says firmly.

"What did you do?" Tom growls, leaning around her.

Lila shoves him again, pushing him back another step, her expression fierce. "I mean it, Tom. You want to fight, take it somewhere else. We have clients watching, for God's sake." Then she whirls to face Blake. "And you," she points, "you're not a client, and this is private property. Next time, I'll have you arrested for trespassing. Leave."

Blake throws up his hands. "I came here to talk, and he assaulted me!" He gestures in my direction.

I smirk at his bloody face and rapidly swelling lip and eye. *Damn right I did.*

"Really?" Her eyes narrow. "Because I just saw a man attack my client at a healthcare clinic for wounded veterans, and the veteran defended himself."

"Are you fucking kidding me?"

"Watch your mouth!" Tom and I bark at the same time.

Blake swipes his arm across his face, smearing blood everywhere. "You're all insane."

Lila advances on him. "No. We're family, and we're not people you want to fuck with. Now get off my property," she says icily. The three of us glare as he gets into his truck, spraying gravel everywhere. Tom picks up my crutches and hands them to me.

"Sorry, man. You alright?" He looks me over.

I snort. "Please. The only thing that fucker hit was the ground." Tom grins broadly.

Lila inspects my hands. "Your knuckles are bleeding."

"It's probably his blood."

She shakes her head. “It looks like you caught his tooth. Let’s get you cleaned up.”

Tom puts a hand on my chest. “Wait. Tell me what he did yesterday.”

I drag my phone out and play the voicemail Blake left for Charlie. Tom’s jaw flexes and his eyes blaze. “I’ll fucking kill him.”

“That’s enough,” Lila snaps. “You guys beating the shit out of him only draws attention to something Charlie wants to forget. You wanna help her? Quit focusing on that asshole.” Lila’s violet eyes pin each of us sternly.

I shrug. “She told him yesterday not to come back to her place of business, and he did anyway. I’ve clearly expressed my feelings about that to him. As long as he doesn’t upset her again, I’ll behave.” She scowls.

Tom doesn’t answer her, and I can tell by his expression that Blake’s bad day isn’t over yet. I’m pretty sure Lila can tell too, because she shakes her head and stabs his broad chest with her index finger, enunciating each word. “Not. Here.” She turns and stalks into the clinic.

I chuckle at her retreating figure. “Tucker’s got his hands full.”

Tom stares after her. “She looks so dainty, but she shoved me backwards. Twice,” he adds, incredulous. “And poked me with those bony little fingers.” He rubs his chest.

I laugh. “Be glad that’s all she did. I’ve seen her take down bigger men than you.”

CHARLIE

It's a workout day, which means I have a houseful of people after work. Tom catches me in the hall. "I'm really sorry. I feel terrible for telling you I thought he was okay. I'm no better at picking guys than Lila."

He pulls me into an unexpected hug, but it doesn't scare me, and that fact makes my bad day significantly better. "It's not your fault he reacted like he did," I assure him. When he releases me, I notice his red knuckles. "What's up with your hands?"

He glances down. "Just a little bare-knuckled boxing."

I study him, realizing who he's likely punched, though his face gives nothing away. "Thanks, Tom," I say quietly. "You didn't need to do that, though."

"I told you, I protect my family, bloodborne and chosen."

I can't say anything else over the lump in my throat, so I hug him, and he chuckles as he hugs me back. "You're getting good at these."

Tom assures me Blake won't come near the clinic again. He also fired him as his assistant coach. I start to protest, because Tom needs the help, but I drop it at his murderous expression. Tom's as furious with Blake as Mark is. Apparently, he knows about Blake's voicemail.

Being surrounded by people is a temporary balm. Lila and I cook a ton of Mexican food for dinner. Maya joins us and catches me up on everything happening in her and Skyler's lives. Skyler's mom is seeing a new guy, but Skyler isn't a fan because, as Maya puts it, "he's all her mom talks about. Dave this, Dave that, Dave, Dave, Dave." I learn that Maya loves her new art teacher at summer camp, but dislikes the nature guide because he smells like "the weird people that lurk at the back of the health food store". I also notice she seems rather fond of a boy named Ben, a fact which makes Tom frown every time she mentions his name – which is often.

It's only after everyone clears out that my dark mood settles back in. I sit beside Mark on the sofa, staring at the television screen, but I'm a million miles away.

Blake's voicemail blasting my response to his apology has led to a couple of insights. For starters, I'm not upset with him for finding my scars appalling. After all, I sprung them on him without warning. Theoretically, his honesty was a good thing. Truth beats lies every day of the week, even if it's painful to hear. How horrible would it have been to keep seeing him if I'd never known how sickened he secretly was by my body? Yes, the way he screamed slurs into my phone was cruel and inappropriate, and it proves he's an asshole. Still, it doesn't change the bottom line: he couldn't cope with my scars, so things couldn't have worked out between us. His reaction simply accelerated the timeline and saved me from getting in any deeper.

My second related-but-not-entirely-Blake's-fault epiphany is that I'm done with dating. No more constantly revolving doors of single guys. I'm uncomfortable being alone with men, and aside from a few butterflies with Blake, I've not felt anything even remotely close to sexual interest since before my assault. I've accepted that in all likelihood, the sexual chapter of my life is over. Without dating, I'm unlikely to build a connection with a man I can trust. Without trust, I can't engage in a physical relationship without having a panic attack.

The whole point of dating is to develop something deeper with the right person, but for me, an intimate relationship is impossible. I have too many scars, both physical and psychological, for most guys to handle. Frankly, my issues are too much for *me* to deal with, let alone saddle an innocent bystander with. For all his bullshit, Blake got one thing right.

I'm meant to be alone.

Having said that, I still intend to work toward becoming more comfortable around men, but it won't be through dating. Tucker hosts a meet-and-greet after-hours at his gym every other month. He sets up a bar, hires a DJ, and people come in to mingle, dance, and network. Tara hosts huge dinner parties most weekends with regional authors, actors, artists, and musicians. Her ridiculously wealthy ex-husband wrote big checks and called himself a patron of the arts, but Tara was the one who got to know them as people, not tax deductions. There are other outlets available to me, too. I might join a local book club or a hiking group or... something. Anything. As long as it's in a group setting, I'll be fine. I'll browse Cedar Ridge's town website for some local groups and activities.

Days pass, and my internal mood sinks. Abandoning my dream of a happily-ever-after chips away at my spirit, piece by piece. On the outside, though, I plaster on my smile and embrace my role. I've had years of practice at pretending I'm fine. I enroll in a kickboxing class at Tucker's gym and join a book club. I'm cheerful with my clients at work. I chat about mundane things with Tom, Tara, and Lila, join them for lunches outside the office, and bring home-baked goodies to share. I even manage to get caught up with the neverending paperwork.

Outside of work, with Lila, Tucker, Tom, and Maya, I'm able to keep up the façade. When they ask how I'm doing, I give a noncommittal but positive answer and shift the conversation. But when it's just Mark and me, I don't pretend. I've stopped wearing a fake smile at home because he sees right through it. Depression engulfs me like a heavy San Francisco fog, reminding me of my secret pain at every opportunity.

Happily-ever-after isn't in the cards for me.

MARK

Charlie gradually slips into a darkening mood. She keeps her disposition light and cheery at the clinic, so only Lila and Tom notice. When it's just us, though, she's quiet. I let it slide for a while, trying to give her time and space to work through things on her own, but after a couple of weeks, I start to worry.

"Have you seen Willow lately?" I ask one night while we're doing dishes.

Charlie chuckles sadly. "Why would I? She's a sex therapist. I'm clearly not in need of one."

"She's a relationship specialist. Maybe she could help."

Charlie intently scrubs a pot. "I'm not in a relationship, nor am I looking for one."

I stop loading the dishwasher and look over. "So you're just giving up?"

She sighs heavily. "I'm done with the revolving door of lousy dates with sketchy strangers. I don't know any decent single guys. And I'm not up to spending weeks getting to trust a new guy just to see if –" she hesitates, blushing "– if I'm able to feel passion." She stares down at the pot in her hands. "Which, I'm pretty sure, I'm not."

I ignore her red face, focusing solely on her words. "So you don't really want a relationship. Not right now, anyway. What you want is a test."

"What?"

"A test. You want to see if you can both create and experience passion, right?"

She glances over. "I guess that's one way to look at it. But I can't fool around with someone I don't trust, and I'm not interested enough to invest my energy into finding a trustworthy guy."

She hands me the pot, and I load it in the dishwasher, considering her words.

It all comes down to insecurity.

Charlie's scars, both psychological and physical, have left her feeling like no man could find her desirable, a belief Blake cemented with his parting shot. Not only that, but the damage those bastards inflicted by using sex as a weapon has left her afraid to trust a man.

Afraid to be vulnerable.

Afraid to let go.

That's the crux of the issue. Charlie can't trust a man enough to let go of her fear because she subconsciously believes her fear keeps her safe. What she needs is to experiment with someone she truly trusts.

She trusts me.

An idea starts to simmer in the back of my mind, intriguing, but forbidden.

I know Charlie trusts me implicitly, but this... this is an unspoken boundary we've never crossed, a subject we've never broached. She and I have never had any non-platonic physical contact, not even once. When I was younger, though, I desperately longed to. It took years to bury those feelings and accept our relationship for what it was – a perfect friendship, with no room for anything outside that boundary.

I look over. "Hand me a dishwasher pod, will you?"

She passes me one from a clear canister and starts wiping down the counters. I bend down and place it in the slot, straighten up, and start the machine, leaning against it to watch her.

Deep breath.

"You trust me," I comment casually.

"Yes," she agrees, scrubbing the counters.

I watch her, but she doesn't make the connection. She moves on to wipe the island.

"I'm a decent single guy. I could be your test subject," I suggest, keeping my tone light.

Her head snaps up, her mouth falling open. "But — but we're friends."

I nod. "Best friends. Closer than most best friends, actually. You know me. You trust me. I'm a man, you're a woman."

"What are you saying?" she asks warily, leaning against the island.

I shrug. "I'm just offering myself as your test subject."

She tilts her head, watching me. "What does that mean, exactly?"

There's no fear in her expression, merely curiosity, so I ease the conversation forward with a soft smile. "It means you and I kiss, and we see if you feel anything."

"From one kiss?"

I chuckle. "Well, I'd probably classify it as making out, but yes. Nothing but kissing," I clarify, "but not just a quick peck, either."

"But we're friends," she repeats.

I nod. "Yeah, we are, and you know I'd never hurt you. You're safe with me. That leaves you free to try things out without being afraid."

She looks at me, her expression indecipherable.

I've gone too far.

"If you're not interested, it's fine. It was just a thought," I say hastily. I don't want to make her uncomfortable. I'm the only guy she's completely relaxed with.

She searches my eyes. "What if it makes things weird?"

"You mean like, what if we kiss and it's like kissing a relative?" I shrug. "Then we stop immediately and never speak of it again." I smile. "Ever."

"No. No, I mean... what if it makes things weird between us afterwards?"

I reach over and lightly take her hand, touching only her fingertips. "Charlie, you and I have literally been to hell and back together. I don't know any two people, not friends, not lovers, not even married couples, that have a stronger relationship than we do. I don't believe a kiss could destroy what's between us. It's not possible."

She nods slowly.

I try to lighten the mood. "I mean, if I really put my back into it -" I grin, "and it does absolutely nothing for you, my pride might be wounded, but that's all."

She laughs, but then worry reaches her eyes. "Mark, I really do think I'm too messed up to respond that way now."

"I'm kidding. My pride will be fine. Besides, it's just a test. If we kiss and you don't feel anything, then you'll know, and if you do, well, you'll know then, too."

She hesitates. When she speaks, her voice is barely a whisper. "What if – what if I do?"

I smile gently. "Then you'll know you aren't as broken as you think."

Long moments pass, and I can see her mind racing as she bites her lip. I let her twist the idea around for a bit before I put her out of her misery.

"The only way to know is to try. I'm offering you a safe option. Just think about it. It's an open-ended offer." I push off from the counter and grab my crutches.

"Okay," she says suddenly. "Okay, let's try it."

Yes. Let's.

A smile spreads slowly across my face. "Okay, then." I move toward her.

"Wait. Now?" she asks hastily.

I pause in front of her. "Did you have somewhere important to be?" I tease gently. She stares up, her eyes wide. She's not frightened. She looks... curious.

Good.

I balance my weight on my left leg and prop my crutches against the island. My right hand grips the counter. I'm less than a foot from her.

Her face is upturned as she studies my face. Her breathing has quickened slightly, but she doesn't look scared. "No," she answers slowly. "Now is fine."

"Good."'

My eyes don't leave hers. Charlie's a fighter. She wants to know if she can move past her fear of physical touch, or if the bastards have truly broken her beyond repair. I know her, though. She's much too strong for them to have beaten her. She just needs to find that out for herself.

"My right hand is going to hold the counter so I don't fall on my ass," I grin as I point to it with my other hand, "and my left hand won't wander. If you feel uncomfortable or want to stop, pull back or tell me, and everything stops."

She nods her agreement. I scrutinize her closely. "You're sure?"

She nods again, looking slightly nervous, but not afraid.

The smile on my face gradually fades as I gaze into her impossibly deep emerald eyes. Her beauty grips me, beauty I've forced myself to ignore for nearly twenty years. "Damn, you're beautiful, Baby Girl." My voice is rough as I lift my left hand and brush the pad of my thumb across her cheek. I slide my hand behind her neck, my thumb beneath her jaw, and tilt her face up, slowly lowering my mouth to hers, giving her time to change her mind.

She doesn't.

My lips skim over hers lightly. She's tense. To be honest, I'm not sure she's still breathing.

"Relax," I whisper, nudging her mouth with my own. I kiss her again, very lightly, and she responds hesitantly, standing up on her tiptoes to meet me.

I pull my mouth away from hers. "Hang on," I tell her, scooping her up beneath her thighs with my left arm. She gasps and slides her hands up to my shoulders. I deposit her gently onto the island countertop so we're face to face.

"That's better," I murmur, giving her a slow smile before my mouth closes over hers again.

She tentatively returns the kiss, still holding back. "Stop overthinking things," I mutter against her lips. "Just let go and feel."

With that, I deepen the kiss, my lips becoming more firm against hers. I move my left hand to the nape of her neck, spearing my fingers through her thick hair, lightly gripping it to tilt her head back. My mouth turns hot, insistent, seeking, and when my tongue gently licks across her lips, she shivers, then parts her lips for me. My tongue sweeps into her mouth. She tastes faintly of vanilla and wine, honey sweet. Over and over, my tongue caresses hers, dancing and circling.

Her anxiety melts away. She leans into me, meeting my tongue stroke for stroke. She slides her hands up to wrap them behind my neck, twisting her fingers into my hair. She tugs at it and pulls my mouth closer, getting lost in the moment, this one perfect moment.

Yes.

Our kisses continue, heated and wet, but I focus on her response. She presses closer to me, pushing her breasts against me. Her nipples tighten against my chest.

Her nipples.

God. I picture them, rosy-brown, pert, straining toward me, desperate for my touch. For my mouth. My teeth.

Hold up. Get a grip.

I can't afford to get too caught up in the heat of the moment.

I move to the safer territory of her neck, trailing steamy kisses down to her collarbone. I feel her sharp intake of breath as my stubble grazes the curve of her throat. Her head falls back as I suck and nibble my way back up, pausing by her earlobe until she shivers again. I chuckle lightly as she reaches for my face and tugs my mouth back to hers. This time she's the aggressor, igniting me with her feverish kisses, demanding more, and I willingly oblige. My left hand drops to tightly grip her hip, sliding her forward against me. My body tightens immediately in response to her closeness. Without hesitation, she takes my left hand and moves it to her right breast, and I groan deep in my throat.

A fiery heat explodes through both of us. Our kisses become more intense, lips and teeth and tongues devouring each other, and when I squeeze her taut nipple, her hands grab my waist, pulling me in as she wraps her legs around my hips. My hardness presses solidly against her inner thigh, and she arches her hips against me.

God, she feels good.

So fucking good.

My hand squeezes her breast as I stroke her nipple. She whimpers before grinding against me again. A growl escapes from somewhere deep in my chest.

She wants this.

We both do.

Shit. No.

You have to stop this.

Now!

I snap back to my senses first. Shocked by the passion blazing between us, I tear my lips away from hers. "Damn, Baby Girl," I say, my voice hoarse. My breathing is ragged as my eyes fix on Charlie. She's the perfect picture of arousal. Her cheeks are flushed, her lips swollen, her pupils dilated. I pull her against my chest, my lips pressed to her forehead, willing my body to calm down. I feel her panting, her chest heaving against mine.

After long moments, I get a handle on myself. I look down. Charlie stares at me with huge green eyes, her lips parted, still breathing hard.

I gently disentangle her legs from around my waist and take her hand. She watches, speechless, as I press it over my heart. It hammers wildly against her palm. "Do you feel this?"

She nods silently.

I move her hand to press it over her own heart. I can tell by the pulse pounding along her throat that it's beating as hard as my own. "Do you feel that?"

She nods again.

"You're not broken, Baby Girl," I murmur, lifting her hand to my lips and kissing her knuckles. "Not by a long shot."

She looks stunned.

I see the instant her emotions change.

Her expression turns to one of mortification. She flushes deep crimson and jerks her hand free, pulling back physically and emotionally.

"No," I say firmly, "don't do this, Charlie. Don't you dare be embarrassed." I shift to make her look directly into my eyes. "That was the sexiest kiss I've had in my entire damn life, but it doesn't change the fact that you're you, and I'm me. It was a test, an agreed-upon, predetermined test. You wanted to see if you could fully engage in a passionate moment, and you did. You wanted to see if you could make a man respond passionately, and you did. Stop second-guessing and kicking yourself. It was a test, nothing more."

She's silent for a long moment. "It was just a test," she finally repeats.

I'm not sure she believes her own words.

I nod. "Just a test. It doesn't change anything between us. Do you still trust me?"

"Of course," she says immediately, a hint of annoyance in her voice.

I suppress my smile. She's back.

"Then we're good. Nothing has changed. We're the same two people we were fifteen minutes ago. We're just two people who answered a question."

I grip the counter tightly with my right hand, leaning over to pick up my crutches. At some point, they clattered unnoticed to the floor.

I help Charlie slide off the counter before tucking my crutches under my arms. "I'm going to go to the weight room for a few minutes and burn off some energy." *God knows I need to.* "Want to meet back in half an hour or so for a movie?"

She smiles uncertainly. "I'll pop the popcorn."

I head down the hall, completely unaware that we've permanently altered our previously rock-solid relationship.

CHAPTER TWENTY-FIVE

CHARLIE

I ESCAPE UPSTAIRS WHILE Mark is in the weight room. I hear pounding music and the clacking of metal weights from behind the closed door. I shut my bedroom door and sag against it, my knees trembling.

What the hell?

What the hell, what the hell, what the hell???

My heart is still pounding from that – that – I don't even know what to call it.

Intense. Passionate. Hot.

And I wasn't afraid. I didn't panic, not even a little.

I head into the bathroom and turn on the shower. I think better in the shower.

I catch a glimpse of my reflection in the mirror. My hair looks sexy and rumpled. My pupils are huge. My lips are swollen, and my face is flushed.

And I'm definitely aroused. There's a heat in my core, a molten fire that I haven't felt before.

Ever.

I swallow hard, remembering, and my heart starts thudding in my chest again.

As soon as I agreed, something in Mark's smile changed. He went from regular Mark to... Sensual Mark? Suggestive Mark? Sexy Mark?

All the above.

I'd taken in his stubbled face, his strong jaw, his full mouth. My stomach churned with anticipatory butterflies.

His eyes softened when he called me Baby Girl and told me I was beautiful, and unlike when Blake called me beautiful, Mark sounded like he meant it, like the sentiment was unearthed from somewhere deep inside him.

My heart pounds harder. I've had boyfriends in the past. I've been kissed before.

But I've never been kissed like that. Slowly. Tenderly. Gradually becoming more inquisitive. Tasting. Teasing. Touching. Caressing.

Electric tingles had coursed through my body, awakening long-forgotten places. A warm ache had begun to slowly build in my body. Tension. Dampness. Heat.

Heat that exploded between us like a volcano, threatening to ignite us both.

I shove my face under the streaming water to stop my mind from taking the path it's begun wandering down, one that wonders what it might be like if he hadn't pulled away.

If we'd just kept going.

Stop.

I can't think about that.

I can't even *consider* it.

Mark is everything to me. My best friend. My rescuer. My *person*.

And even though what just happened was incredibly hot – holy shit, was it hot – and even though it made me want things I've never longed for in my entire life, I'm not willing to throw away our current relationship for really hot sex.

The fact I'm even having an internal conversation about whether or not I should have really hot sex with him proves Mark was right. I'm not broken. Not totally, at least.

And now I'm not sure how to act around him.

I really hope I haven't screwed up the one relationship that matters more to me than life itself.

I finish my shower and dress in my usual shorts and loose shirt. I hear the clatter of weights, signifying he's finishing up. I'm back in the kitchen when he pokes his head in the doorway. His guarded expression throws me for a loop.

"I'm going to run through the shower. Meet you in about ten minutes?"

His tone is light, but something in his eyes isn't right. I nod, ignoring the uncertainty in the pit of my stomach. "I'll have the popcorn and drinks ready."

The tension between us is immediate. We sit side by side watching the movie, but we're careful not to touch, when only yesterday I'd leaned into his side, his arm over my shoulders. We take turns reaching into the popcorn bag so our hands don't graze against each other. I'm pretty sure neither of us could tell you what the movie was about. I know I can't. I was lost in my own thoughts.

My fear.

Fear that I've ruined things between us.

It's even worse at bedtime. I rinse our glasses in the sink and head to his room to join him, hesitating in the doorway. Mark's in bed, leaning against the pillows. He glances up.

"Aren't you coming to bed?"

"Are you sure it's okay?"

"Of course it's okay."

"I could sleep –"

"Don't you dare say on the bench," he says firmly.

"The couch, then."

He frowns, looking like Regular Mark again, and I'm relieved.

"Charlie," he says patiently, "nothing has changed. This was an agreed-upon test. Yes, we kissed. It doesn't change anything. You've slept beside me every night since I got here in case one of us needs the other. Now come to bed. I'm not going to take advantage of you," he adds.

He's intentionally goading me, and even though I know it, it still works. I scowl and pad across the room. "I know that," I snap. "I just didn't want things to be weird."

"Then don't make them weird," he answers sharply. He closes his eyes and draws a deep breath. I pretend not to notice.

I pull the mirror and the massage oil from the closet and climb onto the bed. "Slide the leg of your shorts up so I can work on your quad."

He pauses briefly before pushing his shorts out of my way. I kneel and warm the oil in my palms before gliding them across his muscles. His quad is practically in knots. "You're really tense," I murmur as I begin to massage. I've forgotten my hair tie, and my long hair swings free each time I lean into a stroke, brushing his chest. I kneel above him and lengthen my strokes, working from his knee to the top of his thigh.

I've barely gotten started when he grabs my hands. "I don't want a massage tonight."

I look up in surprise. "Are you sure? Your quad feels pretty tight."

He shakes his head, not meeting my eyes as he pushes my hands away.

Mark doesn't want me to touch him now?

I put away the oil and mirror and wash my hands in the bathroom, his blatant rejection making my face burn. I keep my expression neutral when I re-enter his room. I silently get into bed with my back toward him, careful not to touch him as I face the door.

"Good night, Big Guy," I say quietly.

His voice is equally quiet. "Good night, Baby Girl."

Shit. What have we done?

MARK

I'm sitting in the weight room after the best kiss I've ever had in my entire damn life.

What the hell?

I run my hands through my hair and drop my face into my hands. I didn't think my test-kiss idea through.

I frown. That's not quite true. I did think about it, but not for very long, and I let the brain below my waist make the decision for me.

Sixteen-year-old me is cheering loudly, begging for more. Thirty-five-year-old me is wondering why in the hell I've risked everything I have with Charlie for a few minutes of pleasure.

And damn, was it pleasurable.

My mouth dries as I replay our interlude, and I wonder for a split second what would have happened if I hadn't pulled away from her.

Don't go there.

I get into position on the leg press. I need to strengthen my right leg, and I have some energy I need to burn off. A *lot* of energy.

My interactions with Charlie are immediately strained, even before we sit down to watch the movie. She doesn't scoot next to me on the couch like she usually does, and I keep my hands in my lap instead of leaning back with my arm across the back of the sofa. We make every effort not to touch hands when we share the popcorn bag.

I can't concentrate on the movie at all. I know it's one I mentioned wanting to see, but I can't tell you a damn thing that happened.

Charlie's frustratingly silent after the movie. I settle in bed, leaning back on the pillows to wait for her.

She goes upstairs to brush her teeth even though she keeps a toothbrush in my bathroom now. When she comes back down, she lingers outside my door.

She doesn't want to sleep in here anymore? Have I fucked things up that badly?

"Aren't you coming to bed?"

"Are you sure it's okay?" She looks nervous.

"Of course it's okay."

I'm not going to touch her again.

No matter how much I want to.

I swallow hard.

"I could sleep –"

"Don't you dare say on the bench," I say firmly.

"The couch, then."

I close my eyes and take a deep breath, striving for calm in my voice when I speak.

"Charlie, nothing has changed. This was an agreed-upon test. Yes, we kissed. It doesn't change anything. You've slept beside me every night since I got here in case one of us needs the other. Now come to bed. I'm not going to take advantage of you," I add, my words an unspoken challenge I know she won't back down from.

She scowls as she pads across the room. "I know that," she says, annoyed. "I just didn't want things to be weird."

"Then don't make them weird," I retort sharply.

Too sharply.

I sigh.

She goes to the closet and takes out the mirror and the massage oil.

Shit.

I'm suddenly not sure it's a good idea to have her touch my body right now, but I don't know how to broach the subject with her.

So I don't.

It'll be fine. I'll find a way to distract myself. I'll think about the fights Tucker and I've watched recently.

She has me slide my shorts up to massage my right thigh. I've overworked it between rehab, a long workout with Tucker, and again tonight, after our kiss. My quad muscle is so tight, it's painful.

She kneels over me, her palms gliding up my thigh. Her thick hair swings freely as she moves, and her coconut shampoo mingles with the light fragrance of her body wash. Her eyes drift closed the way they sometimes do when she's massaging, like she's communicating with my muscles, listening to what they need. Her hands work their magic, moving further up my thigh with each stroke.

And my lower brain perks up and starts to pay attention.

A lot of attention.

Shit.

Not now.

And I panic.

I grab her wrists and jerk her hands away before she can see my growing erection. "I don't want a massage tonight," I say quickly.

Too quickly.

She stares in confusion. We both know my muscle is so tense I could bounce quarters off it.

"Are you sure? Your quad feels pretty tight," she says, her brow furrowed slightly.

I shake my head firmly, dropping my eyes. I can't face her questioning gaze as I firmly decline again.

What am I supposed to say? *Your touch is giving me a hard-on I could cut diamonds with?*

Because that wouldn't make things more awkward between us *at all.*

She swallows, then nods and climbs off the bed. She puts away her tools and goes to wash up in my bathroom. I hurriedly rearrange the covers over me, leaving enough messiness to disguise my arousal. Charlie stays in my bathroom longer than usual. When she comes out, she won't look at me, and her face is flushed.

Dammit. I've hurt her feelings.

I don't know how to undo it, either. I sure as hell can't tell her the truth. Things are uncomfortable enough.

She climbs into the bed and lies next to me. She doesn't make contact as she faces the door.

I *have* hurt her.

"Good night, Big Guy," she says quietly.

"Good night, Baby Girl."

Saying my pet name for her makes me remember calling her Baby Girl earlier tonight. Twice. Once before I kissed her, when I told her how beautiful she is to me – how beautiful she's always been to me – and once, when I broke our kiss.

Our steamy kiss.

Her lush curves.

My stroking hands.

Wetness.

Heat.

I rub my hand over my face again in frustration.

It's a long night.

Charlie lies stock-still beside me. Her breathing is even. She wants me to believe she's fallen asleep, but I know she's awake. I've laid beside this woman for months now while she sleeps. Her face relaxes, and her spine melts into me. Unless she's having a nightmare, she's completely at ease.

Right now, she's stiff as a board.

Meanwhile, I'm fighting a different type of stiffness. I've been pretending to read, but I'm caught in the memories replaying in my mind. The taste of her lips. My mouth on her bare skin. Her legs wrapping around my hips, drawing me closer. Her whimper and my answering groan.

The tension grows in my body, and with it, my frustration.

I'm so agitated by the time Charlie gets out of bed an hour before her alarm goes off that I tell her I'm just going to sleep. I can tell she's not slept by the shadows beneath her eyes. She nods and tells me to sleep well, closing my door on her way out.

When I eventually sleep, I dream of her. When I wake, I'm testy, because it's made me want what I can never have.

Charlie.

In every way.

The sexual tension between us is palpable, but neither of us acknowledges it. Not directly, at least.

Charlie's withdrawal started as soon as I stopped her from massaging me. My rejection wounded her, and she's pulling away. The more she withdraws, the more snappish and testy I become, and the more cranky I am, the more she retreats. It's a vicious cycle.

God, I've fucked things up, and I have no idea how to fix them.

I don't even know if we can.

A SNEAK PEEK AT SHATTERED DREAMS

CHARLIE

Pale blue eyes roam over my face before halting to stare deeply into my eyes. The smile on Mark's rugged face melts away as he lifts one hand to caress my cheek.

"Damn, you're beautiful, Baby Girl," he says, his voice husky. One large hand slides behind my neck and tilts my face up to his before he leans in, gently brushing his lips over mine.

"Relax," he whispers against them, and I stretch up on tiptoe to meet him halfway.

I'm startled when he suddenly scoops me up and sets me on the counter, but when I look into his eyes, I forget everything else. He smiles slowly as he dips his head. "That's better," he says as his lips close over mine.

I'm still nervous, though. I feel him smile as he once again mutters against my mouth. "Stop overthinking this. Just let go and feel."

I take the leap and do exactly that.

Mark deepens the kiss, one hand slipping into my hair as his lips touch and tease and taste. When he strokes his tongue across the seam of my lips, I'm all in. Our kisses become hotter. Wetter. Deeper. Excitement spirals through me, and I want more. My fingers somehow end up twisting in his hair, my breasts pressing into the muscled planes of his chest.

He pulls back to kiss his way down my neck before sucking and nibbling his way back up. His perennial five o'clock shadow scrapes over my skin, making me shiver, and I can't help sighing as my head drops back to give him better access.

I need more.

I drag his face back to mine, becoming the aggressor as my lips seek his. A fiery heat engulfs us as our kisses grow more intense. His hand drops from my neck to the curve of my hip, clutching it tightly, pulling me forward. My core grazes his hardness.

Yes...

I tug his hand from my hip and settle it firmly on my right breast. When he squeezes my nipple, my body clenches tightly in response. I wrap my legs around his waist, pulling him closer, arching my hips against him.

God, yes.

My whimpers of excitement mingle with his deep groan as I grind against him again.

Without warning, he tears his lips away from mine. "Damn, Baby Girl," he gasps, his voice rough. His chest heaves like he's just run a marathon. "You're not broken. Not by a long shot."

Oh. My. God.

What have I done?

Test kiss, my ass. I'm an idiot for agreeing to this.

If I'd taken more than thirty seconds to consider it, either common sense or my raging insecurities would have kicked in and made me rethink things. I'd never have made such an impulsive decision, possibly ruining the most important relationship of my life.

I kissed my best friend.

And it was hot. Not just hot – electric. Smoldering. Panty-melting. The hottest, most passionate kiss I've ever experienced.

It wasn't supposed to be like that. It was just supposed to be a test, one I passed with flying colors.

Actually, *failed* is probably the more accurate way to view things, because even though it was by far the hottest kiss I've ever had, it wasn't worth screwing up the relationship Mark and I have. He's my best friend, and that's worth more than all the passion in the world.

That panty-melting kiss was last night. Now I'm in my shower, my brain scrambling for a way to fix things while jasmine-scented steam cocoons me in a thick fog. I brace my arms against the spotless white tiles, dropping my head beneath the hot water.

Maybe if I drown myself in here, I won't have to face my screw-up.

What the hell?

It wasn't supposed to be like that.

Mark and I have been best friends since we were kids. Our parents were best friends, too. His mom died from breast cancer when he was thirteen, and his dad committed suicide a couple of years later, too grief-stricken to go on. My parents immediately brought Mark into our home. When they died in a car accident just after my freshman year of college, he and I were alone, a pair of technically-but-not-really-adults, two kids with no one but each other. We floundered a bit before joining the army. Mark chose infantry and rose quickly through the ranks. I became a medic and loved it, but I missed Mark. I bounced from place to place around the Middle East before I finally scored my transfer to his unit, a platoon embedded deep in a hotspot in Afghanistan.

That's where I met Lila and Tucker. Lila was a fellow medic, and Tucker was Mark's second-in-command and later, Lila's fiance. The four of us became inseparable over our years together, forming our own kinda-sorta-family unit.

Then everything went to hell.

Lila and I were kidnapped by insurgents and imprisoned for eleven days before being rescued. We endured barbaric torture that ended our military careers, and I was left wounded and scarred, traumatized with crippling PTSD.

I functioned on emotional autopilot for years until Mark came to live with me a few months ago. An IED exploded while he was on a mission, leaving him severely injured and missing his right lower leg. After three months in Brooke Army Medical Center, he came here to finish recovering. Lila and I are massage therapists now. We co-own a wellness clinic offering massage, hydrotherapy, and physical therapy for injured veterans. Mark gets PT five days a week, and Tucker, who moved back here and married Lila, spends three afternoons a week helping Mark rebuild his strength.

I brought Mark home with me to heal, but the truth is, he's helped me as much as I've helped him. He's my sounding board, my compass, and my anchor.

After my kidnapping, my persistent male-induced panic attacks convinced me I was too defeated, both physically and emotionally, to feel sexual desire. It seemed obvious I'm meant to be alone. It requires more conscious energy than I possess to force myself to be emotionally and sexually vulnerable. It's just not worth the effort it takes, especially with some of the doorknobs I've gone out with.

That brings me to last night, when Mark urged me not to give up. I declared I didn't know any men I trusted enough to have dinner with, let alone attempt anything physical with to confirm my suspicion that I was irreversibly sexually paralyzed. He suggested a test, a kiss between the two of us. I trust Mark implicitly. He'd die before he'd take advantage of me, and we both know it.

The idea was to let me safely explore whether I was sexually damaged beyond repair.

Well, I'm not.

Definitely not.

My face grows hot as memories scroll through my mind again. Pale blue eyes holding mine. Rough stubble on his strong jawline. Soft lips becoming firm, insistent. Things long forgotten stirring to life. Damp heat. Hardness. Fiery passion.

Jesus, I'm getting turned on again just thinking about it.

No.

I shove my face under the water again to stop my train of thought.

It wasn't supposed to be like that.

It was supposed to be a test, that's all, just verifying I was too damaged to feel aroused after the devastation they'd inflicted. Obviously, I was wrong, and now I've screwed everything up.

Mark and I can barely look at each other. We've always curled up on the sofa together, but last night we avoided all contact. When I set up for his leg massage to stave off his phantom pains, he grabbed my hands and pushed them away, despite the risk of substantial pain later.

Thanks to my overly enthusiastic response, I'm not allowed to touch him now.

We've spent every night since he moved here side by side as a trade-off. I help prevent or ease his phantom pain, and he keeps watch so I feel safe enough to sleep. I didn't sleep last night, though. I couldn't. I was too busy vacillating between remembering every delicious detail of our kiss and worrying I've ruined the most important relationship in my life.

I'm not willing to give up what we have.

I just have no idea how to set things right again.

MARK

I'm cross-legged on my bed, my left leg folded beneath me and what remains of my amputated right leg hanging off the edge of the plush mattress. I'm alone. Charlie's already left for work, scurrying out the side door and across the breezeway to her clinic next door. Meanwhile, I'm taking out my frustrations by pounding a squashy gray pillow and cursing enough to make any sailor blush.

I'm a goddamned idiot.

I've fucked everything up with Charlie. I made a spontaneous suggestion without considering the long-term ramifications, and it's strained things between us.

Our relationship is the most important one in my life. Without Charlie, I have nothing.

Charlie's deeply scarred by a past that's entirely my fault. Four years ago, I sent two teams on a medical mission that turned out to be an ambush. Insurgents killed six of my men before taking Charlie and Lila prisoner. The bastards were savages. Charlie endured unspeakable horrors – beatings, branding, mutilation, and rapes, all because I made the wrong call. It took eleven days for me to locate and rescue them, eleven days and nights of hell that left her with unspeakably deep physical and emotional scars.

When she brought me here to recuperate, I had no clue she struggled with night terrors. Unbeknownst to me, she spent every night on a bench in her hall where she could monitor every entrance, dozing in brief spurts until her nightmares hit. She'd awaken in full combat mode, gun drawn, often firing in the direction she believed her attacker was coming from. Things were so dire, Tucker and Lila installed a remote camera system to alert them so they could help reorient her to her surroundings and calm her.

They never said a word to me.

Not one fucking word.

I get it... sort of. I was half a world away, and a split second of distraction worrying about a problem I couldn't fix could literally have meant life or death for me and my men. I understand their logic, and I'd probably have done the same in their position, but it still upsets me. My best friend needed me, and I had no idea. I'm the one responsible for her night terrors. I'm the one who fucked up and sent my team into a trap.

What's more devastating is that she isn't having regular bad dreams, like falling or standing in front of a crowd in your underwear. During her night terrors, Charlie relives what those fuckers did to her. *Everything* they did to her, as though it's happening in real time, every goddamn night.

I discovered this the hard way my first night here. Charlie cried out, trapped in one of her night terrors, reliving a rape by her attackers. She was still disoriented when I hurried to check on her. If I hadn't struggled with my bedroom door, she'd have shot me in the head. Instead, she planted two bullets in the wall exactly where my head would have been.

Did I mention she's a certified expert marksman?

That horrible night led to a mutually beneficial arrangement. She'd stay with me at night to help manage my phantom pains. In return, she'd hand over her gun and trust me to keep her safe so she could sleep without fear.

When her gun isn't with me, it's in a soft belly-band holster around her waist. She doesn't feel safe without it. Night terrors aren't her only struggle. Unexpected male touch terrifies her. Thanks to those bastards, her mind equates male touch with pain. A mere hug from someone she doesn't trust can instigate a full-blown panic attack, complete with gun drawn. She's only recently begun to initiate affectionate touch with the two males she trusts besides me – Tucker and her friend, Tom. She's working hard to overcome her fears. She was doing really well, even dating one guy for a few weeks until he showed his true colors.

Trust is unbelievably hard for her, and not just with men. Charlie doesn't trust her own judgment now. I think that's why sexual contact has been so challenging, because she can't relax enough to just *feel*. She'd convinced herself she was too broken to feel desire. We'd talked about it a couple of months ago, before she started seeing Blake. I'd hoped the issue would resolve itself, but it didn't, and when things didn't work out, she gave up. She'd decided she was sexually damaged beyond repair, unwilling to risk dating to confirm or disprove her suspicions.

Enter me and my fuck-up of epic proportions.

A thought flitted through my mind while we were discussing her conviction that she could neither feel desire nor arouse a partner. She and I could test her theory – nothing more than kissing, but lasting long enough for her to relax and let go. Charlie trusts me, so the hurdle of finding someone she could be comfortable with was a non-issue. I can read her better than anyone, and I'd stop at her first hint of anxiety or disassociation.

I didn't really think she'd agree, so I never considered the possibility of consequences. I assumed on the off-chance she did consent, we'd make out for a couple of minutes and she'd realize she could enjoy herself with someone once she let go of her fears.

She startled me by accepting my offer.

She stunned me with her passionate response.

My own intense reaction left me reeling.

What the hell?

Where did *that* come from?

Charlie and I have been best friends for nearly twenty-five years. We've been there for each other through everything, from skinned knees to war wounds, bad haircuts to hangovers, losing football games to losing family members. Until last night, we've never once crossed that unspoken boundary, although at sixteen, I'd have loved to.

Sixteen-year-old me was jumping up and down and cheering last night, rooting for more.

Thirty-five-year-old me is mature enough to understand that while sex with Charlie would be mind-blowing, I can't risk what we have. She's my best friend. I can't lose her.

I let my mind drift back to her fervent response, and my lips curl in a slow grin.

Yeah... she's definitely not broken.

CHARLIE

I wake long before my alarm, the only light coming from the bedside lamp on the other side of the bed. I can tell as I shift positions that I'm alone because there's no weight on the mattress behind me. Still, I snake a hand backwards, hoping I'm wrong but finding only cold sheets. I roll over, scanning the room. Pale blue eyes watch me. Mark is perched on his chaise again. His jaw tightens, and his watchful gaze turns to a glare when our eyes meet.

He's definitely not happy to see me.

He used to be.

He always used to be.

But that was before I ruined everything.

Tears spring to my eyes. I leap from the bed, tripping on the edge of the comforter. He instinctively reaches to catch me, but I right myself and pick up my gun from the bedside table.

"I'll get out of your way," I mumble, rushing for the door. After I close it, I hear a crash. I hesitate, wondering if he's fallen, but based on the loud string of curses that follows, he's not injured. His voice isn't coming from floor level. He's just angry.

At me.

God, this week has sucked.

Monday night was the hottest kiss of my life. It was followed by Mark's abrupt withdrawal. He rarely speaks, and if he does, he's crabby. He won't let me massage him at all, not before bed to prevent his phantom pains and not when he's at the clinic, either.

He doesn't want me to touch him.

Maybe I misread things.

Maybe the passion from our kiss was all one-sided.

What if Mark was just trying to prove I still had the capacity to respond?

Oh, God.

It was a *pity* kiss.

And I got carried away.

After that realization sinks in, I can barely make eye contact with him.

At least I've been able to limit my time alone with him. Three evenings a week, Tom and Tucker come over and work out with Mark while Lila and I make dinner, and I've convinced them to watch a movie or hang out afterwards. The other evenings, I've just avoided going home. One night I texted Mark that pizza was being delivered so I could go shopping. I'd rather have bamboo shoved under my nails than shop for clothes, so I played solitaire on my phone and ate a burger in my car. Last night, I hung out with Tom and Maya and sent Chinese food to Mark.

I've even figured out how to circumvent the awkwardness of bedtime. I shower and wait upstairs until I hear him in his own shower, then sneak into his room. I leave my gun on his bedside table and climb into bed, feigning sleep when I hear him moving around the bathroom. He climbs in bed next to me, careful not to make contact. When I sleep, I dream of him in ways I wish I didn't. When I wake, he's never beside me. He's always across the room on his chaise, looking grumpy.

This morning was no different, except for the cursing as soon as I was out of sight.

I've ruined everything.

I shower and dress, escaping to the safety of our clinic. The lights are already on when I get there, though it isn't even seven yet. "Hello?"

"In here," calls Lila.

I follow her voice down the hall to my office, an open room with fluttery white sheers over floor to ceiling windows, soft sage walls, and cherry wood furniture covered in sprawling green plants. A fountain on the buffet behind my desk provides the soothing sound of trickling water. Lila's sorting documents into large piles to fax to physicians' offices and insurance companies. The endless paperwork is my least favorite part of this job. Lila was shocked by the ridiculous amount of redundancy I deal with when she covered for me while I was in Texas with Mark. I've always handled the paperwork because I know she abhors it. Since learning firsthand how much is involved, she's made it a point to help, a task I'm more than happy to share.

"You're here early," Lila greets me. She's cross-legged on the floor, surrounded by precariously high stacks of paper. "I've finally gotten these sorted. We just need to fax those."

"Thanks. I'll send them and work on invoices today. Tara's covering my clients, so I should have time." I examine Lila more closely. Her violet eyes are red-rimmed with dark circles beneath them, and her usually perfect blond curls are twisted up in a clip instead of tumbling down her back. I pick my way across the room, stepping between piles to sit down facing her. "Want to talk about it?"

Her eyes flash to mine in surprise before she sighs. "Is it that obvious?"

"Only to me."

She bites her lip, staring at the floor. "I started my period last night."

Oh.

Lila went off the pill in January to pursue her desire to have a baby, and it hasn't happened as quickly as she'd expected it to. She tracks her ovulation days and peak conception windows obsessively, timing her intercourse with

Tucker to increase the odds. Every unsuccessful month seems to take a little more out of her.

"I'm sorry, Lila." I reach out and squeeze her delicate fingers. "What can I do?"

She shrugs lightly. "Nothing. This is on me, I guess."

I don't address the elephant in the room: her fear that the violent sexual assaults by the bastards who kidnapped us caused enough damage to render her infertile.

Like they did me.

But I don't go there, because neither of us is strong enough for that discussion today. Instead, I shake my head. "This isn't on you. Stress makes it harder to conceive, and this has been a hell of a year. I abandoned you when Mark got injured. You managed the clinic, a gazillion goats and horses, your house, your husband, the renovations to my house – hell, I'm exhausted just listing it all. That's a ton of stress." I pause, gazing at her sad eyes. "I know it's easier said than done, but be patient with yourself. You need to recover, too."

She sighs. "Maybe. But stop saying you abandoned me. Mark was hurt. You did what Tucker and I couldn't do. You were exactly where all of us needed you to be." Then she purses her lips. "Why are you here so early?"

No way in hell can I give Lila one more thing to worry about.

I sidestep her question, tossing my hair and reaching for a piece of paper from one of the piles, pretending to read it. "You know me. Once I'm up, I can't go back to sleep, so I came in to get a head start on this." I gesture around at the stacks of paper. "I had no idea I'd find you here, too." I smile. "I'm glad I did. Makes my day a lot easier."

She eyes me suspiciously, and I'm sure she's going to call bullshit, so I rush to speak before she can. "Why don't you call Tucker and meet him for breakfast? I'll take your morning clients."

"Adam has the flu," she answers, referring to one of our older veterans, a right-sided above-the-knee amputee. "He texted me last night, and Jim has a doctor's appointment this morning, so I don't have a client until noon." She hesitates, and I can tell she's considering my offer. "Maybe I will."

I nod. "Tucker's probably upset, too. Breakfast together will do you both good."

She scoops up her phone. "I hope he doesn't have an early session."

When she's gone, I pull up my knees and tuck my face into them, glad I'm alone so I don't have to pretend everything's fine. I'd give anything to talk to someone about this mess I've gotten myself into.

The problem is, Mark's my go-to person for advice, and he's clearly not an option. Lila's my second, but she's got more than enough to deal with. I could try Tucker, but he'd probably think my kissing Mark was a fantastic idea instead of the giant fuck-up it's become. And Tom is taking the day off, flying to New York with Maya so she can spend the weekend with her mom.

I'm on my own to sort this shit out.

MARK

I'm on the back deck, heaving chunks of charred wood from the firepit at the distant trees lining the lower border of Charlie's property. I'm agitated and desperate to expend some energy. Things are getting out of hand.

The night we kissed, Charlie started massaging my leg as usual, but the feel of her hands gliding over me and her scent as she leaned into her strokes made my cock harden. I hurriedly stopped her, not wanting her to notice my erection. The hurt in her eyes almost made me confess, but I held back, not wanting to freak her out.

She laid beside me all night, stiff as a board, not sleeping a wink. Neither did I, not until she left for work the next morning. When I eventually slept, I dreamed of her. I awoke irritable, wanting what I can never have.

Charlie.

In my bed.

Crying out my name as she comes with my cock deep inside her.

To my dismay, things aren't getting any easier as the nights progress.

The second night, Charlie does fall asleep. She claims my wrist in her sleep and tugs my arm across her body, anchoring my hand so that her full breast nestles perfectly into it. My mouth goes dry and my body tightens instantly.

The third night, she rolls onto me, her head on my shoulder, both breasts pressing into my chest and her leg slung over my groin. I ease out from beneath her, but she immediately shifts back, clinging to me like ivy to a wall as my cock hardens against her thigh.

Last night, she once again pulled my arm around her so her breast ended up in my hand. Our bodies shifted when she rolled, and her luscious backside slid into full contact with my groin. I grabbed a pillow and pushed it between us to hide my immediate erection.

My only respite comes when she's asleep enough for me to escape to the safety of the chaise, out of her reach. Even then, I'm haunted by the images my mind replays. Our steamy kiss. My hand buried in her silky brown hair. Her lush curves. My stroking hands. Wetness and heat. Her green eyes, dilated with desire. And when she moans or makes soft noises in her sleep, it's almost more than I can take.

I don't let her massage me at all, not at home or at the clinic. I'm too afraid she'll see how my body reacts to her touch. Hurt flashes in her eyes, but she says nothing as I traipse past her down the hall every day with Lila or Tara.

In the daytime, Charlie avoids time alone with me like the plague. As soon as her eyes open, she races to her shower before spending even longer hours than usual at her clinic. She's been at work before daylight every day since our kiss. After work, she keeps a cushion of people around so we're never alone. On workout days with Tom, Tucker, and Lila, she acts as though nothing's wrong, and strangely enough, none of them seem to have noticed she and I aren't speaking or making eye contact.

When the guys aren't here to work out, she evades me. One day, she texted she wouldn't be home because she was going shopping. Did she seriously think I'd believe that? She'd rather face a firing squad than go shopping. And all these visits with Tom and Maya? Okay, fine, she does that at least once a week, but she's doing it more frequently now, and it's not like I don't know why. She's even having dinner delivered to me when she's not here. It's like a giant neon sign flashing, "Don't waste your time waiting for me, because I won't be joining you".

We've got to work this out.

I just don't know how.

Every time I try to talk to her, my words come out like growls. I can't stop it, because it pisses me off that she's pulling away. It's become a vicious cycle. The more I snap, the more she withdraws, and the more she withdraws, the more irascible I become. Her injured expression has me wound so tightly that as soon as she leaves the room, I start cursing and throwing things.

I want Charlie to fight for me. For *us*, for what we have together. She fights every other problem head on – why not this one? The only time she reacts honestly is when she's asleep, wrapping her body around mine. Her authentic response proves she wants more between us, even if she won't admit it out loud. The way she reaches for me in her sleep is a problem, though, because it makes me want more. Much more. I allow myself to savor it briefly, but I can't stay that close to her. It's too torturous. As soon as I'm certain I won't wake her, I extricate myself. I can't act on my feelings, so I flee to the safety of the chaise.

I'm not fleeing the same way she is, though.

Definitely not.

She's giving up. I'm just not giving in. There's a difference.

Yeah, right.

Maybe Charlie isn't the only one avoiding the truth.

SHATTERED DREAMS CONTINUES CHARLIE & MARK'S STORY!

If you're enjoying my novels, please visit my website and sign up for my newsletter. You can sign up here: https://phoenix-wolfe.com/ The same page has links to **follow me on Facebook, Instagram, and Twitter!** Pop in and say hello!

If you're enjoying this series, please stop by and leave a review on Amazon. As an indie author, reviews are the best way to get my story out to other people, and to be honest, **there are entirely too many women (and men) dealing with the aftermath of not only sexual assault, but the struggle of self-loathing.** I'd love to put this story in the hands of as many people as I can because I truly believe the message is something most of us need to hear on some level. **If you're willing to help, I'd appreciate it.**

www.ingramcontent.com/pod-product-compliance
Lightning Source LLC
Chambersburg PA
CBHW022021240626
47154CB00007B/2205

* 9 7 9 8 9 8 8 3 5 3 1 1 9 *